MOTHERLAND

G.D. ABSON

Mirror Books

Published by Mirror Books,
an imprint of Trinity Mirror plc,
1 Canada Square,
London E14 5AP, England

www.mirrorbooks.co.uk

ISBN 9781907324833

Printed and bound by CPI Group (UK) Ltd, Croydon, CR0 4YY

First paperback edition

Front cover images: Trevillion, Katya Evdokimova/Millenium Images, UK

For Jenny

Prologue

Saint Petersburg. New Year's Eve, 1999

Her husband's men had been drinking vodka since midday. Through the serving hatch she could see Sasha making a toast with his hand curled around one of her crystal glasses. She had no desire to listen to him and tore apart a head of lettuce at the sink, washing the leaves in the icy water until it numbed her fingers. She heard grunting and dropped the leaves in a salad spinner before returning to the hatch. Now the two men were arm wrestling on her coffee table, their rolled up shirt-sleeves showing off their pale, swollen biceps; the smoke from their untended cigarettes forming cirrus clouds in the stale air. She unscrewed a jar of pickled tomatoes and sliced three on a board then stirred them into a bowl of finely chopped cucumber and onion.

'It's smoky in here.' She wafted her free arm breezily to emphasise the point as she placed the bowl next to a beetroot salad in the adjoining dining room.

Sasha lifted his palm to signal a truce. He tapped the ash off his cigarette then puffed on it. 'Is there more food, Kristina? I'm starving.'

She glanced at him then looked away, conscious of the lie she was about to tell. 'Don't worry, it's coming.' She needed them drunk.

On the floor she gathered up pieces of a jigsaw puzzle – a present for Ksenia's second birthday that spent more time being tossed in frustration than completed – depositing them in the corner of the room reserved for her toys. She raised the blinds. Outside it was black except for the yellow globes of streetlamps and the glow of lights in the apartments on the opposite side of the canal. Ice cracked as she forced open a window and freezing air sucked the cirrus clouds away. She yanked the window shut when the cold began to bite then let down the blinds.

Her eyes flicked to Sasha's brown, wet-gel hair that he teased into tiny spikes. She liked to imagine he'd fixed an otter's pelt to his scalp; it helped to make light of the fact that he had a gun. Usually the dull black pistol was in the inside pocket of his jacket but now it lay by his elbow on the coffee table. On the sofa's arm was an open packet of cigarettes and she helped herself to one. The lighter was next to the gun, so she waited patiently until Vova noticed her lingering and lit the cigarette for her. A strand of the cheap tobacco came free and she absent-mindedly pinched it from the tip of her tongue then wiped it onto the edge of an ashtray.

'This city's messed up,' she said to neither of them in particular, 'I'll never get used to the cold.'

Sasha lit a cigarette and drew on it deeply before picking up a near-empty bottle of Stolichnaya and filling a glass for Vova and himself. She brought out a third from the crystal set in her wooden cabinet and he poured the remainder of the vodka into it until the meniscus was bulging.

She knocked it back, hoping to calm her nerves. 'And up here it's dark from four in the evening.'

Vova settled in her leather sofa and emptied his drink with a flick of the wrist. 'Well, it's good in summer.' He reached for a pickled gherkin, tapped it against the jar to shake off the vinegar then lowered it into his mouth.

She passed the ashtray to Sasha and turned to Vova, whose height barely made it to Sasha's jawline. 'For three months maybe, then there's no night at all. There's just this weird zombie light that makes it hard to sleep.'

Vova licked his fingers. '*Piter*'s always been black or white.'

She wondered then if she had misjudged him. In the daylight it was hard to imagine how any city could shine more brightly than St. Petersburg when it had the Winter Palace and the Mariinsky Theatre, but it was dark too. The city ate boys like Sasha and Vova, turning them into bloated corpses before they reached fat middle age. She'd heard a hundred thousand slaves died building the city, their bones crushed to grit beneath the weight of its wide avenues and fancy European streets. Sometimes she wondered if their spirits had infected the place.

Sasha broke the seal on a fresh bottle of Stolichnaya. 'How long have you been here?'

'Three years.' She pulled on the cigarette and the nicotine made her light-headed. 'We moved after our honeymoon.'

Sasha looked up. 'And how long's it been since Yuri left?'

You should know, she thought. 'Three months.'

It had been the end of September, in that last week of sunshine they call the Peasant Woman's Summer, when Yuri was sent to the prison colony at Krasnoyarsk and Sasha and Vova had arrived. They followed her and Ksenia around from that first day, and within a fortnight had scared off the few friends she'd made in St. Petersburg or "*Piter*" as she'd learned to call it. At first she had been outraged, complaining bitterly to Sasha about the intrusion into her private life, but it had only made them more controlling; more suspicious that her objections meant she had something to hide. They were right to distrust her.

She tried a subtler approach. Back then, they had been plain Alexander and Vladimir and she started calling them by their diminutives. When they followed her to the Leningrad Trade House she asked them to help choose a dress for Ksenia. During the week she bought them biscuits and cakes; at the weekend she treated them to vodka and cigarettes. Sometimes she flirted a little with Sasha, touching him lightly when she brushed past, or complimenting him on his physique.

'Where are you boys from?' she had asked.

'Kupchino,' she remembered Vova volunteering with unnecessary pride.

'South of the city, eh?'

'Yeah,' he muttered, struggling to match her gaze.

'I'm from Volgodonsk,' she had offered. 'From a shitty *Khrushchyovka* block of concrete like yours.'

At the end of October, Sasha told her she could go out alone. Of course, they followed her and Ksenia from a distance, waddling along the pavement like a pair of orphaned bears. She wheeled the pushchair around, pretending not to be aware of their presence. At home, she acted mildly surprised when they returned a minute after her. By mid-November, when it was dark and freezing, they stopped trailing her altogether.

'Are you in there?' Sasha's glassy eyes fixed on hers.

'I was daydreaming.' She forced a smile then watched the two men lean over the table and lock fists again. Sasha's bicep twitched as he strained his arm against Vova's, trying to score a cheap victory. Vova resisted and the legs of her coffee table rattled.

She stubbed the cigarette out. 'I'm going to the *produkti* before it closes.' Alone in her bedroom she'd rehearsed the line but nerves were making her prattle. 'I need cereal too – well, Ksenia does.'

Sasha twisted his thick neck. 'Can you get some Marlboro? The red ones.' He turned his head back to the competition.

She glanced at an open packet of *Peter the Great* and guessed he was taking advantage, but it didn't matter.

'Vodka?'

Sasha kept his bicep locked against Vova's in case of a surprise attack. 'No, we stocked up.' He gave her a queasy smile. 'I bought wine in case you want to join us.'

If her husband had seen that look, he would have cut the idiot's prick off. 'Maybe when I get back,' she replied with a coquettish twist of her shoulders.

'Wait.' He released his hand from Vova's grip, repeatedly stretching his fingers and forming a fist as if they were cramping. 'I'll come with you.'

She felt a momentary panic. 'No, stay, it's freezing outside.'

He looked alarmed. 'What about…?'

'Ksenia? Don't worry, she won't wake up.' The thought of a bull like Sasha terrified at the prospect of looking after a two-year-old girl made her smile.

She pulled on her winter fur, patting its pockets in a rehearsed move. 'Where's my damned purse?'

Instead of going to her bedroom, she went to the nursery and peered through a gap in the blinds at the Zhiguli parked across the street. She had noticed it five days ago, already submerged under a quilt of overnight snow. Now, slush was piled around the pavement where he'd cleared it away, and she could see the car was beige beneath the yellow of the sodium lamp. It was an old model too, with sharp angles. A vehicle that only a child or Soviet engineer might like to draw. There was no movement on the driver's side, no shadows or shapes that told her he was inside; it was too risky to sit and wait for her this close to the apartment.

She scanned the street. A group of revellers, three couples, were starting early on their New Year's celebrations, the women wearing furs and the men in smart three-quarter-length coats with Ushanka hats. He'd be out there too; a muffled figure hiding from the freezing wind. There was a left turn a few metres from the car where he might be keeping out of sight. That narrow road led to the Griboyedov Canal where she'd often stared at a small pool of pure black water that was always the last to resist the ice. Before she became pregnant, and when she realised the kind of man Yuri was, she'd been tempted to do more than stare at it.

She stuffed a pair of Ksenia's thick tights in the bottom of her nylon shopping bag, then added two thin blankets, Felix – Ksenia's favourite bear, and some disposable nappies. It made her feel sick to think of what what she was leaving behind: especially the lace coverlets her grandmother had crocheted as a wedding present.

Ksenia murmured as she pulled a sheepskin hat onto her head before wrapping her tightly in a blanket. Yuri wouldn't harm his own daughter, but *she* wasn't his own flesh, blood and nerves. If Sasha and Vova caught her, well, Yuri was never going to be labelled a cuckold. No doubt they had orders and Sasha would get to use that gun of his. She felt momentary guilt at their fate. If she succeeded they would be sensible to escape too, but she had met boys like Sasha and Vova before, they believed in loyalty the way Baltic sailors drowned – by clinging to the wreckage of their boats when swimming for shore could have saved them.

The handles of the nylon bag cut into her hand as she bent down to pick up Ksenia. Cradling her, she walked softly along the corridor.

'Mama?' Ksenia's eyes blinked open.

'Shh,' she whispered. 'We're going to a magic castle but only if you are very quiet.'

Ksenia nodded solemnly, half in a dream, her eyes flickering as they closed.

There was a triumphant shout from the living room then a pause. 'Don't forget the smokes,' Sasha called, his voice loud with vodka and victory.

She shuffled down two flights of stairs then opened the block's metal apartment door. Instantly, her cheeks burned with the cold and the freezing air made her gasp. She locked the door behind her, nearly stumbling under the weight. The scratching noise of her footsteps on the gritted pavement echoed as she staggered along the street. Ksenia burrowed her head into the fur lapels of the coat.

She stopped for a minute outside a closed magazine kiosk to catch her breath; her arm muscles burned with the effort of holding Ksenia and the shopping bag. Without a scarf, her nose and ears were already stinging; the next stage was numbness, then frostbite. She doubled back towards her apartment. At the familiar hulk of the Zhiguli she squatted, lowering Ksenia.

'Can you stand up for Mama?'

The child nodded slowly and got to her feet.

Kristina took out the blankets from the shopping bag and wrapped them around Ksenia.

'Don't move, darling.'

'Magic?'

'Yes, we're going to the castle now.'

A pair of black leather boots stopped on the path. She couldn't bear to look up.

'Are you all right?'

The voice was slurred and she didn't recognise it. She bobbed her head quickly without making eye contact. 'I'm fine.'

She willed the stranger to go away, her body statue still. It took forever until his footsteps started crunching on the ice and grit. The cold was biting now, sending a thousand icy jabs into the exposed skin on her face. Ksenia's cheeks each bore a perfect red circle and she pulled the edge of the knitted blanket around her until there was only a slit for the eyes.

'Stay there. Be a good girl for Mama.'

'I go bed.'

'Soon, darling.'

She ran a gloved hand along the underside of the Zhiguli's front wheel arch, finding the magnetic box where he'd told her it would be. She braced herself, hugging the top of the tyre with her arm, then gripped the box and yanked it. Her hand slipped off – the damned thing was welded to the metal by ice. She tried again. When that failed, she curled her hand into a fist and jabbed at the little box. Through the wool of her glove, a sharp corner scraped her knuckles, making her eyes water. Needles stabbed as the tears turned to ice. She formed a fist and hit the box again, blinking to stop fresh tears forming, then cradled her hand to mask the fresh pain. She gritted her teeth to suppress a scream, noticing the box had fallen soundlessly onto the snow.

The glove on her right hand was stiff with blood. She peeled it off to pick up the box, her fingers tacky on the freezing metal. She pushed the top edge. It slid open easily, revealing a single, silver key.

When she tried it in the passenger door, barely the tip of the key fitted inside the lock before it stuck.

'Lord Jesus Christ.' She strode to the driver's side in clear view of her apartment.

She resumed the incantation: 'Lord Jesus Christ, Son of God, have mercy on me a sinner. Lord Jesus Christ, Son of God, have mercy on me a sinner. Lord Jesus Christ, Son of God, have mercy on me a sinner.' The prayer did little to calm her mind: all she could think of was Sasha and Vova, and one of them looking outside to see why she was taking so long.

'Mama go home!' Ksenia called from the pavement.

'Shh! Remember the magic castle.'

Ksenia wailed, 'Nooooo – I go home!'

Kristina fought the temptation to comfort her. The cries grew louder. The key slipped into the lock on the driver's door but it too was frozen. She stole a glance at her apartment on the second floor

– the blinds were in shadow and it was impossible to know if they were looking out. She jabbed the key with her palm to try and force it in.

'Lord Jesus Christ, Son of God, have mercy on me a sinner. Lord Jesus Christ, Son of God—'

Ksenia began screaming.

There were hurried footsteps.

A gloved hand pulled the key from her. 'Let me do it.' His breath billowed out like factory smoke.

She looked up. 'Where the fuck were you?' she demanded.

'I needed a piss.'

She smelled alcohol on his breath. 'Is this all a game to you?'

'I was freezing.'

His cheeks were the colour and consistency of cold clay. She nodded to herself. 'Hurry, the lock's frozen.'

He pulled the key out and held a lighter to it. She darted around the Zhiguli's bonnet and picked up Ksenia. 'Shh, we're going to the castle now. There are horses and elephants.'

'I want go home,' Ksenia wailed.

He tried the key in the lock; it opened, and he leant across the seats to open her door from the inside. She cradled Ksenia as she climbed in, then picked up the bag from the pavement. Ksenia's crying tailed off as she became aware of the man sitting next to her and squirmed to see what was happening.

He started the engine. 'Shit, I forgot to bring a child seat.'

'Don't worry, just go.'

Ksenia whimpered, cradled in her arms and cocooned in the blankets. Soon, her soft snores were drowned out by the noise of the engine.

The Alexander Nevsky Bridge was blocked by traffic when they reached it.

'Christ, look at this.' He ran a hand through his hair and stared at three lanes of brake lights. 'When will they come?'

It took her a moment to realise he was talking about Sasha and Vova. 'They'll know by now.'

Prologue

'What are we going to do?'

Two fireworks launched prematurely from a barge on the Neva, their brilliant tips burning like phosphorous flares, illuminating the people in the queueing cars. She squirmed in her seat – they were barely two hundred metres from her apartment on the most obvious route out of the city.

'Hope and pray.'

Red lights winked as the traffic edged forward and she tried to focus on Ksenia's easy breaths.

The spell was broken by his fingers drumming on the steering wheel. 'We could go to the police?'

She snorted in disbelief. 'You want the militia to help you run away with a married woman? They'll take me home and steal your money.'

'Will he come after you?'

'Yuri? He'll never stop...I told him I was leaving.'

'You did what?'

'Relax – I wrote to him in Krasnoyarsk.'

She enjoyed seeing the shock on his face. 'Don't worry, the mail system is shit. We could be anywhere in the world by the time he reads it.'

'What did you say?'

'"Hey husband, you evil bastard. We've gone. Don't bother looking, you'll never find us."' She smiled at him. 'It's not Tolstoy.'

Two hours had gone by since they'd left the city behind. The heater was on full but still she shivered. Out here, away from the water and heading north to Finland, forests threatened the road and the temperature dropped to minus thirty in winter. Ksenia stirred with the noise of the engine and Kristina shifted position, bringing circulation to her numb right arm. The silence was oppressive in the Zhiguli and he broke it by turning on the radio; there was nothing except static and he switched to long-wave. She heard the President's voice and was stunned.

There had been the horror of Chechnya, then everyone's savings had been wiped out when the rouble crashed. And still Yeltsin survived, propped up by Berezovksy and the other oligarchs. He'd gone to America and been discovered drunk outside the White House in his underwear. On the TV puppet show, *Kukly*, she had cringed as he was humiliated again and again.

'He's leaving,' she said in shock. 'Boris Yeltsin is resigning.'

She twisted the volume control to hear it over the Zhiguli's engine and caught phrases:

"I want to ask for your forgiveness because many of our dreams didn't come true… the pain of every one of you, I feel in myself, in my heart... in saying goodbye, I want to say to every one of you: be happy. You deserve happiness. You deserve happiness, and peace."

The old buffoon had made her cry. She dipped her head forwards to dab her tears on the arm of her jacket.

Now the Acting President, a KGB goon called Putin, was promising freedom of speech and freedom of conscience. She wondered if he was smirking while he spoke. At least he didn't drink, maybe he was what the country needed now: someone serious and sober.

They were travelling faster, a hundred kilometres an hour on the empty carriageway; the Zhiguli's lights illuminating cones of snowflakes. She wanted to tell him to slow down but she was just as impatient to get away. The radio announcer cut to a live broadcast outside the Kremlin and they sat in silence as the bells of Spasskaya Tower clock chimed.

'Happy New Year, darling.' She reached across to squeeze his hand. 'To *our* happiness and peace.'

'I love you,' he said.

'I love you too.' She offered a smile to cover up the white lie.

He yanked his hand from hers.

She looked at him, confused, and saw him gripping the steering wheel; his mouth had fallen open.

The Zhiguli slid silently along the iced road. He stamped on the brake pedal; the car jerked to the left. She held Ksenia tightly against her chest. The Zhiguli cut across the opposite carriageway and there was a smashing of steel that thrust her forwards. She floated in clear air and screamed all the way down.

1

The White Nights, June 2017

Zena Dahl tried to focus on her bottle of Nevskoe Pale but it was no good, the damned thing had a life of its own. Beyond it, plates with the remains of pickled herring, salmon in dill, and beetroot salad performed a Day-Glo dance before her eyes. She squinted at her blurred reflection on the metal napkin holder, seeing how her thick blonde hair had curled from the humidity in the bar.

'You shouldn't say that, Zena.'

She looked up. Yulia's face was sliding, presenting multiple images of straightened brown hair and coral lips. Zena screwed up her eyes and a single version of Yulia appeared; it scowled at her then sucked on an e-cigarette, tilted its head back, and blew the steam upwards.

Oh, crap. The conversation came back to her. She'd been talking loudly about corruption – one of her father's stupid arguments.

'Sorry, I can't drink like this.' She puffed her cheeks and blew.

Yulia tucked the e-cigarette into her knock-off Gucci handbag before picking up her bottle of Budweiser Light. 'You're right by the way.'

Zena smiled and clinked her bottle against Yulia's Bud.

'Zdorovye.' The word stumbled from her mouth.

Yulia drained her beer, then looked around. 'Let's get out of here, this place is dull.'

Outside, the heat of the day still lingered and a light breeze brushed against her bare arms without raising goose pimples. The pale light of the sun made Zena check her watch for reference: it was a little after 11 p.m. The street was full of tourists and she sucked in a few deep breaths to try and sober up. Yulia was already ahead, working her way through a small crowd that had slowed to watch a fire-eater. Zena followed her, taking a left onto the main road where a row of SUVs were parked. A group of drivers stood nearby, smoking. A queue stretched along the pavement, the length of six of the enormous cars.

Yulia turned to her. 'This one's new. I've heard good things about it.' Then she added softly, 'You do the talking.'

Zena understood; they had done this before. Foreigners were always in the news: Kazakhs and Uzbeks were stealing jobs, the Chinese were taking over Siberia by stealth, and NATO, as always, was out to destroy Russia; yet being foreign was still an advantage when it came to getting into the city's bars and clubs.

She watched the doorman approach. He had no right to look as relaxed as he did in a pair of navy jodhpurs, a brown shirt with red flashes on the collar, and a red peaked cap. The effect of the vintage uniform was spoiled by a coiled earpiece wire trailing along his neck and disappearing behind his collar. She looked for the name of the bar and saw *Cheka* in the Latin alphabet.

'Hey, you must be the secret police,' she said in English, trying to sound friendly, or at least not as drunk as she was feeling.

'Nice try,' he replied in Russian, twisting his head past her to look Yulia up and down. He shook his head slightly and flicked his eyes to dismiss them.

Zena reached into her purse for her Swedish ID card but the doorman's attention had already shifted to a black Porsche Cayenne. An impassive driver-cum-bodyguard emerged and opened its doors. Two men climbed out, looking decades older than the rest of the clientele.

'Biznismen,' Yulia muttered in distaste as they sloped to the back of the queue.

Zena smiled but the doorman's insinuation had stung; it reminded her of the flea market at Udelnaya where a woman in a tie-dyed shirt had tried to sell her an old propaganda poster.

'It's you,' the woman had said, pulling out a framed picture of a rosy-cheeked girl with straw hair driving a tractor.

She hadn't bought the poster although the likeness had been uncanny – it wasn't flattering and besides, she didn't need a reminder of her own thick hair and broad body.

They made it inside the *Cheka* bar after thirty minutes of queueing.

Chapter 1

Yulia ordered vodka and when the bottle arrived, the waiter, dressed in the khakis of a Second World War soldier, turned it around so Zena could read the label. He enunciated his words carefully, realising he was speaking to a foreigner.

'*Putin-ka,*' he announced, 'it's a joke. An alcoholic drink in honour of our teetotal president.' He smiled good-naturedly. 'Where are you girls from?'

'Here, and she is from Sweden.' Yulia flirted a little.

'Which part?'

Zena watched in silence as he filled their glasses, feeling sorry for the waiter. Usually on their nights out, Yulia was only friendly to the ones she intended to humiliate.

'My friend is from a little town, I don't think you know it.'

'I might do,' he asked.

And then there was the kick in the balls when Yulia would say "It's called Get Back To Work", or if she wanted to pull his wings off first: "Buy me a drink and I might tell you." It wasn't one of her more appealing traits.

'Why don't you—'

'Östermalm,' Zena butted in, 'it's a district in Stockholm. I'm Zena.' She held out her hand and instantly regretted the move as a stuffy habit she'd picked up from her father.

The waiter smiled and shook it. 'I'm Gavril, just ask for me if you need anything. Nice to meet you, Zena.'

Yulia's expression was that of a cat denied the pleasure of torturing a small rodent. 'She's rich,' she said, trying to wrestle the conversation back, 'her father knows the Queen of Sweden.'

'She's joking of course,' Zena said unnecessarily as the waiter was smiling.

'Well, have a good evening.' He tapped his heels together and made a mock salute.

'What a loser,' said Yulia when he had gone.

'I thought he was nice.'

Yulia tilted her head and held out her glass. 'Anyway…To health.'

They tipped the vodka back then Zena stood, feeling the blood drain from her face. 'I need the bathroom.'

When she returned after more queueing, their table was empty but it wasn't hard to find Yulia. She was dancing on the stage and her long, slim arms were raised high in the air; it had the effect, no doubt intended, of pulling up her red mini-dress to reveal a few centimetres of skinny thigh above stay-up stockings. Next to Yulia was a boy, though with chiselled cheekbones and narrow Slavic eyes he was more godlike than human. He wore a brilliant white shirt with the top buttons undone and was throwing his arms around like a bear conducting an invisible orchestra. Zena felt the acid burn in her stomach.

Yulia still hadn't seen her as she climbed on to the stage, and Zena forced her way through a group of five or six drunken men with shaved heads. They laughed and formed a circle around her, then began clapping in time. One of the men entered the circle and squatted on the stage.

'The huge country is rising,' they half-sang, half-shouted over the wailing of the DJ's power ballad.

The one squatting put his hands on his hips and began performing Cossack kicks with some skill. She bumped into his outstretched leg causing him to fall on his back.

'Rising for the deathly battle.'

Zena went to help him from the floor. She realised then, that he'd been looking up her dress. She broke out of the circle and slipped, putting an arm out to stop herself.

'Against the dark fascist force.'

'Fuck, I'm so drunk,' she muttered.

The boy in the white shirt was staring at her, an amused expression on his face. She realised with a shock that her hand was resting on his chest; the tips of her fingers slipping through the sheer material of his shirt onto bare skin. There was no sign of Yulia. They stood there, frozen in time. She tilted her head and smiled.

'Let our noble wrath,' the men shouted, abandoning any attempt to follow the melody of their song.

The boy must be drunk, she thought. Her fingers lingered, then she pulled at a loose thread. 'You've lost a button.'

Chapter 1

He smiled back, and in a moment of insanity she pressed her mouth against his chest. He tasted salty and his skin felt smooth, like plastic. The boy's hand tightened on her waist.

'Against the cursed hordes.'

The arm was gone. He stepped back to increase the distance between them.

Yulia's voice was close and shrill, 'Zena, what were you doing?'

'Seethe like waves.'

She cut through the circle of conscripts. Their singing stopped and she caught a cheer behind her as she climbed off the stage. At the table she grabbed the bottle of Putinka by the neck then ran out into the luminous night, brushing past the tourists milling around Ligovsky Prospekt.

'Hey!'

The doorman with the stupid uniform chased after her. She pushed a hand into her purse and tossed some bank notes on the ground.

'Bitch,' he called out in English.

She waited a safe distance before turning, and caught him pulling at the creases of his jodhpurs before crouching to pick up the notes and tuck them in his wallet.

There were goose pimples on her arms now. She'd been wandering for hours, most of it spent burning off the anger she had directed at herself for behaving like a slut. After that, self-pity had taken hold at losing the only decent friend she'd made after nine months in St. Petersburg. She checked her iPhone then remembered the battery had died somewhere between the tall office blocks that took up both sides of the street. Taking another step, she felt a pull on her left leg.

'Damn it.' She stared at the heel wedged between two pavement slabs.

Easing her foot out of the six hundred dollar velvet pump, she teetered on the remaining heel, then lost her balance.

A grey wall lurched towards her. 'Oh shit.'

She twisted her body in time to take the impact on her shoulder. The Putinka fell from her hand and bounced on the pavement with a chink. It rolled then came to rest a metre from her wedged heel. Putting her back to the wall, she slid down, not thinking of the dress until it crackled with the sound of static. She'd had it less than a day and it was ruined. All those little silk spiders working away for nothing. She squatted on the asphalt and twisted her heel from the grate, then slipped the pump back onto her foot and reached for the bottle. Unscrewing the cap, she put the mouth of the Putinka to her lips.

She heard a blast reverberate through the city and thought it was the cannon from the Peter and Paul Fortress before remembering it was only fired at midday. Craning her neck to see above the office buildings, she saw globes of pink and white fireworks, then watched them fade, leaving clouds of white smoke behind in the pale sky. The air carried the sound of a distant crowd cheering followed by the mournful blast of a ship's foghorn that drowned out their voices. She sipped the vodka more carefully now, seeing the colours of fresh fireworks play on the glass.

Back in Stockholm, she had watched the parades with her father. Those *Konstens Natt* festivals with their dancing girls and marching bands were so lame. She cringed remembering his over-enthusiastic clapping as the Östermalm locals drifted by in their homemade costumes, their heads twisting to get a glimpse of the famous businessman. Konstens Natt marked the start of summer, when the sun stayed above the horizon for three months, but it was pathetic compared to *Belye Nochi*, the White Nights festival in St. Petersburg.

She had heard from Yulia that every year, at the height of the celebrations, a scarlet-coloured tall ship sailed along the Neva to the accompaniment of classical music and enough fireworks to keep factories in China busy for the rest of the year. That was two days away, yet no one seemed to have told the people launching the rockets. She had seen canals filled with splashes of colour, the water churned up by partygoers on motorboats who danced and sang in drunken ecstasy. She sighed – it would continue for weeks and she was already exhausted.

'Pu-tin-ka.' She pushed her lips out and spoke in an exaggerated, deep Russian voice.

Chapter 1

Finally, she screwed the cap onto the half-empty bottle of vodka, leant against the wall and closed her eyes.

An internal alarm made her instantly awake as two boys worked their way towards her, silhouetted by the weak shadows of the office buildings. One of them stopped in a doorway, his face hidden, but the other boy kept coming. He had red Adidas tracksuit bottoms and a stained yellow T-shirt, and even from ten metres she could see his teeth were rotten. The word *gopnik* came into her head; Yulia had used it to describe a street kid they'd seen. She'd asked what it meant.

'A nasty shit with bad fashion sense,' Yulia had replied.

Zena patted down her dress as the *gopnik* approached, conscious of her bare legs, then looked around, trying to pass off the search for an escape route as a casual glance – the place was deserted. Her diaphragm tensed automatically and she rubbed her arms to shake off a shiver. The boy was facing her now, gripping a cigarette between his index finger and thumb. The smoke made her eyes smart.

'You want some?' He moved the cigarette away.

She shook her head.

He squatted until his head was level with hers. She smelled his sickly sweet breath as he took a swig of *Jaguar*. He placed a hand on the back of her head and pushed the can against her mouth.

'Don't touch me.'

She spoke in rapid Russian, making her accent harsh, then shook her head to brush his hand away. The liquid dribbled down her chin.

'Messy girl.' He put the can down and grabbed the strap of her handbag, eyeing her carefully to see her reaction.

She felt the spasm in her diaphragm again.

'Don't...,' she said, then stopped. She stopped to avoid putting the words in his head: *don't hurt me*.

She settled for 'Leave me alone.'

He ignored her and opened the clasp of her purse. A firework exploded into yellow petals that transformed into white trails as they fell. He watched them until they disappeared behind the buildings, his mouth gaping open like a child's.

The twilight resumed and he dipped his head to ground level, twisting his neck to call into the recess of an office block. 'Fuck, Stas, you should see this.'

Her gaze had been fixed on the ground, anxious to avoid eye contact, but now she turned and saw him with a fold of her notes. He was counting them out and she thought of running but the idea was laughable: two boys against a half-drunk girl? Another spasm caught her low in the diaphragm; this time she vomited.

The *gopnik* glanced casually at the puke on the pavement. 'Messy girl,' he repeated, then tutted as if her drunkenness had made him morally superior. He shuffled on his haunches then called over his shoulder, 'Stas, she's got American dollars.'

The other boy came out of the shadows and crouched next to him. She shivered as a breeze blew against her bare legs.

'Leave me alone!' Her voice echoed in the empty street.

Stas's face brushed against hers, and she smelled bitter cigarette smoke and stale sweat as his hands grabbed her thighs.

She glared at him. 'Get your fucking hands off me.'

He grinned back, revealing brown teeth and a stench of decay.

'Or what, princess?' he turned his head in the direction of the empty street in a single sarcastic gesture.

His fingers grabbed at her underwear. She put her hands on his wrists to stop him, digging her nails into his skin. He yanked his arms down, tearing at the flimsy material.

'I said "Get off!"' She lashed out with her right foot, stabbing the heel at his face.

The *gopnik* caught her leg easily, his fingers encircling her ankle.

'Not here Stas.'

He turned his head. While he was distracted she crossed her legs, locking her muscles to keep them together. He lifted her dress and she lashed out with her hand, digging her nails into his cheek. His fist caught her jaw, knocking her head against the wall. There was little strength behind it though, and she felt no more than dazed.

The *gopnik* pulled down his tracksuit pants to reveal pale, hairless legs. 'Open up, messy girl,' he said, oblivious to a trickle of blood on his cheek.

A deep shiver settled inside her. The muscles in her legs were cramping.

A car horn sounded close by and she saw him hesitate.

'Dima?' he hissed. 'Dima? You pussy. Where are you?'

He pulled up his tracksuit bottoms one-handed, his penis solid and twitching inside, then took a phone from his pocket. He turned it over in his hands and she heard the artificial camera sound as he aimed it at her. There were more clicks but it was fine, he could take his porn pictures because he was going to crawl back under his rock soon.

'Stas,' Dima hissed from the shadows, 'someone's coming.'

'Yeah, alright.' He trotted away.

She pulled up her torn underwear then grabbed her handbag.

'Shit,' she said, putting her palms on the brick wall to steady herself as she got to her feet.

'Are you alright?' a voice asked.

Zena pulled her dress down in a single jerky movement then looked up to see jeans and a black leather jacket over a white work shirt.

'I'm fine,' she snapped, wondering how long he'd been there.

She picked up her purse and looked inside.

'Oh no,' she said aloud.

It was empty except for her ID and the keys to her apartment. She guessed the *gopnik* had left them behind so she wouldn't be forced to go to the police. At least he'd been too stupid to steal her watch, she thought, trying to be upbeat – her *Tag Heuer* was worth enough to keep him in Jaguar for the rest of his stunted life.

She'd been planning to spend summer in the city but now realised it was a stupid idea to be hundreds of kilometres from anyone who gave a damn about her. Although she didn't feel so drunk any more it still took a moment of squinting to make out the tiny hands on the watch's numberless dial. It was quarter past two; late, but not too late. There was time to go back to her apartment, catch some sleep, then find an evening flight to Stockholm where she would surprise her father with a late-night call from Arlanda Airport. She would insist they went on holiday to a familiar place, maybe Cap Ferrat, and she would learn to be less fucking stupid.

'You want a lift?'

She'd forgotten he was there, and looked up to see the man's greying hair and lines etched in his broad face. He didn't look like the type of guy to get in a car with, but who was she to judge? Besides, what choice did she have when those *gopnik* pieces of shit had left her without a single rouble?

'Please.'

The man pulled out a key fob and pressed a button. Ten metres away, orange indicators flashed on a black Range Rover Sport and the interior lit up to show pale green leather seats. She headed for his car, willing herself to walk in a straight line. After a few strides, she noticed he wasn't with her. Putting a hand on the wall to steady herself, she turned to watch him stoop, then grab the half-empty bottle of *Putinka* from the pavement.

He jogged up to her. 'You must be a foreigner to leave good drink behind.'

She ignored his hint of a question. Last Thursday, she'd watched the end of a debate on TV about the consequences if Sweden joined NATO. The planted audience were vile; they spoke of squashing, destroying, and nuking. She could almost taste their hatred.

At least the man was making a show of being chivalrous, stepping past her to pull the door open. She gave him a tight-lipped smile as she climbed in to let him know she appreciated the gesture. Getting into a car with a stranger at this time of the morning wasn't stupid, it was *fucking* stupid, she knew that, but it wasn't any worse than wandering the streets alone.

He tossed the vodka bottle onto the seat behind her then went to the driver's side. Her hands were shaking as she fumbled with the seatbelt.

'Here,' he said, leaning over to get the strap into the buckle. Their fingers touched and she pulled her hand away.

'Fuck,' she muttered under her breath as he started the car.

They drove in silence for a moment then she turned to him.

'Thank you,' she said, thinking of how close she had come to being raped.

'That's alright, Zena,' he replied.

2

Natalya Ivanova was sure the woman in the white and purple checked headscarf was holding out. She watched her carefully with the eyes of a practised interrogator. 'What do you mean?'

The woman shrugged, giving little away. 'I mean gone.'

'All gone?'

'Yes.'

'The Parmesan? The real stuff from Italy? I heard you had some.'

Natalya stared at her assembled vegetables and tin cans bunched up at the end of the tiny conveyor belt, wondering if she should make borscht instead of white bean soup, or perhaps she could use another cheese but she wasn't a cook and liked to stick close to recipes. It was a special occasion too – giving up and ordering pizza wasn't an option.

'Still gone.'

Natalya pulled out her wallet, unintentionally revealing her ID card.

'You *menti*?'

She nodded, unoffended by the slang for the police that wasn't exactly respectful but everyone used.

'What type?' the woman asked. 'Militia?'

Natalya caught sight of her tired face in a reflection off the meat counter. The whole afternoon had been wasted on Bolshoi Prospekt interviewing a Svetlana Alkhimovich who had been admitted to Pokrovskaya City hospital with fractures of the left cheek and eye socket. Her husband and likely assailant, Arkady, radiated hostility when she made him stand beyond the perimeter of his wife's bed. Through a gap in the plastic curtain, Natalya saw him eyeing up a nurse as he leant against the cradle of an oxygen cylinder; an unlit cigarette perched in his orange-stained fingers. She was tempted to step out and light it for him just to see if he combusted, but the brute wasn't worth dying for. Instead, she gave Svetlana Alkhimovich the addresses of the few women's refuges that served the city. In her experience, the poor woman had a fight or two left in her before the violence reached a climax and she saved herself – if it wasn't too late then.

It was also clear from the outset that the injuries weren't bad enough for her to intervene. Arresting Mrs Alkhimovich's husband was a joke when her superiors insisted on releasing domestic violence suspects after the statutory three hours' administrative detention – the woman had to be seriously hurt or dead before a criminal case was created. The experience had left her feeling depressed.

'The militia became the regular police five years ago. They are the ones you see with stations in each district.'

The woman scanned her groceries. 'And that's what you do?'

Natalya stifled a yawn. 'No, I work for the Criminal Investigations Directorate, we cover the whole of *Piter* and only deal with serious crimes.'

'How interesting.'

'I used to think so, now I'm just trying to make bean soup before the government bans beans.'

The woman laughed nervously then addressed a rough-bearded man in a foreign language that Natalya figured was Uzbek or Kyrgyz. He left the small shop through a bead-curtained back door then re-emerged clutching a wheel of Parmesan the shape of a small millstone. She saw 'Parmigiano-Reggiano' stencilled on the rind of the cheese and a less convincing 'Made in Belarus' sticker applied to its plastic cover.

'How much do you want?' the woman asked.

'How much is it?'

'Eight thousand a kilo.'

Natalya let out a low whistle. 'I'm not that type of police either.'

The woman shook her head at the bearded man, and he retreated with a rattle of the bead curtain.

Her husband Mikhail, who was also a senior detective in the Criminal Investigations Directorate, was frequently amused by her idealism. Undoubtedly, he would have seized the Parmesan as a contraband item then presented it to her. She thought, ruefully, that his approach made a lot more sense sometimes; judging by the snoring, his conscience didn't bother him too much either.

Inside her apartment block, she dumped her shopping on the lift's mosaic tiles then pressed a button to send it to the third floor; getting out before the doors closed. Like many in the city's pre-Revolution buildings, the lift had been added as an afterthought and couldn't be trusted to transport anything that wanted to stay alive.

As she climbed the marble stairs, she thought of her grand, high-ceilinged apartment with its view of the stone lions on Lviny Bridge. It wasn't the type of place two detectives on meagre salaries could afford, but it had been made possible by Mikhail's mother, Violka, who died of pneumonia brought on by early-onset Alzheimer's. The money had come as a shock considering the old bird had a reputation for being as tight as a tree sparrow; nevertheless, her fifteen million roubles had bought the three-bedroom apartment, and thanks to the property bubble, its value was increasing by more than their combined incomes.

One bedroom was reserved for her stepson, Anton. The arrangement with Mikhail's ex-wife, Dinara, had been for alternate weekends but he had just turned eighteen and was as constant as a cat, often arriving late when he fancied a change of scene. The third bedroom had been kept clear. With the low life expectancy of the average Russian male, Mikhail knew his biological clock was ticking and wanted a child with her before it was too late. At thirty-eight, she was also approaching the age where having a baby could be difficult. Being childless didn't bother her particularly when, after nearly two decades in the police, she had learnt to smother her maternal instincts. Nevertheless, she had been surprised by the ease and speed with which Anton had broken through her natural reserves. No doubt there were explanations that a therapist could uncover but sometimes a cigar was just a cigar, and Anton was just a bright, sweet, funny, boy who she had grown to love.

She dumped her shopping on the kitchen floor then went into the bathroom to take a quick shower. Naked, she appraised herself using the mirrored back of the door and saw more grey hairs in the reddish-brown that she'd need to address soon by dyeing or denial. She put her hands on her hips and tried to tense her stomach only to see faint lines appear. Her body was still slim, though it was more due to neglect than the gym that cost nineteen thousand roubles a year for her non-attendance. She pulled off her underwear then climbed into the shower.

Her hair was still damp after rushing to get dressed. In the kitchen she discovered an old Parmesan rind in the freezer and did a little jig before dropping it whole into the bean soup. Next she retrieved one of the few inherited items from her mother: a steel rolling pin. She took some chilled dough from the fridge, tore it in half and started pressing one of the lumps to make a flat sheet.

She heard the door followed by the sound of shoes being kicked off in the hallway. Mikhail appeared; out of habit he opened the fridge and took out a bottle of Ochakovo. He twisted off the cap before downing half the bottle.

'Don't I get a welcome?'

'Sorry, Angel.' He put his free arm around her waist and kissed her on the mouth.

Mikhail tasted of beer but she didn't mind.

'How was your day?' he asked.

'Better now it's the weekend. This morning I overheard Rogov referring to me as The German to some new recruits.'

Mikhail grinned. 'Well, he is an insolent bastard – you have to hand it to him.'

After the Soviet Union collapsed, her father had taken a job as an administrator on a cultural exchange programme in Hannover. She had loved Germany instantly but it didn't take her mother long to feel uncomfortable with her new life and start complaining about everything, from the language and endless varieties of toothpaste in the supermarkets, to the openness with which any subject could be discussed, including sex and religion. Four years later, when Natalya was sixteen, her mother decided they should all go home. Her father refused, as did her sister, Klavdiya, who at eighteen was old enough to decide her own fate. At the insistence of both her parents, Natalya unhappily returned to Russia with her mother, splitting the family in two. Her father and Klavdiya were now German citizens and she kept in contact regularly, trying to see them at least once a year. Though she was no more German than Rogov, there was something to his insinuations: the more time she spent in Hannover, the more foreign she felt when she returned.

He pointed the neck of his Ochakovo at her. 'Want one?'

'No thanks, I'm on call.'

'OK, I'm going to get changed.'

She looked at him properly, noticing the grey-blue suit that perfectly matched his eyes and complemented his black hair. Naked, she knew Mikhail was a few kilos overweight but his frame was big enough to take it and the buttoned-up suit smoothed out his belly, making it flat to outward appearances.

'You look nice.'

'Day in court.' He took another swig from the bottle.

'How was it?'

'Dull. Did you hear about Colonel Vasiliev?'

'Yeah, he's retiring. It's the worst kept secret in the department.'

Mikhail shrugged with his mouth. 'Well, Rogov told me a new major started today. Some prick called Dostoynov. Before you ask, I already know he's a prick because he's ex-FSB…Vasiliev has put him in my office.'

'What's does that mean?'

Mikhail did the mouth shrug again though she suspected it was more to hide his feelings than to signal that he didn't care. Colonel Vasiliev had a reputation, much like the President's, of pitting his subordinates against each other and awarding the victor the spoils. The prize in this case was control of the Directorate and the only person with the rank to challenge the new major was Mikhail. There was only one snag – if Mikhail got the top job she would have to transfer to another department; it was against regulations to have a supervisory role over a spouse.

He swigged some more of the Ochakovo. 'How was your day – apart from Rogov?'

His eyes flickered momentarily in her direction – she could tell he wasn't interested and decided not to bore him. 'Don't ask.'

She laid the sheet of dough over a *pelmeni* mould.

'What are you cooking?'

'Bean soup and dumplings.'

'Why? We could get a take-out.'

'Anton.' She took out a teaspoon and scooped chopped pork and beef from a frying pan before depositing it in an indentation on the mould. She started on another one.

'What about him?'

'He's staying with us tonight.' She dropped it in the mould and took another from the pan. Thirty more to go.

'So? You don't normally bother.'

'He's bringing his new girlfriend – I put it on the calendar last week. Please tell me you remembered.'

Mikhail pressed his lips together in a mock apology. 'I still don't know why you bother.'

She knew the reason – in all likelihood, Anton was the closest she would get to a child of her own and she intended to take her stepmother duties seriously.

She turned away from the mould and put floury hands on her hips 'OK, if you can tell me her name I'll let you off.'

'What is this?' He took another swig to cover his embarrassment but she saw through it.

'You lose. It's Anna.'

He nodded thoughtfully. 'That's right.'

'You lose again, her name's Tanya, and they'll be here soon.

'Wear something nice,' she said to Mikhail's retreating back.

She returned to the *pelmeni*, wishing she'd bought pizza instead, then heard the key in the door.

'Anton?'

'Yeah, it's me.'

She waited for another voice.

'Tanya's not here.' Anton's head appeared; he was slim and handsome with close-cut hair that was just too long to be a skinhead's. He fixed her with the brown doe eyes he'd inherited from his mother; annoyingly, Dinara was beautiful.

'But she's still coming, right?'

He shuffled in his socks; his arms behind his back. 'There's stuff going on at home, her parents are divorcing...What's for dinner?'

'Don't change the subject. When did Tanya tell you this?'

'What, is this some kind of interrogation?'

She glared at him. 'Just tell me how long you've known so I can decide what object to beat you with.'

'Wait, I can prove my innocence.'

'OK,' she said, picking up the steel rolling pin and tapping the end into an open palm to make a slapping noise, 'but if you lie to me I'll kill you.' She offered a mock-menace scowl. 'You won't be the first.'

Anton had one arm behind his back; he brought it forward: 'She gave me this for you – eleven red roses. She told me to say how sorry she is.'

Mikhail returned to deposit the empty beer bottle. He was wearing a pair of white boxers and his fresh shirt had all the buttons undone. 'What's this about innocence?'

'Tanya's not coming.'

'At least you told me before I put a tie on.'

'So trousers weren't your first thought?' Turning to Anton she said, 'You made me cook so I'm going to make you eat until I hear your stomach tearing.' She fixed him with a bright smile.

Anton groaned then ran a hand over his stubbly hair. 'There's something I need to tell you both. It's bad.'

'Is she pregnant?' Natalya asked. 'Please tell me you're using something.'

Mikhail stared at Anton. 'What is it?' he growled.

She studied her stepson's face, reading reticence. 'Let's talk about it later,' she said, knowing Mikhail was calmer after dinner.

'Whose son is he?' Mikhail had overstepped a boundary and immediately looked contrite.

Chapter 2

Anton studied her face. 'Shall I leave it?'

'Don't look at me, apparently I'm not part of the family.' She raised her eyebrows in a mocking gesture aimed at Mikhail. 'But as I was asking' – she picked dough off her fingers – 'is Tanya pregnant?'

'No,' said Anton, sounding disturbed. 'But it's best if I show you. It came in the mail this morning but you know what Mama is like. She's been happy this last week but anything can send her down. Will you sort it out for me?'

The damned dough was under her fingernails. 'What is it?'

Anton put the roses next to the bottle then went to the hallway to retrieve the small rucksack he seemed to live out of – he revelled in his status as a nomad.

'I've got it here.' Anton unzipped a side pouch and pulled out a creased envelope then held it an equal distance between them as if to maintain his neutrality.

Mikhail immediately snatched the envelope and tore it open. 'Shit,' he said after scanning the letter inside.

'What is it?' she asked. 'Assuming I'm still part of the family.'

Mikhail scowled. 'It's from Professor Litovkin, the Head of Admissions.'

He was quiet as he read. 'To paraphrase, he is informing us that Anton Mikhailovich Ivanov is not academic material.'

Natalya frowned and stared at the *pelmeni* dumplings that would need another hour of preparation. She took the paper from Mikhail. 'I thought you had fixed it?'

Anton looked embarrassed. 'It doesn't matter Natalya, I can find a job. I don't have to go university.'

'I'm talking to your father.'

'I thought I had done it,' Mikhail said quietly.

'What's this about?' Anton asked.

'What do you think?' She put the paper on a worktop and took a knife from the drawer to scrape under her fingernails. 'You're old enough to be conscripted. The only way you can stay out is if you get an exemption certificate; that means you have to be medically unfit or at university. You've heard of dedovshchina, right?'

'Sure, the Rule of Grandfathers, I heard that doesn't happen any more.'

'Yes it does. You could be beaten to death, raped, or pimped out by the older soldiers.'

'It's not so bad.' Mikhail put a hand on her shoulder and squeezed it affectionately. 'I did it.'

She shook his hand off. 'You want to try telling Anton some of your war stories?' She shook her head in wonderment that he'd even brought up the subject. 'You were in Chechnya for Christ's sake, it's a wonder you came back alive.'

'It's different now.'

'Right? So you can promise me he won't get sent to Donetsk, South Ossetia, Syria, or some other place we shouldn't be in. And what if something else starts? Every time the President's popularity falls—'

'Natalya, it won't happen.' Anton's head flicked between the two of them.

'It wasn't supposed to happen. Your father was meant to be fixing it.'

'What are you saying?'

She looked at Mikhail and he shrugged – permission to continue. She wiped dough from the knife onto a piece of kitchen roll. 'Do you remember when you had that fever last year and the doctor saw you straight away?'

Anton ran a hand over his semi-shaved hair. 'Yeah, but what's this got to do with—'

Mikhail jumped in. 'Natalya paid that dried-up bitch of a receptionist eight hundred roubles to jump the queue, that's what.'

'Nice language,' she said.

'Sorry, Angel.' He leaned over and kissed her on the cheek.

'So you're taking driving lessons now.' Mikhail swigged on the Ochakovo. 'If I don't pay the examiner he'll fail you no matter how many times you take it. But if I slip him ten thousand, he'll pass you even if you've never been inside a car.'

'Yeah I know this.'

She scraped the knife under another fingernail. 'And you can be as smart as Andrei Sakharov but you won't get into university without your father opening his wallet.'

'So?'

'So' – she glared at Mikhail – 'your letter means *someone* forgot to pay them. Incidentally, you ought to be more grateful. Your father bought your entrance exam results too. It cost him fifteen thousand roubles. Your real grades wouldn't get you into a state orphanage.'

Anton looked dejected. 'I told you, it doesn't matter. I'll get a job.'

'Then you'll end up in the army. At least they won't have to cut your hair.'

'They won't find me.'

Mikhail's fist gripped the edge of the table. 'Are you going to hide until you're twenty-nine? Don't be stupid.'

Anton looked stung. 'All right, then there are other ways.'

Natalya looked at the dumpling dough. It was getting warm; soon it would stick to the mould then turn to mush when she dropped the *pelmeni* in boiling water.

Mikhail opened the fridge and reached for a second bottle of Ochakovo. 'No son of mine is going into a lunatic asylum. People will think you're crazy.' He picked up the creased letter and waved it. 'I'm sure this Professor Litovkin is just telling us we're late with the payment.' He frowned, showing uncertainty. 'And if not, there are places.'

'We're not going through that again, Misha.' She finished scraping dough from under her nails and dropped the knife in the sink. 'It took us weeks to set up a meeting with Litovkin.'

'OK, OK. Leave it with me, I'll check my accounts but I'm sure I paid the money-grabbing bastard.'

Natalya picked up the *pelmeni* mould and strode towards the pedal bin; she pressed the foot lever to open the lid then tipped the dough inside. She let the lid fall with a clang. Mikhail and Anton looked relieved and she hated them for it.

3

She awoke to Mikhail's crushing weight; his armpit hairs irritating her nose. He was stretched over her diagonally, talking to someone on her mobile.

'No, this is Major Ivanov. Just give me the address, I'll pass it on. She'll be there.'

He hung up. 'For Christ's sake, Natalya, answer your goddam phone next time.'

She pushed her hands underneath his girth to prise him off. 'Misha, you're squashing me.'

His crushing weight lifted as he rolled back; the tang of his armpit lingering in her nostrils. She checked the clock radio, it showed "07:08". For a second she wondered why her alarm hadn't gone off then she remembered, with a sinking feeling, that it was Saturday and she was on call.

'Who was it?'

He turned his back on her. 'Domestic. Some teenager in uniform from Vasilyevsky District; he's waiting for you. The address is on the table.'

Despite being a heavier sleeper than her, Mikhail's constant, low level drinking made him get up several times in the night to urinate and left him tired until midday; yet another reason to stay childless – he would struggle with the demands of a newborn.

From the living room, the day looked bright and she decided on a peach blouse over dark blue jeans; something informal and feminine to narrow the distance between an official and a victim of domestic violence. As an afterthought she grabbed a brown leather jacket from her wardrobe. Whatever she chose, it seemed the city's maritime climate always had other plans.

Chapter 3

She climbed in her ancient Volvo and left Tsentralny – one of the four districts that formed the historic heart of the city. As she crossed the Palace Bridge to Vasilyevsky Island she had an unpleasant memory of being eighteen and getting permission to go out drinking with her friends for the first time. The bar had been on the island and she had decided to walk home, forgetting that all the bridges to the mainland transformed into drawbridges in the early hours of the morning. She had spent the night shivering in a doorway, shooing away drunks who tried to pick her up. It was almost seven when she made it home, her mother adding to her misery by grounding her for a fortnight. Every kitchen noticeboard in the city had the bridge timetable pinned to it but after a few drinks it was easy enough to forget.

It was a little before 8 a.m. when she parked on Sredny Prospekt. The sky was still clear and she locked her jacket in the car boot before checking the address on the slip of paper Mikhail had given her. She hadn't needed to: a uniformed *ment* was waiting conspicuously outside the entrance to an apartment block. On closer inspection, he looked a year or two older than Anton except he had a hardness in his eyes and she wondered momentarily if it had come from military service, a tough childhood, or more likely, both. The policeman had been smoking a cigarette; he tossed it to the pavement and ground it out with his shoe when she stopped at the main door.

'Documents?' he demanded, casting a disdainful eye on her car.

She peered at the rank displayed on his lapel – a private – then took her time pulling out her wallet and showing him her ID badge.

He straightened. 'Sorry, Captain.' His eye twitched with a facial tick. 'Criminal Investigations Directorate? Why did they call you?'

She ignored his impertinence. 'What's going on?'

He spoke in a staccato fashion, 'Fourth floor, third on the left. Renata Shchyotkina. Boyfriend slapped her around. She asked me to wait here in case he came back. Refused to speak to me. Wanted a woman.' He took a breath feeling that he'd given her the salient points. 'This isn't police business, Captain, if we made a criminal of every husband who knocked his wife about there'd be no one left.'

'You're wrong,' she said, giving him a hard stare. 'You represent the state. By doing nothing, you give the cowards permission to continue. And next time you speak to a citizen follow the rules: give them your surname and rank first.'

She brushed past him and steeled herself for four flights of stairs. The private had a point, she thought, even if it was a technical one. There wasn't an offence of domestic violence in the Criminal Code. Worse, a bill had been recently introduced in the Duma to downgrade assaults within the family to an administrative crime. The last time she'd tried to charge a man for beating up his wife he'd been let off with a stern warning, and only one of her cases had resulted in a successful prosecution – then, the sentence of twelve months for disfiguring the poor woman with a hot iron had been unduly lenient.

At the fourth floor she pressed the buzzer on the third door to the left; it was opened by a tall woman, almost one metre eighty and model-slim. One of her eyes had been reduced to a slit and the skin on the upper-part of her face was swollen and already turning blue.

She introduced herself: 'Senior Detective Ivanova.'

Renata Shchyotkina lay down on a white, leather sofa while Natalya took in the apartment. The slate-grey walls and pictures were modern, as was the chandelier with its dozens of filaments glowing orange above an elaborately laid dining table.

'Miss Shchyotkina, you should go to hospital,' she said, pulling on a pair of latex gloves to examine the woman's face. The damage looked superficial, if painful; she'd seen worse. 'Shall I put some ice on that? Or frozen peas?'

'No, leave it like this.'

She understood: Renata Shchyotkina wanted a record of her injuries before they started healing. 'Don't worry about that, in a few days your face will look like you took on Wladimir Klitschko.' She went into the kitchen, gathered ice in a towel then handed it to her.

'Thank you.'

Natalya took out her notepad. 'Does he live with you?'

Renata Shchyotkina pressed the towel over her swollen eye. 'It's his place.'

Chapter 3

This was the moment she hated. 'Move out if you can. What's that saying men are so fond of: "If he beats you he loves you"? He'll come back and apologise but he won't change; they never do.'

Natalya's iPhone started buzzing. She glanced at it, saw Mikhail's name, and tapped the screen to send the call to voicemail.

Renata Shchyotkina shook her head in despair. 'You haven't even asked his name.'

'If I was in charge I'd have all these cowards take a real beating, but I can tell you for certain that nothing will happen to him until he nearly kills you. Miss Shchyotkina, if you have the money start a private prosecution against him.'

'That's a pretty speech,' the woman said, rounding on her. 'Why do you even bother?'

Natalya often wondered the same thing herself. For fifteen years she had worked on serious, violent crimes, and then her career had stalled as less experienced colleagues were promoted over her. There were suggestions in the station that she should put on more makeup or at least wear skirts occasionally. There was even a beauty pageant, Miss Russia Police, and some of the very feminine contestants reached the highest ranks, so undoubtedly she was getting good advice. In return she told her male colleagues to smoke and drink less if they wanted to be sharper and more able to catch criminals.

'Listen to me. Fourteen thousand women are murdered every year by their partners,' she said.

Her phone started buzzing again.

'Why don't you answer it? There's no point you being here anyway.' Renata Shchyotkina said acidly.

Natalya glanced at the screen: it was Mikhail again. 'Excuse me,' she said, and pressed the green circle to accept the call.'

'Hey, Angel.'

'Hello,' she said, guardedly.

Mikhail let out a full yawn. 'Rogov just called me from the station. He heard you were out on that call at Vasilyevsky Island.'

She turned away from Renata Shchyotkina. 'So why didn't he call me directly? Rogov is my subordinate, even if he keeps forgetting.' she said, piqued.

'I'm going out for drinks next week with him. He wanted to tell me about this new sports bar. We are friends, after all.'

She sighed, making it deliberately loud for his benefit. 'So what's the message?'

'Rogov's has been speaking with a duty sergeant from Vasilyevsky District. A girl there has just reported her friend missing. She hasn't heard from her since late Thursday evening.'

Two nights was hardly an emergency unless she was a minor. 'How old?'

'Nineteen.'

So it wasn't important, but Mikhail knew better than to waste her time – unless he was still in bed and half asleep. She looked up to see Renata Shchyotkina roll her open eye in irritation. 'Misha, I can't talk now. Why doesn't Rogov tell him to complete a Missing Person's report?'

Mikhail yawned again, this time loud enough to earn a frown from Renata Shchyotkina. 'Because, my darling, the duty sergeant had the good sense to check out the girl. It turns out her father is seriously rich. Listen, are you still at the address on Vasilyevsky Island?'

'Yes.'

'Then do us all a favour and take a look. The missing girl lives only a few streets from you. Her name is Zena Dahl.'

'Norwegian?'

'Swedish; she's a student at the university and lives on Veselnaya Ulitsa – block eight, apartment two. Can you find out if there's something to it?'

'What about Article 15?'

Mikhail snorted, 'If she's not there make something up. Say you were gaining entry to prevent a crime. Rogov is tracking down her landlord and only a fool would make a fuss. Get back to me as soon as you can, the local *menti* are holding off for now.'

'Mikhail, I can't leave.'

She looked up at Renata Shchyotkina who, judging by the hands on her hips and the scowl on her face, had heard something of the conversation. 'I have to go. I'm really sorry.'

'Just get out,' she spat.

4

Mikhail had been right, the missing girl's apartment was only two streets away. She picked up an apple-filled pastry from a *Teremok* stall at the end of Veselnaya Ulitsa and was still brushing the crumbs off her fingers when she reached Zena Dahl's block. The building was six storeys of Vyborg granite with an impenetrable red metal door. Natalya climbed two stone steps to reach it and pressed all the buzzers next to the keypad. She tapped her foot, anxious to file the report on Renata Shchyotkina's assault then return home before the morning was lost.

There was no answer.

She retreated to the street level and looked around. With these old buildings there was often a courtyard to the rear. She knew, though, the metal door at the back would be equally impenetrable and the lower windows barred. Distrust for banks meant most people kept their jewellery and cash hidden at home; as a result, apartments often had formidable security.

'Yes?'

The door was opened a crack by an old lady with a hooked nose, clear plastic glasses, and a red and white patterned headscarf.

'I'm calling for Zena.'

The woman fiddled with a hearing aid, twisting it around her ear. Natalya presumed she must have been watching her from a window because she wouldn't have heard the bell. She waited as patiently as she could manage for the brown earpiece to be fixed in place.

Natalya resisted taking her ID card out. Especially with the citizens who'd lived through the Soviet era, a call from the police was something to fear and their mouths shut faster than rabbit traps. Another reason for subterfuge was obvious: if Zena had been kidnapped, and for a rich kid it wasn't an unreasonable supposition, the release of information had to be carefully controlled.

'I'm calling for Zena Dahl. Is this her place?'

'Yes, but I don't know where she is.'

'I know,' Natalya thought on her feet, 'she's gone away for a few days. You know what these young girls are like.'

'Then what do you want?' The woman's face hardened and she used her position at the top of the stairs to stare Natalya down.

'I'm a friend of the family. Zena called to say she thinks she left her gas oven on.'

'A man came yesterday too. Is she in trouble?' She eyed Natalya suspiciously.

'Trouble?' Natalya wrinkled her forehead as if the thought hadn't occurred to her. 'What did he look like?'

Up close, the old lady's eyebrows were a burgundy colour, delicately dyed to match the hair hidden under her headscarf. Natalya watched the brows knit together in thought. 'A bureaucrat: grey hair, suit.'

'When was that?'

'Early morning. Seven-thirty? I saw him in the street when I went out at eight. He tried to hide his face in a newspaper but it was him.'

She'd ask her for a better description of the man later, first she needed to have a look inside.

'He called me "*babushka*".'

'I don't know him,' Natalya took the first step, 'but men can be very rude sometimes. Did he say who he was?'

'No.'

'See? We're better off without them. Anyway,' Natalya pushed hair from her eyes and took another step, 'I need to turn her oven off but I just wanted you to know so you don't think I'm a burglar.'

'Do you have a key?' the woman asked, standing back to let Natalya enter.

Like most of the older buildings, the hallway was neglected to the point of abuse and there was a strong, unpleasant smell of ancient tobacco.

'No,' said Natalya stepping inside. There were two doors on the ground level; the one on the right was closing slowly, presumably the old woman's.

'Is that Zena's?' She pointed left at a door that was solid enough to make an OMON riot squad pause for thought.

The woman grunted.

'Then I might need to break a window. I'll send someone to fix it right away, I promise.' She took a step back and offered the woman a reassuring smile.

'I moved here in 1978 with Andrei, my husband. He was a Brezhnev man.'

Natalya groaned inwardly and turned to face her. 'So you've been here a long time then?'

'There used to be another family in Zena's apartment. Irina's man, Vitaly, was an *apparatchik* too. It doesn't matter how much you feed the wolves, they still look at the woods.'

'So they saw other women?'

'Like an affair?' The woman weighed the words, then spat them out in contempt. 'They didn't need to do that. Andrei and Vitaly worked the committees. They said to the young girls with children, you need a place for your new family. You don't want to share the same shithouse with fifty people in a *komunalka*? Excuse my language. Those girls, their men knew what was going on, but what could they do? Andrei and Vitaly made those girls fuck and suck for an apartment, then fuck and suck for a job.'

The woman's top lip curled and Natalya winced.

'They were gone for days and I stayed with Irina in her apartment, or sometimes she came to mine. We cooked together, our children played.'

'That's nice,' said Natalya, edging away.

'She died three years ago last October. Her daughter came to sell the apartment, she told me Irina had a clot on her brain. Come inside.'

'But I—'

'Come inside.' A thick hand touched Natalya's shoulder and she would have had to physically pull away to refuse.

Natalya watched, frustrated, while the woman fumbled with a key to open her door. She followed her into a room with worn parquet flooring covered by a threadbare Persian rug. The only furnishings were a dark-stained wooden wall-unit with cardboard boxes on top and a floral armchair facing a television that was still playing.

'You like Botox?' the woman asked.

'What?'

'Botox. You know, Putin?' The old woman pointed at the television and cackled.

'No, I'm not a fan.'

Natalya looked at the programme. A woman with bright pink lipstick who bore a closer resemblance to a porn star than a TV presenter was explaining why she wanted the president to be her boyfriend. The image on screen cut to show Vladimir Putin inside a mini-submarine off the coast of Crimea.

'I am,' the woman said, nodding resolutely. 'He runs around with his chest out, telling everyone what a tough guy he is. Only a man with a tiny *khui* does that, but he wants to make Russia great again and there are some things you can't argue with.'

Her thick fingers gripped the remote control and she pressed the mute button. 'Here, give me a hand.'

There were open boxes of *matryoshka* dolls by the wall unit and Natalya guessed she sold them to tourists to supplement her pension.

'You want to buy one?' The old lady picked up a doll. 'Do you see? Our leaders. All bald then hairy, bald then hairy, all the way back to Peter the Great. There are only seven in that set. It doesn't sell because it stops at Andropov and no one remembers him. I've also got Harry Potter and Disney princesses – they do much better.'

Natalya took a *matryoshka* doll from the woman and saw Putin's bald head on the outer layer. She opened the doll to find Medvedev inside with his neat brown hair, then a younger Putin, then Yeltsin's white quiff, then Gorbachev with the oxblood birthmark on his bare scalp. She reassembled the doll set and put it back in the box.

'Here, an old ape has an old eye. Look in this drawer for me.'

Natalya opened it to find it crammed full of rubbish.

'What am I looking for?'

'Her keys,' the pensioner said in an exasperated tone as if speaking to an idiot, 'Irina gave me her keys.'

Natalya grinned at the old woman.

5

Natalya waited for the old woman's door to close then she heard the distorted voice of the TV presenter as the volume returned to normal. She took a pair of latex gloves from her handbag and snapped them on before turning the key in Zena Dahl's metal door, careful to avoid the areas of the lock and handle.

Inside it was gloomy; long green curtains were drawn, allowing just enough light to see by. There was a pile of mail on the parquet floor that had been pushed through the door's letterbox, presumably by the *babushka*. Natalya squatted to examine it, picking up the ones with postmarks then returning them to the same position; an envelope that looked like it contained a store card was stamped with the 22nd of June – two days ago. She closed the door behind her, seeing a denim jacket fixed to the hook on the back. Through the gloom she followed the small hallway into a sparsely furnished living room much like the old woman's, with an ancient cabinet, a sofa bed, and a television on a stand.

The taste was random and inexpensive, a pre-furnished student apartment, which came as a surprise considering the funds Zena must have at her disposal. Natalya placed the *matryoshka* doll she had bought from the old woman on a telephone table and sniffed the air. She was glad there were none of the fruity notes of esters that marked the early decomposition stage of a corpse, but nor were there the lingering traces of perfume, cooked food, or artificial fresheners that came with the living.

There were two doors to the right, which she supposed led to the sole bedroom and the bathroom, and an archway on the far side leading to the kitchen. In the living room, next to the sofa-bed, were two empty Heineken bottles resting on a 1970s style smoked-glass table. She picked up each bottle in turn and held them up to a sliver of light to see traces of lipstick on the mouths, reddy-brown on one and pink on the other. There was a small bookcase by the television with titles on International Law and Politics, mainly in Russian; they looked untouched.

Zena's kitchen was pristine compared to her own. She opened the fridge by the door's edge seeing white boxes holding the remnants of a takeaway with the stamp of a Korean restaurant; adjacent to it was a bag of wilting salad leaves. A milk carton had a day left on its 'consume by' stamp. She closed the door and examined a picture postcard fixed by a fridge magnet of Saint Isaac's Cathedral. The card was an old photograph of a man in folk dress standing in a kayak; stylised writing along the bottom edge gave the location away as Östergötland. A few hand-written lines in Swedish were signed off with "Papa" followed by a cross for a kiss. It was dated April. She replaced the card and inspected the rest of the kitchen but it held little interest: a worn but spotless four-ring gas stove; a washer-dryer full of clothes.

A wall calendar of Swedish countryside scenes was pinned to the archway that led back to the living room; it was the type of present an unimaginative parent or grandparent might buy. Taking out her iPhone, she held up the pages and took photographs of any that held appointments. In February, Zena had logged a visit to a dentist; in April, a doctor; both words were written in Russian with no names or addresses – that was a shame. She returned the calendar to the current month, then took a picture of the neat handwriting in the square for Tuesday the 6th of June: "9:30 ZAGS".

Everyone in the country had been to a Zapis Aktov Grazhdanskogo Sostoyaniya, or ZAGS for short, at some point in their lives, it was the civil registration office where births, marriages, divorces and deaths were recorded. They also performed ceremonies. On the 12th of July 2014, she had gone to the one on Furshtatskaya Ulitsa to marry Mikhail at Wedding Palace Number Two. For a girl of nineteen, it was unlikely Zena had gone there for herself.

The bedroom was behind the first of two closed doors, where an ethnic Indian-print quilt covered a neatly made bed. Next to it was an old wood-veneer wardrobe. She pulled on the handles to find it full of clothes. One hanger supported a beautiful rose-coloured dress with tassels; the label displayed "Monique Lhuillier". She flicked through some of the others, finding the names of Brunello Cucinelli, Max Gengos and a few designers she didn't recognise. Below them, an apartment block of shoeboxes held Manolo Blahniks, Jimmy Choos, Valentinos, and a stunning pair of Michael Kors flats. Zena may have shunned a luxurious apartment but the girl had managed to bring a few essentials with her. Natalya stopped when she realised the clothes were becoming a distraction, noting only that there were no obvious signs of burglary since the contents of the wardrobe were worth at least twice her annual salary.

Resting on the bedside table was a pair of gold hair straighteners. She tapped one of the ceramic heating elements – it was cold to the touch. She pulled open the table's single drawer. Inside was a phone charger and a paperback in Swedish which she lifted gingerly to reveal a pink foil pack of birth control pills.

Her phone started buzzing and she saw Rogov's name on the screen. The Sergeant had been Mikhail's best man at his first wedding and seemed to believe his continuing friendship with her husband gave him the right to be overly familiar with her. Normally she welcomed friends of Mikhail, but in her view Rogov epitomised the worst type of policeman; his chauvinism ran as deep as the Volga and the tactics he used to extract confessions made her ashamed to work in the same department. She tried to keep Rogov at a distance and reprimanded him regularly, but he brushed each one away as if she had made an elaborate joke he didn't fully understand.

The phone stopped while she was removing her gloves to avoid cross-contamination. She tapped the screen to return the sergeant's call.

'Rogov?'

'Hey boss, are you in the apartment yet? Misha said you were going to check out the place.'

'Yes, I got the keys from her neighbour. Next time, speak to me.

Don't go through him.'

'Sorry, boss.'

'What did the duty sergeant from Vasilyevsky tell you about the girl who reported Zena missing?'

'Not much – he said she looked like a supermodel.'

'I'll rephrase that. Did he say anything useful?'

'He said she'd tried calling Dahl's phone but it was going to voicemail. Her name is Yulia, no surname offered…from what I heard she was more nervous than a rabbit in a wolf pack. At first he thought it was a joke: a teenager forgets to use social media for a day so it must be an emergency.'

'Until she told him Zena was a rich kid.'

'Yeah.'

She looked at the birth control pills again and observed tiny letters on the blister pack marking the menstrual cycle; they were abbreviations for the days of the week in English. Zena's last pill had been taken on a Thursday. Presumably the day she had gone missing unless the pack was old.

'Does she have any type of transport…a car or motorbike?'

Sergeant Rogov let out a yawn. 'No idea.'

'Well, locate Zena's parents and find out what you can. She may have told them her plans or gone home for the weekend.'

There was a brooding silence. 'Are they Svens?'

'Probably.' Then she realised. 'You don't speak English or Swedish, do you, Rogov?'

'Didn't realise I had to.'

'Well, as you're being so friendly with Misha, can you ask him to do it?' She hid her relief that Rogov wouldn't be interacting directly with Zena's parents.

She kept the phone to her ear and crouched down, careful to keep her shoes and the knees of her jeans away from Zena's fraying Persian rug. Even if the worst had happened, it was unlikely any fibre analysis would be conducted – the facilities existed but they were only used in the most serious cases; and that usually meant a political dimension. Underneath the bed she found a full set of green, vintage-style suitcases.

Chapter 5

'Her luggage is here.'

'Not looking good for the Sven, then.'

'No,' she agreed. It wasn't looking good for Zena but there were still plenty of possibilities to explain a university student spending two nights away from home.

She heard a muffled sound on the phone, then, 'Boss?'

'Wait, Rogov.'

There was one room left to try and she turned the handle with the tip of her index finger. Inside the bathroom was a tub with a detachable shower hose; nearby, a small toilet and sink in white porcelain looked at least fifty years old by the style and loss of enamel. She pulled off a square of toilet paper and dabbed it against the bristles of an electric toothbrush; the tissue came away dry. There were bottles of contact lens solution and an opened lens case. Inside a cupboard she found the same type of medicines that accumulated in her own home: a near-empty bottle of cough syrup, paracetamol and a packet of antihistamines – nothing unusual.

'You still there?' she asked.

'Yes, boss.'

'Who's the expert criminalist on duty?'

'Primakov, I think.'

'Good. Ask him to come here and park around the back. Just Primakov, and tell him to wear normal clothes, none of those fancy white overalls he gets from those websites.'

'Yes, boss,' he said, and she couldn't tell if he was irked or amused.

'Thanks. I'll wait here for him.'

'Anything else?'

'Yes, when you speak to Misha ask him to go to the Dixy. Tell him we're out of toilet rolls and coffee.'

After an hour, she saw the top of the white van from the kitchen window before it disappeared into the courtyard. She left Zena's apartment and undid the bolts of the hallway door that led to the rear yard, still wearing the latex gloves which by now were making her skin itch. She watched Leo Primakov climb out, taking a silver case with him. He wore pale-blue chinos and a dark denim shirt: the type of clothes she'd often tried to get Mikhail into, instead of the plain office shirts and jeans that he favoured. The other difference between Primakov and her husband was that Leo worked-out regularly and his clothes were snug in the right places, revealing every crevice and contour.

She shook her head to dismiss the unfaithful thoughts floating in her mind.

'Leo!' She waved at him. He raised his arm in acknowledgement, then stretched blue overshoes over expensive-looking boots.

Two weeks before, Primakov had lent her a pirated copy of 'CSI: Crime Scene Investigation' and had been evangelical about the scientific techniques the Americans used. She disagreed, finding them unrealistic, but she *was* impressed by the white overalls the police and forensic experts wore even if the *menti* she knew never wore them; her colleagues reminded her of nineteenth century surgeons who eschewed sterilised gowns in favour of gardening clothes.

As a concession to the programme, Primakov had ordered several sets of blue overshoes. He held a pair out for her.

'No, I'm leaving. I was waiting to let you in.'

Primakov drew level with her. 'What's going on? Rogov didn't tell me anything.'

She stepped aside to let him enter. 'I want you to take a look at an apartment rented by a Swedish student. There's money in the family so kidnapping is a possibility. She hasn't been seen since Thursday night.' She drew the bolts behind him. 'There, now you know as much as I do.'

'Two days?'

She shrugged and held up a hand, palm facing him. 'It could be a waste of time, but let's take it seriously for now and hope she doesn't come back while you're picking through her dirty underwear.'

They strolled to the open door of Zena's apartment. 'Anything interesting so far?' Primakov asked.

Chapter 5

'There's a table in the living room with two beer bottles; both have different lipstick marks… I think she had a drink with a girlfriend before going out, possibly the one who reported her missing. It's very neat which makes me think she didn't come home or else she would have cleared them away.'

'I'll try to get some comparison prints from her personal effects.'

She shrugged. 'That makes sense.'

'Anything else?'

'Keep this quiet,' she dropped her voice although there was no need. 'There's a lot of designer gear in her bedroom. Don't let anyone in unless I authorise it. There's a woman in the neighbouring apartment; she's deaf. I told her I'm a friend of the family so she doesn't know anything yet. I'd like to keep it that way until we know more. She thinks Zena has gone away; I'm guessing she was the one pushing her mail through the letterbox.

'What about the rubbish bins?'

She smiled, and tugged on the handle of the back door. 'I thought I'd leave that to you.'

Outside, her phone started playing Elvis Presley's "You're the devil in disguise". She hurried along the yard then answered it. 'Colonel Vasiliev?'

This was bad news. Vasiliev, the head of the city's Criminal Investigations Directorate, wasn't on duty until Monday and he didn't do social calls. He was also close to retirement, preferring to delegate while he planned his next European vacation.

His voice had an icy tone, 'Captain Ivanova, are you having a nice time over there?'

Her car was still parked outside Renata Shchyotkina's apartment and she marched there, anxious to get away in case she was spotted by Zena's elderly neighbour. 'I was asked to look at something urgently.'

'You were asked by Major Ivanov. Is he your direct supervisor?'

'No, sir.'

'So do you always do what your husband tells you?'

The traffic was noisy and she cupped a hand over her free ear. 'No, sir.'

'But in this instance you chose to.'

'Yes, sir. I was in the neighbourhood. Mikhail heard the girl's father is wealthy. If she has been kidnapped or killed it could have political consequences.

'Well, what have you found out?'

'Nothing yet, Colonel. As far as I can determine, there are several possibilities.'

A pedestrian crossing displayed five, then four, then three seconds in large green numbers. She jogged across it as the cars started to nudge their way over the line.

'Then what do you *think*?' she heard him say.

She stood next to a chemist's windowpane and pushed a palm against her ear to blot out the noise of the traffic. 'If the friend is telling the truth then she had an accident that night, or something worse has happened.'

'Thank you, Captain. Well, as you say, it might be political. I've already asked Sergeant Rogov to check local hospitals and I understand Mikhail is trying to find the girl's parents. In the meantime, I'd like you to speak with this Yulia, the one who reported her missing.'

'Yes, sir.'

'See what you can find out by midday then we'll regroup. If there is no obvious criminal element I intend to give it back to the local *menti*.'

She frowned. 'May I ask who is leading the investigation?'

'You are.'

She had expected to hear Mikhail's name or that of the new major, Dostoynov, and almost asked him to repeat it. 'Thank you, Colonel.'

'I suggest you to speak to the girl's family first – once Major Ivanov locates them.'

'Yes, Colonel.'

He hung up.

She continued down the street, located her Volvo outside Renata

Chapter 5

Shchyotkina's apartment, then climbed inside and called Mikhail. He answered after two rings. 'Misha, you bastard, what have you done to me?'

'I don't know what you mean.'

'How did Vasiliev find out I went to the girl's apartment? I was supposed to be doing you a quiet favour.'

He chuckled. 'The Colonel called in and spoke to Rogov. He wanted me to handle it but I said you were the best we had…also Swedes don't usually speak Russian.'

So that was the answer, and it had nothing to do with her superior skills of detection. The girl's father needed regular updates with the person in charge of the investigation. Most of the men in headquarters spoke basic English at best, whereas she had studied it at the Leningrad Oblast Pedagogical Institute and was near fluent. Mikhail's was good enough to establish contact with Zena's parents but to conduct interviews and maintain a relationship, it had to be her.

She heard a clatter of plates and guessed Mikhail had made it as far as breakfast.

'What did Vasiliev say?' he asked.

'Prove there's a crime or he'll give it to the locals…I guess he doesn't want an open-ended missing persons case.'

'What else?'

'He told me to find the girl who reported Zena missing.'

Mikhail mumbled.

'Are you eating?'

There was a chewing noise that made her grimace. 'Breakfast, and I'm having fried eggs before you ask. We need to do some shopping. Have you got a signal on your mobile?'

She held it close to the windscreen then brought it back to her ear. 'Four bars.'

'Good. Can you put me on speakerphone and log onto VKontakte?'

'Misha, I'm busy.'

'Humour me.'

As soon as she clicked the speaker icon, the sound of chewing filled the car, making her feel queasy. She tapped the blue VK symbol on her mobile and the social network software filled the screen, listing recent updates from her friends and pages they had liked.

'Now what?'

The chewing stopped and there was a slurping noise.

'For God's sake put me on speaker phone too so I don't have to listen to that noise.'

There was a soft knock which she guessed was his phone being placed on their dining table. In the background she could hear cupboard doors opening and a murmur of conversation – Anton was up too and she wished she could be there, enjoying a leisurely breakfast with them.

She heard a slight echo when Mikhail spoke again. 'Now look for the missing Sven.'

'She's Swedish, won't she be on Facebook?'

There was another slurp, quieter now. 'She's on both. Have you done it yet?'

'Don't be impatient.' She tapped in "Zena Dahl" then clicked on the search button. Only one profile image returned – a circular profile image of a skier wearing thick goggles and a woollen hat; a stripe of pink zinc oxide cream ran along the length of her nose. Like that, she was indistinguishable from half the girls in St. Petersburg. Maybe it was deliberate – a rich kid craving some anonymity.

'The skier?'

'That's her. She has more pictures on her page.'

Natalya tapped on the image and selected the girl's photos. She flicked through them until she found a clear one of Zena holding up a glass to the camera. 'The wine glass?'

'Yes, that's the best I think. There's been no activity on VKontakte since Wednesday. I've already checked her Facebook account – it hasn't been updated since March and she only has forty-six friends.'

'A loner?'

'Maybe.'

Chapter 5

Another plate clattered on the table, then she heard Mikhail say something indistinguishable. 'What was that?'

'Anton. I told him to eat his breakfast on the sofa while we finish talking.'

'Hi, Natasha,' a distant voice called.

She raised her voice in return, 'Hi Anton.'

'Haven't we finished talking yet?' She asked Mikhail.

'I'll spcak to Rogov and call you back with her address.'

'What are you talking about?'

'Look at your phone again, her security is weak.'

She got the hint and opened Zena Dahl's friends list. There were only four on the VKontakte profile and she studied the circular picture of the first one; it was of a pretty, narrow-faced girl with bright blue hair wearing a cowboy hat.

'You see her?'

'Yes.'

'Meet Yulia,' he said, stuffing egg into his mouth, 'Yulia Federova.'

6

Natalya squinted in the bright sunshine as she drove along the wide highway with its scrub grass borders and grey and brown twenty-storey monoliths in the background. This was Primorsky District, the home of the people who'd never been invited to sit at the city's rigged Roulette table where ruthlessness passed for luck. She turned her Volvo into Komendantsky Prospekt and parked under the shadow of a rusting tower crane whose jib, like an accusing finger, pointed at the centre's Golden Triangle where properties changed hands for five thousand dollars a square metre and upwards.

Mikhail had offered to accompany her but she had insisted he stay at home in case two detectives intimidated Yulia Federova into silence – the woman's brief appearance at Vasilyevsky police station suggested she was nervous. There was also the issue of Anton's university place and she needed Mikhail to check his online account. The consequences of failure were almost too painful to think about: Anton spending years avoiding the soldiers who roamed the city challenging any boy of conscription age. She had heard stories of sons being dragged from Metro trains or plucked from their beds in the middle of the night by uniformed thugs. When she got home, she would check to make sure he'd paid the bribe.

She unlocked the glove compartment and took out her Makarov in its leather holster. First, she checked the clip and safety before fixing it to her belt along with a pair of handcuffs. The barrel of the gun was pressed against her hip bone, ready to tap out a bruise when she started walking; still, it was better than the shoulder harness she had worn earlier in her career which left painful friction marks on her right breast.

Chapter 6

She was putting her leather jacket in the boot when a girl approached the building, pocketing a pair of sunglasses before switching a white holdall to her left hand to tap out a code on the door's security pad.

'Wait!'

The young woman heaved open the metal door and Natalya sprinted for the building, pulling out her police identification card as she ran.

The door closed on her fingers, its metal edges connecting with bone.

Her eyes watered as she strained to pull the door open with her other hand, dropping the identification card to the floor. 'Damn it!' she shouted at the retreating girl. 'Why didn't you hold it?'

She stooped to retrieve her card and saw the girl starting for the stairs.

Mikhail had got the address from Rogov. Yulia Federova was a common enough name but Rogov had got the girl's birthday from her VKontakte profile and reduced the number of matches from nine to one. She looked around the building's foyer, sighing at the "Out of order" sign on the graffiti-tagged lift door: the address was on the twelfth floor.

The girl turned on the landing, the sunshine through a steel-reinforced window framing her fine brown hair like the headshot of a model in a photographer's studio. She was heart-stoppingly beautiful. The only difference was the hair. In her VKontakte profile picture Yulia Federova had been wearing a wig.

'Stay there.'

The girl looked down with a frown then her eyes lowered a fraction to take in the gun and handcuffs.

'Yes?'

She held out the card again, seeing a white line across her fingers where the metal door had closed on them. 'Senior Detective Ivanova, Criminal Investigations Directorate. I need to talk to you.'

Yulia Federova took another step and her neat eyebrows rose in an attitude of indifference. 'I'm in a hurry. Can you come back after lunch?'

Sure, Natalya thought, and then I'll spend the rest of the day trying to find you. 'It's entirely your choice. You can talk now or be charged with obstruction and spend the weekend in a police holding cell.'

'We're already talking, aren't we?' Federova raised her chin in a cocky display that suggested a history with the police. She'd ask Rogov to check Yulia for a criminal record if he hadn't done already. It could explain the girl's reluctance to give her full name and address at the police station.

'Why don't you make some tea?' she checked her watch, it was a little after ten thirty.

'Alright, alright, but the place is a mess and I've only got coffee.'

By the twelfth floor, she was testing the limits of her antiperspirant. They exited onto a long corridor with identical doors; Yulia Federova stopped outside one of them and took out a set of keys from the side-pocket of her bag. Natalya followed her inside.

The bedsit had a tiny partitioned bathroom and a double divan arranged diagonally to take up much of the room's thirty square metres as if the girl was making an ironic statement about the lack of space by reducing it even further. To the left was a built-in wardrobe, incongruously large for the apartment, and to the right, a kitchen with a gas stove and small appliances designed for the single person. Straight ahead, there were windows running along the external wall where a glass door opened to a balcony. Outside, the view was of more tower blocks.

On the wall behind her she saw a framed photograph of a dancer performing a grand jeté, the legs a perfect line and the face an expression of serenity. 'Is that Makarova?' she asked in an obvious attempt to put the girl at ease.

Yulia filled a kettle and switched it on. 'You know ballet?'

'I had lessons until I was ten but I hated the discipline. I saw the gala performance they put on for her at the Mariinsky.'

'Lucky you,' she said.

'So what do you do, Yulia?'

'I take classes in modern dance and Flamenco.'

'And work?'

Chapter 6

Yulia looked in a cupboard then took out a bag of filter coffee. 'A boutique on Nevsky called "Noughts and Kisses". Do you know it?'

She saw Yulia glance at her peach-coloured, short-sleeved shirt, then at the chain store jeans she'd got in a sale at the Galeria shopping mall.

'Perhaps not,' the girl sighed.

She had struggled to place Yulia but now she had her; Yulia was like one of those stick-thin girls who had made fun of her in ballet class until she dropped out because she wasn't cool enough to fit in with their world. She often wondered what had happened to them, and suspected they were unhappily married to rich men or else, like Yulia, worked with high-end clothes that only came in minuscule sizes. From her time in the police she had grown a skin as thick as a sow's hide but had once gone into a shop populated by those little bitches and their snide comments had left her fighting back tears.

She felt herself bristle and glanced at her watch to hide her irritation. 'How long have you been living here, Yulia?'

'Eight months. Before that I was in Tuva.'

'You've come a long way.'

Yulia spooned coffee into a cafetiere and added boiling water. '*Piter*'s the only place if you want to dance.' She pushed the plunger down without waiting; keen to be rid of an unwelcome guest. 'Why don't you ask me?'

'What about?'

Yulia kept her eyes down as she poured the coffee into a single cup then took a Coke Zero for herself. 'Zena. That's why you're here isn't it?'

Natalya took the cup. 'Thanks. You got any milk?'

'Only almond.'

She shook her head and watched Yulia sit on the edge of her bed and toy with the ring-pull of her Coke.

Natalya stood, sipping her coffee; it was very strong and she felt an instant buzz. 'How did you meet her?'

'She was browsing in a boutique I go to sometimes. I can't afford to buy anything but I like trying the clothes on. Zena was shopping there and we got talking. She's interested in fashion so I offered to take her to a few places local designers use.'

'How long have you known her?'

'We met in early February. Zena had just returned for her second semester.' She tugged on the ring pull and sipped the Coke. 'She wore this puffa jacket that made her look like a man. I told her she needed a fur but she thought they were cruel. I suggested she get one anyway and donate some money to an animal charity if she felt bad about it.'

'Has she been here?'

Yulia shook her head and snorted. 'Are you joking? Look at this place, it's a heap of shit. I mean it's only temporary until I get something better but it's embarrassing.'

'What's wrong with it?'

'Nothing…I mean—'

'You were too embarrassed to bring a rich foreigner here?'

Yulia nodded then sipped her Coke. 'Well, wouldn't you be?'

She ignored the question. 'So you've always known Zena had money?'

'The first day I met her, she wanted to buy a pair of Ulyana Sergeenko sunglasses. I showed her where to get them. She didn't even check the price. It was like she was buying an ice cream.'

Natalya put the coffee on a ledge cluttered with magazines then took out a notepad and pen. 'So, you went out on Thursday together. Whose idea was it?'

'Hers. She always calls me at the last moment and assumes I'll drop everything when she does.'

'And do you?'

'Usually.'

'Why?'

Yulia reached into her sports bag and pulled out a pack of Karelia Menthol Slims; she tapped one into her hand and lit it, tilting her head back as she blew the smoke upwards.

'If you must know it's because I can't afford to go out and Zena pays for everything. She was shy and didn't know many people. I didn't have any plans that evening though.'

'So where did you meet? In town?'

Chapter 6

'Her place. She called, I came running. Sounds pathetic, doesn't it?'

'No, isn't that what friends do? Would you call her one?'

'Zena? Sure, she's a friend.'

'What time did you go to hers?'

'Around 8 p.m. We had a beer then went out.'

'What was she wearing?'

Yulia didn't need to think. 'A powder blue dress made from wild silk and a baby blue Hermès Sellier Kelly.'

'That's a handbag, right?'

'Of course.'

She wrote "Hermès Sellier Kelly" in her notepad. 'Describe her apartment.'

'Clean. Really clean.'

Natalya picked up the coffee from the ledge and had another sip before putting it down; the caffeine hit her like a line of cocaine. 'Yours is nice. You've tried hard here. It's easy in a place like this to let go.'

'Yeah well,' Yulia sniffed, 'just because I live here it doesn't mean…'

'No,' Natalya said, not unkindly. 'So where did you go after that?'

'A few bars in town. There's a new one on Ligovsky called Cheka. Have you heard of it?'

'No.' She wrote the name down. 'What time was that?'

'Nine or ten…more like ten. That's where we ended up. First time I've been there too. The staff wear uniforms and call the customers "Comrade". There's the glass bit of a jet—'

'A cockpit?'

Yulia inhaled again. 'Yeah, one of those. They've got it hanging from the ceiling with a dummy inside holding a hammer and sickle.'

Natalya shook her head. She hated all that postmodern bullshit where the past was sanitised and served up as entertainment. 'If they want to re-live the good old days they should put the waiters in charge and stack the place with corpses.'

Yulia rolled her eyes in a gesture that reminded her of Anton's "whatever". Natalya was being rebuked for being too uncool to appreciate irony.

'Then what?'

'What do you mean?'

'Did you share a taxi home, go for a nightcap somewhere, or maybe screw some boys?' She watched to see if Yulia was shocked by the language.

'Oh I see.' She was unperturbed. 'No, Zena was drunk and left.'

'On her own?'

'Yes.'

'Seriously? You let her go home on her own?' Natalya shook her head.

'Yes. There was a guy in the club. We were dancing together. I went to the toilet and when I came back Zena' – Yulia did another eye roll then raised pencil-point thin eyebrows – 'I caught her trying to put her tongue down his throat.'

Yulia reached for an ashtray on a table by her bed. 'Zena was lonely, I tried being nice to her and she repaid me with that.'

Natalya held up her palm. 'We'll get to that. Do you remember what time she left?'

Yulia shook her head. 'Around one o'clock, I think. I was wasted too.' she took a drag on her cigarette and watched Natalya write on the pad. 'I carried on dancing with Maxim – that's the name of the boy – then when I got back to our table the drinks had gone and some strangers were sitting there.' Her brows came together, triggering delicate frown lines between her eyes.

'This Maxim, did he and Zena swap numbers or talk?'

She let out a haughty laugh. 'He wasn't interested in her. Besides, it was too noisy and I was only gone for a moment.'

'Did you go back with him?'

'No, I had work the next day and needed to sleep. The Metro was closed by then so I got a taxi home—'

'Alone?'

'Yes. And I just made it before they raised Liteyny Bridge. Another ten minutes and I'd have been stuck in Tsentralny for the night.'

Chapter 6

'Then what happened?'

'Nothing.' She sucked on the menthol cigarette. 'I went to bed and was late getting to work the next day...yesterday.'

'So why did you report her missing?'

'I kept thinking about the bridges. Zena lives on Vasilyevsky Island and the Lieutenant Schmidt and the Palace are raised before the Liteyny. I was worried she hadn't got home....she was really drunk too. I tried calling but her phone was ringing and ringing. I tried messaging, email...nothing.'

'Was anyone else there who took an interest in her?'

Yulia flicked the ash from her Karelia into the ashtray. 'There were some army boys on leave but they were doing their own thing.' The frown returned. 'There was a waiter who was being familiar. A charmer.'

'I don't want to be rude.' Yulia extended the hand with the cigarette in an exaggerated stretch, 'but is there much more of this? I need to shower and meet my friend.'

Natalya's voice was brisk and businesslike, 'When I've finished. Who was Zena seeing?'

'You mean a boyfriend?'

'Any sexual relationship. Did she have anything casual going on or maybe something long term?'

Yulia shook her head. 'Zena was hopeless. She was shy until she got drunk, and then she made a fool of herself.' She lifted her delicate shoulders in a shrug as if to say, "and that's what got her into trouble."

'No one at all?'

'No one. She wanted a boyfriend but had no confidence. It should have been easy for a girl like her.'

'You mean with the kind of money she had?'

Yulia suppressed a sly smile. 'Of course. But Zena wanted them to love her for herself.' She shook her head quickly as if the idea had been absurd.

'Is that wrong? Natalya asked.

'Doesn't everyone use what they have? Brains, body, looks, or money? You think I'm going to stay here forever?' She pressed her lips together then glanced around the room to emphasise the point. 'As soon as the right opportunity comes along I'll be gone.'

'Is that why you lied to her?'

'What? I didn't say anything.' Natalya noticed the shift in tone. Yulia the boutique girl was losing her veneer.

'You told her you were a student at the State University.'

'I don't remember that. Maybe she misunderstood.'

Natalya held up her iPhone. 'You created a profile on VKontakte saying you were a student; you even posted pictures of the Smolny Convent campus. There are only four friends on your page but my guess is none of them are real. The server has a backup so don't think of deleting anything. Now you want to tell me what you were up to?'

Yulia sneered, 'Look around you. Do you think a girl like Zena would be interested in me if she knew I lived here and worked in a shop?'

'Is that your answer?'

'It's the truth.' The smile had gone, now Yulia looked offended. 'I reported her missing, didn't I?'

'You did. Now I want you to explain why you refused to give your name and address at the station.'

'Why? Because I didn't want to get in trouble. Isn't that what you do? You find someone you like for the crime and—'

'Has a crime been committed here, Yulia?'

Yulia pointed at her with two fingers, the cigarette lodged between them. 'See, that's what I'm talking about. My father was a carpet wholesaler, he ended up in prison because a competitor wanted him out of business. He's still there now, rotting away. The police, the judge, they all took their share. I won't let you do that to me.'

There was one question left, and now Yulia was too angry to cooperate. At least it explained the hostility she had felt on the stairs.

'There are people like that, but I'm not one of them.' She looked at her notepad and flicked back to see what she'd written in Zena's apartment; the word "ZAGS" had been circled. 'I'm nearly finished.'

Yulia tilted her head back to finish the last of her Coke. 'You promise you'll find her?'

'I can't, but I'll do my best. I promise you that.'

Yulia glared but there was less defiance now. 'Ask me another one.'

'OK, was Zena depressed? Did she say anything that made you worry about her?'

'Maybe distracted sometimes...and a little lonely.'

'Enough to take her own life?'

Yulia thought for a moment. 'No, not the type.'

Natalya looked at the pad. 'Can you tell me why Zena went to a ZAGS two weeks ago?'

'I don't know anything about it.'

'She was too young to get married and, as you say, she didn't have a boyfriend anyway. Also, it's unlikely she went there to register a child or get a death certificate. Perhaps she was there to attend a wedding? It's easy enough to verify.'

Yulia had smoked her cigarette down to the filter and the last piece of ash fell away as she stubbed it out. 'I really don't know.'

The silence grew as Natalya studied the girl's face, convinced that for the first time in the interview she had seen a lie. Even Anton was a better liar and he was awful. Yulia was quiet, scared to embellish her answer and make it worse.

'Thanks for the coffee, Yulia. One last question and then I'll leave you alone.'

'What?'

'Can I look inside your wardrobe?'

7

The morning had nearly gone, and what did she have to show for it? Details of the clothing Zena Dahl was wearing; the name of the bar she had been drinking in; the approximate time she had left? All useful information for the local police but nothing to justify the continuing involvement of the Criminal Investigations Directorate. She jogged down the stairs, resting at the main entrance to catch her breath. According to her phone it was 11:35 a.m.; there was a little time left before she needed to report to Colonel Vasiliev and only one lead to follow up.

The sunshine had gone and the sky was grey when she parked on Ligovsky Prospekt. The street was busy with shoppers but she had no trouble finding the bar Yulia had described: the front was painted Tsar's green, and a three-metre-wide sign above it displayed *Cheka* in the Latin alphabet with the lettering altered to resemble Cyrillic. On either side of the word were the obligatory red stars. She was about to knock on a camouflage-patterned metal door when it was opened by a man in a ridiculous vintage secret police uniform. He was tall, perhaps one metre eight-five, and already looked fatigued. The White Nights did that to most people: the parties; the car horns and revelry that went on into morning; the endless light gleaming through curtains and killing any notion of slumber. By September everyone was exhausted enough to sleep through the winter – maybe that was the intention.

'We're closed. Give it a few minutes.'

She held out her identification card. 'Senior Detective Ivanova, Criminal Investigations Directorate.'

He stifled a yawn as he glanced at the card. 'Can I help you, Captain?'

She checked the rank on his fake uniform. 'I hope so…Sergeant.'

'It's only—'

'Yes, I know.'

His red peaked cap tilted as he looked at her quizzically.

'I assume you have this area under surveillance, Sergeant?'

'Huh?'

She raised her eyes to the camera above the doorway.

He looked up too, then gave her a tired smile, warming to the theme. 'Yes, Captain.'

'And inside?'

'Above the bar covering the tills.'

'What was that, Sergeant?'

'Sorry,' he grinned. 'Above the bar, covering the tills, Captain!'

'That's better. Mind if I have a look?'

The grin slid from his face. 'You need to check with the manager.'

'And?'

'And Captain?' he offered.

'No. *And* where is he or she?'

'Sleeping. He comes in around ten in the evening and stays until the takings are checked. You can try Semion, he's in charge when the boss is away.'

'Thanks.' She noticed the gun in his holster, and her gaze hardened as she looked back at him.

He noticed. 'Replica. It fires water.'

She nodded as he pulled the door open. 'Excellent, Sergeant.'

He addressed her back, 'Semion's usually at the bar. Show him your ID and he'll give you a drink on the house. Open to anyone above the rank of corporal.'

'Thank you. Please return to guard duty.'

The interior of the club was dark and humid, and in the corner a man stood over a record deck with a pair of headphones hanging around his neck. She walked towards the bar, thinking of Zena Dahl. If Yulia had told the truth, and there was good reason to doubt it, Zena had left around one a.m. That was early for a St. Petersburg club, when the dancing might be expected to go on until whatever passed for dawn.

She stopped to take in the camouflage net walls and the cockpit of an early MiG jet fixed to the ceiling above the main stage. A waiter approached her; he was wearing Afghanka khaki field dress that she took as a sign the club management were having trouble sourcing Cheka uniforms. There was a bandolier strapped to his chest, modified to hold shot glasses instead of bullets. She held out her identification card as Lyapis Trubetskoy's "Capital" started playing on the sound system. It was a rock number she loved, but the music made it impossible to maintain a conversation.

'Have you seen this girl?' She held up her iPhone to show him the picture of Zena with the glass of red wine from her VKontakte profile.

He shook his head and grimaced to show he hadn't heard, then twisted his body for her to speak directly into his ear.

'She was here on Thursday. A Swede,' Natalya yelled.

He frowned.

'Another girl was with her. Like a model: skinny, brown hair, good tits.' She tapped Zena's friend list and brought up Yulia's picture. 'Ignore the hair in this.'

The waiter cupped his hands to her ear which wasn't necessary. She felt his hot breath. 'Swedish you say?' He turned his head again for her to speak.

'Like Abba and Ikea. Where we park our submarines.' She turned and caught laughter in her ear.

'Blonde?'

Now she wasn't sure if he was trying to help or recording a sexual fantasy. 'Yes.'

'Show me the picture again.'

She tapped the screen of her phone to return to Zena's image and held it up to him. 'Here,' she shouted.

'You got others?' he mouthed.

She swiped the surface of her phone and another picture appeared of Zena posing with her father in a restaurant.

He studied it, then shook his head. 'No, haven't seen her. You want a drink?' He held up a bottle of Putinka in case she hadn't heard.

Chapter 7

She wrinkled her nose. 'On duty.'

He performed a one-shouldered shrug. 'Are you sure you're police?'

She put her mouth to his ear. 'A loyal servant.'

The waiter lingered and she left him for the bar; it was made out of sandbags encased in glass and three recent customers were loitering around it. They were being served by a barmaid who wore the same uniform as the doorman except hers necessitated a lower cut shirt to expose the tops of her breasts and her cap was fixed at a jaunty angle.

Natalya held her card above the customers; eventually the woman noticed. 'Where's Semion?' she shouted.

The barmaid finished serving a half-litre of Carlsberg then lifted the counter top. The two remaining customers scowled at Natalya until they took in the handcuffs and gun, then they pretended to be indifferent to her presence.

Up close, the woman had red eyes and Natalya waited for her to pull out a used tissue from the waistband of her jodhpurs and blow her nose.

'Hay fever. Damned plane trees.' The barmaid tucked what was left of the tissue in her waistband then she tapped on the keypad of a door marked private and Natalya followed her inside.

'Semion, the police want to speak to you.' She addressed a man in another Cheka uniform who was puffing on a cigarette by a barred window.

She closed the door and Lyapis Trubetskoy's majestic song reached a climax. 'Senior Detective Ivanova,' she held out the card to Semion. 'I'd like to see your security camera footage.'

He turned to acknowledge her. 'The manager isn't here,'

She tucked the card back in her wallet. 'I know.'

'He'll be here tonight.'

'Call him.'

He wiped his brow, knocking his cap askew. 'At this time? Seriously? He doesn't get home until 7 a.m.'

She gave him a hard stare. 'It's in the Criminal Code. I ask you respectfully, then you, respectfully, do it.'

'It's just that...Is it an emergency?'

'Show me the footage here and I'll decide?'

He stubbed the cigarette against the wall then flicked it through the bars. 'The hard drive is here, you'll have to take the whole thing if you need it.'

She pulled up a plastic chair while he switched a television on.

'What are you looking for?'

'I'll start with the footage over the entrance. Two girls came in last Thursday' – she extended the times Yulia had given her – 'sometime between 8 p.m. and 2 a.m.'

Semion shook his head and screwed up his face. 'No good.' He winced to convey sympathy. 'The disk fills after twenty-four hours, then it's written over.'

'That's ridiculous.'

'We've only just started,' he shrugged. 'We were meant to get a long record option but the company didn't—'

She held up a hand to stop him wittering. It was the first time she had led an investigation into a serious crime, albeit one that was likely to be downgraded and thrown back to the local police, and she had made little progress so far.

It was well after midday when she left the bar. She looked through the call history on her phone then tapped on Colonel Vasiliev's number. Outside, the cacophony of traffic and people shopping was deafening. She heard Vasiliev's mobile ring three times then his voicemail machine started in.

'Colonel,' she began, 'this is Captain Ivanova, please call me when you get this and I will provide you with an update on the investigation.'

She hung up, pleased that Vasiliev had bought her some time.

8

Natalya found a space on Veselnaya Ulitsa and zipped up her leather jacket to keep the light rain off her blouse before jogging along the leafy side of the road, using the trees for cover. Outside Zena's building a curtain twitched on the ground floor apartment. She waved at the window and waited until the door was opened a crack, observing that the old woman had changed her headscarf for a brown and orange one that did little to complement her burgundy-coloured hair and eyebrows.

'Hey, you didn't give me her keys back.'

Natalya held up her card as rain spattered her face. 'Police.'

She hid her impatience while Zena's elderly neighbour fiddled with her hearing aid to switch it on, then fixed it in place.

'So, you're not a friend of her father?'

'No.'

The old woman pulled open the door and she entered; the stench of old tobacco mingling with the smell of the wet tarmac outside. 'Can I ask your name?'

'Lyudmila Kuznetsova.'

'Mrs Kuznetsova, my name is Natalya Ivanova and I'm a senior detective. May I speak with you, privately?'

Kuznetsova turned without speaking and opened her apartment door as an invitation for her to follow. Outside Zena's apartment, Natalya stopped and felt an impulse to knock on the door. She did, avoiding the buzzer where there might be fingerprints.

There was a pause, which she assumed was Primakov peering through the spy-hole. He emerged wearing his white nylon suit and blue overshoes.

He craned his neck in the direction of Kuznetsova's apartment as the old woman's television blared out. 'She's watching repeats of *Take It Off Immediately*. I can hear everything.'

Natalya shook her head disbelievingly. 'Leo I'm in a hurry.'

He immediately sounded businesslike. 'How can I help, Captain?'

'I'm going to speak to the neighbour, can you brief me in a few minutes?'

'OK, Captain.'

Lyudmila Kuznetsova's door had been left ajar and she knocked on it loudly.

'Come in.'

Natalya took off her jacket and shook it outside then entered. Kuznetsova muted the television as she brushed past the open box of *matryoshka* dolls. 'I'm here because of Zena.'

The old woman showed concern. 'Has she done something?'

'She's missing.'

Kuznetsova's hand went to her mouth, then she crossed herself in the Orthodox style using three fingers from right to left.

'Have you seen anything unusual over the last week? Any people going to Zena's place?'

'Mind if I sit down?' Without waiting for an answer Kuznetsova eased herself back into the armchair facing the muted TV. 'A man in a suit. I told you about him. He called me "*babushka*".'

Natalya checked her notepad. 'Grey hair you said. Was he balding?'

Kuznetsova shook her head.

'Tall?'

'Medium.'

'Fat? Thin?'

'Average. I'll remember if I see him again.'

'Anyone else?'

'Only him.' She dipped her chin and flicked her eyes to indicate Leo Primakov on the other side of the wall. 'The one with bags on his feet. I was going to call the police then I figured that's who he is. I watch Sled on Channel 5 – he looks like one of those people.'

'Forensics?'

'Yes.'

She smiled at how different the Russian version of CSI was to reality. 'He's with me. We don't know if Zena's gone away or if she's had an accident. We just want to make sure she's OK.'

Kuznetsova was distracted by the muted television showing the two presenters on *Take It Off Immediately* appraising a skinny woman in black underwear.

'What about the apartments above?'

The old woman turned her attention from the screen, then shrugged with her mouth. 'Students from the Mining Institute. They keep together… already gone for the holidays.'

'Were they friendly with Zena?'

'I don't think so.' Her mouth moved as if she was chewing on gristle. 'No.'

'What about a boyfriend?'

Kuznetsova shook her head emphatically, then added, 'Unless he's a vampire. I'm in bed at nine and up before six and I've never seen her with a man.'

'What about anyone else?'

'A girl, maybe once a week. Looked a bit like you.'

'But younger and prettier?'

Lyudmila nodded awkwardly.

Her phone had been switched to silent mode and was vibrating. She checked it discreetly and saw Leo Primakov's face on her screen. She thought for a second of answering it to find out why he couldn't wait a few minutes, then tapped the phone to send it to voicemail.

'When was the last time you saw this girl?'

'Thursday evening. I was just getting ready for bed.'

'And before then?'

The old woman frowned. 'Maybe two weeks. She came. She left. Sometime in the afternoon. I remembered because Zena doesn't get many visitors.'

'Did they go out or stay in?' It wasn't important but helped to build up an image of their relationship.

'Out.'

Lyudmila was transfixed by the television as the skinny woman reappeared with a new hairstyle and wearing clothes the presenters had selected. 'These girls never learn, do they?'

Natalya thought it was a callous remark about Zena then realised she was talking about the TV programme. 'No,' she said, checking her watch, 'habits are hard to break.'

She left Lyudmila Kuznetsova watching television and knocked lightly on Zena's door.

Primakov appeared almost instantly, holding a pair of blue overshoes. 'Captain, I've found something.'

She deposited her leather jacket on the stair rail then pulled them on, though it hardly seemed necessary when the department didn't have the fancy equipment that justified it. She snapped on a pair of latex gloves then entered, observing grey fingerprint powder on the door handles and light switches, and a handheld device charging from a socket.

She pointed at it. 'A UV lamp?'

'For Luminol. I bought some off a website. I checked in the bathroom for blood.'

The tone in his voice told her he hadn't found any. 'What is it, Leo?'

'Did you tell the neighbour?'

'Yes.'

'Good. I want to go in the hallway and see if it's the same outside.'

He picked up a white pot with a fine brush resting on the lid; she followed him.

'What is it?'

He dabbed the brush lightly in the pot then touched the door handle, twisting the brush so its delicate hairs produced a swirling motion. Particles of aluminium powder fell to the floor. He continued to whirl the brush, widening the area to cover a ten centimetre circumference around the handle.

'Do you see?'

She peered at it intently. 'No,' she said eventually.

Her phone buzzed and she removed it from her pocket to check the name. It was Vasiliev. 'Sorry Leo, I've got to answer this.'

Chapter 8

She cleared her throat. 'Colonel?'

'Captain, I wanted an update by midday. It's almost 2 p.m. Please make your report now.'

'Colonel, according to her friend Yulia Federova, Zena Dahl was last seen around 1 a.m. leaving a bar on Ligovsky Prospekt. There are no signs that she returned to her apartment, moreover' – Primakov tapped her on the shoulder and beckoned her to go inside – 'there is a possibility she became stranded when the bridges were raised, preventing her from getting to her apartment on Vasilyevsky Island.'

She followed Primakov and watched him point to the inside of a door handle then a light switch on the entrance hall. Both had left a fine sprinkling of aluminium powder on the floor and she was careful to step around them.

'I assume this is your way of admitting that you have found nothing to indicate a crime has been committed.'

Primakov squeezed the nozzle of an imaginary aerosol can then cupped his sleeve in his hand and rotating his wrist in the mime of a window cleaner. She blocked her mobile's microphone with a thumb. 'Who are you, Oleg Popov?' she asked.

'Captain, I need an answer,' she heard Vasiliev squawk.

'Sorry, Colonel. There has been a development…an indication of criminal involvement.' She stared at Primakov who repeated the gesture and gave her a thumbs up sign when she nodded to show she had understood.

There was a longer pause and in the background she could hear the sounds of keyboards and muted conversations.

'OK, come to headquarters. We'll meet in the Zheglov room.'

'Now, Colonel?'

'Yes, now,' he said with ill humour.

9

The enormous five-storey wedge of grey stone and double columns projected strength as well as continuity; ideal attributes for the St. Petersburg headquarters of the Ministry of Internal Affairs. The impression, she often thought, was marred by the air conditioning units that sprouted from every dirty window like alien fungi, lending it an aura of decay. Natalya parked her Volvo at the intersection of Suvorovsky Prospekt and Kavalergardskaya Ulitsa then walked along the main road. Light rain obscured the blue and white confection of Smolny Cathedral in the distance and made her walk faster with her head bent and the collar of her leather jacket turned up.

The building was home to a variety of police units including the city's headquarters for her own Criminal Investigations Directorate. Inside, Sergeant Rogov was waiting for her: 'Boss wants to see you in Zheglov.'

'Thanks, he's already spoken with me.' She was bemused how Mikhail let Rogov stick so doggedly to him. Perhaps he appreciated some irony in his foul behaviour which she had failed to detect.

'Not a problem, Natasha.'

She peeled off her jacket and shook the drips to the floor before holding it under her arm to knock on the door. There was an unintelligible call and she entered. Inside, the walls in the meeting room were still nicotine-coloured from the decades of smoking before the public ban took effect four years ago. One side held a portrait of the President in an action shot, throwing an opponent in a St. Petersburg judo competition; another supported a studio picture of Vladimir Vysotsky, who looked a little like the American actor Steve McQueen. Vysotsky had played Gleb Zheglov, a rough cop in the Soviet-era TV series "The Meeting Place Cannot Be Changed." He was universally worshipped by all the *menti* but she alone seemed to think it was inappropriate to have a photograph of the actor in the room.

Two tables were arranged in a 'T' shape with Colonel Vasiliev sitting in his customary armchair at the head. His steel-wool hair was sculpted into a Teddy Boy quiff making him resemble an ageing rock star rather than the head of a city's serious crimes unit. On the breast of his checked shirt was an enamelled pin badge. From where she stood it was too small to see clearly but she knew it displayed a tiny bear below the tricolour flag with "United Russia" at the bottom. At the adjoining table for subordinates, Mikhail was maintaining an inscrutable expression; opposite him was a well-built man in dress uniform with a layer of stubble for hair.

There were another twenty empty wooden seats widely spaced around the walls of the room for the other detectives in the directorate, and she took one nearest to the three men.

Colonel Vasiliev fingered his United Russia pin badge as he addressed her: 'Captain Ivanova, I'm sure everyone in the Ministry knows that I am retiring at the end of July. As a senior officer with a distinguished career in the security services, we are honoured to have Major Kirill Dostoynov join the Criminal Investigations Directorate.'

The new major stood and extended his hand for her to shake. That was a good sign, she thought – no saluting and no hesitation, unlike many of her male colleagues. Perhaps Mikhail had judged Dostoynov prematurely. There again, he was probably right in calling him a prick – people didn't join the FSB out of altruism.

A minute later Sergeant Rogov came in and sat next to her.

'Captain,' began Vasiliev, 'I have been discussing the Zena Dahl case with your husband and Major Dostoynov. If I may summarise, Yulia Federova reported that her friend has been missing since the early hours of yesterday morning.' He paused for effect. 'Is it serious?'

She pulled out her notepad. 'There has been nothing on the girl's social media and her phone diverts to voicemail. Her suitcases are intact, so are her toiletries. Coupled with this is the testimony of her friend, Yulia Federova, who reported that Miss Dahl has not been returning her calls.'

'Nevertheless, this may change things.' Vasiliev took a paper from his desk. 'Major, please give this to Captain Ivanova.'

Mikhail took the typed sheet from the Colonel and passed it to her; his eyes creased in a smile. The paper had "For Misha" handwritten in a feminine scrawl on the reverse, presumably from a secretary who owed him a favour. For a moment she felt a pang of jealousy wondering what the favour might have been.

All four men were silent while she read it:

MINISTRY OF THE INTERIOR OF RUSSIA
MAIN ADMINISTRATION OF THE INTERIOR OF THE CITY OF SAINT-PETERSBURG
193015, city of Saint-Petersburg,
Suvorovsky Prospekt, 50/52

The Data Processing Centre of the Ministry of the Interior of the Russian Federation, Main Administration of the Interior of the city of Saint-Petersburg and Main Administration of the Interior of Leningrad Oblast hold one conviction for Federova Yulia Vladimirovna (date of birth March 7th, 1996; Veliky Novgorod) under Article 159 (Swindling). Sentence: September 6 2012, 12 months, Volgograd. Juvenile Detention.

She looked up as Major Dostoynov addressed the colonel, 'If I may speak to the Captain?' It made sense. With Vasiliev retiring, Dostoynov would become her superior unless Mikhail took the top job and forced her to transfer. Mikhail was ambitious but she had made it clear she wouldn't go willingly and the harm to their relationship would be significant – the conversation had come after sex two weeks ago when he had been more than a little sanguine about remaining in his present position.

Vasiliev scratched a thumbnail against his *United Russia* badge. 'Permission given.'

Chapter 9

Dostoynov spoke with the slow, confident voice of someone used to having his orders followed: 'Captain, what happened with the two girls that night?'

'According to Yulia Federova, they were both drunk and had an argument over a boy. She said Zena left on her own around 1 a.m.'

'And was she telling the truth?'

'She claimed she didn't give her full name to the duty sergeant at Vasilyevsky station because her father had been falsely imprisoned and she doesn't trust the police.' She held up the typed sheet with the details of Yulia Federova's juvenile record. 'Maybe this was the real reason though.'

'There was something else I found, Major. When I was in Yulia Federova's home she gave me permission to search her wardrobe. Inside there was a pair of Ulyana Sergeenko sunglasses and a trouser-suit that cost well beyond her financial means. Zena's bedroom was full of similar items and my guess is Federova got them from her, one way or another.'

'So you're saying the girl had motive and opportunity? Why didn't you bring her in?'

'Major, I very much doubt she killed her friend.'

Mikhail joined in; his tone was gentle, and a little condescending, 'Natalya, we've met people before who didn't seem capable of murder yet that's exactly what they did. Or if they couldn't bring themselves to do it, they paid a professional to do the job for them.'

'I didn't say she wasn't capable – history shows that most people are. Yulia Federova was angry, not defensive when I spoke to her. She went to the police station voluntarily and even admitted to having an argument with Zena on the night in question. Unless Federova is very cunning, and I don't believe she is, then they are the actions of an innocent woman. Also, if the motive had been theft, then why didn't she steal the clothes in Zena's apartment? There must be thirty to fifty thousand dollars' worth.' She caught a sly smile on Rogov's mouth and made a mental note to ask Primakov to make an inventory of the wardrobe.

Vasiliev chewed on a plastic pen top and she wondered if he had stopped smoking. 'Captain, did you get anything else from this supposed witness?'

'Yulia said Zena was distracted.'

Major Dostoynov opened his palms in a magnanimous motion. 'Perhaps she was drunk and unhappy. A poor, rich girl deciding to end her sea of troubles in the Neva.'

Vasiliev nodded thoughtfully. 'Sergeant, do you have anything to add?'

She twisted in her seat to study Rogov and also to allow the Colonel's full attention to focus on him, rather than her. Rogov was wearing a plain white shirt several sizes too large in order to cover his enormous belly. The cuffs covered his palms and the sleeves hung limply from his arms. There was already a sweat mark at the centre of his chest.

'Colonel,' Sergeant Rogov began, 'I called all the hospitals and mortuaries in a twenty-kilometre radius of the city. There was no one matching Zena Dahl's description.'

Vasiliev scraped his thumbnail against the United Russia badge on his shirt as if there was some dirt on it that couldn't come off it. 'Sergeant, Major Dostoynov asked specifically about drowning.'

Rogov frowned, evidently unhappy to contradict the new major. 'A body in the canals or the Neva floats unless weighted with stones. And then, with the White Nights and the tourists, it's impossible to avoid being seen.'

Natalya hadn't had lunch and also felt a pressing need for tea, something to take away the dryness in her mouth. 'Colonel, I do have some important information. Zena Dahl's neighbour, Lyudmila Kuznetsova, lives in the same block and reported seeing a man calling at her apartment the morning she went missing. She described him as a bureaucrat with grey hair and wearing a suit.'

Vasiliev turned the corners of his mouth down in a shrug. 'Could be anyone. What else do you have?'

'Expert Criminalist Primakov has been assisting me. He checked Zena's apartment for fingerprints.'

'And?' asked Vasiliev.

She thought of Leo Primakov's mimes and hoped she had interpreted them correctly. 'And he didn't find any, Colonel. At least not in the places you might expect.'

'Don't talk in riddles, Captain.'

'Sir, Leo Primakov believes the fingerprints were removed from the door handles as well as from the light switch. Wiping can leave smears but the areas he saw were as clean as virgin snow. There was no dust or grease on them.' She thought of Primakov's mime of using a spray-gun. 'He believes a solvent of some kind was used.'

'Shit,' muttered Vasiliev.

She turned to Rogov who seemed puzzled and she assumed he was having trouble assimilating the information. 'After Zena went missing, we believe someone went into her apartment.'

'I got that,' Vasiliev said acidly. 'But why not use gloves?'

'Maybe they forgot to bring them or thought it looked suspicious to wear gloves in summer.'

'Or perhaps they had been there before,' offered Mikhail, 'and the purpose was to remove all traces of a previous visit.'

'Yes… Major,' she said.

'How did they get in?' Vasiliev asked.

'Primakov is still there, he may be able to confirm.'

'Good. Can you call him?'

She took out her phone and tapped in the number. Somewhere in Zena's apartment, she imagined Primakov trying to remove his latex gloves then wrestle with his nylon suit to extract his mobile.

'Yes, Captain?' he sounded breathless.

'Leo, I'm at headquarters. Can I ask you some more questions?'

'Yes, of course.'

'Was there any sign of a forced entry?'

'Nothing obvious. No drilling or I'd have noticed.' He paused and she assumed he had gone to examine the door.

'Are you still there, Natalya?'

'Yes.' She looked up and was conscious of the men in the room watching her.

'Zena's lock is difficult to bump with a blank key but there are scratches on the mounting. They might be consistent with picking but a professional doesn't usually leave marks behind.'

She thought of the story Zena's elderly neighbour had told about her husband, Andrei, going out on drunken binges with Vitaly, the man who had once lived in Zena's apartment. On nights out with the other *menti* in the station, Mikhail struggled in more ways than one to fit his key into the hole when he got home.

'More like a drunken husband I reckon. Also I doubt a kidnapper or murderer knows how to open a door with a torsion wrench and pick.'

'Then, there's the *babushka* next door,' he said. 'Lyudmila asked if I wanted some tea ten minutes ago. Whoever broke in had to get past her and I bet she doesn't miss anything. My guess is they had a set of keys.'

She thought of Zena's untouched clothes in her wardrobe, tens of thousands of dollars' worth, offering another reason why the visitor wasn't a normal burglar. 'Any idea what they were there for?'

'What does every student have these days?'

She wasn't in the mood, particularly with Vasiliev watching her, but needed to humour him. 'Books, pens, a laptop, writing paper.'

'Try the third one.'

'Computer?'

'Not there, but even poor students have them.'

'It's a little unnecessary,' she said. 'Why steal her computer when we can get the information from her service provider?'

'Maybe there was something stored on it. A document perhaps? The solvent on the door handle suggests they were overzealous so maybe there was nothing.'

'Hmm,' she mused, 'or perhaps they were old fashioned and hadn't realised the extent of technology and police powers. They slipped up in another way.'

'What?' he asked, and she enjoyed the thought of discovering something the ever-diligent Primakov might have missed. Crime scene investigators and detectives may have discrete job descriptions but they knew enough about the other's work to enjoy a little second guessing.

'They left Zena's wall calendar. It's behind the archway as you enter the kitchen.'

'Yes, I noticed that,' he said, a little unconvincingly.

Chapter 9

'Anyway, I'd better get back. Thanks for helping, Leo.'

She hung up and stared at Vasiliev at the top table. 'Primakov agrees. Whoever broke in most likely used a set of keys. Zena's neighbour had some, but she must be in her late seventies.'

The Colonel rested his elbows on the table and studied her. 'So whoever let themselves into her apartment took Zena's keys when they killed or kidnapped her.'

'What were they looking for?' asked Mikhail.

'Maybe the girl had more designer clothes,' offered Rogov.

Vasiliev shook his head dislodging his quiff. 'Nonsense,' he said, 'how many burglars do you know, Sergeant, who are familiar with haute couture?'

'None, sir.'

'None, sir,' Vasiliev repeated. 'The father has money so that makes her an obvious target for criminal elements. Major Ivanov, have you been able to make contact with the family?'

Mikhail straightened in his seat. 'Not yet, Colonel. The father is a well-known businessman, Thorsten Dahl. I left a message at his headquarters in Stockholm…on an answering machine.' He shrugged. 'Last I heard, the Svens were doing a thirty-hour week. Their *menti* weren't much use either.' His eyes flicked up to a wall-clock. 'They took my number two hours ago and promised to get back to me.'

'Of course,' began Vasiliev, 'if the girl has been taken, it's entirely possible the kidnappers have threatened to harm her if the father cooperates with us or his police.' The Colonel turned to her. 'You've handled kidnappings before, Captain. How long, in your experience, does it take before they contact the family?'

Her mouth was drier than the Aral Sea. 'Two days, maximum.'

'And if the motive was sexual. How long if they had intended to kill her?'

'The same,' she croaked, 'often a lot sooner.'

'What about involving the FSB?' Dostoynov volunteered. 'I could always speak with my former colleagues.'

'Or there's the Investigative Committee?' suggested Mikhail.

'As far as we know, this isn't political so let's keep it with us.'

Vasiliev scratched his United Russia badge thoughtfully. 'All right. Captain Ivanova, overtime is authorised. Sergeant Rogov is assigned to you. The rest of you can enjoy the weekend.'

The FSB were as likely to find Zena as they were to shoot her and claim she had been part of a Scandinavian terrorist network. As for the Investigative Committee, or the Russian FBI as they liked to think of themselves, the Colonel knew they were too shrewd to get involved in a case without solid evidence or leads. That left two options: Vasiliev burning his budget to investigate what had happened to Zena, or leaving her fate in the hands of the municipal police on Vasilyevsky Island who she expected to dutifully file a missing person's report then wait for the girl to surface. But Zena Dahl was a wealthy foreigner who had disappeared at the height of *Piter*'s tourist season; if she really had been murdered or abducted and he did nothing, Vasiliev's career would sink lower than the Russian flag on the Arctic seabed.

He caught her staring at him. 'That will be all, Captain.'

10

Ever since she had been a child, Natalya thought the upholstered chair with the wooden back resembled a small throne. Apart from her brown eyes and some jewellery that was too dated to wear, it was the only physical reminder of her mother's existence. After her parents' divorce, the poor woman had worked herself to an early heart attack and died in it. Mikhail was there now and on the table in front of him were half a dozen shopping bags and a plate with slices of sausage and bread that he was eating with gusto.

She picked up his dripping raincoat and fixed it to the hook at the back of the apartment door then unpacked the bags by mutual agreement, knowing he couldn't be trusted to put everything away in the right places

He asked, 'How about some tea, Angel?'

It was an affectation that used to annoy her but the habit was too ingrained. At least she'd managed to stop him calling her "babe", "little fox", and all his other annoying epithets. She frowned briefly then smoothed it away. 'We only have postman's. We forgot to buy loose leaf.'

'*We* forgot?'

'OK, you forgot. But apart from that, you did well.'

There were other things he'd gotten wrong according to *Roscontrol*, a citizens' consumer group she followed. The smoked Odessa sausage he was tucking into was made from animal skin and soya; at the onset of winter, the windscreen cleaning fluid he'd bought would freeze in his Mercedes; and most alarmingly, the bottle of Slavyanovskaya mineral water exceeded alpha radiation limits.

He waved the knife at her. 'You want some?'

'Not hungry. I'll eat later.' She patted her stomach and hoped it wouldn't give her away by growling.

While Mikhail had been shopping she had called Yulia Federova and told her to attend police headquarters on Monday morning for a formal interview. The rest of the afternoon and early evening had been wasted scouring the internet, trying to find a way to contact Zena's father.

'Where's Anton?' he mumbled while chewing.

'Don't know. Maybe at Dinara's? According to the terms of your divorce, he is supposed to live there.'

'Hmm,' he mused, 'more like Tanya's. I hope he's behaving himself.'

She finished unpacking the shopping then switched on the kettle before retreating to the study. Sitting at their computer desk, she typed 'Zena Dahl' on the *Yandex* search engine but it returned little except for links to the missing girl's Facebook and VKontakte pages. She switched to Google, but struggled to find her amidst the other Zena Dahls who had a higher net presence. Next, she tried the father, Thorsten, and followed a link to the landing page she had seen earlier for *GDH Dahl Engineering.* There was nothing of note there and she returned to the search list finding an *InformationWeek* commentary on the liquidity issues the company was facing due to the oil price collapse and increased competition from China. She grew bored of the article's dry, financial language and returned to the main search again, this time coming across an image of the company's main stockholder on the Forbes website. Thorsten Dahl was a blond, big chested Viking wearing a frayed fisherman's jumper. The only concession to his elevated position in Swedish society appeared to be his neat, side-parted hair.

Chapter 10

'Fuck,' she said aloud. Dahl was sandwiched between a pair of Tetra Pak billionaires under the heading of *'The World's Highest Net Worth Swedes.'*

'Thorsten Dahl is rich,' she shouted through.

'Yeah, I told you he is.'

'No, I mean he's rich like an oligarch.'

'The kettle's boiled,' she heard Mikhail shout, already bored with the conversation; presumably he knew already.

'Thanks,' she shouted back, 'I'll have tea.'

She returned to the search results and clicked on a website run by a group of Swedish anarchists. They had posted a picture of Dahl hauling skis outside a villa near Åre and another of him posing with environmentalists in front of an eco-cabin made from recycled glass. She scrolled past photographs of his island retreat on the Sankt Anna archipelago, his six-room pied-à-terre in central Stockholm, and finally, his ancestral pile in Gothenburg. If the online translation was correct, the anarchists were calling him an ugly capitalist boar, but when she looked at Dahl's picture again, she could have sworn he'd become quite handsome.

She heard Mikhail talking and wondered if Anton had returned, his finely honed sixth sense telling him the fridge had been restocked.

The door to the study opened. 'Is that my tea?'

'No,' Mikhail sighed, 'I've just had a call from a lawyer.'

'Criminal…or divorce?' she smiled brightly.

'Commercial, I think. Someone passed on the messages I left for Dahl. He works for him and is based here in *Piter*. The name's Anatoly Lagunov.'

'Did you ask him about Zena?'

'He did all the talking. Dahl was on his way to Düsseldorf when he got my message.'

'So what's the plan?'

It was nearly eight and she hadn't started cooking. With Anton away they might find a restaurant, maybe a romantic one if Mikhail could stomach it.

'His lawyer – Lagunov – is coming here.'

'Here?'

She frowned. To say it was irregular was putting it mildly, but there again the whole investigation had an unofficial tone to it. Until Zena Dahl's disappearance was confirmed as a kidnapping or murder, there could be no teams working shifts in dedicated rooms; instead, she had her husband – when he didn't have better things to do – and an unreliable sergeant.

Mikhail sliced the sausage with the knife. 'I told him we'd see him at the station tomorrow but he's briefing Thorsten Dahl tonight and wanted to talk to us first.'

'And you agreed to this?'

'Not quite.' Mikhail gave her a wolfish smile. 'I told the lawyer to come here then we'll all see Dahl together.'

'So when is this happening?'

'As we speak. Dahl's plane is diverting to Pulkovo. He doesn't have a visa so this way he can talk to us without officially setting foot on Russian soil.'

'Misha, what are you talking about?'

'We're meeting Dahl on his Gulfstream, Angel.'

After fifteen minutes of speed-cooking that produced a green salad and her second pizza in two days, she heard the apartment's buzzer and stuffed a slice of pepperoni in her mouth as Mikhail left to meet Anatoly Lagunov at the main entrance.

She was still chewing a few minutes later when she heard the doorbell. A stream of liquid trickled from the tip of Lagunov's umbrella as he propped it against the exterior wall in the hallway.

Chapter 10

He was wearing a charcoal suit that fitted his stocky frame and had presumably been tailored. As he looked up, sharp eyes covered by rain-spattered, metal-rimmed glasses met hers. He removed his spectacles and wiped them on a lint cloth from his trouser pocket, then smoothed his damp, grey hair with a hand.

The impression she had of him was one of negation. Anatoly Lagunov was the type of man the intelligence services liked to recruit: he looked fit as well as intelligent, but more importantly, his face was utterly unmemorable. He was a person who could never light up a room so much as glide in and out of it unnoticed, extracting all the gossip. Zena's elderly neighbour had offered a similar, bland description of the man who had visited her apartment block the day before.

She swallowed her mouthful. 'What have I missed?'

'Introductions,' Mikhail offered. 'This is my wife, Natalya, and Mister Lagunov is Thorsten Dahl's… what do you call yourself, Anatoly?'

She bristled, hearing Misha strip away her title. Not "Captain", not "Senior Detective", but "my wife". All authority sucked away by the extractor fan she had left whirring in the kitchen.

Lagunov flashed a row of neat, small teeth and pulled out a business card. 'Officially a lawyer, unofficially a fixer.'

She pocketed the card. 'Tea?'

Lagunov sat in her mother's throne chair then checked his watch. 'Please… we have a little time.'

She poured a cup and handed it to him.

'Forgive me,' Lagunov said, addressing Mikhail, 'but I'm here because of your messages. You think something has happened to Thorsten's daughter?'

'Mister Lagunov,' she began, 'Zena was last seen around one o'clock on Friday morning. Are you aware if Mister Dahl, or anyone else, has heard of her since then?'

The lawyer sipped his tea and looked thoughtful. 'I have spoken with Thorsten briefly on the matter; he didn't think so, but you are better speaking to him than me. We do appreciate your concern; is there any cause for it?'

Lagunov removed a wallet from his trouser pocket and placed it on the table as if it had been causing him some discomfort. From her position on his right she could see the notes' section was at least a centimetre thick. 'I mean she is an adult with her own mind. Is there a reason to believe something bad may have happened to her? You are both detectives in the Criminal Investigations Directorate. Has a crime been committed?'

'Not to our knowledge.' Mikhail got up and took an Ochakovo from the fridge. He remained on his feet and eyed the lawyer.

'Then I'm sure there's nothing to worry about. As I said, we do appreciate your concern. Thorsten will thank you himself when you meet him, but the Swedes are more verbal than us when it comes to gratitude.'

As a bribe it wasn't the most subtle she had witnessed, but did it really count as one when they were only doing their jobs? Last year, the end-of-term bottle of cognac she had given to Karpov, Anton's old maths teacher, wasn't just a gift for a hard-working professional, it opened the conversation and allowed an incongruous link to develop between Anton's unwritten school report and the cost of winter tyres for Karpov's new Subaru.

Her eyes flicked to the wallet and away – an indication that, if nothing more, she appreciated the offer. 'Mister Lagunov, can you give me some background on Zena? Did you know Zena personally?'

'We've only met on a few occasions.' The lawyer sipped his tea. 'I can tell you she came here a year ago to take an undergraduate degree in International Relations at the State University.'

'Alone?'

'Yes.'

Chapter 10

'What about security?'

She saw his sheepish expression and laughed with incredulity, letting her professional mask slip. 'She's the daughter of a billionaire, Mister Lagunov. What were you thinking?'

The lawyer's anodyne features sharpened as his small teeth became rodent-like: 'Don't lecture me!' he snapped. 'You know what the Swedes are like – they never got the message that Socialism is dead. I warned him but Zena didn't want to be locked away like a princess in a tower; she wanted to be a normal student.'

A normal student who walked around in designer clothes, she thought. It was as ridiculous as the fisherman's jumper that Dahl wore to project his man-of-the-people image. 'What about friends here?'

Lagunov straightened as he tried to get comfortable; it was a useless gesture. Torquemada might have abandoned the rack had he known of her mother's throne chair. 'There's a student named Yulia; she mentioned her to Thorsten in passing. He doesn't know her surname.'

'Federova,' she offered, 'I've already spoken with her.'

'That was quick work,' there was a flash of intensity from the eyes then he became unremarkable again.

'And has Mister Dahl heard anything at all from Zena?' Lagunov had already told her the answer, but a kidnapper might have forced Dahl to keep quiet.

'No.'

'Is it possible he has but isn't telling you?'

Lagunov frowned. 'Possible, but not probable. I've worked with Thorsten for two decades and I like to think he trusts me.'

'What about her mother or siblings?'

Lagunov shook his head. 'If I may tell you this in strict confidence' – he shuffled in the chair – 'Zena was adopted.'

'By Mister Dahl and his wife?'

'Just Thorsten. He lived here in *Piter* for a few years and supported an orphanage nearby—'

'Which one?'

His eyebrows came together. 'It might have been Krasnoye Selo. To be honest it was so long ago, my memory is hazy.'

'Wasn't that unusual? A single man adopting a child?'

'I was there. They were having an open day and the kids were wearing their best clothes and running around on the grass. They invited relatives of the children and well-meaning locals.'

'To see if they would take on a child?'

'Why not? Thorsten was a patron – back then there was a massive tax advantage in supporting charities – but he took it seriously. Becoming a father was the last thing on his mind... until Zena came along. She was a new arrival, barely eighteen months old and still wearing nappies. Too young to know she had two dead junkies for parents. The day she saw Thorsten she wouldn't let go of his hand. The staff said she was inconsolable when he left. After that it became a joke each time he visited. Zena used to ride on his back and call him her lion. When he was planning to return to Sweden permanently, he discovered he couldn't bear to leave her behind.'

He shrugged. 'So that's how they met. May I ask some questions of you, Detective Ivanova?'

'Of course,' she said, glad at least that he had reinstated her title.

'Have you much experience of this type of thing?'

'I spent fifteen years working violent crimes.'

His voice faltered, 'Murder and abductions?'

'A lot of murders; thirty to forty abductions. It's quieter now than it used to be but it's still not safe enough to leave a rich kid on her own.'

'And you work with your husband in the same department?'

'It's commoner than you'd think; it's only against regulations if he is my supervisor. Mikhail is assisting, but I have operational control of the investigation and report directly to the head of the Criminal Investigations Directorate.'

She watched Mikhail swig from the bottle of Ochakovo and pretend he wasn't part of the conversation. 'My husband has a law degree and will regard himself as a failure if he isn't a colonel in ten years' time, so there may be a crisis then but it's not a concern now.' It wasn't exactly the truth – she was holding up Mikhail's career and could feel his frustration, even if he didn't voice it. Also, he was popular with the other officers and if Dostoynov did take over from Colonel Vasiliev she'd be blamed for allowing it to happen.

Lagunov felt in his pockets and Mikhail, reading the signs, pulled out a packet of his Sobranies and offered him one. 'What have you found so far?' the lawyer asked.

'I'll get an ashtray,' she said, using the excuse to open the kitchen windows. She returned with a misshapen bowl of fired clay that Anton had made in pottery class and they could find no other discernible use for. 'I'll go into the details with Mister Dahl, but Zena left her apartment last Thursday with Yulia Federova and they became separated.'

'Are you sure she hasn't gone away somewhere?'

'No, but there are indications that this didn't happen. Perhaps she is staying with a boyfriend, but no girl I know leaves without taking a few essentials.'

She turned to Mikhail. 'Speaking of which, I'll leave Anton a note, telling him we'll be out this evening.'

Lagunov nodded solemnly then checked his watch. 'It's getting late, Thorsten will be arriving around 11 p.m. and it will take an hour to get there. Shall we go?' He tipped the remnants of the black tea into his mouth and swallowed.

11

Natalya locked up and followed Lagunov outside. The rain had eased off and the sun, occasionally obscured by clouds, hung above the roofs of Tsentralny District's neoclassical apartment blocks. He was waiting by a black Series 6 BMW that smelled of fresh plastic when he opened the door for her. Mikhail, with a couple of Ochakovos under his belt, was almost certainly over the legal alcohol limit as he climbed into his Mercedes on the other side of the road; he performed a neat U-turn to follow them.

Lagunov's eyes flicked to hers then back to the road as he drove. 'Captain, is there really any need for concern? Thorsten will ask me and I don't want him to worry unnecessarily.'

She paused, wishing she'd gone in Mikhail's car and they'd both followed Lagunov. In these situations, searching for the right words only brought platitudes and vague promises but at least she was dealing with a lawyer and not a parent. 'We've already tried the hospitals and the city's morgues. There is nothing in her apartment to suggest she has gone on holiday. Perhaps she's behaving out of character? The first year at university is tough and she's in a strange country.'

'And if not that?'

'She might have had an accident and been unable to get to hospital; there's suicide of course, and murder…all speculation and it doesn't help anyone.'

She leaned forward and pointed left 'You want to get onto Moskovsky Prospekt.'

He tapped the console to show he was following the directions on the car's satnav. 'Let's keep speculating. What else?'

'Abduction. There are four types. Tell me, has Mister Dahl been involved in a custody battle for Zena?'

Lagunov almost smiled as his eyes flicked to hers. 'No, nothing like that.'

'Then that leaves three: terrorists, criminals and sick bastards. Terrorism is rare outside of the Caucasus these days, thanks to Kadyrov and his merry band of psychopaths, and if the motive was sexual or some other twisted reason, then I'm sorry to say this but she was probably killed soon after she was abducted. If she has been taken, then my money is on money. After all, your boss has plenty of it to share around.'

'It seems so far-fetched.'

'As I said, there may be an innocent explanation; kidnapping is just one line of enquiry.'

'What happens if it is a kidnapping?'

'*If* it is, then the people who took her are most likely to be natives with poor English. The university has broken up for summer so they may try to send a message through one of Dahl's companies or to contact him directly. It's the smart thing to do when there's no official cooperation between the Swedish and Russian police. For several reasons I advise you to take the call, not him. Once the kidnappers make contact, notify the consulate here and the Swedish state police, and I will arrange to have a crisis team put in place.'

'How is Zena's Russian?' she added.

'Good. Thorsten felt it was important for Zena to know her ethnic background... some Swedish thing. He hired a tutor and made sure she knew she was a *Russkaya*.'

'That will help her if she has been taken. What about him?'

Lagunov tilted a hand in a see-sawing gesture to indicate it was mixed.

'If his Russian is poor then you must to take the call. Believe me, you don't want misunderstandings that get a kidnapper frustrated. Also, Thorsten will be emotional. So firstly, and this is important, in that call you will establish that Zena is alive and unharmed—'

'And how do I do that?'

'I'll explain that on the plane. Next, assure them that nobody has spoken to the police and nor will they. Third, don't try to negotiate.'

'What the hell am I supposed to do? Discuss the latest SKA game?'

'No, you tell them calmly that you don't currently have the authority to make a deal. Next, you agree a time and method for them to contact you again. Before you hang up, give them a code word – it will prove you're taking it seriously and will stop other criminals posing as the kidnappers.'

'Why delay it for another call? We just want to get Zena back.'

She looked over her shoulder to check Mikhail was still trailing in his light blue Mercedes; he was. 'Because it gives us time to get the bastards without you having to pay a ransom for a girl who may not be returned. If the call is taken in Sweden, get the police to email me a recording. We'll try to identify them but our priority is the same as yours: to get Zena back unharmed. Try to think of it as a business deal.'

'A deal with a gun to Zena's head.' Lagunov sounded irritated.

'Keep in mind they need her alive. You want to buy something; they want to sell it. Start around a third of the ransom amount and work upwards. Try to stay calm. There are three hundred ransom kidnappings a year in this country.'

'They won't hurt her?'

'Zena needs to be smart. If they show their faces, she looks at the floor...she must be respectful, that kind of thing. For you, it means don't renegotiate the ransom once it's agreed. Above all, be careful who you talk to, especially the *menti*. Policemen have been known to supplement their salaries by kidnapping.'

Lagunov grunted. 'But I can trust you?'

She lifted her left arm, waving it at him like a bird with a broken wing. 'Young Pioneer's honour.'

Lagunov smiled though he looked doubtful. She didn't blame him, the police had a bad reputation but most of the time it was undeserved. She watched him take the P-21 on Moskovsky Prospekt, the same direction she had indicated.

'Could it be the mafia?' Lagunov was saying. 'I heard the Tambovski gang own *Piter*.'

She knew what he was insinuating: if it came to it and there was mafia involvement in Zena's disappearance, how far would she go to stop them?

'It's unlikely.'

The lawyer glanced at her. 'Would you go against them…if it comes to it?'

'Believe me, it's not a problem.'

'Why?'

'Because a ransom is Kopecks to them. Twenty years ago, they seized the city's banks and big companies. A kidnapper is more likely to be an individual or belong to a small, unaffiliated group. They might have the funds to bribe a policeman or two, but not enough to stop an investigation.'

She paused. 'So, did I convince you that not all Russian police are corrupt?'

Lagunov stirred in his seat then lit a cigarette, opening the window a crack to let the smoke escape. 'Of course,' he said, turning away from her.

12

At Pulkovo airport, the BMW and Mikhail's Mercedes parked at Terminal 3 – an area of the airport she had never been to before – and they were met by an official with a neat red beard who checked their identification cards before escorting them to a VIP lounge. The experience confirmed her suspicion that the super-rich had broken away and become an entirely separate species of human being altogether.

They sat around a table in leather armchairs where she spotted a barman who was so discreet his presence hadn't registered with her at first. Mikhail was more observant and Lagunov noticed him watching. 'You want a drink? I could do with one…it's been a long day. Thorsten won't mind.'

Mikhail got up. 'Sure.' He looked over his shoulder at her. 'Angel, you want one too? There'll be some good stuff here.'

He appeared to be exhibiting signs of the infectious, anything goes atmosphere that overwhelmed the city during the White Nights but it was important to stay sharp; besides, despite Lagunov's approval she found it distasteful, as well as unprofessional, to meet Zena's father reeking of alcohol. 'I'm good, Misha…thanks.'

The two men were being served champagne when the official with the red beard reappeared. Mikhail cupped his mouth over his flute and swallowed his drink in one mouthful; she noticed Lagunov had left his untouched.

'Please follow me,' the official announced. They were ushered along the concourse and past check-in, then stepped onto the concrete outside. Despite the late hour, the planes were still casting long shadows on the ground.

Natalya eyed two rows of ten business jets on the apron. 'How much do these things cost?'

'Fifty million dollars and up,' the official said. 'You should have been here during the G20 conference a few years ago; there were hundreds then.'

There was a vintage Mercedes, all headlights and sparkles, parked outside one of the planes and some bodyguards, no doubt ex-Spetsnaz or FSB, who eyed them as they walked past.

While mounting the steps to Dahl's Gulfstream it occurred to her that she had never cared about being rich, not *seriously* rich anyway, but her experience so far suggested it was every bit as vulgar as she'd imagined, and at least as enjoyable. The pilot, a middle-aged woman with golden hair and Ray-Bans, and the co-pilot, a pale young man with an easy smile and a crisp white shirt, were waiting at the entrance to greet them. There was even a flight attendant too, a young woman who had dressed in a hurry judging by the brown shoes which didn't complement her navy uniform.

She followed Lagunov inside, seeing a photograph fixed to an interior wall of a wooden jetty leading to a lake. There was a haze over the calm waters and a circumference of trees that reflected the low sun and gave themselves away as silver birch. Along the fuselage she saw Thorsten Dahl seated in a cream leather chair, one of four surrounding a veneer table. He stood up, stooping to avoid the low ceiling, and waved his arm, beckoning them over.

From the internet images, she already knew he was a large man, around two metres tall, but up close it was impressive. He wore a light blue, untucked shirt with the top two buttons undone, hung over worn jeans that had a hole in one knee. An austerity wardrobe for a man-of-the-people billionaire. Even with the advancing years, it was easy to see why the young Zena had called him a lion in the orphanage; his side-parted hair was still blond despite losing some of its colour and his solid frame bulged around the belly where he had developed a paunch.

Dahl's eyes had deep bags and flitted nervously. He twisted his hands and stared at them as they approached. She'd seen it all before, the stages parents went through. It had been ten or twelve hours since Mikhail had left his messages – a long time to dwell on the possibilities, few of which would hold any comfort. He smiled at her awkwardly, giving the impression of a timid man which was at odds with his image as a wealthy industrialist.

She turned away out of awkwardness and saw another picture on a partition wall; it was of coal black cattle grazing on verdant pasture. A well-built farmer with a weather-worn face stood in front of them, his hands on his hips as he stared coolly into the camera's lens. Lagunov twisted to follow the direction of her gaze. 'Wagyu,' he said. 'Mister Dahl's father keeps a herd.'

Dahl rose in his seat to acknowledge them. 'Please sit down,' he said in a voice softer than she had expected. 'Abbie, can you get our guests some refreshments?' The flight attendant who was standing near the entrance approached them.

'None for us,' she said, glancing at Mikhail.

'Then please get me a large malt, and Anatoly…'

Lagunov shook his head.

'Then just mine.'

She sat down, and Mikhail took the seat next to her; he was facing Lagunov who seemed tiny next to Dahl. They watched the flight attendant open a cabinet and pull out an ancient bottle before pouring a centimetre of whisky into a large crystal glass.

'Your malt, sir,' she said, serving it to him straight. Abbie's face, with its hastily applied makeup, looked as inscrutable as a geisha's.

Dahl stared again, unfocused, his thoughts taking him to some dark place. He shook his head slightly to dispel them. 'Thank you for agreeing to meet me,' he said in English, 'and forgive the unorthodox location. It's been a long time since I've been to Russia and I couldn't get a visa at such short notice. Your FSB colleagues have promised not to throw me in prison provided I remain in the confines of Pulkovo airport.'

He held his hand out to her. 'I'm Thorsten Dahl.'

'Senior Detective Ivanova.' She took out her notepad and laid it on a table.

'And this must be your husband, Mikhail. You're a detective too?'

Chapter 12

Mikhail looked relaxed as if he regularly found himself on private jets. 'Yes I am,' he said in his staccato English.

'Have you found her, Captain?' His eyes darted to hers then flicked away.

'No,' she said.

'Then, please tell me what you can.'

She preferred to dictate the flow of information from the start but it didn't matter – cooperation was rarely a problem when a child was missing. 'Of course.'

She shifted in the chair, finding Dahl's nervousness contagious. 'These are my initial findings and will no doubt change as we discover more. The indications are that your daughter was last seen leaving a bar in the early hours of Friday morning.'

Dahl picked up the whisky, swirled the glass, and then tasted it. He didn't seem surprised and she guessed that Anatoly Lagunov or someone else had updated him. 'What indications?'

'Unopened mail, toiletries, and information provided by the female friend she was with that night.'

'Zena mentioned a Yulia to me. I never met her.' Dahl seemed to drift away again as he spoke and she smelled whisky on his breath; more than could be accounted for by a single sip. She would insist he stayed sober until they got his daughter back – one way or another.

'Yulia Federova. She believes Zena may have been stranded by the raising of the bridges. Can I ask a few questions?'

'Please.' He waved his hand expansively.

'Does Zena have any mental or physical illness where she needs medication?'

'No.'

She flashed an annoyed look at Mikhail who was peering past Lagunov and along the plane's fuselage to the cabin. It was unlike him to be so frivolous, particularly when a girl's life was at stake, and she wondered what he was up to.

'Are you aware if Zena had a boyfriend?'

'No – no boyfriend.'

'Sure?'

'Yes. We have a close relationship. She is shy with strangers so she tended to confide in me.'

'Thank you. Do you know if Zena is taking a birth control pill?'

Dahl thought for a moment. 'I do remember something.' He rubbed a hand over his brow. 'Our family doctor in Östermalm prescribed them for her period pains.'

She made a note in her pad. 'And do you have any idea what she was doing at a ZAGS two weeks ago?'

'Which is what?'

'A civil registration office.'

Dahl had withdrawn again, until he noticed her watching him expectantly. 'Oh.' He thought for a moment. 'No, I have no idea.'

Some people were just bad liars; they were defensive when they should be angry, or else they displayed micro-gestures that gave them away. Dahl's head bobbed in an almost imperceptible nod. The movement was nothing more than a weak 'tell' in a poker game and it was possible she had it wrong, yet it was the same question Yulia had reacted to. She remained silent for a while to see if Dahl embroidered his answer but it was an old trick he was no doubt familiar with.

'Is there anyone she mentioned recently? Someone new, perhaps someone she was afraid of?'

'No one she mentioned.'

'And what about you?'

'I run a large company. There are always people who wish ill of me but none I know who would take it this far.'

'What do you do?'

Dahl sat back a little as if surprised that she didn't know; it made her wonder just how much whisky he had been drinking to display his feelings so readily. 'I run the family business – GDH Dahl Engineering. My grandfather set up the company after the war, then my father took the helm in the 1980s until his retirement. The focus is on shipbuilding now. Obviously the Far East is the main market.'

So that explained his timid manner; Dahl's wealth was inherited. 'And Russia?' she asked, trying to make the question as casual as she could.

Now he was talking he seemed less withdrawn. 'Do you know *Kungsträdgården*?'

'No.'

Dahl shrugged his wide shoulders. 'There's no reason you should I suppose, it's a park in Stockholm with a famous statue of King Karl the Twelfth. He has a drawn sword in one hand; with the other he points a finger at Russia. I used to think differently, but now I'm with him. Eighteen years ago I invested in your country. Now...'

'You prefer to point swords at us?'

Dahl gave her a slight smile. 'It might be hard for an outsider to understand, but I've never had a problem with the people here. Sure, you've had dreadful governments since the dawn of creation, but the general public are wonderful, so full of life. The mistake most foreigners make is they don't make the effort to understand the Russian psyche.'

'Or they patronise us?'

He spoke automatically, his mind elsewhere. 'Yes, we certainly do that.'

'Tell me about Zena.'

'What do you want to know?'

'How is your relationship?'

'Close, but Zena never understood why an inorganic thing like a company had to take precedence over flesh and blood...companies are living creatures too.' Dahl sipped his whisky. 'Sixty thousand families depend on me, Captain Ivanova. I have to be there for them.'

'Is it possible Zena has gone away...perhaps deliberately?'

'To punish me for being absent?'

'Yes.'

'No, I don't believe so.' Dahl straightened up. 'I really don't. As she got older, Zena came to understand my position. After all, the company will be hers one day. Recently, people like Anatoly here' – he patted the lawyer's shoulder – 'have been taking more operational control and allowing me more time to be a better father.'

A missing person, she thought, was a puzzle with a hundred different combinations and only one resolution; first, she had to get inside Zena's head. 'Do you speak often?'

'We got into the habit of making Skype calls about three years ago when I spent a fortnight in Nagasaki. Since then, we always put aside time to catch up. After moving to St. Petersburg, I confess the communication has been sporadic.'

'Are you the problem or she?' asked Mikhail.

Natalya frowned. 'Was that her fault or yours?' she interpreted.

Dahl stared out of the window as if weighing up how honest he should be. 'She was distant when she came home for the winter holidays. I thought perhaps she had found a boyfriend or was struggling at the university. When she returned for the spring term I tried to Skype her, perhaps three or four times in as many months, but she was often unavailable.'

'What do you think was the cause?'

He shrugged. 'I have no idea.'

'And can you think of any places she might have gone to?'

'I honestly don't know. Of course I'm grateful that you're taking this so seriously and will help in any way I can.'

'Does Zena have money of her own?'

She caught Anatoly Lagunov raise his eyebrows in a "what do you think?' gesture.

'OK, silly question. What banks or credit card companies does she use?'

'A few in Sweden. I believe she has a Russian checking account too – I don't have the details.'

She made a note to ask Primakov if he found anything in Zena's apartment. That was an easy way to rule out an impromptu holiday.

'When did you last speak with her?'

'Three or four weeks ago. Sometime at the end of May.'

'And what was her state of mind?'

Dahl stared at the whisky glass then picked it up and swallowed the remainder. 'As I said, Zena was distant. We didn't speak long. She told me she was busy at university and couldn't talk.'

'Mister Lagunov explained that Zena was adopted. Is it possible she is looking for her natural parents?'

'No.' Dahl smiled to himself accentuating the bags under his glacier-blue eyes. 'As I'm sure Anatoly told you, they are both dead.'

'And Zena is aware of that?'

He spoke while staring into his empty glass. 'Yes, she knows the truth, and there were no reliable relatives either. I would never have taken her out of the country otherwise.'

'What about you? Is there an ex-wife or girlfriend she is fond of?'

'There have been a few girlfriends over the years but no one of significance. Zena is all I have, and I am all she has.'

As much as she'd gone through the whole kidnapping scenario with Lagunov, one key fact didn't fit: the ransom demand was overdue. Dahl was a hard person to get hold of though, perhaps it was that, or maybe her abductors were taking their time getting Zena to a secure location. Two days, she mused, then studied Dahl's pained expression as he stared at his glass. He was already assuming the worst possibilities.

He looked up and seemed to struggle to meet her gaze. 'I called her yesterday and got her voicemail. I was going to try again tonight.' He patted his pockets then removed a business card from his wallet. 'This is my private number. Contact me any time.'

'Thank you.'

She turned to see Mikhail typing on the screen of his phone and nudged him with her knee. 'Misha, do you have something to add?'

'Not yet, I think you're covering all the bases,' he replied in Russian.

She tapped her fingers on the veneer table in irritation then stopped when she realised she was doing it. 'Can you think of anywhere she may be?' she asked again.

'No. Apart from this Yulia, I don't know any of her friends. Have you tried the hospitals?' he asked, clasping his hands together as he became more animated.

'Yes, we've done that.' She watched Dahl deflate again.

'And where do you think she might be, Captain?' asked Anatoly Lagunov.

'As you say, there's probably a normal explanation but I'd like to discuss the possibility that someone may have taken her.'

'Do you think it's possible?' Dahl ran a hand through his hair, 'Is there anything I can do?'

Mikhail stopped tapping his phone, 'Speak to your police.'

She glared at him, willing him to shut up. 'Major Ivanov is right. They will record your calls and advise you to keep your mobile phone on and always charged. Make sure someone who can speak Russian is available to answer it. That goes for house phones too – twenty-four hours a day. Monitor Skype, Facebook, Instagram, and any other social media that Zena uses. I suggest Mister Lagunov deals with any contact initially but it's up to the Swedish police to advise you. I also suggest you think of a proof of life question.'

She needed to slow down. It was a bad idea to send Dahl into a panic. He needed time to process the information.

The Swede waved his glass. 'Abbie?'

The flight attendant took his glass and replaced it.

'By that, I mean you should think of a question that only Zena knows the answer to. It will prove they have her; more importantly, it will prove she is alive.'

Anatoly Lagunov shuffled in his seat. 'Do you really think she has been kidnapped?'

'As I said, it's a definite possibility considering Mister Dahl's wealth.'

Mikhail stretched in his chair, pushing his back into its contours. 'That said, it is unusual now.'

'He's right,' she said, 'there are fewer kidnappings now than when you might remember from eighteen years ago. In the meantime we will do everything to find her.'

'Before we go,' Mikhail stood up to leave, 'OK if I take picture of airplane? I like to collect them.'

She frowned. Mikhail had no pastimes that weren't sports-related.

Dahl seemed to brighten at the frivolousness of the request, and suddenly he was the rich man in poor man's clothing embarrassed by his wealth and eager to share it, if only vicariously. 'Yes, please do.'

They stood and moved to the aisle. Mikhail stepped deeper into the aircraft's fuselage before turning so his back was behind the open cabin door. The pilot and co-pilot were busying themselves then stopped and put their arms on each other's shoulders; Mikhail joined them, holding his phone at arm's length. She remained with Dahl and Lagunov, quietly furious as she watched the grotesque spectacle, but even Lagunov was amused, showing a row of his small, even teeth.

There was a click, then one of the pilots frowned and said something to Mikhail, who shook his head as if reprimanding himself.

'Sorry. Wrong way, I must take one more.'

Lagunov smiled again, Dahl looked contemplative, and she projected a look of pure disgust.

There was a click then Mikhail returned, looking pleased with himself. 'We will be back,' he said.

As they climbed down the steps, she turned and caught the Swede brushing tears from his eyes.

Lagunov accompanied them to the terminal building where they were allowed inside after showing their identification cards to two FSB guards manning the security desk. Mikhail scanned the concourse furtively, looking for somewhere to smoke. He pulled out a packet of Sobranie Classics and offered one to the lawyer as they passed through a set of sliding doors.

She addressed Lagunov, 'While you're here. I'd like to ask you a few more questions.'

'Anything to help.' He cupped his hands around Mikhail's to receive a light.

She pulled out her notepad. 'Can you tell me when you first met Thorsten Dahl?'

Lagunov exhaled then frowned slightly. 'It was in the spring of 1999. March or April.'

'How?'

He frowned again, this time the wrinkles showed his age. 'I was hired by Thorsten's father, Gustav. Thorsten was given five million dollars in seed money and sent to Russia. It was the end of the fire sale but there were still bargains to be had.'

'Were you hired because Mister Dahl doesn't speak Russian?'

'Yes.'

She paused to study Lagunov's solid frame. 'And to keep him out of trouble?'

'That too. I had a firearms licence and could take care of myself. It's easy to forget now that Chechen terrorists were setting off bombs and the mafia held gunfights in the street like actors in an action movie.'

'So you were a bodyguard, a fixer, and a lawyer?'

'Why not? Vladislav Surkov was an oligarch's bodyguard before he became the president's advisor.'

'And this orphanage that Thorsten Dahl regularly visited, where was it?'

Lagunov watched a car in the liveries of a New York cab pull up; two skinny girls in sequined tops climbed out, tottering on heels. 'As I told you, it was at Krasnoye Selo.'

She held her pen over her pad. 'Describe it to me.'

'You may be better speaking to Thorsten. I can't remember the details.'

'In the car earlier, you told me Zena called Mister Dahl' – she checked her notepad – '"her lion" when they first met. Presumably you were there that day?'

He exhaled smoke into the pale night air. 'Not at all. Thorsten is fond of telling it; he's repeated it so often I feel as if I must have been there.'

He smiled to himself displaying his neat teeth.

'So when you said you were there earlier today it was a mistake?'

'I misunderstood the question. I went to the orphanage on other occasions.'

'Zena isn't a Russian name; what was she called before the adoption?'

'I'm afraid I don't know.'

Was he lying? She couldn't tell. Lawyers and policemen had too much practice but it was hard to believe his memory could be that poor or that he was innocently contradicting his earlier answers. 'So you don't remember what must have been the most significant event during his time here. On top of that, you were his fixer – you must have helped him with the paperwork and any bribes.'

He pushed his lips together. 'It would be foolish of me to admit to anything like that in front of a police officer.'

'Of course.' She tapped her pen on her notepad. 'So when did Mister Dahl leave?'

'Towards the end of 1999.'

'Was he back for Christmas?'

'I don't remember.'

'Did you have Christmas with him here or had he gone by then?'

Lagunov looked at Mikhail quizzically, hoping he would interrupt. 'Look, Natalya—'

'Captain,' Mikhail reminded him.

'Alright, Captain. I don't know what you want me to say. All this happened a long time ago and these questions are of no relevance that I can see.'

'Might your powers of recall improve if you came to police headquarters for a formal interview on Monday?'

'I thought you wanted me to answer Thorsten's phone in case the kidnapper calls?'

'Well, that was contingent on your cooperation. May I continue?'

He raised a palm towards her in a sarcastic gesture. 'Please do.'

'So, you spent the Christmas of 1999 together?'

'Thorsten stayed with me and my wife; we divorced a few years later.'

She noted his answer.

'And what did you do with Zena?'

'Zena wasn't there.'

Natalya looked up. 'So this story of the open day and Zena clinging to his leg. That was in the summer?'

'Perhaps...'

'Yet you set the scene fairly well earlier. I imagined children running around on the grass; maybe a little wine to loosen up the prospective parents. That doesn't sound like winter to me. So where did Zena spend Christmas? The Swedes are big on Christmas and I don't believe for a second he left his new daughter behind.'

He shrugged. 'Perhaps she left the orphanage between then and the New Year. Our government is twitchy about foreigners adopting Russian children so you can understand if Thorsten is reticent about giving away too many details.'

'We should go.' Mikhail stubbed his cigarette out.

Lagunov did the same and she let the lawyer separate from them as he hurried for his BMW.

'Misha,' she scowled as they walked towards the car park, 'what were you doing on the plane?'

'What do you mean?' he grinned.

'Dahl's daughter might be dead and you took a selfie with the pilots.'

'Oh, that,' he said smoothly, taking out his mobile, 'Do you really think I'm that shallow?'

'I'm beginning to wonder.'

'Here, I'll send it to you. Have a look for yourself.' He tapped some buttons on his phone and she heard hers buzz.

'It's late, Misha. I'm too tired to play games.'

'Remember when you spoke to our good colonel. You told him someone called at Zena's on the Friday morning. The *babushka* said he wore a suit and had grey hair.'

'Yeah, she called him a bureaucrat.'

'Sounds to me like Dahl's lawyer.'

She shrugged. 'Or a salesman.'

'Well,' he said, 'there's one way you can find out.'

She unlocked her phone then opened the message to see a photograph. It was of Anatoly Lagunov smiling condescendingly at the stupid policeman who wanted to impress his friends. Mikhail hadn't taken a selfie – the camera had been pointing the other way.

13

As Mikhail parked, she observed it was 1:10 a.m. according to the clock in his Mercedes. Outside, the sun was lolling drunkenly over the horizon, and she could see silvery splashes on the streets where its dim light was reflected on puddles. She took the stairs before finding their apartment as dark as a coal bunker from the blackout curtains that Mikhail installed during the White Nights. She took off her shoes in the hallway and stepped on a half-full beer can that crushed under her foot; the cold liquid soaked her sock.

She peeled it off and held it gingerly in her hand. 'Misha, you bastard.'

'What have I done?' he said, behind her.

She felt for the light switch. The can had spilled from a plastic bag filled with bottles, cans, and the contents of several ashtrays; next to it were three empty pizza boxes. It was cold enough to give her goose pimples and she felt behind the curtains and blinds to find the windows wide open; no doubt to clear the air of cigarette smoke before they got home.

While Mikhail stormed into Anton's bedroom she went to the bathroom and rolled up the leg of her jeans.

'You irresponsible little shit.' She heard him shout as she directed the bath's shower attachment at her beer-soaked foot.

There was a murmur from Anton then a yelp of indignation. She cleaned her teeth then went to their bedroom and closed the curtains before switching on the light. Mikhail came in and started pulling off his clothes, dropping them on the floor as he changed.

'Your sister left a message with him.' Mikhail, she noticed, was unable to say Anton's name. 'She's working a night shift in the hospital. She said you can call any time.'

'What happened?'

Mikhail fiddled with his belt buckle, his hands yanking at it. 'What?'

'The mess.'

He glared at his discarded shirt on the floor then realised she was talking about the beer bottles and pizza boxes. 'Anton.' He pulled the belt free and shrugged off his trousers.

She wanted to laugh at the incongruous sight of him being angry in his underwear and socks.

'Your fault,' he hissed.

'Mine?' her voice rose in pitch.

'You left that note telling him we were going to the airport. He thought it meant we were going away and he decided to invite some friends around. Luckily they left for a club an hour ago.'

'At least he tried to clean up.'

He glared at her again, then dropped his underwear to save his socks for last.

'Did you check the bribe today?'

'Because I feel like doing him a favour?'

She realised he was better left to himself. 'Don't worry about it, Misha. I'll call Klavdiya.'

She undressed and pulled on a dressing gown before switching the light off. In the living room, she sat on the sofa and dialled her sister's number from memory.

'Claudia?' she said, using the Germanic version of the name that her sister preferred.

'Yes.' Claudia sounded officious and she guessed there was someone close by.

'You want me to call back?'

'It's fine. I'm giving a patient some water, they are going now.'

'How's life in Hannover?'

She heard the sigh. 'Too many Russians. They hear of a nurse who can speak their mother tongue and all day they want me to tell them what the doctor is saying. I tell them to fuck off and learn German if they want to live here, but they don't care. They all watch cable TV and speak Russian with their friends. There's no incentive.'

Chapter 13

'Damned Russians.' Natalya laughed. 'How's Papa?'

'Old and cantankerous. He misses his Natashenka – so do I. When are we going to see you?'

She wondered how long it would take before Claudia brought up the subject. Living in Germany as children, they had both been given dual citizenship but she had relinquished hers to join the police. Despite the complaints, being an expatriate had made Claudia more Russian; returning to St. Petersburg had the opposite effect on her though. The mafia, the chauvinism, the bureaucracy, the incompetence; it made her despair. Spending her teenage years in Germany had turned her into an alien, a fifth columnist.

'Natashenka?'

'I'm still here. Can you wait a second?'

She crossed into the study and switched on the desktop computer. If Mikhail couldn't be relied on, she would do it herself. It was late, but another day might be lost before she or Mikhail had another opportunity to check if Anton's university bribe had been paid. That was another thing – bribes. What sane society was based on paying and receiving bribes? Newly qualified doctors couldn't locate the body's organs because they had bought their medical degree; children wanted to be tax officials and prosecutors when they grew up. There was even an app for a mobile phone that calculated the appropriate bribe to offer for a traffic violation. The whole damned thing was ridiculous.

'How's my favourite nephew?' she asked.

'He's a little swine. Yesterday an AfD candidate came to our door canvassing for the local elections; Oskar dropped his trousers and did a shit on the hallway floor – right in front of him.'

Natalya laughed.

'I was scrubbing the tiles all day and I can still smell it. Don't ever have children.'

'I'm not intending to.'

Claudia's voice dropped, 'Oh, I didn't mean it like that.'

'That's alright, I'm not offended.'

'How's Mikhail?'

'Usual. You should come over, we've got the space now.'

There was silence on the other end then an exchange in German. Natalya used the lull in the conversation to enter the Windows password on the computer, then she checked the ring file where Mikhail kept his bank details. She opened the webpage for the North-Western then typed in his account name and password.

'Are you happy, Natalya?'

'I'm tired. There's a new case: a missing girl, I've been working on it all day.'

A page came up and she clicked on a button to show Mikhail's transaction history. The balance showed 49,534 roubles, less than her monthly salary, and not enough for him to pay the bribe. There was a chance though that the Admissions Head had made a mistake and it had been paid some time ago.

'I know you'd need to reapply for citizenship, but I have a friend at the kindergarten, one of the mothers, her husband is a Russian who joined the police. I can speak to her and find out how difficult it was.'

'I'm nearly forty, Claudia – that's too old to start again.' On the screen she flicked through the last month of Mikhail's transactions. She remembered the bribe had been for five thousand dollars. Since the economic sanctions, the exchange rate had nearly doubled, so she was expecting to find a transfer of approximately three hundred and twenty thousand roubles.

'Nonsense,' her sister said, 'I'm sure they'll take your experience into account.'

There was nothing in Mikhail's account for a withdrawal of that size in May, then she remembered they had accompanied Anton to the university last September. He could have transferred the money any time since then and it might explain why Mikhail or the Admissions Head had forgotten about it.

'Claudia, do you remember that wedding you went to in St. Petersburg, sometime in the summer of 2014? Mikhail and I were standing in front of the priest holding candles. I was the one dressed in white?'

Her sister grunted. 'Well, I'm sure Misha could get a job too. He might have to learn German but, like I said, there are a lot who don't and they get along fine.'

She had a point, Natalya thought; her circle of friends was becoming smaller as people packed their bags for America, Germany, Israel, and Britain. Mikhail was sure to be the last to go though, at heart he was a Russian cop who would never feel at home anywhere else.

'And Anton too,' her sister said unconvincingly.

That was fantasy. Anton was legally an adult and he didn't have the transferable skills to get himself a one-way ticket. On top of that, he wasn't her son. Mikhail leaving without Anton was a joke, and she wouldn't go without them.

'Maybe,' she said, to kill the conversation.

She looked at the screen again and tapped the mouse button to take her to the April transactions. Mikhail's salary was there, as were the debits for most of their household bills. She tapped the mouse button again for March. Nothing there. She tapped it again, and again. On the January statement she saw it: an amount of three hundred and fifteen thousand roubles leaving the account, no doubt to pay off the Head of Admissions. She looked closer, unable to believe what she was seeing. Her heart started pumping and her mouth felt dry: a few days before, a sum of three hundred thousand had been deposited into his account.

'Well, think about it anyway,' Claudia said.

She was confident Mikhail had no other bank accounts, or at least none that he'd mentioned. In addition, he didn't gamble and had never mentioned receiving a payout. There was no reason for anyone to give him such a large sum of money.

She clicked on the highlighted transaction to see where it had come from. There was no name, only a long string of digits that she realised was an international payment number: an IBAN. The payment had come from abroad.

'I will.'

She opened a new tab, and the default Yandex browser appeared. She typed in "IBAN calculator" then copied and pasted the digits from Mikhail's online account.

'Do you know the story of frogs in boiling water?' Claudia asked.

'People always leave things until it's too late.'

After taking a deep breath, she hit send. A name came up with a fresh link for *The Limassol Trading Bank*.

'Shit,' she whispered under her breath.

The bank's website opened in a new tab when she clicked on the link. There was a small, square icon at the top of the page; a tricolour of white, blue and red. She tapped the flag and the page translated into Russian.

'Are you there, Natalya?'

She copied the sort code and account number from the IBAN calculator and pasted them into the fields on the bank's web page and clicked the 'Go' button.

'Yeah, I'm here.'

A welcome page appeared and she tapped the flag again. This time there was an empty field asking for a six-digit passcode and an account name. She typed in "Mikhail Ivanov" and used his birthdate for the code, then clicked 'Go'. An error message appeared explaining there was an error in the details entered and she had two tries left.

'You don't sound there.'

'I was just thinking about the frogs,' Natalya said, staring at the screen.

Her mind was reeling. Was this Mikhail's account or did it belong to someone who owed him money? If it belonged to him then it was clearly illegal – public officials were banned from having overseas bank accounts. Worse than that, it was an offshore one of the type the mafia used to launder their dirty money. If it belonged to Mikhail then he was corrupt. There was no doubt about it.

'What about the frogs?' she heard Claudia say.

'It's not true,' Natalya said after a moment. 'The frogs don't leave it too late. Some twisted scientist tried it with live ones. They all jumped out when it got too hot.'

14

She heard the alarm on Mikhail's phone but it sounded distant; an echo in another room. She yawned, keen to dispel the nightmare floating inside her head: Anton in danger and she unable to do anything about it.

The alarm stopped. She was tired and sensed a cool trail of saliva running from the corner of her mouth to her jaw line. Without opening her eyes, she wiped it with the back of her hand but it came away dry. What time had she returned? Around four she guessed. It was coming back to her in flashes. She had left the apartment; too shocked at seeing the offshore bank account to climb into bed with Mikhail and pretend nothing had happened. There was another memory – she had gone to the Cheka bar and Semion the barman had flirted with her, offering free vodka. She had driven home drunk. Her fingers made contact with an upholstered wall as she reached for Mikhail, wondering what to say to him. She opened her eyes, puzzled, and stared at the edge of the sofa bed. She frowned, then remembered assembling it and lying down fully clothed because the bedding was at the top of the wardrobe in Anton's room and she hadn't wanted to disturb him.

At least it was Sunday and she could afford to deal with it all later. She closed her eyes and drifted off. There was a noise in her face, a metallic whine of a fly. She opened her eyes and saw Mikhail standing over her, an electric toothbrush in his mouth.

'Oh God, what time is it?

'Nearly ten,' he mumbled.

She felt stiff and in need of a hot shower.

He was wearing the grey shirt his ex-wife Dinara had bought for him in the dying days of their relationship; it was a bad omen.

'What the hell happened to you?

'I couldn't sleep so I went to the bar…the one Yulia said she had gone to with Zena.'

'And?'

'And I wasted my time. No witnesses and the security tapes have been reused.'

'You told me that last time.'

'This time I checked with the manager.' She yawned to cover the lie.

He switched off the toothbrush and gave her a look that was more sad than angry. 'Then why didn't you come to bed?'

'It was late and I didn't want to wake you.' Another lie, Mikhail could sleep through the tank section of a May Day parade.

'Do we have a problem?' he asked.

The question wasn't a surprise considering she was exuding vodka from every pore and Mikhail was no fool.

Anton stepped into the living room wearing a pair of yellow boxer shorts. 'Natasha, have we got any juice?'

'No,' she said, addressing no one in particular and watching Mikhail frown as he wondered whom she had replied to.

Outside it was overcast and Natalya took the Metro to Vasileostrovskaya station then walked for a kilometre along Sredny Prospekt before turning onto Veselnaya Ulitsa. It was quiet outside Zena's apartment; there was no twitch of the curtains from the neighbour, Lyudmila Kuznetsova, and she let herself in. She slipped on a pair of latex gloves and looked around. The food in the fridge, what there had been of it, was starting to smell and she was glad Primakov had taken the rubbish away. The heavy green curtains that had come with the apartment were still drawn but now the room felt like a mausoleum – a tomb without a body. It was hard to imagine the girl coming back to breathe life into the place. She stepped into the bedroom and opened the wardrobe, surprised to find the designer clothes still there. If Zena didn't return, one day they too would disappear, leaving another mystery to solve.

Chapter 14

She heard the door in the adjacent apartment open and called out, 'Mrs Kuznetsova?'

'Yes?'

There was a shuffle and in the hallway she saw the old woman wearing a black headscarf and clear plastic glasses. 'Still no news?'

Natalya shook her head. 'May I ask you a question?' She tried to keep the eagerness out of her voice – it was the first lead she had on the case. Following regulations, she ought to bring Lyudmila Kuznetsova to headquarters and present her with a range of images but she sensed the old woman spoke more freely at home.

'May I?' The soft wrinkles on Kuznetsova's face cracked into a smile as she impersonated Natalya. 'You are so polite. Are you sure you're a ment?'

'I wonder it myself.' Natalya took out her phone. 'I'd like to show you someone. You said a man came to Zena's door two days ago.'

'The bureaucrat, yes. He was waiting for me to leave.'

Natalya flicked through the saved pictures and selected the one Mikhail had taken of Anatoly Lagunov on Dahl's Gulfstream. She kept her voice level, 'Is that him?'

The old woman pulled off her glasses then peered at it. 'Can you make it bigger?'

Natalya tapped the image twice and it enlarged. 'Is that better?'

'These phones are a miracle.'

'Yes they are. Is that the man you saw?'

'Wait. Patience and work will grind down everything.' Lyudmila Kuznetsova squinted. 'I knocked on the window and he looked up.' She put a thick hand over the phone to push it away. 'My eyesight isn't so good now but I'm sure it was him.'

She was walking halfway along Sredny Prospekt when her phone started ringing. She fumbled for it in her handbag then pressed her palm against her exposed ear to block out the surrounding traffic. 'Yes?'

'It's Primakov, Captain.'

'I can see that.' His VKontakte image showed him running; the photograph taken mid-stride as if he was floating on air. She tried to shake the tiredness out of her voice. 'Sorry Leo, how can I help?'

'Major Ivanov asked me to call.'

'He did?' A driver beeped his horn at the car in front for being a millisecond too slow at pulling away from the traffic lights.

'I left a preliminary report on my findings on your desk. Mikhail saw me, he was in his office.'

She thought hard to remember what Primakov must be calling for. There had been a conversation in the plane. Where was her notepad?

'Leo, can I call you back? It's hard to hear you—'

'He asked about bank details.' Primakov got in fast before she ended the call.

Not Mikhail's surely. Something to do with Zena. An image flashed in her mind of sitting in the staff room behind the bar in Cheka bar and one of the doormen telling her something. She had written it down.

'Zena's bank details,' Primakov said. He was always polite but there was a hint of exasperation in his voice.

She stepped inside a café and felt a chill of air conditioning. A waitress approached and she waved her away. 'What about them?'

'Mikhail asked me to let you know. There was nothing in her apartment. No statements, cards or bills. She was tidy, so maybe everything was online.'

'What about you?' she asked. 'You hate mess. If a burglar broke into your place would they find your bank details?'

'Maybe.'

On Monday, she'd ask Rogov to call the main banks and see if any held Zena's checking account. He was off duty now and only she had been authorised to continue working. Mikhail shouldn't have been in either but he often used the weekend to catch up on his paperwork when the office was quiet.

'Leo?' She took a table by the window and mouthed "Cappuccino" at the waitress. 'I need some advice.'

'Captain?'

She had little reason to doubt that Primakov was on her side, he had never done anything to make her think otherwise, but he was a very private individual and she wondered how much to tell him. 'It's probably nothing.'

She heard heavy breathing on the other end of the line. 'Leo, what are you doing?'

'Going up the stairs.' She heard a door close. 'Now I'm home.'

She shook her head. It felt too ridiculous to voice her thoughts. Inexplicably, there were tears forming and she blotted them with her fingertips, annoyed at her emotional incontinence. 'If I ask this, promise it will go no further?'

'Unless you've killed someone.'

'You watch too much TV.'

'True.'

She looked around to make sure no one was in listening range then dropped her voice to make sure. 'I have a friend, she's worried her husband has got another woman set up in an apartment. She's found a secret bank account but can't get past the security questions.'

'Then what do you want me to do?'

'Nothing illegal, just some advice. She promised me she won't take any money from the account; she only wants to poke around and see what else he's been doing. How can she hack into it?'

Primakov's reply was instant, 'It can't be done.' There was a pause and she heard the sound of a meow then the clatter of what could have been a saucer – she didn't know he had a cat. 'Or at least,' Primakov added, 'it can't be done the way you think. Usually the bank locks a user out after three attempts then send a warning email or text message to the account holder.'

'So, what do I do?'

'You get Mikhail to give it to you.'

Primakov, as usual, was too smart, but it annoyed her that he hadn't spared her feelings by going along with the subterfuge. 'Well, if it's impossible—'

'I didn't say that, Captain. Your…friend needs to think like a cybercriminal. Give me half an hour and I'll send you an email. Make sure you disable the spyware option on your… I mean her antivirus software if she has one on the computer. Tell her to run the program in the email and follow the instructions. Make sure she deletes everything afterwards and empties the trash folder.'

'It's not for me, Leo.'

'Of course.' She could almost hear the bastard smile.

'What are you sending?'

'A keylogger. It will sit invisibly on your…friend's machine and copy everything her husband types.'

'Thanks, Leo.'

The afternoon had gone in a blur. Instead of taking the Metro she decided to clear her head with a walk and somehow ended up at the Peter and Paul Fortress. The temperature was barely warm enough for shorts yet middle-aged men and women, their bodies a luminous white or else the colour of oiled cedar, lay like basking seals on the banks of the Neva. She followed the road entrance and passed two young women with a gold 'K' on their shoulders. They wore white blouses, both had blonde hair half-way down their backs and tottered on platform heels at least ten centimetres high. She had been one of those girls once: a police cadet who appeared to exist solely as bait for the instructors or, according to the boys in her class, to fulfil an equal opportunities quota.

In hindsight, joining the police had been an effect with more than one cause: an act of supreme rebellion against her mother who had impressed on her the need to find an office job, get married, and have a baby at the earliest opportunity. Enrolling as a police cadet after university had seemed the most efficient way to deal with the issue of finding a job, while postponing marriage and motherhood for as long as she could. Blaming the dead was never satisfying though, they never argue back.

She walked around the fortress, stopping at the old jail where many of the country's historical figures had been incarcerated, including Alexei, Peter the Great's own son whom he'd had tortured to death. After a while, she crossed Troitsky Bridge thinking of Anatoly Lagunov. In the airport, he'd displayed stunning ignorance when she asked him about the orphanage. He'd also been unable to recall Zena's birth name, when the adoption had taken place, or even what the orphanage had looked like. It did make sense if he was covering for Dahl. At a time when Russia was falling apart, adoptions were often informal or beset by bribery. If Zena's had been one of them, Dahl was laid open to blackmail or criminal charges.

At the midpoint of the bridge, she paused and stared over the Neva. Another thing Lagunov would struggle to explain was his presence outside Zena's apartment on the Friday morning, a full twenty-four hours before Yulia Federova reported her friend missing – assuming it was him that Lyudmila Kuznetsova had seen. It didn't mean Anatoly Lagunov was complicit in the abduction of his boss's daughter – not necessarily. An even more likely possibility was the kidnapper had already made contact with Dahl, and Lagunov had merely been summoned to check Zena's apartment to see if she really had been abducted. She had seen it before: parents colluded with kidnappers and withheld information from the police, sometimes telling outright lies in a dubious attempt to protect the missing child. It made the job twice as difficult. On Monday, she'd insist Anatoly Lagunov and Yulia Federova come to headquarters for a formal interview. Until she was convinced that Lagunov wasn't involved, she would instruct Thorsten Dahl to keep him out of any ransom negotiations. She knew she needed to make that phone call urgently, but it required treading carefully and her head was too full of last night's vodka to find the right words.

Back at home, she made herself a coffee using instant granules before switching on the computer in the study. The email from Leo Primakov was already waiting for her; it had no title or contents except for a single executable file. She was relieved to note that their anti-virus software was a free download Mikhail had obtained from the internet and it had no Spyware option unless, it suggested, she pay fourteen hundred roubles to upgrade it to the *Elite* version.

The front door creaked as it opened and her hand flashed to the mouse to minimise the window on the screen. There was silence, then the sound of shoes being kicked off. Her hand hovered over the 'off' switch.

'Hello?' she called out.

There was a girl's voice; lively and giggling, then a hiss of "Shh!"

The door to the study opened. 'Natasha? You're home.'

She noticed Anton's glistening eyes and red lips; he rocked on his heels with his hands behind his back. A smile creased the corners of his mouth.

'Anton, have you been drinking?' Her eyes flashed to the clock on the computer. 'It's not even six.'

'Sorry, I—'

A younger, moon-face appeared and a bare arm grasped the door frame for support. 'You must be Tanya.'

'Hello, Mrs Ivanova.' The girl grinned.

'You can call me Natalya, I'm not his mother.'

'Please don't send her home, Natasha, it's my fault.' Anton tapped his chest and nearly lost his balance.

'Just drink lots of water and make sure you're quiet when your father gets back.' She spoke to Tanya and the girl blushed, 'And come over for dinner. Don't worry about last time. Just let me know,' she smiled, 'and don't listen to Anton if he tells you I'm an awful cook – he's lying.'

The two teenagers left and she heard Anton's bedroom door close. She hoped they were being sensible but girls were rarely on the pill, and boys with condoms were regarded with suspicion as if they had a sexually transmitted disease. Despite improvements in the last few decades, abortions were still one of the main methods of birth control. She would speak with Anton when he was alone, Mikhail couldn't be relied on: the first time they tried to have sex, she had insisted on him using a prophylactic and it had ended in an argument when he questioned her on her sexual health.

Now she was alone, she heaved a sigh and felt her chest shake. The questions ran through her mind. What could she do if Mikhail was corrupt? Was the offence serious enough to leave him for? In her mind an affair deserved an automatic disqualification but money in a secret account? Numbers stored electronically didn't carry the weight of a lipstick smear or a hotel receipt. What the hell was she supposed to do with it? And what of Anton, the boy-not-yet-a-man? If she left Mikhail could they still have a relationship?

Chapter 14

She took a deep breath and returned to the computer, re-opened Primakov's email then clicked on the attachment. The computer asked for permission to install the software he had sent. She tapped "OK", then again to run it. A box appeared requesting a new password. She typed in "Heidelberg" remembering it as the last place she had seen her own parents truly happy. She confirmed the password then closed the box, The keylogger flashed a message to confirm it was now running invisibly in the background. A pang of guilt came from nowhere. Why didn't she just ask Mikhail about it? She was accusing him of being secretive and yet was doing exactly the same thing herself.

Her phone started buzzing. She deleted Primakov's email, then emptied her virtual waste bin to remove all trace of it. She glanced at her iPhone and tapped the green circle to take the call. Instantly there was the urgent wail of a police siren.

'Mikhail?'

'Just a minute, Angel...Hey, get out of the way, shit-for-brains!'

She heard him let loose more obscenities. As a senior officer, he was entitled to use a blue light on his own car but it didn't always help when many of the ancient streets were narrow and there were traffic lights and crossings at every intersection.

The siren stopped. 'Drop everything,' he shouted. 'Get to the Maritime Victory Park on Krestovsky Island.'

'What is it?'

'I said "Get out the fucking way!"'

She was deafened by the simultaneous blast of a car horn and the wail of the siren through the phone's earpiece; they stopped abruptly.

'There's a body.'

She sat up straight. 'Zena?'

The siren started again and she heard him fumble with his phone. 'No idea. I'll see you there.'

She ran down the stairs, taking several steps at a time. At the entrance hall, she burst through the block door and ran to her Volvo. She stopped. To get there quickly she needed a car with emergency lights but that meant going back to headquarters. Then, it was painfully time consuming to wait in line to be breathalysed. Instead, she could travel to Krestovsky Island in her Volvo, or get there even quicker if she took the Metro.

The gun tapped against her hip as she ran towards the entrance of Admiralteyskaya station, pausing to swipe her *Podorozhnik* card on the barrier. Feeling the warm air envelop her, she descended on a ribbon of steel into the city's underground station; one of many built deeper than normal so *Piter*'s population could survive a nuclear attack. She switched to the left of the escalator and started jogging down it. After a hundred metres, a young family of four, each with a suitcase proportional to their size, blocked her way and she observed a booth at the bottom where a guard, stupefied by boredom, was monitoring the CCTV cameras fixed to the sloping ceiling. She heard a commotion and turned to see a group of four OMON in their grey-blue uniforms pushing their way down and coming to a halt a few steps above her. At the bottom, she passed the woman in the booth then took another escalator, this time shorter, and she came out in a wide, marble corridor with arches on both sides and a nautical-themed mural at the end.

The family were slow to get off and the travellers disgorged around them; a stream circumventing a rock. A uniformed sleeve went to brush her aside, and she quickly identified the owner as a major in the National Guard. It was a new army of four hundred thousand with the authority to shoot into crowds in the event that people stopped believing the propaganda on TV and decided to get rid of the president. The man would be a pauper or a millionaire, depending on his honesty, and the stony face and neat brown hair gave nothing away.

The train was already at the platform and she rushed for the doors, feeling a momentary panic for not checking which direction she was heading. A sign on the train told her she was on the *Frunzensko-Primorskaya* line, but that was hardly a surprise when it was the only one serving the station. She saw a diagram, a line dotted with locations, and after the first stop she knew it was heading for Krestovsky Island.

15

Outside the Metro station, she was momentarily blinded by the bright sun. A distant siren cut through the sounds of traffic and tourists and made her wonder if it was Mikhail. She jogged down the steps and crossed the road where two empty police cars were parked on the pavement at the open gates of the Maritime Victory Park. She skirted between them and then resumed her running pace, soon drawing alongside *Divo Ostrov*, the Miracle Island amusement park. A child's electric car darted in front of her, nearly tripping her up; inside its single seat was a capuchin monkey clinging to the doors, its teeth bared and eyes wide in terror. The animal's owner twisted the tiny steering wheel on the miniature BMW's remote control, and the monkey shrieked as it sped towards a group of teenage girls. Natalya jogged on and heard screams as a crude rocket ship arced above her, supporting wires fixed to a massive metal arm like a spinning crane. There were more screams and she glanced up to see a couple being catapulted fifty metres in the air by a human slingshot.

Ahead, the myriad of lanes and groves of exotic tree species revealed no clue to the crime scene. There were happily oblivious tourists everywhere, thousands of them.

'Damn it,' she cursed out loud. The park was at least two square kilometres and Mikhail had given her little in the way of directions; it was going to take forever to search on foot. She pulled out her mobile to call him then stopped herself, wondering if he was expecting it. Vasiliev had given her the case yet Mikhail was always hovering in the background, ready to help out. She knew Misha cared and was looking out for her, ready to catch her if she fell; that made her oversensitive, paranoid even, that the other *menti*, like

Rogov, didn't take her seriously because she was married to a senior officer.

Her breathing became ragged. She slowed, following the path as it joined the central fountain, bordered by beds of marigolds and benches where the park cleaners sat in their blue plastic boots and waterproofs sharing a flask of something steaming. They were relaxed, their demeanour suggesting they were unaware a dead body had been found nearby.

She doubled over, placing her palms flat on her thighs to catch her breath. A uniformed policeman was observing her from ten metres away. She beckoned him with her arm and watched as he pinched out a cigarette then discreetly pocketed it. The armpits of his light blue shirt were stained dark with sweat and she was aware of the dampness on her own blouse. She held up her hand while she got her breathing under control, then reached inside her purse.

'I'm looking for —'

'The body?' he said, scrutinising her ID. 'Follow the central path for a hundred and fifty metres and look for a Cosmonaut.'

She held a hand over her eyes to block out the bright sun. 'Thanks.'

In less than a minute she came across a bulky OMON officer in the standard camouflage blue. Because of the distinctive round helmets and padded gear they wore when attending demonstrations, the OMON Special Purpose Police were known as "Cosmonauts" – it made them sound benign, but many of them had performed counter-terrorist assignments in the Caucasus, leaving behind nothing but graves and grieving mothers.

He checked her card. 'You can go,' he said, despite the fact she was several ranks above him.

She followed a gravel path for fifteen metres until she reached a treeline where a uniformed corporal was laying out police tape. She watched him for a moment as he tied it to a Maritime Victory Park sign that said "Entry for Authorised Persons Only." There was a haze in the air that smelled pleasantly of sweet wood smoke and barbecue.

She held out the card again. 'Where are you from?'

Chapter 15

He looked up and adjusted the peak of his cap. 'Petrogradsky District.'

'Where's the body?'

'You've got an interest?'

'Missing person.'

He held the tape up for her. 'Keep going, and good luck. You won't see much.'

She ducked under it then straightened up. 'Who's in charge?'

'Senior Lieutenant Gorokhov.'

'Thanks.'

She looked down at her dusty shoes and worried about contaminating the scene; maybe Primakov's prissiness was starting to rub off on her.

'Don't worry about those,' the corporal sniffed. 'Some workman found the body; there's nothing they haven't stepped on or pissed over.'

It was colder under the canopy of the trees and a light breeze brought goose pimples to her arms. Despite the corporal's advice, she walked along the edge of the path, keen to avoid the mass of shoe and boot prints already on the ground.

She stopped at a clearing where six workmen were sitting cross-legged with their hands underneath their buttocks. They were all silently miserable under the shade of an ancient Siberian Oak; their darker skins and cheap clothing giving them away as immigrants. Another OMON stood over them, his rubber-coated steel baton poised at shoulder height, ready to lash out for the slightest infraction.

'Go through there.' The OMON officer tipped his head towards another path. 'That's where these baboons came from.'

She outranked him too but wasn't tempted to reply. Following his instructions, she heard voices before seeing a group of three uniformed policemen standing around a fire-pit. Closer, the smell of wood smoke was damp and acrid.

'Welcome to the party.' An officer with a drawn face held out his hand. 'Ilya Gorokhov, Senior Lieutenant.' He smelled of a freshly smoked cigarette.

'Senior Detective Captain Ivanova. I've got a missing person.'

He raised his eyebrows. 'Not enough robberies and murders for you these days?'

She shook her head then ran her first two fingers against her thumb in the international sign for money: 'Rich kid.'

Gorokhov flicked his eyebrows in a conspiratorial gesture. 'That would do it I guess.'

'Mind if I take a look?'

He stepped aside to give her a view of the pit. All traces of Gorokhov's cigarette breath were soon obliterated by the stink of burnt meat and the damp, bitter smell of the extinguished fire that had smelled so pleasantly outside the clearing. Closer, there was something else too. 'Petrol or kerosene?' she asked.

He shook his head. 'I'm a chain smoker – my sense of smell was taken out and shot a long time ago.'

She peered into the pit then walked around the circumference. 'Where is it?'

'Most of the logs are in place, we only moved a few to make sure it was human.'

'How do you know?'

'So you see' – he extended a nicotine-stained finger and traced an outline over the pit – 'this is the body.'

She leaned over, cupping a hand to her brow to shield her eyes from the sun cutting through the clearing. The logs were blackened and glistening 'I can't...'

'Look closer.'

Then she saw it, half-covered in ash and curled grotesquely, the head almost touching the knees. She shifted position to get a better view of the face, of muscles and sinews shrunk against a black skull like a mummy's. The fat in the lips was gone leaving a macabre grin on an eyeless skull. She turned away sharply.

'There you go,' he added, drily.

'Any idea of gender?' she asked, warming to the Lieutenant.

'We're waiting for the pathologist. Apparently you can tell by the hips. Women are designed for childbirth.' He stopped and looked at her awkwardly. 'I didn't mean—'

Chapter 15

'That's OK, and you're right, it is how they tell if the victim is female. That, and the larger brain capacity.'

Gorokhov grinned.

She stepped back. 'Did anyone see or hear anything?'

He pulled on his jacket. 'Potentially hundreds. The few we spoke to saw smoke around 5 p.m. We're in a designated area for park wardens so no one cared to investigate.' He pointed to a green metal shed with a smashed padlock. 'Normally they use the pit to burn off excess foliage and lock up anything decent for seasoning in there.'

'So no witnesses?'

'None I found, but my instructions were to secure the scene.'

'Who are the men sitting on their hands?'

'Contractors building the new stadium. Got here an hour after the fire started. There's a dispute over pay so they've been kicking their heels, refusing to work until their boss sorts the mess out. They brought food and drink for a picnic then saw the smoke and thought they'd take a look.'

'What about the sign telling them it was off limits?'

'Their supervisor said none of them read Russian. I doubt it though, they all learn it at school.'

'What did they see?'

The sound of two men sharing a joke carried on the air; she recognised Rogov's voice and hoped Mikhail was there too.

Gorokhov was nonplussed, 'They smelled burning meat. One of them is a medical school dropout; he took a closer look and told them it was human. They put out the fire with water bottles while their supervisor called the police. The despatch operator told them to stay here, so that's what they did…and wiped out the crime scene.'

'Who called in the Cosmonauts?'

'Despatch. Someone heard the word "immigrant" and prematurely ejaculated.'

She found herself warming to Gorokhov. 'Mind if I speak to the contractors?'

'Be my guest.'

She went back to the first clearing and saw Mikhail and Rogov sharing cigarettes with the Cosmonaut. Mikhail cupped his hands around a flame as Rogov offered him a light. He tilted his head in her direction and exhaled smoke. 'Is it her?'

She shrugged. 'Too early to say. Can't even tell if it's male or female.'

Rogov rubbed the stubble on his chin. 'Surprised this lot came running in when they smelled pork'. He pulled his foot back as if to kick one of the men on the ground. His intended target was around the same age as Anton; he screwed up his eyes in anticipation of an impact which never came. Rogov chuckled to himself.

'Sergeant,' Mikhail said sharply, 'behave yourself.'

Rogov looked crestfallen at being reprimanded by his friend.

She addressed the contractors, 'Who reported the body?'

A man in a worn, red Zenit T-shirt raised his hand. 'We have papers. Not illegals.'

'No,' she said, 'you wouldn't have called the police if you were.' Though the sensible course of action had been for them to run away and leave the body for someone else to find.

The Cosmonaut grunted and spat on the floor, mistaking her comment for a criticism of the worker.

She squared up to the OMON cop and glanced at the two stripes on his shoulder lapel, 'Junior Sergeant,' she said, emphasising the *junior*, 'have you examined their papers?'

'No...Captain.'

'Then where are they?'

'They were playing football earlier and took everything out of their pockets.' He tilted his head to indicate a group of small rucksacks assembled at the base of a linden tree.

'OK, let's get this over with.' She stepped over to the pile of bags and picked up one at random. 'Whose is this?'

Mikhail puffed on his cigarette. 'Come on…Captain, I don't think this is your job.'

She glared at Mikhail and he shut up.

'Come on, whose is it?'

A boy wearing a sports vest glanced at the OMON cop before

pulling his hands from underneath his buttocks. He raised an arm and she tossed the bag to him. 'OK. Next?' She worked through them until none were left.

'Now please remove your work permits and passports.'

She took the foreman's first and barely glanced at his documents before handing them back. The boy of Anton's age was visibly shaking and she saw his permit had expired in April. 'That's all in order,' she said, returning it to him with a pointed look.

A man with a muscle-etched face flashed a gold incisor as he spoke. 'I forget my bag.'

The Zenit-shirted foreman spoke to him rapidly with building anger.

Natalya waited for him to finish then addressed the supervisor, 'Thank you for reporting the body. I'm sorry for the trouble here. Was it worth it?'

'Worth what?'

'Coming to Russia and being treated like this?'

'We send money home,' he shrugged. 'Most of time it's OK.'

'Can you tell me what you just said to this man?'

He eyed the other contractor. 'I told him he makes everything worse.'

'Because he forgot his papers.'

'No, because he has papers. I checked them this morning.'

'Where are they?'

'In his bag.'

'Where is it?'

He raised his palms in another shrug.

Mikhail turned to her. 'Natasha, can you show me the body.'

'Can't it wait? I'm nearly done.'

'Five minutes, then perhaps we can all go home.'

She led him through the path to the second clearing where Ilya Gorokhov, the Senior Lieutenant, was sitting on a tree stump smoking a cigarette and collecting the ash in a cupped hand. His two men were sitting on grass a metre away from the clearing, their backs resting against tree boughs.'

'This is Major Ivanov.' Natalya explained to the group and the three stood smartly. 'Lieutenant Gorokhov, please show him the body.'

Mikhail peered into the fire pit while Gorokhov stood next to him, tracing an outline in the air as he had done for her.

There was a cry from the first clearing and she rushed back with Gorokhov and Mikhail. The contractors were still under the shade of the Linden, most had lowered their heads. She scanned the clearing. She couldn't see Rogov and the gold-toothed man without papers was gone too.

'Where are they?' she demanded of the Cosmonaut.

'I didn't see anything.' He smirked, delivering his thug's answer.

There was another cry, this time muffled. Rogov appeared at the edge of the clearing dragging the missing worker by his shirt collar; blood was dripping from the man's nose and staining his shirt-front.

'Sergeant Rogov!' she yelled. 'Do you want to explain yourself?'

'He ran into a tree. Isn't that right, Mohammed, or whatever the fuck your name is?'

'Let him go, Stepan,' ordered Mikhail.

Rogov dragged the man into the clearing and pushed his face down in the dirt. 'Shall I show the nice captain, Mohammed?'

She noticed, then, that Rogov had a holdall in his other fist. 'I saw him run away. His bag was hidden under a bush. I saw him take it and keep running. When I caught him I thought he was about to yell "Allahu Akbar" and send us both to paradise.' He tossed the bag on the floor near the contractor's head, then spat on his knuckles and wiped away a bloody smear. 'But no, it's because Mohammed here doesn't trust the *menti*. He thought we were going to steal his things.'

She knelt beside the man with the bloody nose. 'What's your name?'

'I am Kanat Aliyev,' he looked at her defiantly, 'not Mohammed.'

'Show me your papers, Mister Aliyev.'

He unzipped a side compartment on the bag and pulled them out. She scanned the dates of the permit and checked the name against the one in the passport, then studied his bloodied face against the photograph: everything was in order.

The papers shook in his hand after she gave them back and she noticed he had shifted the bag under his knees. 'What did you buy? Nothing will be stolen, I assure you.'

Rogov lit a new cigarette then pointed at the man on the ground. 'Don't bother. I looked myself. Mohammed got himself a fucking handbag, didn't he. Some knock-off piece of shit for his wife.'

'Show me.'

Aliyev was still, barely breathing.

Her voice hardened, 'Show me. Now.'

The Cosmonaut raised his baton and she stepped into his path. 'Put that down, Junior Sergeant, we're not fascists – at least, not yet.' The OMON cop looked to Mikhail as the ranking officer, expecting him to overrule her. 'This is my case and he's my fucking husband,' she added.

Mikhail nodded. 'She makes two sound points.'

The Cosmonaut lowered his baton and she bent down to the man. 'Let me see inside.'

Aliyev gave up the bag and she unzipped the main compartment. There was an empty drinks container and a pair of hard-wearing gloves; underneath them her fingers touched a leather strap. She snapped on a pair of latex gloves then opened it fully, careful to avoid rubbing the exterior of the handbag as she pulled it free.

Rogov leaned forward, blowing smoke in her face as he did. 'It's a fake,' he announced to the men standing in the clearing, 'I got one for Oksana last year from an Arab in a subway; cost me eight hundred roubles and the piece of shit fell apart after two months.'

She held the bag up to eye level, then twisted the clasp and opened it by the corner of a flap. It was empty inside.

'Rogov, get a van. We need witness statements from everyone except him' – she pointed at the man with the bloody nose – 'He gets charged.'

'Can't immigration deal with this?'

'No, and don't involve them. I've already checked their papers.'

'You want me to help?'

She studied Mikhail's face for evidence of condescension but he seemed genuine. 'No, you go home.' She thought of the keylogging software. 'Can you make sure you pay the Admissions Head tonight? We'll talk later.' She decided needing answers mattered more than paying some official twice, especially if it got Anton into university.

'Sure.'

She unclipped her handcuffs from her belt. 'Hold your hands out,' she said to Aliyev. 'I'm arresting you for theft and Article 294: Interfering in the Activities of an Investigator.' She turned to Rogov. 'Get his fingerprints on AFIS,' she said, referring to the automated fingerprint identification system. 'Do it as soon as you can and arrange for him to see a doctor and a lawyer – if you can find one on a Sunday. And Rogov, if he looks any worse in the station I'll hold you personally responsible.'

'Wait, Captain,' said Gorokhov, 'it's still my jurisdiction.'

'Not any more.' She held up the pale blue handbag on a latex-covered index finger. 'This is a Hermès Sellier Kelly worth at least a million roubles. More to the point, my missing person had one the night she disappeared.'

She flicked through the address book on her mobile, then dialled the station. It rang three times, then was answered as the voicemail was about to cut in.

'Colonel,' she said before he could speak, 'it's Captain Ivanova. I think we've found her.'

'Is she…?'

'Dead? Yes, and murdered.'

16

The evening was clear and the late sun cast long shadows in the park. The coroner had arrived and was directing Gorokhov's men to remove the logs and place them next to a plastic sheet. At the base of the pit where pale ash swirled in eddies, Zena Dahl's body lay exposed. The muscles of her glistening, charcoal limbs had contracted into an exaggerated foetal position. Strands of hair, now carbon filaments, disintegrated into dust as the light breeze touched them. Primakov, who had arrived before the coroner, was standing over the pit taking photographs of her body.

Natalya stepped into the first clearing where the immigrants and the OMON officer had been. They were all gone now: the contractors taken away by a prisoner transport vehicle, and the Cosmonaut was on the main path, supporting his colleague to keep a meagre crowd away. She took out Dahl's business card and called his private line; it was answered immediately.

'Captain Ivanova?'

The line was bad but serviceable enough for her to recognise Anatoly Lagunov's voice. She remembered asking him to screen Dahl's calls in case of a ransom demand.

'Will you be able to stay with Mister Dahl this evening?'

'Can you repeat,' she heard through the static.

'Are you staying with him tonight?'

'No,' he enunciated each word carefully, 'I'm driving. His calls have been routed to my phone. I am not sure where he is. Do you have news?'

'Will you ask him to call me?'

The line went dead and she had no way of knowing if he had heard her. The phone was a poor way to break bad news and she preferred to do it in person or have the Swedish police visit Dahl; unfortunately reporters would pick up the story soon and it was better to hear it from her than see it on television.

Through the clearing she watched the Senior Lieutenant's men. They were making karate chop movements with their hands and she realised they were playing rock-paper-scissors. The loser received a pat on the back from Primakov before lowering himself into the pit.

Her phone rang.

'Misha?' she felt a twinge of guilt that she was snooping into his private affairs even if his secretive behaviour had driven her to it.

'Hi Angel, how's it looking?'

The uniform in the pit was tugging the plastic sheet underneath the body. The other policemen laughed in horror as Zena's rigid arm tapped his face in a ghoulish slap; even Gorokhov smiled.

'Just waiting. Leo Primakov is here and the men from Petrogradsky are getting her body out. It was fun earlier, we must do it again sometime.'

'You shouldn't be too hard on Stepan.' Hearing Rogov's first name was always a shock, almost as much as knowing he had a mother.

'I'm not. I'm being as hard as he deserves.'

There was silence and she could feel Mikhail's smile through the phone.

'He shouldn't have done it but you're too sensitive about these things. Your Mister Aliyev will get much worse in prison.'

She shook her head lightly. 'I'm surprised Rogov hasn't made him confess to murdering her.'

'Oh, he will. Stepan's threatening to bite Aliyev's balls off as we speak. I think he might actually do it.'

'Misha!' she shouted in horror. The men in the second clearing turned their heads.

'It's a joke, Natasha, the doctor is there, fixing the stupid bastard's nose.'

'What has Aliyev admitted to?'

'He was first in the clearing and found the handbag resting

against the woodshed door. He was planning to give it to the park authorities but when the body was discovered he panicked because his fingerprints were all over it and Aliyev knew he'd be in the shit if he told anyone.'

'You believe him?'

'Some of it. Stepan reckons the guy knew it was a real Hermès because all the immigrants sell fake handbags to tourists.'

'Rogov is a liability.' She watched another uniform climb into the pit then both men pushed their hands underneath the plastic to lift the body. She was glad her uniform days were behind her.

'You underestimate him. He got Aliyev to admit he's got a wife in Tashkent and a mistress in *Piter.* He said his girlfriend would be sucking his khui out of gratitude when he gave her the handbag.'

'That still sounds like Rogov.'

'What about you?'

She wondered for a moment what he meant. 'A blowjob for a Hermès?' She looked around to make sure no one was listening. 'I'm cheaper than that – try a weekend in Tallinn. Have they recovered any prints?'

'Covered in them. Popovich is staying late to record them on AFIS. We'll know by tomorrow if there's anything.'

'Thanks.' She was unconvinced. The other expert criminalist in the department, Pavel Popovich, may have had the same name as a famous Cosmonaut but he was a red-faced alcoholic whose work was shoddy. Given the choice, she preferred Primakov to handle the fingerprints after finishing at the site, even if it meant delaying the results.

'I'm checking out, Angel. I'll see you at home. We still need to speak about last night.'

He hung up and she watched the uniforms carry a black body-bag on a stretcher to the coroner's van.

There had been plenty to find in the first clearing: broken glass from a smashed bottle of Privet vodka, a dozen gold cans of Zhigulevskoye beer crushed flat, greaseproof wrappers and Cellophane from packed lunches; though she suspected by their state of decomposition that they would yield no useful clues. She ducked under the police tape taking the thing she would have been most glad to leave behind – the smell of sweet, burnt flesh that lingered in her nostrils as she crossed the gravel path.

There were a few teenagers loitering near the grass, now being monitored by some fresh-faced recruits she recognised from headquarters. In the night air, the sound of distorted music and shrieks drifted from the amusement park. Her eyes adjusted to the metallic light of the evening and she saw the flying chairs of *Divo Ostrov*, Miracle Island. She checked her watch; it was after nine and she was tired.

Behind her she heard footsteps and turned to see Primakov clutching his silver case. 'You want a drink? I need one,' he asked.

'Did you drive here?'

'Yes, I'm parked near the athletics arena. Do you want a lift?'

She'd been hoping they could have taken the Metro together. Primakov's Samara was an ex-police car he'd bought at an auction last winter. It was only as the weather improved that the urine and vomit embedded in the upholstery became apparent. Augmenting the bitter odour of Zena's body with a trip in his Samara wasn't an attractive thought.

'I need to walk. There's a café around the corner from Krestovsky Metro, I'll see you there.'

The noise of the amusement park had drowned out her phone and she noticed it by the buzzing in her pocket. She pulled it out and saw a warning message that the battery was at ten per cent. She checked the display: the number was unknown but she answered it anyway.

'Is that Captain Ivanova?'

She recognised Thorsten Dahl's nervous voice and held up her hand to Primakov with the fingers splayed to indicate she would meet him in five minutes.

'Mister Dahl, there has been a development.'

The screams from the amusement park in the background were inappropriate in the extreme but there was little she could do about them.

He exhaled heavily. 'Tell me what it is, Captain.'

Chapter 16

'Mister Dahl—'

The phone beeped to warn the battery was at five per cent.

'Thorsten.'

She had never broken the news to anyone on the phone before. 'Thorsten, have you got someone with you?'

'Yes, just tell me…please.'

She cupped a hand over the receiver to shut out the shrieks of glee as the rocket ship passed overhead. 'Mister Dahl, I'm in the Victory Maritime Park on Krestovsky Island. Some workmen discovered a body here this evening.'

His voice had dropped to the level of a whisper. 'Is it her? Is it Zena?'

'I think so, yes.' Don't say *think*, that gives him hope. 'We found a handbag near the body. It matches the description of the one we believe Zena had when she went missing.'

'Do you need me there…to identify her?'

'There's something else, Thorsten.'

She heard the heavy breath again as he steeled himself to take whatever she was about to say.

'The body was burned, Thorsten. It wouldn't be possible for you to identify her.'

'Will you find whoever did this?'

'I'll do everything in my power to get them.'

'What can I do to help?'

She thought for a moment. Zena had been adopted, so a DNA match was no good. 'Thorsten, you really don't know Zena's natural parents?'

'No.'

'Then can you send me her dental records?'

The pause was so profound she thought her battery had died. 'Thorsten?'

'May I call you Natalya?'

'Yes.'

'Do you believe in God, Natalya?'

It was an odd question but appropriate given the circumstances. She remembered attending a ceremony in St. Isaac's where her mother crossed herself as if she had been doing it all her life instead of practising it for the first time that morning.

'No,' she replied.

'"The darker the night, the brighter the stars. The deeper the grief, the closer is God."'

'That's beautiful.'

'One of yours… Dostoyevsky,' he said. There was another silence and she checked her phone to realise the battery had died.

17

In the café near Krestovsky Metro, the plexi-glass counter was decorated in bank notes from half the countries of the world. Natalya stared at them half-heartedly. Had she agreed to meet Leo Primakov in order to delay going home? She didn't want to confront Mikhail, not yet; not until the keylogger could get to work and invisibly steal his passwords. Then, she would know the extent of his corruption. What she did with the information was more of a problem.

While the bookish girl with braces poured her wheat beer, she examined a cork wall covered in photographs of smiling teenagers. In one of them, a group of kids with puffy eyes were eating breakfast wearing thick pullovers and she guessed they'd gone there after pulling an all-nighter. One of them could have been Zena; she had the same shade of blonde hair and appeared to be tagging along with a group of five or six others. The automatic focus of the camera had been attracted to a candle flame, though, and the girl's face was blurred as a result.

The coffee shop appeared to be a place for rich kids to hang out. Her theory was confirmed when a five-hundred-rouble note bought her a half-litre of beer and no change.

'You look good,' she said as Leo Primakov entered. He was wearing a brown leather jacket over blue jeans and, apart from the silver case, looked as if he'd just stepped out of a menswear catalogue. She guessed he'd kept a change of clothes in his car.

'Thanks, you too,' he said automatically, though she knew it was a lie. One look in the mirror of the café's unisex toilet had confirmed there were yellow armpit stains on her shirt and her hair was greasy with neglect.

She listened to Primakov order a decaffeinated Ethiopian Chelba, then waited for him to join her.

'Did you get that email I sent?' he asked.

'Thanks,' she said, not wanting to elaborate.

'Good. Whatever happens, that stuff is illegal. I don't want it to ever come back to me.'

'It won't, I promise. Do you still take pictures?'

He ladled sugar into his cup of coffee. 'Yeah, you know how it is.'

'I do,' she touched his arm.

Under the Medvedev reforms, the *menti* were better paid than they used to be but it still wasn't enough to survive in the city. The honest ones lived on the outskirts in high rises or had second jobs; the dishonest, well, that depended on where you were in the hierarchy. Primakov had a photography business on the side but things weren't working out for him. Earlier in May, she'd tried to help out by ordering some family portraits. The results had been excellent.

She drank a quarter of her beer in one go. 'Did you find anything?'

A bell above the door rang and they both looked up to see a young woman wearing the student uniform of jeans, T shirt, and an expression of casual indifference. Primakov opened his case and removed his camera.

He passed it to Natalya. 'Have a look.'

She leaned over, cupping her hand to shield the camera's display from an overhead light.

'The last ones are from the pit.' She flicked through them, not seeing anything new, then saw a close-up of Zena's head.

'I've taken some of her teeth. One of the upper incisors is chipped but the heat from the fire could have done it.' He sipped his coffee.

The door buzzer rang and Natalya glanced up to see the young woman leaving the café; she had been looking for a friend.

'Go back a few more, there's something interesting.'

She scrolled to pictures of Zena Dahl's handbag, its baby blue colour would soon have a brushed aluminium finish from the fingerprint powder. 'Mikhail said Popovich found some prints.'

Chapter 17

Primakov sipped his coffee. 'He's discounted the ones belonging to Rogov and the immigrant who took the bag. Zena Dahl's are due tomorrow morning.'

'From the Swedes?'

He shook his head. 'Federal Migration Service. They recorded her biometric data when she applied for a visa. I have some from her apartment too but we may as well do it right. Popovich is putting what's left through the AFIS computer.'

She nodded. 'You said you found something interesting?'

Primakov took the camera from her and flicked through the images then passed it back. She stared at an enlarged picture of a broken heel on the forest floor.

'One of the Petrogradsky District boys found it behind the woodshed. There was a metal pin in the pit and burnt fabric so my guess is the rest of her shoes burned with her.'

She thought of Yulia's description. 'What about her clothes? Zena was wearing a silk dress.'

'Didn't see anything like that. They used an accelerant, maybe petrol or kerosene.'

'So nothing left?'

'No.'

'I doubt her father will survive it. No one gets over their child being murdered, but when it's just the two of them...'

'What about Dahl's wife?'

'Never married; Zena was adopted. Her biological parents died when she was a baby. Sad, but it's a relief…telling a mother they have a dead kid is the worst part of the job.'

Primakov took the camera from her and flicked through the pictures before passing it to her. 'OK, you need to look carefully at this. We know the contractors trampled on everything, but I found these coming from the opposite direction.'

The image was an expanse of green. 'I don't see anything.'

'Wait.' Primakov handed the camera to her. 'Try this one'.

She stared at a semi-circular heel print. 'Zena's?'

'It looked fresh so it's likely, though it doesn't match the heel the Petrogradsky boys found.'

'So where do you think she was going?'

'The Southern lake is on the other side, maybe she was cutting through.'

'To...?'

'There's the *Karl & Friedrich*, a German restaurant that sells sausages and beer. They have a huge windmill. I'm surprised you haven't been there.'

'For Christ's sake, I only lived in Germany for four years. Besides' – she sniffed – 'Windmills are Dutch. I'll ask Rogov to find out if anyone had a reservation today but didn't show.'

'And I'll get the tip checked for DNA but there's a six week backlog. The lab is swamped with requests from the Israeli consulate. The mafia have been forging birth certificates for Russian citizens so they can emigrate there.'

'And let me guess, they aren't Jewish.'

'About as much as Easter cheese.'

'Did you find any other footprints besides hers?'

Primakov switched off the camera and laid it on the table. 'None.'

She frowned. 'She was on her own?'

He nodded.

'So Zena was going somewhere, maybe to the restaurant or the lake,' Natalya finished the wheat beer. 'But it's Sunday now and she's been missing since Thursday night.'

'Maybe she wasn't going anywhere. What if she was escaping?'

'On Krestovsky Island?' Natalya shook her head dismissively, 'Too many people; someone would have saved her or called us.'

The woman behind the counter was reading a novel and Natalya made eye contact to order another beer, then decided against it and shook her head.

'What if she was dead already?' asked Primakov.

'Then the footprints aren't hers.' She switched the camera back on and examined the photograph. 'How fresh were they?'

'Impossible to say without recreating the conditions...maybe a few hours.'

'The lieutenant at the scene – Gorokhov – he said people noticed the smoke around 5 p.m. Let's say it took the killer an hour to kill Zena and build the funeral pyre. If someone else had made those footprints then they must have seen Zena being killed and we'd be dealing with a distressed witness or another body.'

Primakov drained his coffee. 'That makes sense.'

'So let's say they were hers. Where was she coming from?'

'The South-East. I'd guess she came through the main gates.'

'That was the same direction as me. If Zena took the Metro she would have been in Krestovsky Ostrov station.'

18

In the café near Krestovsky Metro, the plexi-glass counter was decorated in bank notes from half the countries of the world. Natalya stared at them half-heartedly. Had she agreed to meet Leo Primakov in order to delay going home? She didn't want to confront Mikhail, not yet; not until the keylogger could get to work and invisibly steal his passwords. Then, she would know the extent of his corruption. What she did with the information was more of a problem.

While the bookish girl with braces poured her wheat beer, she examined a cork wall covered in photographs of smiling teenagers. In one of them, a group of kids with puffy eyes were eating breakfast wearing thick pullovers and she guessed they'd gone there after pulling an all-nighter. One of them could have been Zena; she had the same shade of blonde hair and appeared to be tagging along with a group of five or six others. The automatic focus of the camera had been attracted to a candle flame, though, and the girl's face was blurred as a result.

The coffee shop appeared to be a place for rich kids to hang out. Her theory was confirmed when a five-hundred-rouble note bought her a half-litre of beer and no change.

'You look good,' she said as Leo Primakov entered. He was wearing a brown leather jacket over blue jeans and, apart from the silver case, looked as if he'd just stepped out of a menswear catalogue. She guessed he'd kept a change of clothes in his car.

'Thanks, you too,' he said automatically, though she knew it was a lie. One look in the mirror of the café's unisex toilet had confirmed there were yellow armpit stains on her shirt and her hair was greasy with neglect.

Chapter 18

She listened to Primakov order a decaffeinated Ethiopian Chelba, then waited for him to join her.

'Did you get that email I sent?' he asked.

'Thanks,' she said, not wanting to elaborate.

'Good. Whatever happens, that stuff is illegal. I don't want it to ever come back to me.'

'It won't, I promise. Do you still take pictures?'

He ladled sugar into his cup of coffee. 'Yeah, you know how it is.'

'I do,' she touched his arm.

Under the Medvedev reforms, the *menti* were better paid than they used to be but it still wasn't enough to survive in the city. The honest ones lived on the outskirts in high rises or had second jobs; the dishonest, well, that depended on where you were in the hierarchy. Primakov had a photography business on the side but things weren't working out for him. Earlier in May, she'd tried to help out by ordering some family portraits. The results had been excellent.

She drank a quarter of her beer in one go. 'Did you find anything?'

A bell above the door rang and they both looked up to see a young woman wearing the student uniform of jeans, T shirt, and an expression of casual indifference. Primakov opened his case and removed his camera.

He passed it to Natalya. 'Have a look.'

She leaned over, cupping her hand to shield the camera's display from an overhead light.

'The last ones are from the pit.' She flicked through them, not seeing anything new, then saw a close-up of Zena's head.

'I've taken some of her teeth. One of the upper incisors is chipped but the heat from the fire could have done it.' He sipped his coffee.

The door buzzer rang and Natalya glanced up to see the young woman leaving the café; she had been looking for a friend.

'Go back a few more, there's something interesting.'

She scrolled to pictures of Zena Dahl's handbag, its baby blue colour would soon have a brushed aluminium finish from the fingerprint powder. 'Mikhail said Popovich found some prints.'

Primakov sipped his coffee. 'He's discounted the ones belonging to Rogov and the immigrant who took the bag. Zena Dahl's are due tomorrow morning.'

'From the Swedes?'

He shook his head. 'Federal Migration Service. They recorded her biometric data when she applied for a visa. I have some from her apartment too but we may as well do it right. Popovich is putting what's left through the AFIS computer.'

She nodded. 'You said you found something interesting?'

Primakov took the camera from her and flicked through the images then passed it back. She stared at an enlarged picture of a broken heel on the forest floor.

'One of the Petrogradsky District boys found it behind the woodshed. There was a metal pin in the pit and burnt fabric so my guess is the rest of her shoes burned with her.'

She thought of Yulia's description. 'What about her clothes? Zena was wearing a silk dress.'

'Didn't see anything like that. They used an accelerant, maybe petrol or kerosene.'

'So nothing left?'

'No.'

'I doubt her father will survive it. No one gets over their child being murdered, but when it's just the two of them...'

'What about Dahl's wife?'

'Never married; Zena was adopted. Her biological parents died when she was a baby. Sad, but it's a relief...telling a mother they have a dead kid is the worst part of the job.'

Primakov took the camera from her and flicked through the pictures before passing it to her. 'OK, you need to look carefully at this. We know the contractors trampled on everything, but I found these coming from the opposite direction.'

The image was an expanse of green. 'I don't see anything.'

'Wait.' Primakov handed the camera to her. 'Try this one'.

She stared at a semi-circular heel print. 'Zena's?'

'It looked fresh so it's likely, though it doesn't match the heel the Petrogradsky boys found.'

Chapter 18

'So where do you think she was going?'

'The Southern lake is on the other side, maybe she was cutting through.'

'To...?'

'There's the *Karl & Friedrich*, a German restaurant that sells sausages and beer. They have a huge windmill. I'm surprised you haven't been there.'

'For Christ's sake, I only lived in Germany for four years. Besides' – she sniffed – 'Windmills are Dutch. I'll ask Rogov to find out if anyone had a reservation today but didn't show.'

'And I'll get the tip checked for DNA but there's a six week backlog. The lab is swamped with requests from the Israeli consulate. The mafia have been forging birth certificates for Russian citizens so they can emigrate there.'

'And let me guess, they aren't Jewish.'

'About as much as Easter cheese.'

'Did you find any other footprints besides hers?'

Primakov switched off the camera and laid it on the table. 'None.'

She frowned. 'She was on her own?'

He nodded.

'So Zena was going somewhere, maybe to the restaurant or the lake,' Natalya finished the wheat beer. 'But it's Sunday now and she's been missing since Thursday night.'

'Maybe she wasn't going anywhere. What if she was escaping?'

'On Krestovsky Island?' Natalya shook her head dismissively, 'Too many people; someone would have saved her or called us.'

The woman behind the counter was reading a novel and Natalya made eye contact to order another beer, then decided against it and shook her head.

'What if she was dead already?' asked Primakov.

'Then the footprints aren't hers.' She switched the camera back on and examined the photograph. 'How fresh were they?'

'Impossible to say without recreating the conditions...maybe a few hours.'

'The lieutenant at the scene – Gorokhov – he said people noticed the smoke around 5 p.m. Let's say it took the killer an hour to kill Zena and build the funeral pyre. If someone else had made those footprints then they must have seen Zena being killed and we'd be dealing with a distressed witness or another body.'

Primakov drained his coffee. 'That makes sense.'

'So let's say they were hers. Where was she coming from?'

'The South-East. I'd guess she came through the main gates.'

'That was the same direction as me. If Zena took the Metro she would have been in Krestovsky Ostrov station.'

19

After putting out some cereal for Anton's breakfast she left early for the office. She had expected to find Mikhail sleeping on the sofa but there was no sign of him. If he hadn't appeared by roll call she would check with Oksana and see if he had stayed at Rogov's. Now that she thought about it, she would call anyway to make sure he hadn't had an accident – it was odd considering what she had discovered about Mikhail, but when it came to other women she trusted him. After fifteen years in the department she had a very good idea of who screwed around and who didn't. For all his faults, Mikhail was more respectful to women than any other male *ment* she had known.

Outside it was grey and wet, and the spray from the Neva mingled with the fine rain to make them indistinguishable: the ideal weather for a Monday morning. From home, Suvorovsky Prospekt was an unpleasant one kilometre walk from the Ploshchad Vosstaniya Metro station or two bus journeys, and so the Volvo was her only option when the weather was bad. Luckily the traffic was light and she was in the station by eight.

The area reserved for detectives was quiet and she found a Post-It note stuck to the receiver of her desk phone. It was from Semion, the barman at Cheka, asking her to call him for another interview. The note was an unsubtle attempt at seduction and she screwed up the message and dropped it in the bin. She made herself a coffee, avoiding the machine which produced something that tasted like ground acorns in mud. Back at her desk, there was a backlog of eighty emails and she started clearing them down.

After half an hour, the rest of the day shift appeared and she kept her head down, not wanting to engage in the joking and teasing that came with the job. She took out a notepad and made a list of her follow-up activities: the civil registration office, ZAGS, might tell her what Zena's appointment with them had been about; the girl's last movements, and possibly her assailant's too, might be on the CCTV footage of the Krestovsky Island Metro; then there were the fingerprints on Zena's Hermès handbag that Pavel Popovich would need a chase call on; finally, she had to finish the phone conversation with Thorsten Dahl and get him to mail over Zena's dental records.

At ten minutes to nine, Rogov appeared and sat on the edge of her desk creasing the papers underneath. The smell of mouthwash on him was so strong he could have bathed in peppermint oil.

'Did Misha find you last night?'

'Being friendly now?' He stretched a hand over his face and yawned into it. 'Yeah, we went out for a little one. He's gone home for a wash and change.'

She nodded. 'Thanks.'

Rogov paused, agony corrugating his simple brow. 'It's not my place to say this, Natalya, but Misha's a good man. You two need to talk.'

'Yeah, you're right, Rogov.' She studied his stricken features. 'It's not your place to say it.' She yanked her keyboard from underneath one of his buttocks. 'Now get off my desk and do some work.'

At roll call in the Zheglov meeting room, she sat on one of the chairs placed against the wall and tuned out her thoughts to focus on Colonel Vasiliev as he addressed the Directorate's detectives. 'Captain Ivanova is working on the Dahl case. For those of you unfamiliar with it, Zena Dahl, a nineteen-year-old student from Sweden was last seen on Thursday night, and is believed to be the body discovered in the Maritime Victory Park.'

Vasiliev smoothed hair that required no smoothing. 'Captain Ivanov, please provide an update to Major Dostoynov on your progress.'

This was new, she thought. Had the new major already succeeded in becoming Vasiliev's replacement? She shifted in her chair feeling the eyes in the room on her. 'Major, there are no suspects yet;

however, a handbag was found at the scene and Expert Criminalist Popovich will report today with his analysis of the fingerprints. In addition, I will be following up on a number of leads.'

'Do you need assistance?' asked Dostoynov.

'Yes, sir, I need a team to make street enquiries and to—'

'Good, Captain.' He looked to Colonel Vasiliev for approval. 'You can keep Sergeant Rogov. The need for additional manpower will be reviewed this evening. In the meantime, your main priority is the identification.'

'Yes, Major.' Her tone was upbeat but she felt anything but optimistic. The Colonel had clearly spoken with the new major before the meeting and put him in charge of the case.

With roll call over she went to the equipment desk and took several deep breaths before wiping her mouth with the back of her hand. The corporal behind the counter handed her a breathalyzer and she blew into the nozzle, conscious that the bottle of Satrapezo she'd been drinking until midnight could deprive her of a departmental car as well as her Makarov. After visiting Yulia Federova she had kept the gun for the weekend – there was no rule requiring her to return the Makarov at the end of her shift – though all the *menti* generally checked in their weapons to avoid the wrath of senior management; there had been too many incidents involving off-duty policemen.

The corporal rotated a clipboard in her direction. 'Please sign... and don't drink so much next time, Captain. You were just under.'

She took her Makarov and the key then found Rogov, who was conspicuously absent from the equipment desk; she presumed because he was over the limit. At the car park she held out the fob at arm's length and pressed the unlock button to find the vehicle assigned to her. Rogov read it as an invitation and raised his hand for the key. She shook her head and decided not to mention that the mouthwash he had been swilling would be enough to fail a breathalyzer test on its own. 'We'll split. I'll drive first.'

'OK, boss. Where are we going?'

She held her arm in a different direction and pressed the button on the fob again. This time, the indicators on a dark grey Nissan

Primera flashed.

'To ZAGS.'

'I didn't think you cared.'

As she climbed inside, she was hit by the smell of greasy food with the vinegar tang of vomit.

'Zena went to one of their offices before she disappeared. I want to know which one.'

'What about Dostoynov's order?'

'The one where we behave like a pair of Moscow Watchdogs and leave the detective work to someone else?'

'That one,' he smiled.

Had Rogov agreed to keep Dostoynov updated? She didn't think so; Rogov was Mikhail's man and – at least for the moment – that guaranteed her some loyalty too.

She started the engine and drove out of the car park, waving at the guard on the barrier. 'You're an insubordinate bastard, aren't you, Rogov?'

'Yeah,' he nodded enthusiastically then paused to think and she could almost hear the machinery turning, 'but I'm with you. I don't want anyone else taking the credit.'

'It won't happen. Thorsten—'

'Zena's father, right?'

'Yes. Misha and I met Dahl on his plane.'

'I heard.' Rogov scratched his chin.

'Well, I've asked him for Zena's dental records. We have a little time before they get here.'

'Misha said Dahl couldn't leave the airport because he didn't have a visa.' Rogov frowned, 'But I heard he's rich.'

'Like an oligarch.'

'So why did he lie?' Rogov whistled through his teeth. 'With the cabbage he's got, Dahl could turn up naked at the Russian embassy and expect the ambassador to fix a visa to his puckered *zhopa*.'

It wasn't a pleasant image of a bereaved father, but Rogov was right. At the junction to Suvorovsky she teased her phone from her jeans pocket then gestured with a finger for Rogov to be quiet while she called Mikhail.

Chapter 19

He answered it immediately. 'Tasha?'

'How's the head?'

He groaned. 'Like there's a wolf inside tearing at a reindeer.'

'What do you know about this new major?'

'Dostoynov? I have to share an office with him. He doesn't fart or smoke but there's still a sulphurous smell to him.'

'Has Vasiliev anointed Dostoynov yet?'

'No, but the colonel knows I don't want the job.'

'I'm sorry, Misha, it's my fault. If it wasn't for me—'

'Yeah, well. Natasha, I've got a lot of work, and the grandfather of all hangovers. How can I help?'

'I was reminiscing with Sergeant Rogov about the wonderful time we spent on Dahl's Gulfstream.'

She could hear laughter in the background and wondered how busy Mikhail really was. 'What about it?'

'Do you think we were taken in? Rogov thinks Dahl lied about the visa and for once I think he might be right. Surely Dahl could have got one easily enough.'

'Maybe he was scared to leave the airport. He was here in the nineties and you know what they say about the oligarchs?'

'What?'

'Never ask how they made their first million.'

'Could be…thanks. Can you stay on the line?'

'Because I've got nothing better to do?'

Natalya parked the Nissan then tapped Rogov on the shoulder and pointed out the red-orange building on the opposite street. With its stucco façade and pilasters the civil registration office had the appearance of a wedding cake. 'Try this ZAGS first.'

Rogov wound down his window then tapped out a cigarette from a soft pack.

'Wait a minute.' She tapped Rogov on the shoulder again, then narrowed her eyes and flicked the back of her hand imperiously in the direction of the car door. He took the hint and she watched him dash out into the rain then huddle under the gated archway of the ZAGS building. Soon, smoke billowed out, lending him a demonic aura.

'Tasha, are you there?' asked Mikhail.

'Yes.' She stared through the water-mottled window of the Primera. 'I was thinking…on Saturday we all thought Zena had been kidnapped, not murdered. What would you do if someone abducted Anton?'

There was the sound of footsteps over the earpiece and she presumed Mikhail was moving somewhere safer to talk. 'I'd use a low powered bullet to ricochet inside the skull and turn the brain into soup.'

She felt a chill from his answer. 'Wrong question. I meant, what if you were Thorsten?'

Mikhail exhaled deeply and she wondered if he and Rogov were subconsciously in tune with their cigarette breaks the same way women aligned their menstrual cycles.

'OK, Dahl won't trust us. All those nice Sven newspapers will tell him the *menti* are no better than crooks.'

She almost gasped at Mikhail's hypocrisy. 'So…if you were Thorsten?'

'I'd hire a Sven to sniff around, or maybe that Russian lawyer of his, Lagunov. Someone who knew how to keep his mouth shut. You'd do the same so why the phone call?'

'I want to know when Dahl applied for a visa.'

'The FSB look after immigration now. Ask Dostoynov to check with his old buddies.'

'He only wants me to get an identification for the body.'

'It's sensible. Unless he's certain of getting the killer he'll try to ditch the case. If you start digging and bigger dogs get involved, they'll be able to blame you for fucking it up if they don't find her killer.'

She snorted. 'Doesn't anyone care about Zena?'

'I didn't say I agree. I'm just saying Dostoynov will be too used to the FSB's Machiavellian ways to think like a real policeman.'

She heard him laugh and wasn't sure if something had happened in the office. 'I don't care about getting blamed, I want to make sure we get the bastard who killed her before he does it to someone else. The right bastard too.'

Chapter 19

He sighed. 'OK. I know someone in the Big House: Viktor. He's FSB but doesn't stink like the rest of them. We studied law together. I'll do it on one condition.'

Mikhail did favours the same way cats left pigeons on doorsteps. 'What?'

'We'll stay in tonight and talk. I love you, Angel, I don't want anything coming between us.'

She glanced at Rogov who was still huddled under the ZAGS archway.

'Of course…me too.'

Mikhail hung up and she called Rogov over. He tossed the cigarette then pulled the corners of his light blue suit jacket over his head as he walked up to her.

'If I remember, ZAGS have a centralised booking system. See if you can find out which one Zena went to on June 6th. The appointment was for 9:30 a.m.'

'Me?'

'Yes, I've got a call to make. Oh, and Rogov' – she smiled at him – 'you need to make lots of noise, I don't think they open on Mondays.'

Rogov rang the bell, the interior of his jacket already stained dark by the rain. After ten seconds he started banging on the door with a fist. There was no answer and he jogged down the street to find a rear entrance, moving surprisingly nimbly for an overweight man.

She stared out of the window, not focusing on anything in particular. Certainly, Mikhail preferred her to be a loyal wife and ignore his dirty money; that wasn't an option when he'd chosen to make her an accomplice by buying their apartment with it. There was still a hundred thousand euros in the account. All told, that was too much for the occasional bribe. It was the kind of money that put innocent people away in the hell-holes that passed for prisons, and let the guilty go free to rob or kill again.

After ten minutes the door of the ZAGS building was opened by an earnest young man and a sodden Rogov stepped out of it without acknowledgement then paced to the car. He pulled on the Nissan's door huffily and sat down, his brow streaked by rainwater. She waited for his laboured breathing to calm. 'What did you find out?'

'It's an hour's drive away,' he mumbled. 'The appointment was in fucking Sestroretsk.'

'The seaside, Rogov. That's just what you need for a hangover.'

'You're not coming?'

'No, drop me off at Krestovsky Metro. I'll meet you at the station in two hours – call me if you find anything interesting.'

'Are you going to be like this all the time?'

'Like what?' she smiled.

The spray turned to heavier rain as she started the car and followed the road alongside the tree-lined gardens of Tauride Palace.

'How about I smoke with the window open?' he asked.

'No.'

Rogov was brooding for a few minutes before he spoke again. 'What will you do?'

She scrutinised him to see if it was more than a casual question but his expression gave nothing away. 'There's nothing more I can do. I told you I've already asked Dahl for Zena's dental records. She was adopted so DNA is no good.'

'What about the Sven *menti*?'

She shook her head. 'There's been little cooperation since last year.'

He gave her a malicious grin. 'I guess we threatened to melt their little snow kingdom one time too many.'

Rogov scratched his foot and she saw the bottom of an ankle holster. Most likely it held an OSA, a traumatic pistol that fired a steel–core rubber bullet and was completely legal for any citizen to own. She hoped it was anyway, and nothing deadlier.

'Natalya?' Rogov looked to the floor. 'I was talking with Misha last night.'

'That's it!' Her eyes flashed to the mirror then she stamped on the brakes. The car pitched Rogov forward.

'What the fuck was that for?' He rolled back in his seat.

'We need rules.' She glared at him, and she could tell he was trying very hard not to smirk. 'You take the litter out of my house and I'll return the favour. Don't talk to me about my personal shit and we won't discuss yours.'

'Like what?'

'Like Oksana married a racist, chauvinist arsehole who screws around.'

He blustered, 'I—'

'Come on, Rogov, everybody knows. That brothel you go to… The Depot, isn't it? You've got a Chinese girl there. Good luck to her if she's not being coerced, but whatever you're paying her isn't enough.'

The smirk had frozen on his face.

'Oksana is my friend, but I won't say anything because you've got your personal shit and I've got mine. Ready?'

'For what?'

'Another rule. I've earned the right to be called "Captain". When the shift is over, I don't care. In the car like this, I don't care – unless you're being an arsehole, which is most of the time. But in public, or at the station, it's "Captain". Got it?'

He nodded. 'She's called Duckweed.'

'Who is?'

'The girl. That's what her name means in Chinese.'

She shook her head, then indicated to rejoin the traffic. 'Rogov, did you hear anything I said?'

'You know, you can be meaner than Oksana when she's waving the red flag.'

They took a right then a left and followed the grey Neva. Rogov lapsed into a silence that soon became awkward, but not as awkward as maintaining a conversation with him.

At Gorkovskaya station she pulled over, leaving the keys in the ignition.

'Now you can drive. Get to the ZAGS in Sestroretsk before you get caught in the lunchtime traffic.'

'Yes, boss,' he replied.

On the Metro she changed at Sadovaya for Krestovsky Ostrov then took the escalator to the glass-fronted exit. Outside, a group of four conscript catchers were questioning a boy in cut-off jeans clutching a skateboard. The youth was scared, and whatever documents he possessed hadn't convinced them he was exempt from military service. One in an ill-fitting army uniform grabbed him by the neck of his T-shirt, wrapping it round his fist to stop him running. The boy tried to yank the hand away, letting out a cry as his arm was forced up his back to the point of dislocation. She glared at the one clutching the boy's T-shirt until he noticed her, but she was powerless to intervene.

At the only populated ticket booth she flashed her ID. 'Where's the security office?'

The matronly woman picked up a phone and she waited. A man in an ill-fitting uniform appeared. He picked at rotten teeth and wiped the resulting issue on his trouser leg. 'Nina, you stay here, I'll take her.'

The station guard escorted her past the row of empty ticket booths and pushed on a door to the left of them. Inside, a man in a grey camouflage uniform was slouching in a leather chair, he was puffing on a cigarette and eyeing a bank of screens. He looked at his watch, then at the guard.

'Thanks,' he said to the ill-fitting uniform. 'Have you searched her?'

Her phone started ringing. 'Ivanova, Captain,' she answered, not recognising the number. There was a wry smile on her lips as she saw the security guard in the chair straighten up.

'It's Pavel, Captain,' she heard and had to think for a moment before recognising the voice of Popovich, the other expert criminalist.

'What is it?'

The line went quiet and she could hear Colonel Vasiliev talking in the background. While waiting, she waved her ID at the man in the grey uniform then pressed the mute button on the call. 'I'd like the footage between 3 p.m. and 7 p.m. yesterday.'

'Is this about the girl in the fire?'

She shrugged noncommittally, then pointed at the security cameras. 'How do you store the images? A hard drive?'

'DVDs. There might be a camera on the train too. If you come back with an exact time I can get the train number for you, but you'll have to go through central admin to get the footage.'

'Thanks.'

There was distortion over the phone that sounded like a cheer.

She passed her identification card for him to copy her details. It was rare for anyone to insist on a search warrant for camera footage since its specific purpose was to prevent crime. The guard flicked through a DVD holder mounted on the wall, then removed four disks. He slipped them into a plastic wallet and passed them to her. She tucked it in her handbag and nodded a thanks.

The phone was still pressed to her ear as she left, nodding again at the young man with the unfortunate teeth. The noise of the station increased and she clicked the mute button again to enable the sound. When she returned the mobile to her ear, the applause in the station had gone and Popovich was asking if she was there.

'Yes, it's me.'

'You'd better get back. The Major was asking where you and Rogov had gone.'

'Rogov's on a job. What's happening?'

'Captain,' Popovich said, barely able to contain his excitement. 'Zena Dahl's handbag. We got a hit on AFIS.'

20

Her clothes were soaked. The walk from the Ploshchad Vosstaniya Metro to Suvorovsky Prospekt had taken fifteen minutes, and it had been fifteen minutes of unrelenting rain that stuck her cotton trousers to her legs and turned her white blouse indecent. Her arms were folded to cover her breasts as she stood at the back of a crowd of local and national press who were gathering outside the Ministry of the Interior building.

She ducked under the umbrella of a photographer who was wiping a lens with a lint cloth. 'Hey, what's going on?'

His hand poised over the camera. 'Press conference. That Swedish girl.' He assessed her, taking in the handcuffs and gun, and his manner became less gruff. 'You're a detective, are you working on it?'

She shook her head, 'They don't let me do anything serious like that. I only saw what was on television.'

'Well, if you don't mind…?' He lifted the lens to inspect it.

She walked away and cut through the small crowd. Ahead, she saw Major Dostoynov in dress uniform at the top of the steps and Colonel Vasiliev standing beside him like a benevolent uncle – albeit one with an ageing Teddy Boy quiff. Mikhail was nowhere to be seen and she guessed it had been deliberate to send a signal that he wasn't going to compete with Dostoynov for the top job. She felt a pang of guilt as a camera team clambered out of a Channel One News van parked on the pavement and cut to the front of the assembled press.

When the microphones and cameras were in position, Dostoynov descended, the wide brim of his peaked cap keeping the rain off his stubble length pate. He stared into the middle-distance as he spoke:

Chapter 20

'Following the discovery of a deceased female at the Maritime Victory Park on Krestovsky Island yesterday at approximately 6 p.m., we have identified a suspect.'

Dostoynov held up a picture and a blond, broad man with a Channel One camera on his shoulder edged forwards, blocking her view. 'Dmitry Dmitrievich Bezzubtsev,' continued the Major, 'is twenty-one years old, slim, and has brown hair. He should not be approached. A reward has been offered of one million Roubles for information leading to his arrest.'

She rushed away from the conference and took the Suvorovsky entrance. Inside, she saw Mikhail instructing a group of young men with shaved heads and grey-blue uniforms who had gathered in a meeting room where desks were being hastily pushed together.

'Get the numbers for this room and have the switchboard route them,' he directed to a uniform.

'Mikhail?' she called.

He waved at a sergeant. 'Here take over.' He stepped outside the room and closed the door behind him. 'Tasha, are you entering a wet T-shirt competition?

She folded her arms self-consciously. 'Misha, what the hell is going on?'

'Popovich got a match on AFIS: some missed abortion called Bezzubtsev who did eighteen months for a string of street robberies. He's not at his registered address so Dostoynov suggested Dahl offer a reward.'

'I thought Dostoynov wanted someone else to take the case?'

'Not now there's a target in his crosshairs.'

'So instead of finding him ourselves, we've given out a hotline to every chancer in *Piter*.' She shook her head in disbelief at the idiocy of the move.

Mikhail sniffed. 'An inferior mind might imagine Dostoynov was doing it to boost his profile.'

She flicked her thumb at the room. 'And who are they?'

'Conscripts on loan from an army engineering unit.'

'That's great.'

'Did anyone speak to Dahl?'

Mikhail shrugged. 'No, the request went through his lawyer, Lagunov. You got a change of clothes in your locker?'

'Just gym gear.'

'Well, you'd better find something before you give Rogov a hard-on. Let's go to my office first, while Dostoynov's out.' He grimaced. 'I hate sharing it with the uptight prick.'

She followed him into a plain, grey room with a wall-mounted safe and a filing cabinet. At the far side was a dirt-streaked window with an air conditioning unit fixed to the outside. There were two swivel-chairs at opposite ends of a table. 'This half is mine,' he said, unlocking a desk drawer. He took out a torn page from a notepad and handed it to her.

She tried to decipher Mikhail's scrawls, and made out the name of the Astoria hotel in Admiralty District. 'What is this?'

'It means Rogov was right.' He sat behind the desk and pulled out a packet of Sobranies then lit one. 'Dostoynov doesn't like me lighting up in *his* office.' Mikhail gave her his finest wolfish grin. 'The man's turning me into quite a chain smoker.'

'Maybe he's not so bad then. Dostoynov, I mean, not Rogov – he's a complete arsehole. So what is it?' She dangled the torn page from the notepad for emphasis.

He took a deep lungful of smoke and blew smoke into the weave of Dostoynov's chair. 'It's from my friend Viktor in FSB Immigration. Turn it over.'

She saw a name on the back: "Felix Axelsson". 'Who is he?'

'I had to look him up on Yandex. Apparently, Axelsson is a freelance security advisor based in Stockholm. Advertises himself as ex-Säpo, which means he probably isn't.' He picked up a mug with the departmental crest and flicked cigarette ash into it; she guessed it belonged to Dostoynov.

'Wait.' He went to the printer and took a sheet from the out-tray. 'I got this off his company site.'

It was a picture of Axelsson; he had a lean soldier's face: broad and healthy. His short-cropped red hair added to the impression, along with the combat trousers and a black polo shirt with a military logo on the breast pocket. Maybe, as Mikhail said, he was trying to look the part; in that case it was a convincing act.

'He looks like he'd be useful in a fight.' She folded Axelsson's picture and put it in her pocket then turned over the slip of paper.

Mikhail picked up Dostoynov's cup and went over to the window; he opened it and peered out. 'Press conference still going on. Christ knows what they can still find to talk about.' He puffed on the Sobranie. 'Viktor matched the flight manifest against FSB records to see who cleared immigration.'

She paused and turned the paper to study the address on the cover. The excitement was obvious in her tone. 'Are you saying this Felix Axelsson got off Dahl's jet before we arrived?'

'I am.' He stubbed the cigarette out in the mug. 'According to Viktor, the Gulfstream continued to Arlanda with two pilots and a flight attendant.' Mikhail held the mug out of the window then upended it.

She stared at him. 'The plane returned to Sweden without Dahl or Axelsson?'

He nodded.

'So he lied to us; Thorsten had a visa?'

'Yep.'

'So where are they?'

Mikhail shrugged as he placed the mug on Dostoynov's side of the desk. 'I don't know. The Astoria is the registered address but the reservation was cancelled. Dahl and Axelsson are hiding out in *Piter* like a pair of squirrels at a fur farm.'

She watched Mikhail spit into Dostoynov's mug then take a tissue from a box on the desk and wipe it clean. She left as he was returning it to the exact position he had found it.

After towel-drying her hair and putting on an opaque sports bra from her gym bag, she returned to the meeting room where Mikhail had routed the press conference response calls. Of the six conscripts who had been assigned to help, four had gone to lunch at midday. It was nearly two o'clock now and she suspected they were gone for good. One was somewhere in the building and the remaining conscript was writing details down on a pad while he spoke with a caller.

She watched the boy for a moment as he spoke with the phone wedged between his shoulder and cheek – the shaved hair; the jug ears; the olive green summer uniform. He hung up and looked at her.

'Any good?' she asked.

'Yes' – out of habit he glanced at her shoulder looking for rank insignia – 'A man reporting his neighbour's son, says he's been putting graffiti tags on their building.'

'Was the boy called Bezzubtsev?'

'No,' he checked what he'd written, 'Ilya Ryazantsev. But the neighbour swore it was his picture on Channel One.'

'If he calls again, threaten him with wasting police time.'

The five deserted desks were littered with Post-It notes and she started gathering them up. 'The crazies go here.' She wrote *"Niet"* on a Post-It and stuck it to the desk. 'If they look promising, put them here.' She scribbled, *"Da"*. 'And if you can't tell, add them to this pile.' She drew a question mark. She flicked through the notes and sorted them. One of the young soldiers had such poor handwriting, all his notes went under the question mark – she hoped there wasn't a genuine tip-off among them.

The phone on another desk started ringing and the conscript leant over to pick it up. 'Hello, um…police investigation,' he said, making her smile. She'd find out his name and put in a good word if he was interested in joining the force.

Her mobile vibrated and she saw Rogov's pale, smiling face on the screen. She took the call. 'Sergeant?'

There was a siren in the background which was cut off abruptly and she guessed he was breaking regulations by using it to cut through traffic. 'I'm on my way back from Sestroretsk.'

'Wait a moment.' It was noisy outside, and she closed the door to the meeting room. She asked, 'What did you find?'

'I got the office manager's number from the directory then made her open up the ZAGS and go through the system. She was a sixty-year-old virgin: all glasses and girly habits. If she'd been younger I might have offered to put her out of her misery.'

She felt herself bristle. 'And?'

Chapter 20

'And Zena called a month or so ago. The old maid was the one who dealt with her, but she didn't understand what she wanted.'

'A waste of time then.'

'No, Zena came back with a friend who was better at explaining things.'

'Yulia Federova?'

'Could be. The duty sergeant in Vasilyevsky said she had a good pair on her.'

She ignored the comment. 'So Zena brought her to negotiate?'

'Yeah, I reckon the Sven needed someone more worldly. Yulia was there to give the queen a gift.'

'Surely not for a wedding, Zena was only nineteen?'

She watched the young conscript hang up the phone and add a note to her *"Niet"* pile.

'No,' began Rogov, 'Zena wasn't looking to get married.'

'What was it then?'

'She was looking for a death certificate.'

'Whose?'

'The queen didn't remember, but she was sure it wasn't for a Sven or that would have stuck in her mind. Told me she went into the storage room with them where they keep the microfiche. The Sestroretsk ZAGS went digital around fifteen years ago.'

'Then she's looking for her natural parents. I spoke to Yulia on Saturday.'

'Yeah, you said she was stealing Zena's clothes.'

'We don't know that for certain. What if Zena had given them to Yulia as a present for helping out, or they had an arrangement?'

'We should bring her in.'

'I asked her to come in today.'

'You asked her?'

'She's not a suspect. If you've got a problem with that?'

'No—'

'Actually Rogov, I've got a better idea.' She flicked through her notepad. 'Find me at headquarters. Federova works on Nevsky Prospekt; a place called "Noughts and Kisses", pick me up and we'll bring her in.'

'Yes, boss,' he said, exhaling heavily.
'Rogov, are you smoking in the car?'
'No, boss,' he said, too quickly.

21

Nevsky Prospekt was as quiet as it got. Rogov turned off the four lane highway, then parked the Nissan in the courtyard of an army surplus shop. She leant over to lock her Makarov in the glove compartment then they crossed over to the shade of the massive wheat-coloured monolith of the Gostiny Dvor shopping centre. This time she had brought a jacket, a light raincoat she kept in her locker, which had the effect of scaring off the rainclouds and drawing out a hot sun from nowhere.

Rogov stopped to roll up the long sleeves of his tent-like shirt and peered at a window display of amber jewellery in one of the Gostiny Dvor arcades.

'Something for the mistress, perhaps?'

He scowled. 'It's Oksana's birthday on Thursday.'

'What about an amber necklace?'

'Not here…not on my salary.'

'Really?' she arched an eyebrow.

'I know what you think of me, Natalya.'

Her hands shifted and settled on her hips. 'Well, while we're being honest, I think you're a bigot.' She raised one arm to point at an amber teardrop on a silver chain. 'There…that one matches Oksana's eyes don't you think?'

'I'm a bigot? Christ, boss, where did that come from?'

'For a start you kept calling Aliyev "Mohammed."'

He lit a Winston and puffed on it thoughtfully. Somewhere in the universe Mikhail would be feeling an unconquerable urge to smoke too.

'You know Oksana's a Muslim, don't you?'

At the back of her mind, she did know. Rogov's wife didn't drink;

there again, Oksana didn't wear a veil either and swore like a priest on a sabbatical.

'But you're not.'

He sighed unhappily, sending a plume of smoke into the face of a passing schoolgirl. 'I'm supposed to be. Oksana's family are from Kazan, her brothers are *menti* too…they made me convert – I had to recite the *Shahada* in front of an imam.'

She laughed out loud. 'This is such shit, Rogov, if you're a Muslim, you're the worst example I've ever seen. Next you'll say you didn't break Aliyev's nose.'

'He ran into a tree, I swear.' Rogov pushed the Winston in between his lips to hide the twitch on them.

'Sure.'

'You have to believe me.'

'No I don't. This isn't one of those films where you play the racist, sexist, drunk and I get to be the one with a rod up my *zhopa*. When this is over we won't be slapping each other on the back and celebrating.'

She strode ahead, taking the stairs to an underpass. It was full of stalls: a newsagents, a downmarket amber shop, an obligatory display of *matryoshka* dolls, a *Teremok* selling blinis and salads. There was more life in the subway than above it.

'OK, OK…wait up.'

She slowed.

'I admit, I did give Aliyev a few slaps but he withheld important evidence. Now we'll get the little shit who killed her because I got him to talk.' He sucked on his Winston. 'Honestly, I would have done it to anyone.'

A woman was dragging her pushchair up the subway steps. She nodded a thank you as Natalya bent down to grab a strap between the wheels to lift the front. Rogov walked alongside them, puffing on his cigarette.

'That's magnanimous,' she said. 'Don't you think I would have got the truth out of him?'

'Not by playing by your nice EU rules. We had a dead girl three metres away.'

Chapter 21

The woman holding the rear of the pushchair stared at the top of her child's head, anxious not to make eye contact with Rogov.

'My EU rules?' she began. 'A murdered Sven... a German boss... Mohammed the contractor... but, oh no, you're not a bigot.'

They reached the top and Natalya let go of the strap. The mother walked away briskly, then looked over her shoulder at them.

'Next you'll say I'm not a feminist, boss. That hurts.'

Instead of answering, she flicked her eyes at a store front where, in place of a name, were hundreds of twenty-centimetre-high "O"s and "X"s acid-etched in rows. 'Tuck your shirt in, Rogov, we're here.'

Inside *Noughts & Kisses*, a woman in her early twenties with perfectly straight blonde hair stood less than a metre from them but she could have been a mile away so assiduously was she ignoring them. She had a button nose, a BMI in single figures, and was staring at a single handbag on a wooden rhomboid floor display with the intense focus of an artist arranging pieces for an exhibition. Another shop assistant stood behind the counter, appearing like a clone of the first with her adolescent boy body and perfect face, except her hair was a luminous white and cut in a Sixties bob.

Rogov picked up a knitted thong from a rail and twirled it on his index finger 'Hey, how much are these things? There's no price tag.' The blonde didn't turn her head and he frowned, disappointed not to see a look of disgust on her face.

Natalya went to the counter. 'Are you the manager?'

The woman was friendly enough if she focused on the mouth; the eyes, however, were as vacant as a salmon's at Kuznechny market.

'No, I'm Maya, the senior sales assistant.'

'You'll do.' She held up her ID card. 'I'm looking for Yulia Federova.'

'Oh,' the woman spoke with effortless cool. 'We're really, really not sure. She might be sick. She was supposed to be in today but we haven't seen her.'

Rogov joined in, 'Hey, what's with your hair?'

'Oh,' Maya spoke again and her eyes did a little roll as if he'd asked a more thought-provoking question. 'Well, it's obviously a dye, but you can get this shampoo that makes it glow.' She scrutinised Rogov's pepper-and-salt hair. 'I think it'll work on yours.'

'Did Yulia call in sick?' Natalya asked.

'Oh no, she didn't say anything at all. She just didn't come in.'

'Is that normal?'

Maya's head tilted to one side as if considering the upcoming presidential election. 'I haven't been here long enough to say.' She looked over Natalya's shoulder and called to the blonde. 'Olesia, is it normal, you know…for Yulia?'

The blonde turned then frowned; her concentration on the rhomboid broken forever. She shook her head then spoke in a voice barely above a whisper. 'No, not normal.'

'Sure?' asked Natalya.

'Oh yes,' said Olesia, 'I think so.'

'Fuck,' Rogov sighed when they left the boutique. 'Where do they find these people?' He lit another Winston. 'So what's the plan now, boss?'

'Primorsky District. Let's get personal.'

She parked in the same spot outside Yulia Federova's apartment block and under the shadow of the crane. Rogov worked his way through all the buzzers on the intercom calling "Police! Open the door!" until finally someone relented and there was a rasping sound as an anonymous inhabitant pressed a button to release the lock. They started climbing the stairs and Natalya soon found herself on her own. By the sixth floor she stopped to catch her breath.

'Rogov,' she called below, 'are you alright?'

She heard a retching cough followed by a scuffing of shoes. A minute later he appeared, red-faced, his translucent shirt stuck to his body by sweat. He sat on the landing, his feet on the lower steps, and put his head in his hands. 'Boss…Natalya, I'm going to shit my lungs if you don't stop.'

'Then stay here. I'm not carrying you down if you have a heart attack.'

She left him and started walking again…seven…eight…nine…ten. With each floor, the smell of tarry tobacco became more pungent and she found herself holding her breath until she couldn't keep it in any longer.

At Yulia Federova's apartment she rang the bell, keeping her finger on it longer than necessary. She stepped back and smoothed her hair. Far below, she could hear Rogov's slow shuffle on a landing then his heavy, lumbering steps as he mounted another set of stairs. The smell brought bile in her throat and for a second she wondered if she might be pregnant before dismissing the idea – that would only happen if Mikhail had been switching her pills.

Rogov's footsteps had stopped. 'Are you OK?' she called down, her voice echoing in the stairwell.

She heard another retching cough.

The wallet with the four DVDs from the Krestovsky Island Metro was still in her handbag and she reached past it for her notebook. She flicked through the pages to find the entry with Yulia Federova's number and entered it into her mobile. The phone in the apartment rang three times then stopped. In her ear she heard the girl explaining that she was out and to leave a message. Natalya hung up and banged on the door with her fist.

'Yulia! Open up!'

A short, squat man appeared in the door opposite. He was wearing a white vest and smelled of fresh sweat that was at least an improvement on the cloying stench of tobacco in the hallway. She felt for her ID and held it out. 'Police – have you seen your neighbour, Yulia Federova?'

'Not for a few days,' he scratched an armpit. 'Last weekend… Saturday morning.'

The neighbour scratched his armpit again then surreptitiously sniffed at his fingers. 'Seven forty-five; that's when I get my Sport Express.' He ran the same hand through the grey strands of his thinning hair. 'She leaves for her dance class at the same time,' he added, and Natalya had an image of him spying through his peephole then emerging to "accidentally" bump into his pretty neighbour on the way to buy his paper.

Natalya nodded thoughtfully and wrote the details in her notepad though there was little reason to when she had seen Yulia herself after the dance class had finished.

'Is she in trouble?'

She gave him a tight smile to avoid the question. 'Have you got some water?'

He left in a haze of sweat and she inserted her ID card between the jamb and door of Yulia's apartment. It stopped at the strike plate and she pushed it firmly with the heel of her hand, feeling the lock part.

The neighbour appeared and held out a beer glass with a double-headed eagle logo.

She put her notepad away then took it from him. 'Thanks, it's not for me.'

After a minute, Rogov appeared, wheezing. He leaned heavily on the metal railing and she handed the water to him. 'Here, drink this.'

His jowls shook as he nodded gravely, then poured the water down his neck in one swallow.

'You want another? You don't look too good.' The neighbour asked.

'Nah, I'm fine.' Rogov returned the glass, then wiped his mouth with the back of his hand. 'You know who her landlord is?' he wheezed.

The neighbour shook his head.

'Alright, you can go now. Thanks for your cooperation.' Natalya said.

Rogov waited for the man's door to close. 'I take it Federova isn't in?'

'She is, but I thought I'd wait in case you wanted to beat a confession out of her.'

He grinned, then wheezed as he exhaled. 'Seriously, what are we doing here? Every policeman in *Piter* is out searching for that

Bezzubtsev piece of shit. You know, the one who actually killed the girl.'

'Yulia lied to me, Rogov, that's why. I asked her about Zena's trip to ZAGS and she said she didn't know anything about it.'

'So? Federova's got a record and doesn't like talking to the *menti*. I bet the hairs on Misha's balls, she'll show up once we have Bezzubtsev in a pair of bracelets.'

Rogov's cheeks were turning to their normal pasty colour. 'Unless,' he added, 'Federova was stealing from Zena. Is that what you think? Did she hire Bezzubtsev to stop Zena turning her in? Someone with a taste of prison would do anything not to go back.'

'No, Yulia reported Zena missing. If she had her friend killed that's the last thing she'd do. When I spoke to her she was genuinely worried.'

Rogov scuffed the floor with his shoe. 'Well, fuck this. She's not here…shall we join the search for Bezzubtsev?'

'Rogov, she was hiding something.'

His eyes took in the ID card sticking out of the door and shook his head. 'What are you doing?'

'Taking a look. Keep it quiet?'

'Sure, boss.'

'If anyone asks, we thought the girl was in danger.' She twisted the handle and her ID card fell to the floor as the door swung open.

22

A kitchen drawer was wide open, scattering cutlery to the floor; assorted clothes were spilled over the bed. Natalya snapped on a pair of latex gloves and told Rogov to do the same.

'I left mine,' he said and stuffed his hands in his pockets.

The framed picture of Natalia Makarova performing a grand jeté was on the floor, smashed. To avoid the broken glass, she placed her feet carefully then flicked through the clothes on the bed.

'Christ!' Rogov ran a hand over his damp brow. 'Looks like she left in a hurry.'

He stepped to the kitchen side of the bedsit. 'There's a knife-holder here with a gap where the big one is missing.' He looked in the sink then squatted on the floor, nudging the cutlery with his foot. 'Yeah. Can't see it.'

She picked through the clothes. 'When I was here before she had a navy blue trouser suit and a pair of sunglasses, both Ulyana Sergeenko.'

Rogov shrugged. 'Who?'

'Fashion designer. Rihanna, Lady Gaga, Kim Kardashian … they all wear her stuff. Thc sunglasses were in a pink box.'

He pulled open the wardrobe. 'Nothing here. She emptied everything.'

'OK.' She watched Rogov lower himself to examine a cabinet, nudging the door open with an elbow to avoid leaving fingerprints. Leo Primakov would not have been impressed.

'Anything there?'

'No. Just old magazines.'

Sun broke through a cloud, sending a column of light through the balcony and illuminating motes of dust.

Chapter 22

He asked, 'What's going on?'

'Let me think.'

There was an obvious narrative: A fight had occurred and Yulia Federova had fled, grabbing what she could. Except, Natalya had seen the aftermaths of too many violent confrontations to believe it. There was nothing she could swear to but the spilt cutlery was scattered in too neat an area and rooms were usually in a worse state by the time they reached the picture smashing stage.

'She believes her father was sent to prison on false charges.'

'What are you saying?'

'She staged it.'

'Why?'

Natalya shrugged. 'Maybe she was worried we were going to blame her for Zena's murder and decided to disappear.'

'Did you say anything to make her nervous?'

She didn't like his insinuation. 'That's enough, Rogov. She made me a coffee and we spoke about Zena, I didn't give her any indication the *menti* were taking a hard look at her. At that stage we didn't know anything.'

'And the way I see it, she didn't need to run. With those bazookas, even Dostoynov would believe her – she could be a serial killer and get away with it.' He held his hands out, palms facing her. 'I'm only telling the truth.'

'Rogov, I worry what's in your head.'

'You should, it's disgusting in there...Natalya, do you trust the new major?'

'Dostoynov?' She shook her head instinctively. 'If we tell him Yulia staged her own disappearance he'll insist we charge her for wasting our time. For a murder case she'll go to prison. It's ridiculous, she didn't need to run. If anything I was trying to protect her.'

'Then we won't say anything.'

'No, we have to report it.'

'Boss, it's nearly five. I'm going back to HQ, where – with your permission – I will take a leisurely shit, then go home.'

She checked the time on her phone and heaved a sigh. 'You're right, Rogov, let's get out of here.'

At Suvorovsky Prospekt, she remembered the Krestovsky Island Metro footage and checked it in as evidence, leaving Rogov walking in the direction of the toilet block. In the meeting room six desks had been pushed together; a conscript sat at each, looking almost identical with stubble for hair. She approached the one she had spoken to before, though she wasn't sure it was him until she took a furtive look at his jug ears.

'They came back from lunch?'

He looked puzzled for a moment. 'There was a colonel' – he dropped his voice – 'the one with hair.'

'Colonel Vasiliev?'

'Maybe…I don't know. He had a word with our CO.'

In the middle of the desks were the piles of telephone response categories she had started. She flicked through them, adding most to a new discard pile.

'You want to do some overtime?'

Three of the conscripts looked at her as if she was being wilfully stupid. She understood immediately: what was the point of volunteering when their commanding officer would take their money – they did as they were ordered, no more.

Looking through an internal window, she saw Mikhail in the office he shared with Dostoynov; both men were sitting on opposite lengths of the same desk. They looked uncomfortable, like Siberian tigers in a zoo who had resolved to ignore each other because the constant aggression was wearisome. Both were typing on laptops. Walking over, she knocked then waited.

'Come in,' they said together.

The air conditioning was fierce although Mikhail didn't like to use it; she wondered if it was Dostoynov's revenge for making the room smell of cigarette smoke.

'The conscripts, Major. Will they be working late?'

Dostoynov turned. 'It's already arranged, Captain, thank you. I was hoping to see you supervise them today. You are supposed to be in charge of this case.'

Mikhail scowled at the Major; expressing unhappiness that his wife was being criticised. It made her wonder if his dislike of Dostoynov ran deeper than the fact that the man was ex-FSB. Was the real reason closer to home? Mikhail was giving up his chance to run the department for her but she couldn't be blamed so he heaped it all on Dostoynov. Only, the new major didn't look like the type of man to put up with abuse for long. Would she be humiliated in front of Mikhail as a casualty in their cold war?

'I was following up a lead.'

'Was it to speak to the girl's father? Because I made that call.' Dostoynov waited for her to fill in the silence; she waited for him too, badly wanting to know what Thorsten Dahl had said. Mikhail ducked behind his laptop screen.

She gave in first: 'What did he say, Major?'

Dostoynov checked the document on his screen and she realised he was writing up a report. 'Dahl was unavailable. I spoke with the lawyer – Anatoly Lagunov – he said it will take at least a week for the dental records.'

She was going to speak when she saw Mikhail frown at her. He was signalling her to be careful.

Dostoynov looked up from his screen. 'What was the lead?'

'A waste of time.' She remembered the phone call the conscript had taken. 'Someone thought Bezzubtsev was a neighbour's son.'

'And that took you all day?'

'I also tried to see if Zena was registered to a dentist in the city.' She shrugged again as if it too had been a dead end and left the lie unembellished.

'Good. No going home tonight. Tell your sergeant the same.'

Dostoynov returned to the laptop and she took his response as a dismissal. She left their office and walked straight into the conscript.

'Captain,' he said, breathlessly, 'it's about the girl. Someone called from Gatchinsky District this afternoon; he didn't make much sense...he was wasted.'

'What's your name?'

'Morozov, Alexei Yurievich.'

She gave him an encouraging smile, which she hoped wasn't too patronising. 'Well, Alexei Yurievich, it's unlikely someone will be calling from the Winter Palace, if that's what you were expecting?'

The conscript scratched his head and she wondered if he had lice. 'He said his name was Petya,' the boy began, 'but he didn't mention Bezzubtsev, just kept asking about the ransom and if it was real. I told him not to waste our time. I got rid of him...then he called again.'

Morozov rubbed a finger along the collar of his shirt. 'He told me there's a group of squatters in an old schoolhouse in Novvy Svet. Two more joined them last Monday. Called themselves Stas and Dima. On Friday night they were flashing around money. Stas said he'd banged an American and she was so grateful she gave him two hundred dollars. Petya thought they were whistling until he showed them a picture.'

'I asked him to send it to me.' Morozov held up his mobile phone and his cheeks coloured. 'Is this the girl who was killed?'

She took Morozov's mobile and stared at the picture. The camera flash had bleached the image though it was easy enough to make out the bottom half of a girl lying on a pavement, her pale underwear visible above crossed legs. There was some of her dress in it too, but it had been rendered grey, not powder blue as Yulia had described. The face was visible though; Zena Dahl could be seen glaring angrily at the photographer.

The tiredness of the day was gone. She left Morozov watching her expectantly and burst back into the office. Dostoynov scowled instantly; Mikhail expressed paternal disapproval with a frown.

'We've got the bastard,' she said.

23

The dark grey OMON truck led the four vehicle procession, its six massive tyres and heavy suspension easily negotiating the narrow, broken road. In its wake, three police cars weaved around the ruts as if driven by children. Mikhail's Mercedes was last, the blue light attached to his roof no longer flashing; his sirens no longer blaring now the city was behind him.

He gripped the wheel one-handed while he lit a Sobranie. 'You lost Stepan because he went for a shit?'

'I shouted outside the door. His mobile was off too. Maybe he had a heart attack on the toilet. I thought he was going to have one this afternoon.'

He twisted his head to the left and exhaled smoke through the open window. 'Angel, I don't believe a word you said to Dostoynov in my office. Where were you and Rogov today?'

'I can be good at lying too,' she said. It was apparently too enigmatic for Mikhail as his expression remained unchanged. 'We were looking for Yulia Federova.'

'Where was she?'

'No idea – I think she ran away.'

He flicked his cigarette ash out the window. 'Seems everyone is hiding from us. Perhaps she's with Dahl and his security man having caviar and champagne?'

'More like she doesn't want to get involved.' Behind her, she noticed a pair of pressed jackets on the back seat.

'What the hell are they?'

'Got them from the dry cleaners earlier.' He looked ashamed.

'No, you brought them along in case the press turn up. I thought you were giving Dostoynov a free pass. If you take Vasiliev's job, I'll have to leave – there's no other way. I'll end up in the municipal police fishing drunks out of the Moika. Why can't you keep things as they are?'

He shook his head slightly. 'I don't know what I want, Natalya, but I do know the man drives me to it. Did you know Dostoynov turned down a lift with me so he could ride with the OMON?'

'That's your fault for baiting him. He'll damage you if he gets Vasiliev's chair.'

He grinned. 'I know, Angel, but I can't stop myself.'

They were quiet for a while and Mikhail pressed the button for a preset station on the radio. A young man's voice filled the Mercedes; he was being interviewed about the Geiger counter measurements he took every winter of the chemical sludge they sprayed on the roads. Barely a minute later and the presenter deftly steered the topic to immigration. It was always about immigration. Or gay people. Or liberals. Or Ukrainians, Georgians, the EU, NATO, Britain, or America. It was never the fault of the incompetents who were too busy robbing the country to run it properly.

She stabbed at the off button. 'We could always split up.'

Mikhail was bluff, 'That will make it even worse. They definitely won't let me supervise you.'

'You really want this, don't you?'

'I want you more.'

'Listen, Dostoynov's ahead after that press conference. This will make you even.' She peered again at his suits on the back seat. 'If you're trying to upstage him wear the blue one, it's more assertive; grey is too corporate.'

He tapped his fingers nervously on the steering wheel. 'Why are you doing this?'

His tone softened, 'Angel, what's got into you?'

The procession turned right and the car began to shake as the road deteriorated. She saw a huge slab of concrete, cracked and deformed by tree roots.

'Christ!' he shouted, swerving around it. He looked at her, his face humourless. 'Want to hear a joke.'

'Sure.'

Chapter 23

'Did you know the Russians invented time travel?'

She gave him a mock disparaging look.

'Sure you do. If you want to go back to the time of the tsars just drive an hour out of Moscow or *Piter*.' He had a pull on his cigarette. 'Jesus, will you look at this place?'

They were passing two houses on the right with neat vegetable gardens. As the procession drew level, she saw their pretty red roofs transmute into corrugated iron coated in rust treatment paint. The walls were bare concrete and half-timbers that offered little protection from the swarms of mosquitoes in summer or the ravaging winds in winter. A horse waited on the lane outside while its wizened owner fixed a tarpaulin to the cart. The man looked up briefly, then pulled on a rope, unbothered by the sight of the convoy.

'I can't be your boss. If I take it you'll be re-assigned to a district station and coming home smelling of puke and piss each day. Is that what you want?'

She needed more time to decide. She needed to find out if Mikhail was still the person she had married. If he wasn't, well… she hadn't got that far in her thinking but it didn't look good. Divorce felt inconceivable – she didn't want to be with anyone else – but if he was corrupt, how could she stay? 'I'm not saying that, but if you don't put yourself forward he'll win for certain.'

'But you don't want me to win.'

He risked another look at her then pulled his eyes back to the road. 'Natashenka, you can't quit just so I can chase a promotion.'

'I'm not.' She took a deep breath and exhaled. 'I'm just saying let's not decide now.'

The OMON truck caught dried mud on the road and sprayed a cloud of dust behind it. Visibility dropped to a few metres. Mikhail pressed a button to close his window then stubbed out the Sobranie. 'What's going on?'

Red lights leapt out of the gloom. Mikhail stamped on the brakes then manoeuvred around them. She looked over her shoulder to see a police car merge into the dust.

'Flat tyre I bet,' he said. 'Should have watched the road.'

Her heart fluttered like a trapped bird. 'You're dirty, Misha.'

'Angel, what the hell are you talking about?'

Now the bird was thrashing, snapping its wings. 'Tell me about your secret bank account. Tell me about *Misha Buratino*.'

'How—'

'Mikhail!'

The car in front swerved but he was too slow. The Mercedes buckled as it hit a pothole, then righted itself.

'Are you trying to kill us?'

He slowed and craned his neck, she assumed to listen for the rumble of a burst tyre. There was nothing above the heavy diesel engine of the OMON truck ahead, and he accelerated to catch up with the convoy.

Mikhail was calmer than she had expected: 'What makes you think I'm dirty?'

'I found your secret account when I checked to see if you'd paid Anton's university bribe.'

His chest shook as he chuckled to himself. 'Then you'll be amused to hear Professor Litovkin called this afternoon…he has the money and is adamant the rejection letter was no more than a clerical error. He sounded very appreciative.'

No wonder, she thought, Mikhail had paid the man twice. 'My congratulations.'

'So tell me, Natalya, how did you find out about *Misha Buratino*?'

'I put a keylogger on our computer; it captured your passwords.' She felt her voice rise in pitch, 'You bought our apartment with dirty money, Misha.'

They passed a sign indicating the village of Novvy Svet was two kilometres away and the Mercedes gathered speed as the road became smooth tarmac. On the right was a drainage ditch; she thought about ripping the steering wheel from his hands and dragging the car into it so the rest of her body could experience the jagged, visceral pain in her gut.

Mikhail was frustratingly calm, he pressed another preset and "Radio Zenit" displayed on the dashboard. The airwaves filled with the sound of a crowd cheering.

'Turn it off. Football is caveman shit.'

Chapter 23

He touched the button and twisted the volume control by mistake. Suddenly the roar of the crowd was personal. They weren't cheering for points on some league table, they were cheering him on; it was his victory over her. She stabbed at the button again to switch it off.

'Talk to me, Misha. What did you do, get someone off murder?'

He pressed his lips together. 'You've got it wrong, Angel. It wasn't me.'

'You control the account, don't be ridiculous.'

He went to speak and she rolled her eyes in anticipation of the lies that were going to come. 'There's nothing you can say.'

'Oh I think there is,' he spoke urbanely, smoothing his collar. 'My mother.'

She let out a short laugh. 'What did Violka do?'

'I told you before. She left me her money.'

'Don't lie, I deserve better than that.'

'If you'd just listen!' He took a breath. 'Didn't you ever see *The Adventures of Buratino*?'

She unlocked her arms and waved a hand. 'Of course, who hasn't?' It still appeared on the listings for the cable channels that sold nostalgia.

'Well, it came out just before I was born. When I was six or seven, I had these stupid blond curls like Dima Iosifov, the boy who played *Buratino* – I couldn't wait to have the fucking things cut off – I was always getting into trouble too. Before my mother started losing her mind, she set up the account and transferred her assets to me; it was her idea of a joke: *Misha Buratino* was my childhood nickname.'

'Then how was it you never told me?'

'Because, my darling, it is illegal for an official to have a foreign bank account. More importantly, I was hiding it from those felons in the Federal Tax Service who are in league with the mafia.'

'So why didn't you tell me?' she asked again.

He let out a weary sigh. 'Because you're too honest and I didn't need the shit.'

She looked out of the windscreen at the OMON truck; it was

pulling over. Mikhail parked behind the remaining police car, almost dropping the Mercedes into a hole in the tarmac so perfectly spherical it could have been made by the impact of a meteorite.

Already, Cosmonauts wearing blue and grey uniforms, black belts and boots, were climbing out. Mikhail stopped the engine and pulled on his door handle.

'Definitely the blue jacket.' She flicked her head in the direction of the men assembling outside the six-wheeled OMON vehicle. Dostoynov stood with them, affecting their easy, masculine stance. 'I bet he warned the press.'

She climbed out and pointed her Makarov at the ground as she racked the slide. To anyone else, she was sure Mikhail's explanation sounded reasonable – all the money had come from his mother and the foreign account was to protect his inheritance – but it didn't sound right. There was no reason to conceal the fact it was held offshore. Sure, tax evasion was illegal, but so was bribery, and hadn't they done just that to get Anton into college? Mikhail was lying: he hadn't told her about the account because it was stuffed with dirty money. Buratino was the boy who told lies.

'Are we good, Angel?' he asked.

There was a sting of histamine and she sucked in air to stop the tears welling. 'No, we're not.'

The old school house stood on the opposite side of the road. It was a two-storey block of concrete with plywood for windows, surrounded by a tall brick wall that, perversely, looked like the only part of the building made with any real affection. She instantly pitied the poor children who had passed through it, then wondered if the squatters occupying it had once been students there; now returning, subconsciously or otherwise, to wreak revenge on the place.

The wall wasn't high enough to obscure the OMON truck but subterfuge wasn't necessary when the open fields surrounding the schoolhouse would merely provide sport for the police if the squatters ran for cover. She disengaged the safety on her Makarov then tucked the gun back in her holster. It wasn't the way she'd been taught but the guard was good enough to prevent an accidental discharge.

Chapter 23

Next to a lamppost in the shape of a dandelion seed, a too-thin, too-pale boy was fidgeting with his phone. She took out her mobile and called the number the conscript had given her.

The boy was startled when his phone rang and he stared at it for a full two seconds before answering.

'Petya?'

'Yeah?'

'You see a woman waving?'

'Yeah.'

'That's me. Come over.' She saw a couple of OMON officers taking an interest as they clipped their batons in place. 'And don't go anywhere near the thing that looks like a tank, you'll regret it.'

She watched him walk briskly across the road and saw his face was covered in yellow-pitted acne as he came closer.

'Are they still there?' she asked.

He frowned then rubbed his nose with the back of his forearm leaving a glistening trail on it. 'Yeah, Stas and Dima are cooking.' He sniffed, 'You got the reward?'

'Don't be stupid, son.' Mikhail appeared, grabbing the boy by the wrist before he could run. 'You think we'd give it to a junkie.' He pulled out a nylon tie to fix the boy's wrists.

'Leave him, Misha. Give me the keys, I'll take him back.'

He shook his head. 'You can't. This is your case. It's a major arrest, Natalya, and it's all yours. Everyone else is here to support you, even Dostoynov and the Cosmonauts.'

'I'm not going in there.' She re-engaged the safety on her Makarov. 'Make sure you get to them before Dostoynov realises what's happening – it'll make you even with him.'

She heard a motor and expected to see the police car that had burst a tyre; instead, a van drove past with an outsized satellite dish fixed to the roof and a blue "1" on its side for Channel One. They either had a supernatural sense that a major arrest was about to happen or someone was feeding them information; Dostoynov, she imagined.

'Angel, I don't care about that.'

'You should. I'll see you at home.' She couldn't focus on his eyes, couldn't bear to.

The OMON had split into two rows and Dostoynov was addressing them.

'You let him make the arrests and you may as well resign – he'll make your life miserable. Give me your car keys, you can go back in that stupid troop carrier.'

His voice sounded distant. 'In the ignition…I'll see you at home, right?'

She mumbled a reply then removed Mikhail's blue jacket from the back seat and tossed it to him. 'Put this on. You look handsome in it.'

Turning to the boy, she said, 'Get in the car, and if you leave any bodily fluids behind then he' – she tilted her eyes at Mikhail who adopted a menacing look on cue – 'will do bad things to you.'

She watched Mikhail pull on the jacket, then take out his Makarov and hold it in a two-handed position at the ground. He crossed the road, hugging the contours of the wall before disappearing from view. A Channel One reporter she vaguely recognised chased after Mikhail followed by a flustered cameraman.

'Right, Petya,' she said, climbing in, 'let's go find your mother and see what she wants to do with you.'

24

Natalya glared at her alarm clock before realising the harsh buzzing sound was coming from her intercom. She ignored it, assuming a caller had pressed the buttons to several apartments in order to get past the block door. The noise stopped. She frowned. A bottle of Satrapezo to wash down a family-size packet of mushroom and sour cream crisps had seemed like the perfect formula last night. Then she remembered her first glass had been early evening and it hadn't been one bottle of Satrapezo either. At least she got the flavour of the crisps right.

She contemplated going back to sleep but had no desire to return to her dark dreams, so she got dressed. It was already Wednesday, the last of the two days' compassionate leave Colonel Vasiliev had authorised. Early on Tuesday morning, when Mikhail had got home after the arrests at the old schoolhouse, she had told him to leave. She arranged for him to stay with Rogov and Oksana until he was ready to tell her the truth. He had protested meekly but nevertheless had packed a bag before work – another indication of his guilt considering it was his money that had bought the apartment and, by rights, she should have been the one to move out. Unfortunately, on the few occasions she had spoken to him on the phone, Mikhail had stuck rigidly to his story and she had to make a decision soon whether to take him back and ignore his dishonesty or make the separation permanent.

The buzzer sounded again. This time, it was the one on her apartment door.

She squinted through the eyepiece to see Mikhail wearing a suit; he had also shaved. After a quick check in the mirror, she smoothed her unironed checked shirt before opening the door.

'Misha, what a surprise.'

'I left my keys.' He looked around and rocked on his heels awkwardly.

She let him in. 'Take off your shoes, you're making me nervous.'

He did, then craned his neck as he looked around. 'I like what you've done with the place.'

After two days, the sink was overflowing with dirty dishes and there was a heap of clothes piled up on the sofa near an ironing board. Mikhail was the tidy one in their relationship. 'I've been busy.'

'I can tell.'

She stared at Mikhail's discarded shoes; a hint that he was beginning to outstay his welcome. 'How can I help, Misha?'

'Did you see Channel One?

'Last night *and* yesterday. You looked a real hero. I reckon they might offer you the Medal for Valour.'

Somewhere between her first bottle of Satrapezo and an old episode of Spets, a news item had shown him shoulder-barge the kitchen door of the schoolhouse. Inside, he confronted two teenage boys in their underwear cooking up the dirty opiate junkies call *krokodil* that was supposedly more addictive than heroin. The report had included a slow motion action shot of Mikhail pulling out his gun and forcing the two boys to the floor. The camera panned to show packets of codeine pills and industrial chemicals.

'Thanks… reports going to the prosecutor's office. I can't see them objecting. Early this morning they both confessed to killing the Sven.'

'Did Rogov handle it?'

'Yeah, but don't get down on Stepan. We found pictures of Zena Dahl on one of their phones with her dress around her waist.' Mikhail's mouth twisted into a grimace. 'You can only imagine what the sick fucks did to her.'

'Still, I'd like to read their confessions.'

She thought of the two boys withdrawing from the *krokodil* and Rogov offering to give them whatever they craved as long as they put their names to a statement – one that he'd probably written himself. Mikhail had a point though, suspects were convicted on less and they were a pair of nasty shits that the world wouldn't miss.

He snorted and pulled out a packet of Sobranie Classics. 'It's been two days now and I still can't get the damned smell of iodine out of my nose. Jesus, Tasha, have you ever seen kids on *krokodil* before? When Bezzubtsev put his hands up I could see his actual arm bone moving inside – the phosphorous rots their flesh. It was the freakiest thing I've ever seen. Don't be surprised if he's dead before trial.'

Mikhail tapped the end of his cigarette and looked around; she pointed to the balcony door.

He frowned. 'You're banning me from smoking in my own apartment?'

'Just clearing the air.' She followed him out and pulled the handle behind her to keep the smoke out. 'So who was his friend?'

'Stanislav Stanislavovich Mamanov. Called himself Stas. He has a juvenile conviction for indecent assault.' He smiled grimly. 'Looks like they had a charming double act going – one robbed and the other raped. Poor Zena, it's terrible to think they were her last experience on Earth. The two of them stank like railway tramps too…they hadn't washed in weeks.'

'What did they smell of?'

'Just unclean, why?'

She watched him tap the ash of his cigarette over the balcony and waited until she had his attention. 'You didn't notice wood smoke or petrol?'

'Don't think so, why?'

'Misha, if they hadn't washed in weeks how did they get the smell of wood smoke and petrol off without washing away the rest of their stink?'

'You got a better idea?'

She leaned on the railings and stared at the street below. The light was sharp and it brought a pain behind her eyeballs.

'So why did they kill her?' she asked.

Mikhail stared into space and puffed on his cigarette thoughtfully. 'Prison rules, perhaps? Raping a stranger carries a death sentence inside. By killing her then burning the body I guess they wanted to improve their chances.'

'What's the timeline? Where did they hold Zena between Friday morning and Sunday evening? Did you check with the others at the squat to account for their movements?'

'We don't need to. Are you saying they didn't do it?'

'Anything's possible,' she said, realising how absurd it sounded.

'Sure, so is teaching a dog to tap dance.'

'So they raped and robbed Zena, kept her for three days, then took her to one of the most public parks in the city. They got the fire going with petrol, threw her on, and then hurried back to their squat. Right?'

He nodded. 'If you've got more questions you can file them under "Who gives a shit about a pair of *gopniks*?". The prosecutor has the case and Dostoynov won't thank you for interfering. That's why I'm here.'

He looked at her so gravely she wanted to burst out laughing.

'What is it, Misha?'

'You remember asking me to find out about Dahl's visa?'

'Sure, you said you knew someone from law school at the Big House.'

'Viktor.' He puffed on his Sobranie and stared thoughtfully at the pedestrians posing for photographs by the stone lions on the opposite side of the Griboyedov Canal. 'He was waiting for me outside the car park this morning. There was this look on his face you don't often see outside an interrogation room. Like a tough guy who knows he's in the shit. Only when these guys get in the shit it can end very badly for them.'

'What did he say?'

Mikhail took another drag. 'A woman – an FSB major from the Economic Crimes Directorate – called him from Moscow.'

'Who are they?'

'Basically, thieves. She wanted to know what business he had checking the manifest of Dahl's Gulfstream. He made up some excuse but he could tell she didn't believe him. Natasha, if the FSB have an interest in the Zena Dahl case then wash your hands of it, and don't look back. I'm telling you' – he gave her the earnest look again – 'for all our sakes.'

'Did Viktor warn you off?'

'That's why I came here. I assured him the case was already closed and I was the only one asking, but…for Christ's sake, Natalya, leave it alone.' He stubbed the cigarette out on the underside of the railing then held it in his palm and flicked it into space.

25

She parked her Volvo on Vosstaniya Ulitsa and strolled past the street's shop fronts inhaling deeply the fresh, if fume-tinged, air to help shake off her hangover. Officially she was off duty until Thursday but she owed it to Zena to find a few more answers and put the case to bed. The FSB involvement intrigued her as much as it scared her, but she reassured herself that they would have no interest in a police murder investigation. Most likely it was high politics that had drawn them in, and she could keep her distance from anything that smelled dangerous.

The business card Anatoly Lagunov had presented to her in his BMW displayed no company name or logo, and neither did Thorsten Dahl's headquarters – there was only the number etched in black on a brass plaque. The doors were locked and she noticed a slot where a swipe card allowed the employees to gain entry. She rang the bell then heard a click and went inside.

As much as the building was anonymous on the outside, inside it was stunning. An atrium extended to the full height of the six-floor edifice. Under her feet there was an ancient map of the heavens tiled in brown and blue marble. Ten metres above her head hung a chandelier, its yellow and orange crystals forming a sun. Even the reception desk was a greyish-white and shaped to resemble a crescent moon. A security guard-cum-receptionist watched her calmly from it. His fine hair was red and she wondered how much he must hate putting on his chocolate-brown uniform each day.

She pulled out her ID card. 'I'd like to speak with Anatoly Lagunov.'

While he picked up the phone she examined an aluminium wall mosaic of Yuri Gagarin peering through his Vostok-1 porthole from half a century ago.

Two minutes later, a set of Art Deco varnished doors parted, and a woman exited a lift on the far side of the crescent-shaped desk. She had a blonde bob and curves accentuated by a tight red suit, making her the image of an Aeroflot flight attendant. A swipe card hung on a lanyard and swung between her breasts,

'Hello, I'm Daria, Anatoly's secretary.' She held out her hand to Natalya.

They crossed the expanse of marble to the Art Deco lift. 'Nice place.'

'We like it here.'

The lift opened on the second floor into a large office where around fifty people, mostly men, were sitting in cubicles staring at computer screens or talking.

'Who are they?'

'This floor it's the accountants; above us is marketing, below is IT. Don't ask more than that, I couldn't tell you.'

They weaved through the cubicles to a smoked glass wall and Daria pulled on a door handle. Inside was a narrow reception area containing a small desk and three swivel chairs. Beyond it, there was a closed door. Daria knocked on it lightly and Anatoly Lagunov emerged, beckoning Natalya inside.

On the wall was a framed certificate of a law degree from Leningrad State University that dated Lagunov's student days to the premiership of Yuri Andropov, the Butcher of Budapest.

'I can barely remember my time there,' Anatoly Lagunov said, noticing her gaze at it. He held out his hand.

She shook it and studied the lawyer, realising he must be older than he looked. A grey silk shirt showed off the contours of his physique and she felt his sharp eyes study her in return, no doubt reaching a less favourable conclusion after a night of drinking fine Georgian wine.

'Captain Ivanova, it's nice to see you.' Lagunov flashed those small teeth. 'Something to drink?'

'Coffee: black, no sugar. Thank you.'

Daria had been hovering in the background and turned smartly, closing the adjoining door. Natalya took a cappuccino-coloured rocket chair that put her several inches below the lawyer's, then pulled out her notepad.

'How can I help?' Lagunov took up his seat and she noticed the framed portrait of the president adjacent to a wall safe.

'Are you sure your money is secure next to him?'

He laughed, baring his teeth, then leant forwards and planted his elbows on his desk. 'Quite secure…I must congratulate you on the resolution of your case.'

'Thank you. Please pass on my condolences to Mister Dahl, I haven't spoken to him since the evening we found Zena.' She edged forwards in the chair. 'If you don't mind, there are a few loose ends I need to tidy up.'

Lagunov pressed his hands together. 'Please, Captain, whatever I can do.'

'We haven't been able to speak to Mister Dahl recently so perhaps you can pass on any questions that you are unable to answer?'

He shuffled in his seat. 'As long as you don't ask about Zena's adoption again.' He gave her a tight smile. 'That's a private matter I'd prefer not to be discuss again.'

She maintained a neutral expression. 'First, I'd like to explain what will happen to Zena's body. There's a backlog for autopsies but due to the importance of this case, it's likely the state pathologist, Doctor Fedyushina, will want to start this week. After that, Zena will be held until the identification process is complete. A dental specialist will be called once we have her records.'

He unclasped his hands. 'I'll pass that on and make sure Thorsten expedites your request for her records.'

'Thank you. I imagine he'll want to start making funeral arrangements soon.'

'Yes, he will.' Lagunov looked flustered and she watched his hands knit together again.

'Also, I'll be happy to escort him to Zena's apartment to retrieve her belongings. In cases like these, I hear it helps family members to accept the reality of the situation.'

'That is kind. Again, I'll pass it on.'

'Thank you.'

Now the niceties were over she asked, 'Has Thorsten been to Zena's apartment before?'

'I don't believe so.'

'As I said, I'd be happy to take him there. Unless you want to do it yourself…I assume you know where she lives?' She glanced at him casually.

'No…but I have the address somewhere.'

Now she studied his face for the lie; it was impassive as he contradicted Zena's elderly neighbour. 'Then perhaps you could accompany Thorsten.'

'Was there anything else?'

'How will you get in? I presume someone has a set of her keys?' Again, she behaved nonchalantly. If Lagunov had been the one inside Zena's apartment, then he had got her keys from somewhere. Was it possible he had hired the two boys to kill his boss's daughter?

He shrugged with his mouth. 'We don't. Could you arrange for a copy to be made?'

'I can do that. Incidentally, how will you get hold of Thorsten? We've been trying since Monday and it seems all roads to him go via you.'

'He's grieving the loss of his daughter and prefers not be disturbed. I will pass the message on.'

'Mister Lagunov, where is he?'

'I don't see what relevance—'

She decided to go in as heavy as a steel pile driver. 'You can answer the question here or in an interview room. If you remember, on Saturday I said the same. You're wearing my patience.'

Lagunov's face blanched. 'But that was before Zena was found – I assumed that changed everything. Thorsten's a busy man; he could be anywhere.'

'Yet a moment ago you said he didn't want to be disturbed. Which is he – busy or seeking solitudc, and how do you know if you're not in contact with him?'

Daria entered with a coffee. She handed it to Natalya, and

Lagunov waited until the door was closed again. 'Is this another interrogation?'

She shuffled forwards and put the cup on the edge of his desk. 'There's always a journalist or two waiting outside headquarters, if I bring you in it will be hard to avoid them. I imagine someone like you must hate to be seen by the press.'

Lagunov bared his little, neat teeth again. 'I'm cooperating, aren't I?'

'I hope so. Tell me, is Thorsten in Sweden?'

'I don't know.'

She sipped her coffee. 'You don't know which country he's in?' She frowned. 'I thought you were cooperating. Aren't you supposed to be his right-hand man?'

'I'm his lawyer which means I don't have to answer these questions under commercial secrecy.'

'So the abduction and murder of his daughter is a commercial secret?'

'Why are you being so difficult, for God's sake? I'm trying to help you but my hands are tied. I can't say anything. He's lost a child. Try to have some sympathy.'

'No need to be bad tempered. We all want to get to the truth, don't we? The fact is, I already know Thorsten is somewhere in St. Petersburg. He's with a man called Felix Axelsson who works as a freelance security advisor. So I have two questions for you – think carefully before you answer: where is he, and what is he up to?'

She watched Lagunov squirm. 'He's not doing anything illegal.'

She scribbled in her pad. 'I'm noting that you refused to answer both questions.'

'I'm not refusing, I'm not allowed to.'

She nodded as if satisfied with his answer – which was far from the truth. 'Then whatever he's doing, ask him to call me. I'm sure you can do that. My sole interest is making sure the case against Zena's killers is watertight. I have no interest in any minor laws he may have broken. What's that expression?'

Her question earned a frown from Lagunov.

'You must have heard it: "The severity of the law is offset by its lack of observance." In other words, I can be unobservant when I need to be. I my mind, there is a difference between citizens who break minor laws as a matter of necessity and those who commit acts of serious criminality. Removing a child from an orphanage without the requisite paperwork' – she waved her hand dismissively – 'doesn't interest me at all.'

'I'll pass your message on.'

'Thank you.'

Lagunov leaned back in his chair. 'Honesty is admirable in an honest society but here' – he snorted – 'it destroys you. As you say, everyone breaks the law sometimes; it's a matter of doing what your conscience allows.'

'What do you mean?'

'I don't want to open a newspaper and read how those boys burned Zena to destroy the physical evidence of a rape. Journalists pay well for insider knowledge like that: the tragic life and death of a billionaire's daughter. If I told you Thorsten was willing to protect Zena's dignity would you be surprised?'

'He'll pay me not to talk to the press?'

'You don't need to do anything. Honesty ought to be rewarded. The Svens are very big on that kind of thing.'

She took another sip of the coffee. 'But then I'm compromised. For instance, you could threaten to tell my superiors about your generous gift unless I stop asking difficult questions. Try this one as an example: how did you know Zena was missing before anyone else did?'

Lagunov looked as if he'd been slapped. 'I don't know what you're talking about.'

'But you do. A witness saw you outside her apartment. Tell me what you were doing between seven and eight on Friday morning.'

'I was at the office but I should also remind you I have legal privilege.'

'Not if I determine that you are a suspect.'

He held both hands up, halfway to a surrender. 'Let's calm down. Whoever you spoke to was mistaken. I always get to the office early on Friday. I was here between seven and eight; in fact, I was here all day.'

She poised with her pen over her notepad. 'I want you to understand that you are giving me an alibi. Is there anyone who can corroborate it?'

'Ask anyone who gets in that early, they'll tell you the same thing. There again I'm not under any kind of suspicion so you can do what you like with my so-called alibi.' He snorted. 'Why are you persisting when you already have her killers? If I make some calls it won't be me facing difficult questions.'

'If that's a threat you'd better be very careful.'

'Not a threat – mere curiosity.'

'A girl is drunk on the streets when the two suspects—'

'Call them what they are,' Lagunov spat, '*gopniks*.'

She ignored him. 'The two suspects find her drunk on the street. The one hooked on *krokodil* steals her money, the other sexually assaults her. They take her somewhere for nearly three days then they kill her and burn the body.'

'That's what the police are saying.'

'But there are still unanswered questions. If they dragged her to the park, alive or dead, someone would have seen them. The only way she got there was voluntarily.'

'Voluntarily?' Lagunov smirked. 'She danced to the park hand-in-hand with those *gopnik* scum? That's ridiculous.'

'Then how did they get her there without being seen? It's the White Nights, remember, no one sleeps. Teenagers are out there all night. Someone would have called the *menti*. Besides, it's a stupid place. Why not dump her on a building site or wasteland, wherever was nearest…unless…'

She trailed off but Lagunov had no interest in prompting her; he tapped his fingers on the desk in irritation.

'Unless…it was deliberate. Her killers wanted it to be public,' she added.

He sighed. 'You give too much credit to a pair of junkies. From what I read they were high on *krokodil*. Who knows what goes on in their addled brains? Maybe they carried her between them and everyone mistook them for drunks.' Lagunov folded his hands behind his head. 'Just let it go and Thorsten will thank you.'

She was amused by his persistence. 'And how much would he offer? Ten thousand dollars?'

Lagunov laughed out loud. 'That's kopeks to him.'

'Then what about fifty?'

She anticipated laughter but Lagunov was matter-of-fact. 'Now I'll answer your questions,' he began. 'Thorsten isn't the man you saw on the plane. He's tired and withdrawn. Yes, he's in *Piter* but there's a media circus waiting for him in Stockholm and no one knows him here. *Piter* is also the last place Zena knew before she died and that gives him great comfort. As for Felix Axelsson, the security advisor that got you so excited, well, it would be insane for Thorsten to travel around the city without a bodyguard. There's no mystery to any of this. The *gopniks* confessed, they left their prints on Zena's handbag, and they took indecent pictures of her.'

'I'm not saying they didn't do it, but there's more to this case than a pair of wasted teenagers. Where was Zena kept? How did they get her to the park? Why go to the trouble of burning her body to destroy the evidence when they go and leave her handbag behind with their sticky fingerprints on it. You know what my favourite one is?'

'Humour me.'

'They hadn't washed for days when they were caught but they didn't they smell of smoke.'

Lagunov exhaled heavily. 'So what's your theory?'

'Someone else was involved, and he set them up.'

Lagunov was incredulous. 'For what reason?'

'I don't know.'

'Natalya…Captain, this is beneath you. You should keep these ill-considered ideas to yourself. You're not going to exploit Thorsten or get his hopes up. In fact you're not going to do anything. As we discussed I'm happy to come to an arrangement so that you leave Zena Dahl to rest in peace and let a father grieve for his daughter.'

She pulled out her mobile and studied it as if there had been a missed call then tapped the screen for voice memos. Instead of pocketing it, she shoved it under the chair's cushion.

Lagunov stood then turned to face the wall and pressed the keypad of his safe. 'Enough. I've got euros and dollars. Euros are worth more right now so have them if you like. Fifty thousand to leave the case alone, agreed?'

She watched, hypnotised, as he pulled out bank-fresh bundles of notes and piled them on his desk.

26

At reception she nodded a curt goodbye to Daria then waited until the lift doors had closed and Lagunov's secretary had disappeared from view. A man with thinning hair and a briefcase brushed past her and swiped his card through a slot in the door to exit the building.

She took out her ID card but the red-haired receptionist waved it away. 'You're Oleg, right?'

'Yes, Detective.'

'Those things.' She pointed at the slot by the door. 'Do you have to use a pass to get in and out of the building?'

'Unless I let you in.'

'Do they record who uses them?'

'On here.' He lowered his head and she peered over his desk to see a blue screen in front of him.

She spoke *sotto voce*, 'Oleg, this is confidential: Mister Lagunov thinks his wallet was stolen last Thursday evening. Can you check if his pass has been used?'

'When?'

'Friday morning. It's possible he had it then but he's not sure.'

'The *menti* come out for a stolen wallet now?'

She spoke in a monotone as if the subject bored her. 'It's a new initiative: we crack down on street crime to stop petty thieves becoming bigger ones.' She shook her head to suggest her superiors were idiots for thinking of it.

He fixed his concentration on the screen and pressed a few keys. 'Anything else you need?'

'No, thanks…Oleg.' She patted her pockets. 'I've left my phone upstairs.'

He took out a temporary pass and handed it to her, 'You'd better take this.'

'I'll be back in a minute.' She started walking away.

'Wait…they are just coming now.' He gathered several sheets of A4 paper from a printer and stapled them together. 'This is everyone from Friday morning. Mister Lagunov's code is C13284.'

'Thanks.'

She took the papers and headed for the stairs, continuing until she reached the floor above Lagunov's office. On the landing, she examined the sheets of A4, noting each had the same three columns: "ID Code", "Entry Timestamp" and "Exit Timestamp". She knelt and flicked through them until she saw the first occurrence of C13284. Taking out an old biro, she made a mark against Anatoly Lagunov's ID Code then drew a line to find the corresponding time. It stopped on an entry timestamp of "07:05:37". She checked the date to confirm Oleg had printed a log for the right date – he had.

It was disappointing but these things happened. Early on the Friday morning, Lagunov had gone to work half an hour before Lyudmila Kuznetsova reported seeing the grey-haired bureaucrat from her window. Sometimes, by being overly helpful, witnesses caused more trouble than those who kept quiet. The old woman's hearing was clearly bad, maybe her eyesight was too.

To complete the task Natalya scrolled through the remaining pages. There was another instance of C13284 and she drew a fresh line to find the corresponding timestamp. It was "07:12:04". She stared at the paper and smiled. Lagunov had been at work for less than seven minutes, barely enough time to establish an alibi by talking to a few early birds. Further down the list she found another C13284 and tracked it with her pen to see when he had returned: "10:15:48" – three hours later.

In Zena's apartment, Leo Primakov had mimed a solvent being used to wipe the fingerprints from Zena's light switches and door handles. Lagunov wasn't a professional burglar, perhaps he had forgotten to bring gloves and had called in at the office, not to establish an alibi but to find a stationery cupboard and pick up one of those sprays used for cleaning dirty finger marks off computer screens.

The pass Oleg had given her came with a lanyard and she pushed it over her neck then ran her fingers through her hair. She found a toilet and reapplied her lipstick before tucking her checked shirt tightly in her skirt to pull out the creases. She hid her Makarov and handcuffs in her handbag and headed onto the office floor. There was an open-plan design segregated into six areas that were in turn divided into cubicles. A banner suspended from the ceiling displayed the name of a steel town in the Urals, another the name of Segezha, a prison town with a large paper mill.

She strolled to a coffee machine and watched a woman feeding coins into it. 'Is this finance?'

The woman turned and Natalya saw that her upper lip was short, leaving her with a permanent pout. 'Marketing. You need the second floor.'

'Actually,' Natalya dropped her voice and held out the temporary pass, 'I've just started and the coffee there tastes like an unflushed toilet. I was hoping it might be better here.'

'No chance of that,' the woman said.

Natalya continued in a whisper. 'As I said, I've just started and there's a rumour that the company is being sold. No one will tell me anything and I don't want to ask in case I get in trouble. Am I wasting my time here?'

The woman pressed a button for lemon tea. 'That's finance for you. I heard the deal was off.'

'So my job is safe?' Natalya looked relieved, 'My husband works in offshore exploration. He's stuck at home looking after the kids until the oil price goes up.'

The woman took her plastic cup from the machine then glanced around the room. 'There were irregularities.'

Natalya leaned closer. 'What do you mean?'

'The buyer dropped out because the accounts didn't balance'.

'What do you mean?' she repeated.

The woman's eyes narrowed, 'I thought you were in Finance?'

'I'm admin.'

'Well, everyone is talking about it…up here at least. Millions are missing. If you hear anything more, will you tell me? I've got kids too.'

Natalya screwed up her face to look pained. 'Of course.'

She left the woman pouting and returned to the second floor, cutting a path between the accountants' desks. Lagunov's secretary had seen her and was making her way across the floor, ready to intercept her. 'Daria, I need to speak with Anatoly. It's urgent.'

'Please wait there.'

Daria took a few paces to his inner office before Natalya brushed past her and burst in.

Lagunov whirled round. 'Captain, what are you doing?'

He looked over her shoulder at the open door to his office and his secretary. 'Daria, it's fine,' he said. 'Please leave us.'

She heard the door close behind her.

'Did you change your mind?' he asked.

She frowned. 'About the money? No' – she shook her head for emphasis – 'I don't take bribes. I left something behind.' She bent over the chair to retrieve her mobile from the side of the cushion. 'I accidentally left it recording.' She showed him the screen so he could see the moving bar of the voice recorder. She tapped the stop button.

'Time to start talking.' She put her palms flat on his desk.

'You can keep recording us if it makes you feel better,' he sneered. 'I can even incriminate myself and it will make no difference, I assure you. Would you have taken more if I'd offered it?'

More than fifty thousand dollars? Her eyebrows lifted in surprise. 'No.'

Lagunov shook his head slowly in disappointment. 'Then let me give you some good fucking advice: visit your sister in Germany. This is bigger than you.'

She stared at him, too shocked to speak. Finally she found the words. 'Who the hell do you think you are?'

'No, Captain. *Where* the hell do you think you are? This is Russia. The case is closed, don't attempt to lift the lid.'

Mikhail, and now Lagunov. Two warnings in one day. One from State Security, which was insane to ignore; the other, from

Chapter 26

Dahl's lawyer, which was more perplexing than anything else. She had enough to arrest him for the false alibi and attempted bribery except she could tell by his cockiness that it would backfire. Lagunov was one of those hard, clever men who would prove to be as slippery as a Baltic eel when she brought him to headquarters. And for what? Lying over an alibi for a case that was already with the prosecutor? Attempting to bribe her? Well, there were many in the department who saw bribes as a perk of the job and they would be furious if she caused mixed messages to be sent out.

'You lied to me. You left the office almost as soon as you arrived. Why don't you tell me what you were doing in Zena's apartment on Friday morning?'

The lawyer sighed. 'I know you are just doing your job but it's of no concern to you.'

Natalya stared at him and felt an almost insatiable desire to slap him around the head. 'What are you keeping from me, Lagunov?' she shouted.

The lawyer was close enough for her to grab him by the collar. She did; he was as solid as a statue. 'Tell me what's going on.'

'Control yourself. I'm helping you.'

She let go of Lagunov and watched him straighten his shirt. Her phone started ringing and she glanced at it to see Primakov's name and the picture from his VK profile of him crossing the line at last year's St. Petersburg Half Marathon. She answered it while glowering at the lawyer.

'Leo, this is a bad time.'

In the background she heard a raw wind blowing and what sounded like a ship horn. 'Sorry, Captain. I know it's your day off but it's important.'

'Hold on, Leo.'

She held up a finger to Lagunov then stepped into Daria's outer office.

'OK, carry on.'

Primakov sounded breathless, 'Major Dostoynov said you were off duty. He's going to send someone else. He told me not to involve you.'

'What is it, Leo?'

'Well, can you come anyway? I'm just off Morskaya Naberezhnaya, there's an old boatyard before the Petrovsky Fairway Bridge.'

'I'm busy, Leo, why don't you call later?'

'It's not that…Look, you need to see this. We've found a body. I think it's connected to Zena Dahl's murder.'

27

Natalya turned off Morskaya Naberezhnaya at the north end of Vasilyevsky Island; the rough, compacted earth of the derelict boatyard soon forcing her to drive at a walking pace. Attached to a concrete post by heavy chains, a pair of German Shepherds stopped their intense sniffing of Primakov's Samara to watch her with mild interest. She edged past them, and ten metres on saw an ancient Zhiguli police car parked next to a civilian hatchback with an unnecessary "Doctor on call" sign in the windscreen. The path narrowed, and what appeared to be sand dunes mutated before her eyes into banks of builder's aggregate sprouting wild grass.

She stopped by a grey-blue amphibious troop carrier with a track missing that was losing its battle against the elements. To save explaining herself to the uniforms from the Zhiguli, she fixed her handcuffs and Makarov in place before walking down a cracked concrete lane. A grey sky hung overhead, threatening rain, and she had the strongest desire for a cigarette that she had felt in years. This, she thought, was a much better place to find a corpse.

Two *menti* were gazing thoughtfully across the Malaya Neva river at the construction of the massive, half-finished, cable-stayed bridge to link the island with the tip of Krestovsky and then across the Bolshaya Neva to the mainland. Next to the policemen was a skinny, unkempt man with white hair who was sucking on a hand-rolled, broken exhaust of a cigarette.

She took out her notepad, 'Did you call the police?'

The man jumped and twisted his head.

'Me? Yes, I came here an hour ago to feed the dogs.'

'You own this place?'

'No.' He stretched an arm in the direction of the two German

Shepherds, 'Kolya and Kazan do security. I look after the dogs.' He rubbed two fingers together.

'So not official. What did you see?'

'I came by to feed them, also to take Kolya for a walk. He takes a shit at this time – there's a spot by the river he likes. I saw a new mound of gravel. Kolya got excited and started digging at it…then I saw the hand.'

'I'll come to that. Tell me, when were you last here?'

'Seven this morning. It wasn't there then.' He shifted the cigarette to a corner of his mouth.

'How can you be sure?'

'The landowner has a boat moored here. I check it every day at the same time.'

'Thanks.'

One of the policeman standing near the dog owner glanced casually at her Makarov and handcuffs, then spent too long working his way up to her eyes.

'Where is it?' she asked.

'Over there by the water with Grandfather Frost and the Snow Maiden.' The policeman laughed to himself, and she smelled alcohol.

The Snow Maiden, Leo Primakov, was in his white, nylon oversuit taking pictures of the ground. Near his feet was Grandfather Frost, a grey-bearded doctor, who was pressing two fingers against the wrist of a hand poking from a low mound of gravel.

'Dead?' she asked.

The doctor looked up, seeing her for the first time, 'As a Syrian peace negotiation.'

The two uniforms were still studying the bridge construction and she inserted her little fingers into the corners of her mouth and blew hard. The noise was piercing. 'Hey, Holmes and Watson – Over here!'

Primakov pulled down his mask, 'Captain. Thank you for coming.'

'You said it was connected to Zena?'

'I said it might be.' He stepped back to let the two *menti* join the group. 'The corpse has Scandinavian tastes.'

She addressed the two men, 'Put on some gloves and start piling the gravel to one side. Anything you find – a dog end or a piece of fingernail – call me. Do not lean over the body. Do not touch the victim or his clothing. Understand?'

Turning away from them without waiting for a reply, she asked, 'Leo, why?'

'There's a black sneaker…over there.' She saw the shoe next to a small flag with a number one on it; no doubt something else he had ordered from the internet.

'It's a size forty-seven Axel Arigato.'

'Who?'

'Swedish designer—'

The policeman smelling of alcohol was at her elbow. 'So? I've got an IKEA kitchen but that doesn't make me a Sven.'

'Are you still here?' She frowned to convey sarcasm. The smile on his face faded and he slunk away to join his colleague.

For a minute she watched the two policemen scooping gravel with their gloved hands and depositing it in a pile between them.

Primakov shrugged, 'Well, it was only a thought.'

'And I'm not dismissing it,' she mused, 'with feet that big it could be Dahl.'

Primakov's oversuit rustled in the wind, 'I heard he's built like a defenceman.'

She recognised the term from Mikhail's love of ice hockey and her high estimation of Primakov slipped a few notches. 'Either way, he was murdered. Suicides don't bury themselves in gravel.'

'No, obviously not.' Primakov sounded offended.

'Sorry, Leo, that was patronising.'

He shrugged it off, 'I just thought those mafia days were behind us.'

'Could be political.'

'Is there a difference?' he asked.

It brought back Mikhail's warning about FSB involvement. If this body proved to be Thorsten's she had definitely strayed into their territory.

The wind was whipping her hair and she tied it back.

'So what do you think happened?' he asked.

'See that?' She pointed to a concrete slipway. 'There's plenty of big rocks around. If the killer had brought rope and rolled him into the river, the eels would be the only ones to know.'

Primakov nodded thoughtfully, 'So the killer improvised; he didn't intend to kill him, or to kill him here.'

'I agree.' She watched the two uniforms for a moment; the mound of gravel had become human-shaped. 'OK, stop there,' she called out, 'I'll take over. One of you take a statement from the dog owner.' They passed her without a word.

She pulled on her last pair of latex gloves before kneeling down, then scooped gravel from an area where, judging by the position of the hand, the head was likely to be. Every now and again she heard Primakov's camera click. There was reddish-blond hair now and she picked away at the gravel, placing it in a new pile. A face emerged.

Primakov peered at the body. 'The father?'

The hair wasn't blood-tinged, it was red. The relief she felt was absurd when this man's death would cause no less misery to his loved ones. At least there had been no wedding ring on the protruding hand. It was Felix Axelsson, Dahl's security expert. She examined a handful of gravel then let it fall through her fingers to the new mound she had created.

'No, it's not him.'

There was another click of Primakov's camera and she picked off a few more stones. 'Doctor?' she called, 'I can see a bullet entry wound between the jaw and the left cheekbone. Can you take a look? Also I could do with an approximate time of death.'

The doctor's bones cracked as he knelt beside her, 'That's definitely lead poisoning. If you want the time it's best not to delay. I've got a thermometer if you can find me an arsehole?'

'I can find one for you.' She looked for the policemen; one was interviewing the night watchman while his partner, the joking ment, was staring at the bridge again. 'Hey,' she called. 'Doctor's got a job for you.'

Chapter 27

She pushed the gravel off the torso then checked the pockets. There was no phone, keys, or wallet which meant the killer wasn't a complete amateur or Axelsson had deliberately hidden his identity. She smelled alcohol as the uniformed *ment* and Primakov joined her. Together they heaved him onto his side, then she checked his back pockets. They looked empty and she rubbed a latexed finger along the inside seam to make sure. There was nothing.

'You see that corona bruise?' the doctor beckoned her over.

She crouched by him and watched him rotate a finger over Axelsson's face. Whoever killed him had made it personal. They had jammed a gun into his face then pulled the trigger – using enough force to leave a ring-shaped mark behind. With his bodyguard dead Dahl must be in fear of his life. She needed to find him before anyone else did, assuming they hadn't already.

'Do you recognise him, Captain?' Primakov asked. Had he picked up on the fact that she had stared at the body for too long? If the FSB were involved she didn't want to put him in danger.

'No,' she lied.

There was a quizzical expression on the criminalist's face. 'Thanks, Captain. I'm sorry to waste your time.'

'If anyone asks, tell them I was passing on my way home. Come visit when you're done.'

She climbed into her Volvo and saw fat raindrops fall on the path. The amphibious vehicle with the broken tracks resumed its fight against entropy, and as she navigated around them, the dogs, Kolya and Kazan, finished spraying Primakov's Samara to waddle back to their position by the concrete post.

Three cars, all with flashing lights, passed her at the boatyard entrance. She was about to pull out when Mikhail's blue Mercedes joined them. He had a grim expression and was alone. Someone else was dead now. She didn't have a clue what was going on and somehow the FSB were involved as well. She felt a surge of anger and opened her glove compartment to select the album *For Millions* by the rock group *Leningrad*. She pushed the CD into the slot below her radio and drove towards Tsentralny District as the ska-punk track "My name is Shnur" started playing. She twisted the volume control all the way and the first eight words of the song started as she accelerated along the highway. She screamed along to them: "Fuck! Fuck! Fuck! Fuck! Fuck! Fuck! Fuck! Fuck!"

28

Anton was sitting on the living room floor when she returned to her apartment. His back was resting against the sofa and his skinny legs were folded underneath him. He looked shifty and she noticed the balcony door was open where a faint smell of cigarette smoke was wafting inside.

'Hey Natalya.' He glanced casually at the Makarov that she had meant to check in on Monday. 'You ever kill anyone with that?'

'No,' she lied for the second time in the morning, before offering a hand to pull him to standing, 'usually my cooking is fatal.'

The smile he returned was thin and he looked stressed.

'Have you been here long?'

'Ten minutes. Papa told me you were on holiday today.'

'I thought I was too.'

She watched his eyes flick from the mounds of clothes on the sofa. 'I like what you've done to the place.'

'Your father said the same thing. I'm thinking of spraying graffiti on the walls next.' She noticed the red light flashing on her answer machine.

'Natasha, how long are things going to be like this?'

'I've got no plans.'

He stretched, then bent to touch his toes. 'Will Papa come home soon…do you think?'

'It's his decision. I just threw him out temporarily.'

Anton picked at a hole in the knee of his jeans. 'He told me.'

She scowled. 'What did he tell you?'

'About the money.'

She shook her head. 'Fuck it, let's go outside. Bring your jacket, it's wet.'

The balcony floor of the apartment above offered some shelter and she peered down into the swirling rain over the Griboyedov Canal.

'Got one of those cigarettes you've been smoking?'

Anton smiled sheepishly and took out a crumpled pack of Sobranie Classics from his rain coat.

'Interesting brand.'

'Yeah, I went to see Papa at Uncle Stepan's last night. They were both wasted; they didn't see me take them.' He lit his Sobranie and coughed on the first drag.

'Haven't had one in years.' She took the lighter from him. 'As your stepmother I am obliged to tell you that you will regret smoking more than anything else in your life.'

'I know. I know,' he said with the ennui of a hardened addict.

'So you know they can prevent your penis from working when you get older?'

'Natasha, stop now.'

'I'm only saying.' She lit hers and puffed on the cigarette. The nicotine made her light-headed and a little nauseous. 'Do you know where he is?'

'At work?'

'He's by the Malaya Neva. Someone was murdered there this morning.'

'Really?' he said, his voice rising in pride.

'Really.'

She puffed on the cigarette then pinched it out and dropped it on the floor.

'Hey, that's a waste.'

'Depends on your perspective. Now tell me what you want to say.'

Anton looked away from her. 'I heard about the money back when Baboulya died.' Anton sucked on his cigarette then looked away.

'Does he know you're here?'

He flicked ash on the balcony floor then smeared it with a twist of his foot. 'Don't think so. Does it matter?'

Chapter 28

She could understand that Anton might feel excluded. When her own parents had separated, there had been no affairs to her knowledge, or cruelty, yet they hadn't sought out marriage guidance counselling or even tried to be kinder to each other. It was as if she and Claudia had simply not been worth the effort.

'So did he tell you or did you find out?'

He shrugged. 'I told you it doesn't matter? I'm just letting you know.'

She waited for him to stub out the Sobranie. 'OK, thanks for letting me know.'

'So things will be like they were before?'

She sighed. 'I don't want to make you feel bad but your father shouldn't have made you come here.' She opened the glass door for him.

Inside, Anton picked up a framed photograph resting on the television. In it, he had a beaming smile as he sat on his father's red *Ducati Monster.* Mikhail had been so fond of the damned motorbike he'd cut down on his drinking so he could ride it more often. He'd even let Anton sit on it and click through the gears with the engine running and the clutch lever pulled in. A few months later, a car went through a red light and hit the Ducati side-on. The bike was wrecked, but Mikhail was thrown clear with a few minor scratches. The car driver had been unharmed; at least until Mikhail found him.

Anton put the photograph down. 'I like this picture.'

'So do I.'

He stuffed his hands in his pockets. 'Papa didn't tell me to come here. I thought you should know the truth.'

'How did you get here?'

'The Metro.'

'Then you must be a magician.'

'What do you mean?' he said warily.

'You manage to walk a hundred metres in the rain without getting your coat wet.'

Anton adopted his default sulk. 'OK, Papa gave me a lift but you wouldn't believe me if I told you that. He didn't tell me what to say.'

'Let's leave it there, I'm touched you came.'

'So does the toilet still work or do I need to use a bucket?'

She smiled, glad at the change of conversation. 'I'm in the middle of cleaning,' she lied, 'that's why everything's a mess.'

He closed the door and she pressed the button on the answering machine. "You have one message" it began, then she heard her sister's voice with the same Russian accent despite all the years in Hannover. "Natasha, it's Claudia. Do you remember I was going to ask my friend's husband, the police sergeant, about working here? He told me all the states have their own rules and you have to apply for citizenship first. Basically, it's complicated. Anyway, speak soon, kisses."

The bathroom door opened. 'You lied to me.' Anton grabbed his jacket. 'You told me you had no plans. You're leaving the country.'

'No, it was about all of us. I—'

He pulled on the door then slammed it.

She pushed aside a pile of clothes to slump in front of the TV, flicking through one channel after another. Too upset to focus on anything. She left it on a fake documentary about the rise of fascism in Ukraine and it made her feel even more dispirited. She retrieved her discarded cigarette from the balcony, then lit it off the stove. It was the last day of her compassionate leave and things were no clearer. Mikhail couldn't stay at Rogov's indefinitely and nor could her marriage carry on as before, not until she felt he was being honest with her. This last trick hadn't helped. Mikhail had coached Anton to talk about the inheritance but it was a cynical move, a poor attempt to shift the debate from what it was really about – dirty money.

She stared into space. Her career of fifteen years in the Criminal Investigations Directorate was over if Mikhail took Vasiliev's job. She puffed on the cigarette feeling the nicotine work on her brain. If Zena Dahl's murder was going to be her last case, the least she could do was get some justice for the poor girl even if that meant ignoring Mikhail's warning about FSB involvement. It was hard to believe the *gopniks*, as everyone else called them, weren't involved in Zena's murder but the official explanation left too many questions unanswered.

In the study she switched on the computer. While it powered up, she flicked through her notepad for Thorsten's company, then typed "GDH Dahl Engineering" into Yandex. There were pages of links even after she used the advanced options to exclude everything except news items. She applied a filter to restrict the results to the last week. First on the list was a Swedish business site and she clicked to read the rest of the item, then clicked again to translate it into Russian. The corporate language had been rendered almost unintelligible by the online translator but she managed to understand the gist of the article.

At first, the journalist expressed sympathy for the loss of Zena Dahl ("a tragic defeat"), then having established that his motives were pure, he proceeded to drag Thorsten's reputation through the dirt. Dahl, he claimed, owned a portfolio of Russian companies that he was having difficulty selling to an unnamed buyer ("a mysterious shopper") for eight hundred million euros. Yesterday, the price had been lowered to six hundred and fifty million to stop them walking away. A lawyer representing the company, one Anatoly Lagunov, denied the figures were correct then accused the journalist, according to the translation software, of making "obvious, prodigious falsifications."

She sat back and puffed on the remainder of the cigarette. So that was the mystery of Lagunov and his generous bribe. Fifty thousand dollars was nothing compared to the money Dahl was losing each day to a jittery buyer. The last thing they needed was a detective calling at the office unannounced asking awkward questions.

Her mobile rang and she saw another picture of Mikhail's Ducati; this time from a road trip to Finland. She muted the television and accepted the call.

'Angel?'

It felt trivial to correct him. 'Misha?'

'As we speak I'm watching them wheel the Sven away. You know who I'm talking about.'

'Yeah, Felix Axelsson.'

There was an uncomfortable silence and she got the feeling Mikhail wasn't entirely happy about hearing the man's name being spoken on an open network. 'Well, I never said anything so he's an Ivan Ivanovich now. Did you tell Primakov?'

'No, I didn't want to get him in trouble.'

On her laptop she typed the name of Felix Axelsson into Yandex. It brought up his company website: 'Axelsson Logistics.'

'You there, Angel?'

'I'm here.'

There were tabs at the top of the page, and she clicked on the one displaying Axelsson's qualifications. A list appeared, headed by recent experience as a contractor in Afghanistan; all in muted language to suggest his real role had been far more dangerous.

'Anton called, he's upset. He said you're moving to Germany.'

She clicked on another tab that listed testimonials from Axelsson's happy clients with blanked out names.

'That's just Claudia. You know she's always wanted us to emigrate. Anton heard a message she left and overreacted.'

'I'll tell him it's nothing to worry about. We can still sort this out, Angel, whatever it is.'

'You know what it's about, and don't involve Anton next time. It's not fair.'

There was a pause and she thought he was going to deny it. 'OK, Angel, I won't. Just tell me how I can make everything better.'

Another tab on Axelsson's site was headed "Contact Details". She clicked on it and saw an address in Stockholm along with a phone number.

'Women hate the lie more than what it conceals – did you know that, Misha? We can handle the odd obstacle on the road but we don't like driving in rough country. Men are different. You just keep on blindly and pretend everything's fine until your head smashes through the windscreen.'

'So what do you propose?'

'Just tell me the truth. I can't do anything until I know that.'

Chapter 28

'I'm not,' he began, then stopped himself. 'We'll do that another time. I'm calling to warn you Dahl's lawyer has complained to Colonel Vasiliev about you. Lagunov said you went to see him this morning. He's accusing you of harassment.'

'He offered me fifty thousand dollars to go away.'

Mikhail chuckled. 'The sly bastard. Then I guess that means you turned him down.'

'Of course. And I taped it.'

'Well, aren't you the Young Pioneer? I'll let Vasiliev know.' Mikhail paused. 'Listen, Angel, whatever happens to us, do this one thing for me. The FSB have got an interest in the Dahl case, get far away from it.'

'Don't you ever get tired of it, Misha?'

'What? Breathing?'

'The FSB are criminals. Why do we roll over each time and let them do what they want?'

'Because they kill people and they are above the law.'

'Then why are they sniffing around my murder case?'

'Does it matter? Leave it alone. Do it for Anton if not for yourself.' He hung up.

On the computer, she stared at the office number for Felix Axelsson for a full minute then found her house phone and dialled it.

Her call was answered instantly by a woman with a deep voice: '*Hos Axelsson*.'

'Do you speak English?' she asked.

'Yes,' she heard in a heavy, Swedish accent.

'My name is Captain Natalya Ivanova. I'm from the Criminal Investigations Directorate in St. Petersburg.'

There was a pause. 'Yes, how can I help you?'

'I am trying to find Mister Felix Axelsson.'

'He is my husband. Is he in trouble?'

In the background, Natalya could hear the high energy sounds of a television cartoon show. She hadn't expected his wife to answer the office number he had provided on his website or to discover he had young children. She softened her tone. 'I understand Mister Axelsson is working with Thorsten Dahl.'

Mrs Axelsson sounded surprised. 'For Dahl?'

'Yes.'

'Wait one moment.' The sound of the television went quiet and there was the moan of a disappointed boy.

She came back on the line. 'You are the police?'

'Yes.'

'Is there a problem?'

She hated using subterfuge but telling the truth often raised more questions, and Axelsson's wife didn't deserve to hear about her husband's death this way. 'Only with his visa. Does he have a mobile? I need to contact him.'

His wife recited a number and Natalya wrote it down then thanked her.

After hanging up, she called Rogov.

'Boss? I thought you were on holiday.'

'I am. If I text you a number, can you contact Telecoms and tell me where it is.'

'Which case?' he asked too quickly.

So Rogov had also been warned to leave the case alone, either officially from Dostoynov, or via a friendly word from Mikhail.

'Renata Shchyotkina.' She gave him a plausible lie in case he checked up. 'It's a domestic abuse case. The number is a Swedish mobile because her boyfriend is a Sven. She thinks he's stalking her. Can you get back to me immediately?'

'Sure, boss.'

She ended the call, then turned up the sound on the television news in case Axelsson's murder had been picked up. She caught the end of an item about how sanctions hadn't affected the economy. "Nope", the reader could have said, "it doesn't bother us; not one little bit."

She filled a steam iron with water then set about clearing the mountain of clothes. After an hour, a row of neatly pressed dresses and shirts were on hangers and she contemplated starting on the mess in the kitchen when the house phone rang.

'Boss, it's Rogov. I've got the details for that number.'

'That was quick.'

Chapter 28

'I called in personally. Your woman has got nothing to worry about. They traced her piece of shit boyfriend to some place in Stockholm.'

'Was it called Östermalm?'

She heard a rustle of paper,

'Yeah, that's it.'

'Thanks Rogov.'

She hung up, then took a deep breath before tapping in the number for Axelsson's mobile phone. She was surprised to hear it ring when the killer should have dumped it in the Malaya Neva.

When the call was answered she heard a fumbling noise in the background as if the phone had been hidden and hurriedly located. There was a hiss of static then the sound of traffic. She pressed her ear to the phone, listening intently. No one spoke.

She decided to break the impasse. 'Hello?' she said in English.

The line went dead.

29

She took the M10 to Pulkovo, abandoning her Volvo in the airport's car park before emptying her personal account for a handful of krona at the currency exchange. The flight to Sweden was direct and it was still early evening when she arrived to a colder, brighter sun. She took the Arlanda Express into Stockholm then caught a taxi outside the train station. The driver took her across bridges and islands that reminded her of home then pointed to a number on his meter that was almost equal to all her converted money.

The building, like its owner, wasn't as grand as she had expected. It was a narrow, four-storey house on the Strandvägen Boulevard in Östermalm that didn't seem large enough to house six bedrooms. Outside Zena's apartment there hadn't been a single security camera and her father's house was no different. After ringing the bell, she stepped back and waited.

A young woman with spiky blonde hair and a surprisingly formal black and white uniform opened the door. She appraised Natalya then spoke in English, 'Yes, can I help?'

'I want to speak to Thorsten.'

'He's not—'

She pushed her way inside, passing a metre-high model of a sailing ship in a glass cabinet.

'Leave immediately or I will call the police,' the maid demanded.

'Where is he?'

A man in his fifties with slicked-back hair and a chef's apron appeared at the end of the hallway; he blocked it off with his arms slightly raised, ready to intercept her if she tried to push past. 'Please, you must leave.'

'Thorsten!' she yelled. 'Where the hell are you?'

Chapter 29

The maid picked up a phone from the hall table. 'Do you want me to call the police or will you go now?'

'I'll stay. Your boss can explain how he stole a child from an orphanage.'

The girl gave a slight shrug and started dialling.

'Gunvor, let her pass.' She heard Dahl's voice from a room to the left, 'I know this lady. Show her in.'

The chef dropped his arms and walked along the hallway, stopping at an open door where blue silk curtains shimmered and a white china dining set was laid out on an oak table stained white. Dahl was standing inside the doorway, wearing his trademark jeans and a fisherman's sweater; he looked more exhausted than when she'd seen him on his Gulfstream.

'It's alright, Gunvor. Maria, please leave us alone.'

The maid and chef walked away. Dahl was about to speak and she decided to get in first. 'Did you have a good flight, Thorsten?'

'Let's go upstairs for some privacy.' He opened a pair of teak doors to reveal a small lift.

She stepped inside, feeling awkward at being in such close proximity to Dahl. At the third floor she followed him through a reception room and out through a set of glass doors. She stepped onto a roof garden with immaculately trimmed grass dotted with small trees contained by earthenware pots; cast iron daisies were interwoven at the buildings edge to form a barrier.

'I had this built for Zena when she first came here. She loved throwing paper planes from the roof.'

He pulled out a metal chair and she sat down by a black lacquered table with a Japanese motif. 'Now, how can I help you, Captain Ivanova?'

'I want to know why you've been hiding away in St. Petersburg with your security advisor, Felix Axelsson.'

She watched the muscles tighten in his jaw and he repeated the phrase that was already becoming worn: 'I don't know what you're talking about.'

'Of course you do, we found Axelsson's name on your Gulfstream's flight manifest."

'I don't know who you mean.'

'Then can you explain how I traced his mobile phone to this address?'

'He's not here.'

'Now we make some progress. I know he's not here. Why do you have Axelsson's phone, Thorsten?'

'He left it here.'

'Look I've just destroyed my bank account to see you. Believe it or not we're on the same side.'

'Captain…Natalya, you shouldn't have come. I don't want you getting involved.'

Now, he was trying to protect her, but from what?

'I'm not moving, Thorsten, call the police if you want to but Sweden isn't Russia, you can't buy your way out of trouble here.'

'Oh?' He tilted his head. 'I think you'd be surprised.'

'You want to test me?'

He ran a hand through his hair. 'A Russian detective questioning a Swedish citizen without any authorisation? Yes, I think I would be surprised. They'll put you on the next flight to Pulkovo and your people will reprimand you.'

'Don't pretend to be a tough guy, Thorsten, you're better than that. Let's agree that we can both make life difficult for each other. Isn't that called mutually assured destruction?'

'No, it's called me telling you what I can and you working out the rest for yourself. Agreed?' He took the chair opposite her and stretched out his legs without waiting for an answer. 'You know there are nice views of *Djurgården* from here.'

'Never mind that. Start at the beginning.'

'When?'

'The day you met Zena.'

He snorted. 'Why?'

'Because all I've had from you and Lagunov are lies.'

He stared through the wrought ironwork at the scene below. She followed his gaze to see a family cycling along the harbour path: a mother, father, and two young boys. It made her stomach ache to watch them.

Chapter 29

'I'm sure Anatoly told you. I met Zena in an orphanage. She clung onto my leg. We were outside having a picnic.'

'Was that the one in Lisy Nos?'

'No, Krasnoye Selo.'

'At least that part of your story matches his. What was her birth name?'

'I don't remember.'

'That's not a problem. Show me a copy of the adoption certificate and we can clear it up?'

'I don't have it any more.'

'Then where did you spend Christmas that year?'

'Orthodox?'

'Non-orthodox.'

'I had a suite in the Astoria.'

'With Zena?'

'Of course.'

'Lagunov said you spent it alone with him and his ex-wife. Thorsten, we can keep going like this but it doesn't profit either of us and I know it's not the truth.'

The doors to the balcony garden opened and the maid appeared with a teapot, cups and pastries.

'Thank you, Maria.'

He waited until the maid pulled the glass doors behind her then laughed to himself. 'They are checking up on us…I didn't ask for tea. Nevertheless' – he poured it into two cups – 'it would be rude to refuse.'

'I thought you were going to talk to me.'

'No, I said I'd tell you what I can. I'll give you this: Zena's surname was Volkova and I didn't spend that Christmas with her. Now don't ask me any more on the subject.'

Dahl closed his eyes momentarily and seemed to struggle to open them; he was exhausted.

'Then let's jump to Felix Axelsson. Why did you involve him?'

'When Anatoly told me the Russian police had reported Zena missing, I assumed she had been kidnapped – just as you had. I hired Felix to assist. The idea was to use Anatoly in the negotiations and keep Felix in reserve for his more earthy skills – he speaks Russian and has a military background. Also I wanted someone unconnected to the company. My father is retired but he is likely to interfere.'

'Then Zena was killed.'

'Yes,' he rocked in the chair and exhaled slowly, 'and then my daughter was murdered.'

'But that was Sunday evening. Why did you stay in St. Petersburg until today?'

Dahl flashed teeth. 'Because I wanted to find who killed her and I don't trust the Russian police to do their job.'

She ignored the barb. 'So where were you hiding?'

'Alright, I'll give you that' – he took a breath – 'I rented an apartment in Admiralty District and gave the owner a little extra to keep my name off the books.'

'What did you discover?'

He stopped rocking. 'Nothing…or at least nothing until yesterday.' Dahl's pale eyes caught hers and held onto them; their intensity made her break away after a few seconds. 'Anatoly took the call at his office. He said the man had a Russian accent and used that criminal slang.'

'*Fenya*?'

'Yes. He said Zena was alive but not for long. Anatoly told him to call back, when we would ask him a proof of life question. Imagine how I felt hearing Zena had been murdered then being offered the tantalising possibility that it had all been a lie.'

'I heard of a case recently,' she said. 'A businessman took a call and heard his son screaming in the background. They told him to stay on the line and transfer eight million roubles online or listen to him die. After he paid, the father called his son's school and spoke to the headmaster. The boy had been there all day – someone had imitated him.'

Dahl waved his hand dismissively. 'Felix was with me when Anatoly called. He suspected it was a trick but I insisted we went ahead with it. I thought of a question that only Zena and I could know. I even checked the internet to make sure it wasn't public knowledge. When the man called Anatoly again, he was ready with the question.'

'What was it?'

'Zena had two friends called Benny and Bo. I asked who they were. He hung up saying he would call back in five minutes with the answer.'

'And he did?'

'Yes, he said "It's the same fucking horse".'

'Was he right?'

'Yes. Bo was a gelding I bought for Zena's tenth birthday. I named him after Bo Widerberg, the film director, but Zena didn't like it. After a few weeks she changed his name to Benny.'

'Did he convince you she was alive?'

He shrugged. 'I didn't know what to think. The only other possibility was that he had access to someone who knew Zena intimately. I thought of that girl who reported her missing—'

'Yulia Federova.'

'Yes, maybe she helped him but I couldn't see how that was possible. How could she answer any question I asked about Zena?'

'Perhaps the man bugged your phone or that apartment in Admiralty and listened to you and Axelsson discussing what questions you were going to put to him.'

'I hadn't thought of that.'

'You didn't need to, it was Axelsson's job. What happened next?'

'I instructed Anatoly to offer him two million roubles to let me speak to Zena directly but he wasn't interested. He said' – Dahl looked away – 'if we wanted more proof he would take a blowtorch to Zena's face and send me the Polaroids.'

Using "Polaroids" in common speech, she thought, put the man in his forties or older. 'What did you do?'

Dahl's foot started tapping erratically, then he stood, unable to contain himself any longer; he paced alongside the daisy chain barriers. 'What do you think I did?'

'You gave him everything he asked for.'

He rubbed his eyes then stared at her. 'Of course I did.'

She followed him to the barrier and stood alongside him, staring out to the sea. 'What did he want?'

'Articles of incorporation, the presses for my company seals, banking and tax details. All to be delivered by me personally – Anatoly told me the man was very insistent about that.'

'He stole your Russian companies.'

Dahl twisted his head to look at her; his eyes were red-rimmed. 'Believe it or not, I gave them up willingly.'

She had wanted to be easier on him but the omissions were making her angry. 'Here's something you forgot to mention in that story: you sent Axelsson to the handover. It was this morning at a boatyard near the Petrovsky Fairway Bridge.'

Dahl shook his head in disbelief. 'If you knew all this, why did you make me tell you?'

'I don't have the full picture yet. What happened, Thorsten?'

He took two paces away from her, then gripped the rail of the bannister. For a second she thought he might vault over it; he stuffed his hands in his pockets as if the thought had occurred to him too.

He shuffled towards her. 'It was arranged for 10 a.m. If Felix found Zena I instructed him to take her to the Anglican Church on Malaya Konyushennaya. Do you know it?'

'No.'

'It was my idea. The church is next to the Swedish Consulate. I thought I could get Zena to safety there then obtain emergency papers to get her out of the country. Instead, I sat for two hours on a wooden bench. I even prayed a little. Believe me, an atheist praying is an ugly sight.' His chest heaved as he chuckled to himself but his face betrayed little humour. 'I told Felix not to take chances. I told him to leave immediately if she wasn't there.'

'Why do you have Axelsson's phone?'

'I also have his wallet and wedding ring. Felix said it was standard procedure to remove any proofs of identity prior to an operation. He bought a prepaid phone for the handover.'

'I'll need the number.'

'I've been calling it all morning. It's no longer in use.'

'Most likely at the bottom of the Malaya Neva.'

'Felix said that if I didn't hear from him, I was to leave the country and take his possessions home for his wife.'

She sipped her tea. 'So you know he's dead?'

Dahl pulled his hands out of his pockets and leaned over the bannister at the harbour below. 'I know you think I'm a fool. I got an innocent man killed because someone conned me.'

'Zena's in a mortuary,' she said gently. 'Thorsten, there's no shame in what happened. These criminals are clever and ruthless. They spend all day thinking up nasty con tricks. Now will you promise to trust me?'

He stared at her. 'Yes, I think I can do that.'

'Good,' her voice was brisk. 'I need you to return to St. Petersburg. Take the land border through Finland and use the smallest crossing you can find. Don't use your credit cards and leave your mobile phone behind. I'll give you an address. Whatever you do, keep away from the FSB – they handle immigration so be careful.'

'You too, Captain,' he said, with a melancholic smile.

30

At Arlanda, Natalya caught an *AirBaltic* flight. With the stopover at Riga it was well after twelve when she queued outside the row of sentry boxes that marked passport control at Pulkovo airport. Despite the half-empty plane, nearly an hour passed before she found herself facing a woman wearing a gunmetal grey uniform and possessing a pair of eyebrows that had been plucked clean then pencilled in a high arch; combined with the sour mouth it made her look permanently sarcastic.

'Documents.'

Natalya handed over her passport then waited. The woman studiously avoided her gaze and tapped numbers into a computer keyboard one finger at a time. There was a clock on the wall and her mind habitually ran to the bridge timetables. Around this time, six days ago, Zena Dahl had walked out of the Cheka bar and her troubles began.

'Will this help?' Natalya took out her police ID card.

The official glanced at it. 'No…Captain.'

Now she was the last passenger from the small propeller plane and still the woman tapped on the keyboard.

Another uniformed official entered the booth, this time a man with a red band on his peaked cap. She glanced at the two adjacent stars on his epaulettes to check his rank: a lieutenant; then she glanced at the open pores on his veined nose: a drinker.

The woman's eyebrows were raised even higher on her forehead as she handed Natalya's passport to the officer. He examined it then tucked it in his breast pocket. 'Any baggage in the hold?' he asked.

'No.' Natalya twisted one shoulder to show a small rucksack.

He left the booth to face her. 'Then come with me.'

Chapter 30

'I'm a captain in the Criminal Investigations Directorate, what's the delay?'

'No delay.' He opened his mouth and sprayed breath freshener onto a yellowing tongue.

She followed him to a white-walled room with no windows. There was a desk and two chairs. Next to a fluorescent strip light she noticed a black plastic sphere masking a security camera.

'Someone will be with you soon,' he said, then left, closing the door. She heard a lock click into place.

She didn't believe him, having tried the same trick often enough to unnerve a suspect. Well, it wouldn't work on her. She was too tired to be stressed let alone wonder why she was being detained. Slumping in one of the chairs, she dropped her head on her forearms and instantly fell asleep.

A spasm in her neck woke her. She checked her phone: it was approaching three in the morning. Her body was craving nutrition and more sleep; her mobile battery was almost flat.

She flicked through her contacts wondering who would take a call at this time: Mikhail? She selected his number and listened to his voice as it diverted straight to the answerphone. Who next? Rogov? Too unreliable. Claudia? Certainly, but Germany may as well be on another planet. Anton? Well, it was safer for him if she didn't call. She tapped a number and saw beads of sweat caught on muscled, golden legs. Despite the oppressive room, she chuckled to herself; only Primakov could run a half-marathon and look as if he was modelling sportswear.

She tapped her phone again and heard his ring tone. She pressed an index finger and thumb to the corners of her eyes to help her focus, then wedged the mobile to her ear with her left hand. At this time of the morning she had expected him to take longer to answer but he picked it up almost immediately.

'Leo? I'm stuck in an interrogation room in Pulkovo—'

'Forgot to put it on silent,' Primakov was saying, not to her though. Instead of hanging up, he left the line open.

Knowing Leo's fastidious nature he wouldn't be careless enough to keep the line connected accidentally – he was telling her something.

She shut her eyes and shrank the world to the voices in her ear. There was a murmur of conversation then, 'Major, how long are we going to be here?' The voice might have belonged to Rogov but it was hard to tell because something was rubbing against the microphone. It sounded like a zipper being pulled up and down. Was that Leo's nylon oversuit?

'Don't forget you're a fucking Sergeant.' That was Dostoynov, she was sure of it; so Dostoynov and Rogov.

There was fumbling and before the line went dead, Primakov's voice came through at so low a whisper it was barely audible: 'Federova's apartment.'

She switched off her phone to save the battery then closed her eyes. A vacuum cleaner started outside her door. It wasn't moving and she wondered if it was an attempt to unsettle her, along with the too-bright fluorescent light. Well, they could try, but they would have to pull out her fingernails just to keep her awake. Two freckles on her right forearm; fine, translucent hairs. She focussed on them, feeling sleep draw her away. Her skinny arm became a pillow; the red of the fluorescent light through her eyelids became a desert tent at sunset; the motor of the vacuum cleaner turned to white noise; white noise was the best noise of all.

A hand smacked on the table, hard. 'Wake up!'

'Go away.'

Silence, then her shoulders were gripped from behind. She was shaken violently, the back of her skull connected with her spine. Her head ached and the nerves in her neck screamed. She twisted her shoulders to see a man the size of a weightlifter. He was wearing a shoulder harness with a black Grach pistol tucked in it. That was as good as an identification card. The police had been waiting for years to get their aging Makarovs updated to Grachs – the excuse they had been given was there were too many guns already in circulation. It wasn't a problem for the FSB though; they already had them. He pushed her shoulders against the desk then did it again.

Chapter 30

She tried to turn and punch him but his thick hands held her rigidly.

'I swear I'll shoot you if you do that again,' she said.

Fingers as hard as wooden stakes pressed under her collar bone making her eyes tear up. She sucked up the pain, refusing to give him the satisfaction of knowing it was working. Her attention fixed on the black globe on the ceiling, appealing to the person watching the thinly disguised camera to intervene.

She twisted a shoulder free from his grip; he replaced the hand and shook her again. The room was spinning; she could hardly breathe. She locked the muscles in her neck, lifted her head, and twisted to spew the meagre contents of her stomach over his trousers.

'You—'

He stopped whatever insult was coming. The weight released from her shoulders and she turned to see black hair, thick, tanned skin and an impassive face.

'What the hell are you doing? I'm a—'

'Nosey bitch. What were you doing in Sweden?'

He had intelligent eyes, she could see that, even if he an objectionable personality.

The hands gripped her shoulders again and he shook her body sideways. The bones in her neck cracked. 'This gives you brain damage. Do you want to be a vegetable? What were you doing?'

'Stop and I'll tell you.'

He withdrew his hands and she rubbed her neck. 'A woman I know, Renata Shchyotkina. Her boyfriend is a bastard like you; I went to have a word with him unofficially.'

'A Sven?'

'Yeah, except they actually have laws against beating women over there.'

'That bitch, was her boyfriend called Thorsten Dahl?'

He wrapped her shirt into his fist and dragged her to standing. 'I have a story for you, it's called "you ignored the fucking warning". If you didn't have a uniform you would be dead already.' He uncurled his fist and she tensed her body to prepare for another assault. It never came; he walked out of the room without looking back.

Over the Tannoy she heard an announcement for a late Aeroflot arrival from Moscow and checked the door. The handle twisted – he'd left it unlocked. Next to a silent vacuum cleaner she saw a plastic chair with a rucksack and her belongings spilling out of it. On top was her passport, splayed open to show her photograph. She pushed everything back into the bag and slung it over her shoulder then followed the line of closed sentry boxes marking passport control. A hubbub of passengers grew louder, then they came into view. There were no immigration officials for the domestic flight and Natalya attached herself to a middle-aged woman pulling a small silver case and wearing too many clothes for the mild morning, presumably to avoid paying for an additional bag. At the exit doors of Terminal 1, she left the woman at the taxi rank and went to the car park for her Volvo.

On the way home, she thought about a lot of things. In another life, Primakov's message might have passed for intriguing, now it was damned sinister. What the hell was he doing in Yulia Federova's apartment in the middle of the night with Dostoynov and Rogov? At least he had warned her, so there was still someone she could trust. She rubbed the aching muscles on her neck and tried to think clearly, but she was exhausted and whoever that bastard was, he'd left her with a *katyusha* firing inside her skull.

She drove back to Tsentralny District and parked on the road outside her apartment. A BMW X5 pulled up behind her. The driver remained at the wheel while his passenger got out and casually sat on the bonnet to smoke a cigarette. It was the weightlifter from the airport. He waved at her gaily like an old friend. Knowing they were FSB, it was safe to assume they were using her phone to track her movements and maybe listening to her calls too. "You ignored the fucking warning" she thought. Well, she couldn't fault him there.

On the floor above hers, she saw a light and heard "Everything's going to be alright" sung at a quarter speed. She could see Sergei, the old violin teacher, as he meandered from room to room, his head bobbing in and out of view.

The men in the X5 had a clear view of the block door but she had no alternative. She started walking towards it, her rucksack draped over her shoulder. She bent to tie her shoelace and saw the driver had his face tilted in her direction and a mobile phone pressed to his ear. She picked up pace but they didn't follow. That was good – they didn't have orders to take her in; at least not yet. At the metal door she pulled out her keys from her rucksack and pressed a magnetic disk against the lock. There was a soft click and she was in.

Until now she had never used the lift in the apartment block but she was too weary for the stairs. It took her to the fourth floor and she tugged on a tarnished brass bell. In the confines of the corridor, the noise rang out like an old fashioned fire alarm. She could feel herself being observed through the peephole and wondered when the two men in the street would receive new orders.

'Goooooiingng to beeeee allllll-riiiigggghhht!'

Sergei, her old neighbour, yanked the door open on the final word. Beneath the violin teacher's neat brown goatee he was topless, wearing only a pair of blue jeans on which he was hastily fastening the fly buttons.

'What's up, darling?'

'I'm in serious trouble, Sergei,' she said, letting herself in. 'I need your help.'

31

The sun was already up but the city was still asleep. From the shadows of his bedroom, she watched Sergei cross the street below. She'd told him to behave naturally but he was an ex-violin teacher not an expert in counter surveillance and she saw him turn his face away from the X5 as if the building's wall held some fascination for him. With good reason, the men in the car would be intrigued by his self-conscious behaviour, wondering if they should question him, particularly now her phone had stopped transmitting its position.

'Everything's going to be alright,' she sang to herself.

Sergei kept walking until he disappeared from view. Ten minutes later, the X5 suddenly came to life. Its headlights flashed on, and it performed a sharp U-turn in the street and accelerated away. She dashed out of Sergei's apartment and took the stairs.

On the third floor she opened the door with a key, smelling cigarette smoke and fried food. The comforting wood-saw of Mikhail's snores cut through the silence. She stepped over a bag of empty Ochakovo bottles to reach the bathroom and had a quick shower. As she reached for a towel the door burst open sending the flimsy lock flying to the far wall.

The steam iron was in Mikhail's fist; his aggression offset by the pair of fake tiger-skin underpants she had bought for his fortieth birthday.

'It's OK, it's just me.' She finished tucking the towel over her breasts then found a wide-toothed comb and pulled it through her hair.

'Tasha?' He rubbed his face. 'What the hell are you doing here?'

'Can you put the iron down? Actually I'm surprised you knew

where to find it.'

'Funny.' He rubbed his hand against his cheek making a rasping noise against the stubble. 'Anyway, you left it out.'

'Still, what are you doing here, Misha?'

'I'd come to warn you again, but you weren't in so I decided to wait. It appears Dostoynov is acting for his old friends… Stepan told me.' He scrutinised her. 'Jesus, you look terrible.'

'I was interrogated by the FSB. They followed me here.'

He ran the fingers of his free hand through his hair, 'Tasha, I told you to leave it alone, now you've brought them to our home.'

'They aren't there now.'

'What do you mean?'

She pointed a finger skywards. 'Sergei got rid of them.'

'What were you thinking? He'll be killed.'

'Misha, I was desperate. I told him the risks and he agreed to help. I took the SIM and battery out of my phone and asked Sergei to reassemble it at Finlyandsky station. He's going to hide it on the first *elektrichka* he finds. It was the only way I could get rid of them.'

Apart from the risk Sergei was taking, it made her feel sick thinking of the FSB getting hold of her phone with its calls to Dahl as well as the recording she had taken from Lagunov's office. She may as well write them a note telling them everything she knew. Almost as bad, without her mobile she had few means of contacting anyone.

Mikhail looked deadly serious. 'The FSB are paranoid fucks but they are not morons. When they know you've been playing with them they'll designate you an enemy agent. I told you to stay away.' Saliva flecked his chin. 'I fucking told you, Natalya.'

The thought of being hunted down by the FSB made her spine freeze. The successor organisation to the KGB was barely twenty years old but they were already up to their elbows in blood and had displayed little concern about killing far more important people than her. 'Where's Anton?' she asked, her voice rising in panic.

'So now you think of him. I told him to stay at Dinara's until you stop using State Security to commit suicide.' He looked at her sternly. 'I love you, Natalya, but I don't want Anton dragged into this. Those pricks will ruin his life just to ruin yours. Now tell me where have you been?'

'It was my day off, why should you care?'

'I do care. Answer the question.'

'Alright, I went to Stockholm to see Dahl, then I spent the night stuck at Pulkovo being entertained by an FSB gorilla.'

'What did he say?'

'Dahl? He told me he'd sent Axelsson to a ransom exchange at the boatyard.'

'For what?'

'Zena.'

Mikhail rubbed the stubble on his chin. 'Did he forget his daughter was dead? I suppose it's easily done.'

'He's not stupid but some conman pretended to be a kidnapper and answered a proof of life question. He thought it was worth taking a chance—'

'Sure, with someone else's life. How did they know the answer?'

'I'm guessing they eavesdropped on him while he discussed what question to ask.'

'What were they after?'

'The deeds to Dahl's Russian companies.'

Mikhail let out a low whistle. 'Christ. They got them, I suppose.'

'Yes.'

'How much are they worth?'

She shrugged, 'Maybe half a billion dollars.'

Mikhail's mouth slid open. 'That's a good con trick.'

'At least it explains the FSB interest. They don't get out of bed for a few million.'

He frowned briefly. 'So what did the gorilla in the airport want?'

'To scare me off.'

'Then be scared. Get away while you can. Go see Claudia and come back when they have what they want.'

'Misha, what's going on? I called Primakov a few hours ago; he was in Yulia Federova's apartment.'

'Dostoynov heard the girl is missing and he's scrabbling around to connect you to it. You forget our new major is ex-FSB, and any fool knows there's no such thing as ex-FSB. I'm guessing someone whispered in his ear that you need to be put away.'

She put the comb down and stared at him. 'Rogov was the only one who knew Yulia had gone away.'

He put the iron down in the sink. 'Angel, Dostoynov threatened to fire Stepan this afternoon for insubordination. Don't be too hard on him, his balls are in a vice.'

She shook her head, incredulous that Mikhail was defending Rogov.

'And there's a witness. Federova's neighbour has gone on record claiming he heard you threatening the girl.'

'Is this the guy in the apartment opposite hers – the one with poor personal hygiene?'

'I think so.'

'Misha, this is ridiculous.' She felt the urge to scream. 'Isn't Vasiliev doing anything?'

'He's keeping his head down. Those bastards in the FSB could make a church mouse look like it stole the Patriarch's Breguet.'

'I didn't do anything.'

'You think they care? Half the unmarked graves in Russia are full of the innocent; the other half hold their defence lawyers.' He smiled grimly. 'Your only hope is to get away and leave the Dahl case alone. Will you do that for me?'

'I can't.'

'You mean you won't.'

'Those two boys didn't kill Zena Dahl on their own. They were set up or helped. When did we decide to stop going after murderers because it got difficult?'

Mikhail looked away momentarily and she wondered if it had something to do with his secret bank account. How had he been compromised?

He nodded solemnly. 'As long as Anton's safe I'm here for you.'

'If that's true, I want three things from you.'

'Whatever you want.'

'You promise?'

'Promise.'

'One, tell me where your money came from. I can't trust you until you do that. If it's bad I won't forgive you, but I get to decide.'

'Agreed. What else?'

'Two doesn't happen without one.' She put a hand on his chest. 'I'm tired and I don't intend to sleep on the sofa.'

'And three?' Mikhail asked instantly.

'That comes after two.' She dropped the towel and watched a greedy smile break across his face.

Mikhail had a tenderness in bed that was a contradiction to his bluff personality. He ran his fat fingers through her hair and cupped her buttocks with his other hand. She pushed her body against him, feeling him harden.

'How's tiger?'

'Elephantine.'

'Tell me about the money first.'

'You want to ruin the moment?'

She gave him a sour look.

'OK, but now?'

She maintained the look.

He pushed himself onto the pillows and patted the table. His hand came away with a fresh pack of Sobranie Classics.'

'When did you start smoking in bed?'

'I picked up some bad habits at Rogov's.' He climbed out to look for a lighter.

'Is it an African or Indian one?'

'What?'

She peered at his penis and he grunted. After he left, she heard the cooker ignition; he returned trailing smoke.

He climbed back in bed and drew deeply on the cigarette. 'What I told you about the account was the truth – just not all of it. Most of the money came from my mother. She came up with *Misha Buratino*. It really was my childhood nickname, you know.'

'You said "most". What about the rest of the money?'

He sucked on the cigarette. 'Do you remember a murder case

around eight years ago? Artur Romakhin.'

She thought for a moment then shook her head.

'It wasn't big news at the time.' He spoke nonchalantly, 'Romakhin was a pawnbroker, his wife found him dead on the shop floor with his skull cracked.'

She ripped the cigarette from Mikhail's hand and put it to her lips, flicking her eyebrows in a "so what?" expression before he challenged her.

'It was my first big case. You know what that's like. You've got uniforms and detectives running around asking for orders and all you can think of is not screwing up. Well, the dead guy's wife, Yana, she told me Romakhin was an actual pawnbroker.'

She looked at him in amazement. 'You mean he wasn't money laundering?'

'Can you believe it? He'd made a lot of cabbage running a shop in Veliky Novgorod and liked his chances in *Piter.* By all accounts, he was a good citizen.'

She took a final drag on the cigarette and passed it back to him.

'Romakhin started getting smashed windows and thought someone was going to break in so he bought a camera off the internet. Yana showed it to me – it was built into a smoke monitor in the ceiling and streamed to a laptop. I watched everything in the storeroom.'

Mikhail puffed on the Sobranie and blew the smoke away from her. 'Imagine that? It was my first murder case and I'd solved it in five minutes. On the laptop, I saw these two *bratki*, mafia bulls, come in and start an intense discussion with Romakhin.'

'Let me guess, they didn't believe he was legitimate.'

'Exactly.' Mikhail sucked on the cigarette. 'Big misunderstanding. They wanted to know whose cash he was rinsing. He told them he was legitimate. They didn't believe him and pressed a little harder. All the while, Romakhin thought it was safe to push back because he was making his little movie with them in the starring roles. After a bit of this dancing, one of the *bratki* took exception to a member of a prey species pointing a finger in his face. He punched Romakhin and his head hit the marble counter. End of Romakhin.'

Mikhail flicked ash into a coffee cup he'd been using for an ashtray.

'Before the day was over, I had both *bratki* charged with murder, aggravated by racketeering. One of them was built like a cage fighter, he hands me this paper with a phone number on it. "What's this, dick for brains?" I ask. "Get out of jail free card" he says. So out of curiosity I called it.'

'Who was it?'

'An *avtoritet* for the Tambovski mafia. I mean this guy was off the fucking scale. The cage fighter happened to be his new wife's nephew. We exchanged pleasantries then he asked me to choose between silver and lead.'

The lightness in Mikhail's voice had gone. 'The silver was a hundred thousand dollars to get the two *bratki* out of the shit and put someone in their place. The lead, well, you know what that is.'

'Jesus Christ, Misha.'

'I know, Angel. If it had been just me I'd have told him to get lost, respectfully of course, but I was with Dinara then and she was already unstable. Anton was in his first year of senior school too.'

Her voice rose in pitch as she spoke: 'You set someone up?'

'On the laptop footage, after Romakhin was killed this kid called Pyotr Voloshyn comes running in. He was a *shestyorka*, a mafia novice they were using as a lookout. Voloshyn was eighteen; he had a juvenile record but nothing serious. I lost the laptop and the *avtoritet* offered him an incentive to do the time for Romakhin's murder. The widow knew what I was doing, so did everyone; even the kid's mother. She cried all the way through the trial.' He pursed his lips and stared into space. 'The prosecutor and judge had been bought. Everyone was lined up like toy soldiers. The *avtoritet* even gave me a bonus of twenty thousand for making it look good.'

'What did the boy get?'

'Ten years in Ulyanovsk. I make enquiries every now and again, he's still there.'

'He'll be out soon then.'

Mikhail's eyes looked glassy though she didn't know if it was from drinking. 'I came in as an idealist and then suddenly I was one of those *menti* I always despised.'

Somewhere in the early morning, she'd fallen asleep in his arms before they had twisted apart to take up their usual positions. They hadn't made love in the end. After his confession, the mood had changed. Her lungs felt tight from the few cigarettes she'd smoked but she still leaned over Mikhail for his pack of Sobranies. If she had made that call to the *avtoritet* and been offered silver or lead, could she have refused if Anton had been her child? She lit the cigarette off the stove and climbed back into bed. There was something existential about lying in bed naked with another human being. Exposed and vulnerable with all weaknesses on display, just as theirs were. Silver or lead, she thought. At least it took the threat of a bullet to make him dishonest. Real criminals didn't need encouraging.

Mikhail stirred. 'You're smoking.'

'Your detective skills are an inspiration to me.'

He re-arranged his pillow to lie on his side and watch her. 'I've missed this. I've missed you.'

'Me too.'

His eyes flicked to her breasts then back to her face. 'Are we getting back together?'

'I think so – I haven't decided.'

He passed her the cup to flick her ash into. 'What would it take?'

'An act of atonement maybe? Could you give Romakhin's widow your blood money?'

'She despises me.'

'Well, that's a surprise.'

'Anything else?'

'You remember this morning I wanted you to do three things? Here's the third: I need a lift to headquarters.'

He shook his head. 'That's not funny.'

She got out and gathered her clothes from the floor. 'I'm going to take on Dostoynov. Just make sure Anton is safe.'

32

The interview room was older and dirtier than the one in the airport. It had a large paint-chipped radiator and a grime-smeared wire-reinforced window. Across the bolted table sat Dostoynov and Colonel Vasiliev – who had said little.

'Major, what am I to be charged with?' She rested her elbows on the table.

'That's not how it works, Ivanova.'

'And what approach are you planning on using? The Reid technique gets results or you could try the "good cop, bad cop" routine.' – she scanned the room – 'there's an electrical socket if you want to try a "phone call to Putin"?'

'You shouldn't believe everything you read in the Novaya Gazeta.'

'I'm just saying you haven't got any evidence so your only option is a confession. I'm a terrible story-teller, though. My nephew is always complaining. Last time I told him Koschei the Deathless I forgot what happens when it gets to Baba Yaga.'

Dostoynov turned, exasperated, to Vasiliev who merely smoothed his quiff with a palm.

'Ivanova, let's see what you can remember, starting with your movements last Saturday morning.'

'Yes, Major. I went to interview Renata Shchyotkina, a domestic violence victim, when I was asked to check Zena Dahl's apartment. I arrived there around eight fifteen and conducted a search.'

'How did you get in?'

'Her elderly neighbour gave me a key.'

'But first you gained permission from Dahl's landlord?'

'No, sir. There was reason to be concerned for the girl's safety.'

Chapter 32

'An insufficient reason. I will consider a referral to the prosecutor under Article 165 of the Criminal Procedural Code.'

Colonel Vasiliev interrupted. 'It will be hard to justify a prosecution considering the Dahl girl was murdered.'

'Good point, sir.' Dostoynov's eyes twitched in a micro gesture of annoyance. 'Ivanova, what time did you leave?'

'Expert Criminalist Primakov joined me between nine thirty and ten. I left shortly after to interview Miss Federova at her apartment.'

'Another irregularity. Why didn't you bring her to the station for a formal interview?'

'She wasn't a suspect at the time.'

'But you were aware she has a criminal record.'

'Not until later, as you recall, when I returned to brief the Colonel.'

'So when did you get to Federova's?'

'Around ten thirty.'

'And what did you discuss?'

'Yulia Federova gave me a description of Zena Dahl's clothing and her last whereabouts.'

'I hear she had some designer items that took your interest.'

She tried to display no emotion at his inference that she had a motive to harm the girl. 'Yulia Federova had a pair of Ulyana Sergeenko sunglasses and a trouser suit. After a moment's consideration I decided they weren't enough to kill her for.'

'Is this funny, Ivanova?'

'Only if you think Kafka wrote comedies.'

Dostoynov rested his arms on the table and leaned forwards. 'You threatened her?'

'No, it was civil. She made me a coffee; we spoke about ballet and how she met Zena.'

'Then, when you returned to her apartment the second time you found it in disarray. A violent struggle had taken place.' His voice took on a snide tone. 'Yulia Federova was a witness. Wasn't that worth reporting to me?'

'I believe the struggle had been staged. Yulia claimed her father was sent to prison on false charges and thought the same might happen to her. I believe she ran to avoid arrest.' She looked Dostoynov in the eye. 'Innocent people get convicted all the time.'

Dostoynov matched her stare. 'Nevertheless, Ivanova, the accusation stands that you failed to report it.'

'Agreed,' said Vasiliev.

'Now let's go back to that first home visit when you found those designer clothes in her wardrobe: a trouser suit and a pair of sunglasses. Obviously the girl was stealing from Dahl.'

'They may have been gifts to thank her. Yulia was helping Zena to trace her parents.'

'And you know that as a fact?'

'Yes – I sent Sergeant Rogov to the ZAGS in Sestroretsk. He said the two women went there to look for a death certificate.'

'Against my specific order to concentrate on the body's identification.'

'Zena was adopted so a DNA match wasn't possible. I requested the dental records from Thorsten Dahl. There was nothing further to do.'

'Then you should have asked for new orders. Likewise, why did you return to Yulia Federova's apartment with Sergeant Rogov?'

'Because Miss Federova hadn't mentioned that she was helping Zena Dahl to trace her parents – I wanted to find out why.'

'So why didn't she mention it?'

It was the first decent question she'd heard from Dostoynov. Presumably Zena had told her friend not to say anything, but for what reason? 'I never found out, Major. She had gone when we returned.'

'There is a witness who claimed you threatened to kill her.'

'He's lying.'

'That's easy to say.'

'It's easy to make someone say it too. Why would I blackmail Federova? She didn't have any money.'

'Why did you enter her apartment without permission? This is becoming a habit of yours.'

'I thought she was in danger.'

Chapter 32

'Enough,' Dostoynov announced. 'All I hear is lie after lie. The prosecuting authorities have agreed to open criminal case 144 128.'

'For what?'

'Extortion.'

She felt her voice rise. 'You have no evidence.'

There was a knock at the door. 'Enter,' shouted Dostoynov.

Rogov was holding a portable TV by the handle. 'Colonel… Major… there has been a development.'

She stared at him, daring Rogov to look away out of shame. To his credit, he did.

'Sergeant what have you got?' asked Dostoynov.

'You need to see this, Major.'

He set the TV on the desk and plugged it in, then retrieved a remote control from his back pocket.

'Rogov,' she hissed, 'not you too.'

He looked hurt by the accusation. 'I'm sorry, Captain.'

The TV screen displayed static and he pressed a button on the remote control. 'I found this logged under the case as evidence.'

A frown formed on her forehead then quickly disappeared. 'It's the camera footage from the Krestovsky Island Metro,' she offered. 'I thought it might show Zena Dahl or her killers. That was before I heard about the two boys—'

'Save your excuse until we've seen it,' Dostoynov snapped. 'Sergeant, please?'

Rogov touched the TV with a nicotine stained finger. 'The screen is split into four. The two at the top cover the platforms—'

'Where do they go?' asked Dostoynov.

Rogov pointed at the screen again. 'There's only one line. One train goes to Primorsky, the other runs in the opposite direction to Frunzensky. The two images below cover the escalators; there's a camera suspended from the ceiling to capture the faces of passengers.'

'That's what it's designed for,' she said acidly, earning a disapproving glance from Dostoynov.

'I simply fast-forwarded until a train came in, then looked at the platform to see who got on or off. If there was anyone interesting I got a better look at them on the escalator as they left.'

'What did you find?' asked Dostoynov.

'One moment, Major.' Rogov fast forwarded the footage, then stopped it with the remote. 'She arrived just after four from the direction of Primorsky.'

'Who?'

He pointed to a frozen image of a young, slim-hipped woman stepping off a train. He pressed 'play' and she came to life, strolling confidently along the platform in her heels. His finger moved to track her when she first appeared as a blurred collection of pixels at the bottom of the picture. Ten seconds later, she was closest to the escalator's camera. The girl looked up and Rogov pressed the pause button on the remote control.

'There she is,' he said, triumphantly.

Vasiliev peered at the image of the girl's face bleached by the sun's rays. 'Well, that's not the Dahl girl.'

'No, Colonel.' Rogov wetted his lips with his tongue. 'It's Yulia Federova.'

She focussed on Rogov again; his face still flushed with excitement. 'Sergeant, when was this footage was taken?'

'Natalya, just tell them what they need to know.'

'Don't worry, Rogov, there's a timestamp.' She leaned forwards to read it. '4:04 p.m. Twenty-fifth of June. That was last Sunday. Did you go through all the footage?'

'Yes.'

'And are you still a Muslim, Rogov or was that bullshit too?'

'I don't know what you're talking about.'

'OK, that was bullshit.' She sat back. 'Did you recognise anyone else?'

'Just Federova.'

Dostoynov said, 'You're not asking the questions here, Captain, I am.'

'Apologies Major, I'm finished now.'

Vasiliev took out a packet of cigarettes from his jacket pocket and offered them around. Rogov was the only one to take one. He bent down to get a light off the colonel then leaned on the edge of the table, puffing on it guiltily.

Dostoynov frowned at Rogov smoking before turning to her. 'Was Federova going to meet you? Is that why you hid the footage?'

'Yes, instead of destroying it I hid it in the evidence room logged under the case. I figured no one would ever discover it there.

'There is no need for sarcasm. The fact you found footage of her suggests you were interested in her movements.'

'Yulia Federova is dead.'

Dostoynov pushed his lips together then nodded solemnly. 'Sergeant, please record the Captain's confession.'

Rogov left the cigarette in his mouth and patted his pockets before coming away with a pen. He pulled a notepad from his shirt pocket and leaned over the table.

'Good, now we can begin,' encouraged Vasiliev. 'Captain, how did it happen?'

'Yulia Federova is dead,' she repeated.

She watched Rogov scribble in the pad. 'Am I going too fast for you?'

He scowled.

'You see that?' – she pointed at the screen – 'Yulia is wearing the Ulyana Sergeenko trouser suit and her hair looks perfect. She was going somewhere.'

'A date?' asked Vasiliev.

'Or a modelling assignment. She was beautiful and needed her luck to change. She was murdered an hour later, then her killer used her keys to enter her apartment and make it look like she'd run away. That's why it looked staged.'

Rogov looked up. 'Keep writing,' she urged, 'there could be a confession at the end of it.'

'Continue, Captain,' said Dostoynov, 'but be aware you're digging a hole.'

'Yulia was Zena's only friend in *Piter.* I wonder if she was killed for discovering something. It could be those ZAGS records that she was helping Zena with.'

Dostoynov put a hand on Rogov's arm to stop him writing. 'I thought you said you were no good at stories.'

'Then let me tell you another one, it's a mystery called "The death of Zena Dahl". First question: why does a murderer burn a body?'

She looked to Rogov but he was hunched over his notepad, writing.

'To destroy physical evidence,' volunteered Dostoynov.

'Then the killer was an idiot – he left her handbag behind at the scene.'

'This is old ground and your description of an idiot matches either of the *gopniks*. In case you have forgotten, it was your husband who arrested them.'

'Here's another theory. The body in the park was burned, not to destroy evidence but to disguise the victim. The killer needed to destroy the hair and face, and to make those long legs curl up. Zena Dahl was adopted and we don't know who her natural parents are – that means we can't match on DNA.' She smiled sweetly at Rogov. 'Make sure you write this in capitals: The body in the park is Yulia Federova, not Zena Dahl.'

There was silence in the room, then 'That's some imagination,' said Dostoynov.

She shook her head. 'Yulia Federova left the Krestovsky Island Metro an hour before witnesses reported seeing smoke. And no one puts a body in the Maritime Victory Park unless the purpose is to draw attention to it.'

Dostoynov snorted. 'So someone killed Yulia Federova and turned her into Zena Dahl. You expect me to believe that?'

'Zena had been missing for nearly four days by then. All we needed was a burned body and a handbag to be convinced it was her.'

'Why?' asked Vasiliev, tapping his cigarette over an aluminium foil ashtray.

'I don't know yet, Colonel, but it's easy enough to prove. Yulia Federova's father is in prison, you can compare his DNA to that of the body in the woods.'

Dostoynov grinned. 'This is better than Koschei the Deathless. Aren't you forgetting the two *gopniks*? Setting a murder like this is beyond their intellectual capacity.'

'Rogov?' she waited until he lifted his head. 'You questioned the two boys.'

'Scum,' he spat.

'Before you forced a confession out of them, what was their story?'

'Colonel, Major,' he blustered, 'I didn't coerce them.'

'Sergeant, answer the question,' said Vasiliev.

Rogov put his hands on his hips. 'They told me lies. Popovich found their fingerprints on the purse. They told the truth soon enough.'

'Sergeant, answer the question,' Vasiliev repeated.

'The *gopniks* told me they found her on the street and robbed her.'

'We know that, then what?'

'They heard someone coming and ran away. It doesn't make sense.'

'It does if a kidnapper was tracking Zena's movements,' she said. 'Whoever abducted her saw the robbery and decided to intervene. They knew the boys would have left fingerprints behind on her handbag.'

Rogov wobbled his jowls as he shook his head. 'Why bother?'

'Because someone has made the daughter of a billionaire disappear and all you can think of is how to frame the only person trying to solve the case.'

'What about the *gopniks*?' asked Rogov.

'Knowing our justice system they'll be stuck in pre-trial detention for months. They were a pair of nasty shits though, so I'm not going to lose sleep over it.' She paused for breath. 'So, gentlemen, do you want me to find Zena Dahl, as well as Yulia Federova's killer, or would you prefer to keep me here on false charges?'

Vasiliev patted his Teddy Boy quiff. 'Thank you, Major… Sergeant, I wish to speak with the Captain alone.'

'I don't think you realise—'

'That's enough, Major Dostoynov.'

Vasiliev waited until the door was closed. 'I apologise for all that unpleasantness… it's not what I wanted.' He stubbed his cigarette out in the foil ashtray. 'Natalya, did you ever hear of an Aleksey Mikheyev?'

'No, Colonel.'

'It's a true story.' Vasiliev pulled his chair opposite hers. 'Mikheyev was a traffic *ment* in Nizhny Novgorod who offered a girl a lift out of town. Soon she is reported missing. The local police discover Mikheyev was the last person to see her so they charge him with her rape and murder. He refuses to admit what he did with her body so they put a few volts through his brain to improve his memory. Mikheyev thinks they are going to kill him so he jumps out of a third floor window and breaks his back in the fall. Now he's in a wheelchair for life. Two weeks later, the girl turns up unharmed – she'd been staying with friends.'

If the case was a jigsaw, it would go back to the shop minus its missing pieces. Colonel Vasiliev wasn't helping either.

'You're saying the uniform won't protect me.'

'Well, it didn't do a lot for Mikheyev. What is your objective?'

'I want to find Zena – if she's still alive – and get the bastard who killed Yulia Federova. It would be nice to stay alive too. The FSB want me to leave it alone.'

'Dostoynov's one of them of course.'

'But not you?'

'Listen.' Vasiliev leaned forwards over the desk. 'You ever seen this?' He tapped the United Russia pin badge on the lapel of his jacket.

'Yes, Colonel.'

United Russia was the political party created as a vehicle to keep President Putin in power. It was Vasiliev's way of informing his subordinates that he was plugged in to the administration..

'You breathe a word of this, Ivanova, and I'll let the FSB do whatever they want with you – is that clear?'

She nodded. 'Yes, Colonel.'

He opened his wallet and removed an ancient piece of card; he held it up for her to see. 'Now, look closely.'

Some of the lettering had disintegrated but it was still readable.

Chapter 32

'You were in *The People's Freedom Party*?'

'Don't sound so surprised.'

'My father supported them too – weren't they one of the early pro-democracy movements?'

Vasiliev returned the tattered card to his wallet with care. 'That's who I am; one of the original members too. I kept my head down when they were de-registered.' He tapped the pin badge. 'How could I join the party of crooks and thieves for God's sake? I'm a policeman.'

'So you're helping me?'

'Helping, but mostly arse-covering. If I let you walk out of here, the FSB will know I helped you and I could lose my pension… or worse. Dostoynov has raised a criminal case against you, but until he presents evidence to the prosecutor it's just a number, nothing more.'

'So I'm screwed.'

'Not necessarily.' Vasiliev smoothed the sides of his quiff. 'I think there's a way out for all of us. I want you to sign something.'

'You're still after my confession?'

'Why would you say that?' He removed a sheet of paper from a manila folder and passed it to her.

'What is it?'

'Take a look. It's your resignation. I had it typed this morning when I heard Dostoynov was looking for evidence against you.'

She scanned it quickly, unable to believe what she was seeing. 'I won't sign it.'

'Look at the top.'

Her eyes flicked upwards. 'It's backdated to last Saturday.'

'The day you walked into Zena Dahl's apartment.'

'You're forcing me out?'

'No, disowning you, and I'll only do it if the FSB catch or kill you. I'll show the letter to Dostoynov too and tell him exactly the same. He won't like it any more than you but the FSB will be off my back, and if you sign it' – Vasiliev extended his hand towards the door – 'you'll be free to go.'

'Why are you helping me?' she asked, suspicious that Vasiliev could process her resignation the moment she walked out.

'Because I think you're right. Find Zena Dahl and get Yulia Federova's killer.'

For the first time in several hours she smiled, then picked up Rogov's discarded pen and signed the letter.

Vasiliev took it from her and placed it inside the manila folder. 'And for God's sake, Ivanova, keep away from the FSB.'

33

She counted the floors of the building, stopping at the fourth. The living room window had drawn blinds and heavy curtains to block the daylight entering Sergei's bedroom while he slept off his nocturnal activities. Below his apartment, there were no lights. Not that she could see anything inside it from the coffee shop on the opposite side of the street.

If they hadn't already, the FSB men would soon find her iPhone in its hiding place on the *elektrichka*. She lowered her line of sight to the pavement and watched a white van with "Vadim's Art Collective" stencilled on the side and a woman with unkempt red hair in the driver's seat. It was parked where the grey BMW X5 had been earlier and she wondered if it was there innocently or the FSB were taking a stealthier approach. She dismissed the idea; the woman looked more likely to be an agitator than an agent.

She ducked down as she approached her Volvo, five cars behind the van, not caring how conspicuous she looked to passers-by. Her door opened with a clunk that echoed down the street and she lifted her head momentarily to check for activity then removed her Makarov from the glove compartment. She fixed the holster to her belt, then, on impulse, lay down on the pavement and examined the underside of her car, running her hand against the dirt-crusted metal to check for a tracking device. There was nothing she could feel, but that didn't mean there wasn't something there.

There were footsteps behind her and she turned abruptly, her thumb touching the top of her belt for the Makarov.

'Captain?'

'Jesus, Leo.'

Primakov, for once, was dressed to unimpress, his jeans were dirty and frayed at the bottoms, and he wore a T-shirt with a green, circular Starbucks logo beneath an open, flapping anorak with the hood pulled over his blond hair.

She wrapped her arms around him without thinking. 'It's good to see you.'

He patted her back stiffly. 'You too, Captain.'

She let go and stepped back. 'What's with the clothes?'

'Disguise. There are a lot of strange people around.'

'You mean FSB?'

'Yes,' he fidgeted with his car keys, looking more anxious than she had ever seen him before, 'one of them came to my apartment – a major from Moscow. She was asking questions about you. They scare me; *she* scared me.' Primakov looked around. 'The fact is, we should get away from here. Far away.'

They jogged to his Samara.

'You had any offers?' she pointed at a "For Sale" sign taped to his dashboard. Above it, dangling from the mirror, were a collection of air fresheners in the shape of pine trees.

'We don't need to talk about it.'

'I'd prefer a little distraction.'

'Oh, well, one man was interested.'

'Until he took it for a test drive and complained it smelled like a toilet?'

'Exactly that.'

'You bought it in winter, try selling it then.' She climbed in and immediately wound down the window.

He started driving. 'Where are we going?'

'To Zena's place.'

'What were you doing outside my apartment?'

'Major Ivanov asked me to find you. He told me not to call you.'

'The FSB have my phone.'

He nodded, satisfied. 'Why?'

'It's something to do with the Zena Dahl case. They want me out of the way, I don't know why. Also, I think—'

'She's alive? I heard. Do you know where she is?'

Natalya shook her head. 'No idea.'

Chapter 33

'I also heard the body in the woods is her friend, Yulia Federova.'

'Who told you?'

'Major Ivanov.'

'Leo?'

Primakov nodded thoughtfully. 'Yes, Captain?'

'You can call me Natalya, I don't think I'm going to be in a job much longer.' – or alive, she thought – 'If it's not a rude question, why are you helping?' She leaned out of the open window to suck in sweet air as they crossed Blagoveshchensky Bridge to Vasilyevsky Island.

She pulled her head back in to hear him.

'Scales of grey,' Primakov was saying. 'I have a mild obsessive compulsive disorder. It's simpler to keep things as black or white. Tidier.'

'And poorer.'

He smiled. 'That too. Dostoynov is trying to throw some dirt on you.'

'You don't believe him?'

'Major Ivanov moved in with Rogov after I sent you that keylogger. My conclusion is you found something you didn't like. That makes you more honest than most. Also, the FSB aren't interested in conspiracy theorists but they are very interested in you. Unfortunately for me, wanting everything black or white means a sliver of white and a whole lot of black.'

She took a breath, inhaling pine and an undercurrent of urine.

'Thank you.'

He waved it away and they lapsed into silence. Primakov checked his mirror nervously, driving twice along Veselnaya Ulitsa before pulling up outside the eighth block. He stopped to tie his shoelace and she went on. The curtains in the apartment of Zena's neighbour twitched before she could climb the steps to the metal door; it opened as she took out the key.

Natalya peered at a pair of burgundy eyebrows and burgundy hair scraped back into a bun. 'Mrs Kuznetsova, do you remember me?' she asked, reached for her identification card.

'Yes, I've been expecting you.'

'And this is Expert Criminalist Primakov.'

Lyudmila Kuznetsova gave him a flirtatious grin, showing teeth that were too white and even to be real.

'Come in, he's been here all afternoon.' The old woman pulled the door open wide then turned for her apartment, calling out to Primakov behind her: 'And close it behind you, handsome.'

Natalya followed the old woman, half-listening to her voice as it competed with the high volume of the television. 'He speaks Russian like a donkey but he bought food and vodka.'

Kuznetsova was animated and, coupled with the flirtation over Primakov, Natalya reached the conclusion the old woman had already started drinking.

The door to the apartment was ajar. She watched Thorsten Dahl climb out of the armchair facing the television. He bent down to kiss Natalya's cheek then thought better of it and offered his hand. 'Captain Ivanova, it's good to meet you again,' he said, raising his voice to be heard over the current affairs programme on TV.

'You made it alright?' she asked.

He moved away from the television to speak. 'I flew to Helsinki then took a hire car. I've been driving all night.'

'Thorsten. Let me introduce,' she stepped aside, 'Expert Criminalist Leo Primakov, a crime scene investigator.'

Primakov held out his hand to Dahl. 'Pleased to meet you and before you ask,' he said drily, 'it's nothing like CSI.'

Kuznetsova tried to beckon them all towards a table laden with food but Natalya resisted; she moved her head from Primakov to the old woman as a hint he should go and keep the old woman happy.

'Come with me,' she said to Dahl, taking out Zena's key. 'It's too noisy with that TV.'

Dahl yawned. 'Yes, I think her hearing aid is broken.'

They walked into the landing. 'Have you ever been here before?'

'No,' he said.

'What about Anatoly Lagunov?'

'I doubt it.' The Swede shook his head. 'Anatoly barely knew Zena. Perhaps he met her once or twice at my house in Stockholm.'

Chapter 33

Natalya turned the key in the door and pushed it open. 'Well, I thought you might appreciate seeing her place.'

'Yes, I do. Thank you.'

She stepped into the living room and drew the curtains, scattering dust and clearing the gloom.

'It's not what I expected.'

'Trust me, this is upmarket for a student – I shared with four girls who swore like sailors and drank like it was their last day on Earth.' Her hand went to her mouth. 'Sorry, poor taste.'

'It doesn't matter.'

She sat on the edge of Zena's sofa. 'Thorsten, I wanted to speak to you privately.' She touched his arm. 'I found camera footage of Zena's friend, Yulia Federova. She was walking towards the park where the body was found.'

'You think she's implicated.'

'No, this happened an hour before smoke was seen.' She spoke carefully, 'I must tell you some of my colleagues have a different opinion but I have reason to believe it was Yulia Federova who was killed, not Zena.'

Dahl's eye's performed a little roll as if he couldn't believe what he was hearing. 'You mean Zena's alive? What about the two boys who admitted killing her?'

'There were coerced into confessing.' She held out her palms to temper his enthusiasm. 'There's no guarantee I'm right, but if someone went to the effort of making us think Zena is dead, then it's a good indication that she isn't.'

'Why do that?' He ran his hand through his hair. 'It's sick.'

'I only have theories, Thorsten. Perhaps, Zena's abductor got nervous and gave us a body to stop the police investigation.'

'Why not pick any girl off the street and kill her? Why her friend?'

'Perhaps Yulia knew Zena's kidnapper without realising it? When I spoke to Yulia she told me she didn't know what Zena had been doing at a ZAGS office. Later I found out she had gone there with your daughter. When I asked you and Anatoly Lagunov about the same subject, you were uncomfortable too.'

Dahl waved his hand dismissively. 'Do we have to go over that again?'

'I think so.'

He sighed. 'Her adoption wasn't completely legal. There wasn't time to get the paperwork arranged. I didn't want to tell you because I didn't know if I could trust you.'

'If that's all there is, I won't mention it to my superiors.' She stared at Dahl, wondering if he was telling the truth.

'So you think a kidnapper has been holding her all this time? The man who spoke to Anatoly, was that him?'

'Yes,' she said. 'I think it might have been genuine.'

'Does he still have her?'

'It's possible.'

'And he killed Felix Axelsson?'

'That's another thing I don't understand. Why did the kidnapper kill Axelsson unless he made them nervous?'

'Felix was a professional—'

'I wasn't criticising,' she said, though she was. 'When I saw his body' – she pointed at a spot between Dahl's cheek and jaw – 'there was the imprint of a gun barrel. His killer had jammed a pistol in his face then fired. That was rage. Didn't you tell me they asked for you personally?'

'Yes.'

'Then I think the kidnapper intended to kill you at the handover. When Axelsson showed up he was angry because he had been cheated.'

'Why? Were they afraid I was going to report the loss of the documents?'

'No,' she mused. 'That doesn't account for the rage; it was too personal. Did you upset someone when you were here in the nineties?'

He frowned. 'I implemented western standards of governance on companies that were being driven into the ground by petty thieving and inefficiency.'

'That would do it. I bet there's a long list of people that bear a grudge against you. We should go back, Lyudmila has made dinner and she'll be offended if we take any longer.'

'There's a line in Corinthians, if I remember my Bible,' he said. '"Let us eat and drink for tomorrow we may die."'

'I'd prefer to survive another day with indigestion and a hangover.'

He looked around the apartment. 'May I have some time alone? What you say makes sense, Zena could be alive, but I can't allow myself the possibility. And what if they hurt her or do something worse? I will have lost her again.'

She left him with his thoughts and returned to Lyudmila Kuznetsova's apartment. Leo Primakov had already charmed the old woman into letting him mute her television, and the dining table had more plates of food as well as an open bottle of vodka with two crystal glasses. She dumped her jacket and Makarov on the armchair then followed the sound of low conversation to the kitchen where Leo and Lyudmila were sat together on a kitchen top, alternately flicking ash out of an open window. She smiled watching them, glad of the distraction.

Primakov looked up in surprise like a naughty boy caught smoking. 'Natalya, Lyudmila here was telling me she was nominated by her school to give a bouquet to Nikita Khrushchev.'

'It was 1958,' the old woman picked up the prompt, 'and my mother made this blue and cream dress for the occasion. She woke me up at five to braid my hair. In the assembly hall, these big, fat, old men were sitting behind a row of tables on the stage. I had to walk past them when the whole school was watching...they made me so nervous.' She shook her head at the memory. 'As I curtseyed, I broke wind in front of Premier Khrushchev. I died of shame. I gave him the flowers and ran away to the sound of him laughing. Khrushchev was a peasant.'

Natalya pushed her lips together in mock sympathy then waited for them to finish their cigarettes. At the table, Thorsten Dahl joined them and she made a toast to Zena's safe return. The potato cakes were good and the vodka was better. For the first time in days she found herself relaxing. Lyudmila Kuznetsova proposed a new toast, this time to her youthful intestines. They all tapped their glasses and drank before Natalya was forced to translate to a bemused Dahl about the old woman meeting Khrushchev.

An hour later, just as she thought her stomach would tear open, Lyudmila brought out a Lomonosov porcelain ashtray for the cigarettes that were now permitted at the table. Natalya looked at the old woman's pink cheeks and smiled. Even Dahl, despite the uncertainty over Zena's fate, was transformed by the atmosphere. He opened a sealed bottle of whisky – the same type he had been drinking on the plane – and passed it around. Lyudmila sniffed it gingerly then poured some in her tea, earning a horrified look from Primakov. More glasses were filled. Natalya raised hers. 'To Yulia Federova.'

Dahl followed with a toast for Felix Axelsson's family. Primakov, she noticed, had become silent.

34

Lyudmila Kuznetsova thumped the near-empty bottle of vodka on the table, spilling her tea. 'Ah come on, I thought we were having a party.'

'Someone's here,' Primakov spoke in a low voice.

Natalya turned to see a man in a leather jacket blocking the open door. It was the one built like a weightlifter from the airport.

'Hey! Get out!' Lyudmila shouted.

He took two steps in and raised his Grach, pointing it at Natalya's head. 'Captain Ivanova, put your gun on the table.'

'I'm raising my hands.' She lifted them slowly with the palms facing out; they were shaking. 'Now I'm going to stand so you can see I'm not armed.'

She stood and turned slowly to show the waistband of her jeans.

'Anyone else?'

'No one,' she said.

He focused his gun on Dahl, then Primakov, watching them flinch in turn. The arc of his arm continuing until it returned to her.

'Clear,' he called out.

A lean man in his early twenties squeezed past the weightlifter, pocketing his sunglasses at the same time. She recognised him as the driver of the BMW X5. Behind him followed a woman with a bleached blonde bob and a voice sharp enough to pickle a salted cucumber: 'Detective Ivanova, place your hands flat on the table. Move them and he will shoot without hesitation.'

Natalya did as she was ordered. Dahl, she noticed, was sweating.

'She's FSB…the one who came to my apartment,' Primakov whispered.

'Nahodkin, check for weapons.'

The stocky man frisked her thoroughly. Scanning the room, he found her Makarov on Kuznetsova's armchair. He removed its clip and dropped it in his jacket pocket then waddled up to her. He pulled his hand back under the pretext of reaching for his jacket pocket then drove a fist into the side of her ribs.

'Natalya,' yelled Dahl.

She dropped to the floor, pain searing through her body. There were voices around but she couldn't hear them. After a few breaths she dragged herself onto her hands and knees then grabbed the edge of the table for support.

'That was unnecessary,' she gasped, pulling herself to standing.

'Give him cause and he'll put you on a liver transplant list,' the blonde woman said. 'Now sit and have a drink.'

Natalya took a sip of the malt. Its sweet, peaty taste filled her mouth, leaving a pleasant heat behind. It was easily the best whisky she had ever tasted. Fine as it was, it did little to calm her nerves or take the edge off Nahodkin's punch.

'Who are you?' demanded Dahl. 'You try anything, you'd better be prepared to shoot me.'

'That won't be a problem. My name is Major Belikova and I work for the FSB's Economic Crimes Directorate, in Moscow.'

'What's that?'

'Licensed thieves,' Natalya said under her breath.

Dahl nodded solemnly but Nahodkin heard her and edged closer.

Natalya scowled at him. 'What? Are you going to hit me again for that?'

Nahodkin shrugged his massive shoulders.

'He's gone soft on you,' said Belikova.

'Are you ours, or theirs?' Nahodkin asked.

Natalya shook her head hearing the same question the KGB used on dissidents. You were on their side or you were an enemy; no other option was permitted. 'I'm a patriot. Can you say that?'

Major Belikova shook her head. 'Children, please.' She approached the lean agent. 'Demutsky, take the *babushka* next door.

Let our homosexual friend go home.'

Primakov stared at the grain on the table, his cheeks burning with indignation. 'You told me you wouldn't tell anyone.'

'Oh, I'm sorry, was it a secret? Don't worry, the Captain here will keep it to herself. I understand she has liberal attitudes. Now she knows you're a homo she'll want to go out dancing with you and your boyfriends.'

Primakov stood; he looked glum as if his world had collapsed. 'Please don't say anything Captain,' he begged, 'they'll destroy me at headquarters.'

'Don't worry, Leo. I think I've always known; it's hardly a surprise.' He didn't look any less relieved and a thought occurred to her, a bad one. 'Leo, how did she know we were here?' A new thought followed on the last: 'You were the last to come in. How did they get past the door?'

'And I heard a rumour you were a decent detective,' Major Belikova said. 'Hey, Demutsky, hurry up.'

'Leo, you led them here, didn't you? You left the door unlocked.'

Primakov put his hands over his eyes as if trying to blot out what he had done. 'I'm so sorry, Captain. She made me do it. She told me they only wanted to talk.'

'You should know homos can't be trusted,' said Belikova. 'One threat to tell Papa and' – she snapped an imaginary biscuit between her fingers – 'this one turned into Tula gingerbread.'

'Hey, Demutsky, get moving.'

'Major.' The young agent helped Kuznetsova to stand then escorted her and Primakov out. Nahodkin closed the door behind them.

'I need to try this.' The Major leaned over the table to examine Dahl's whisky. 'Nahodkin, get me a glass. While I remember, Detective, here's your phone. You don't want to hear what Nahodkin said when he found it on the *elektrichka*.'

Natalya took it. 'You charged it.'

'All part of the service. I dare you to lose it again.'

Nahodkin returned with two glasses.

The Major poured a shot of whisky and sipped it. 'Yeah,' she sniffed, 'I don't like this foreign shit. You say potato, I say pass me the fucking Stolichnaya.' She tilted her head back to finish the glass.

'Hey, Nahodkin, I didn't ask for vodka. It was a figure of—'

Major Belikova froze in mid-sentence and stared past Natalya. 'Sweet sinless fucking Mary, was that...'

Natalya followed her line of sight. On the television screen, a reporter was outside a white-walled clinic with a luminous red cross on the side; he was interviewing a stocky man with grey, bristly hair. There was light scarring on the man's face and he had the cocksure swagger of a gangster. A woman was in the background, her head twisted away from the camera. The man beckoned her to join him, then, when she resisted, he grabbed her by the arm and pulled her into view.

'Someone turn the sound on. Now!' shouted Belikova.

Nahodkin's gun tracked Natalya as she dashed for the remote control on the armchair. She fumbled it, dislodging a battery that had been held in place by sticky tape. The battery dropped to the floor.

'Hey, ment? Get out the way!' Nahodkin shouted.

'What's going on?' demanded Dahl.

'Quiet everyone,' ordered the Major, though the volume was muted.

The girl on the television was approximately twenty years old, had thick, blonde hair and looked dazed. Natalya saw her mumble something in reply.

'Hey, isn't that your daughter?' asked the Major. 'I have to say, for a corpse she looks fresh.'

'Jesus Christ,' muttered Natalya.

The outside broadcast cut to the studio where a balding news reader raised his eyebrows to emphasise a joke that was lost on the people in the room. Behind him, on a brilliant blue background, a photograph of Thorsten Dahl appeared; he was standing on a dais in an auditorium and looked a decade younger.

'You must be famous. Can I have your autograph?' Nahodkin asked.

Chapter 34

Along with the time, there was a news ticker at the bottom of the screen, and Natalya read a bulletin as it drifted past:

Dead Swedish Student Is Alive! Local businessman taking paternity test.

Dahl's mouth was gaping, showing white, capped teeth. 'Volkov,' he uttered, finally.

The Major took Primakov's chair then clapped her hands in delight. 'I can't wait to hear this. It's going to be fantastic.'

'Thorsten, what the fuck is going on?' Natalya asked.

Dahl's voice was distant. 'Natalya,' he managed, 'I haven't told you the truth.'

'Wait. I need to get comfortable.' Belikova helped herself to one of Lyudmila's cigarettes before pouring a vodka. She had a malicious grin. 'I'm ready.'

Natalya slumped in her chair, anger and fear turning to despair. She was used to being lied to but Zena wasn't a runaway being abused by her father. Thorsten had no excuse to hide anything from her. 'Tell me the truth now,' she said in a controlled voice.

Thorsten Dahl held his glass in one hand and stared at it morosely as if the crystal had revealed his destiny. 'We missed someone out.' He held his drink up in an outstretched arm. 'To Kristina, and what might have been.'

He brought his arm back and finished his whisky alone.

'Who the hell is Kristina?' asked Natalya.

He exhaled heavily. 'She was a receptionist at the Astoria hotel. I had a suite there for most of 1999. One evening she found a pretext to come to my room. She was married, I'm not proud of it.'

'What happened?'

'We saw each other until the end of September then she left. At first I thought she had gone on holiday then one of the chambermaids told me she had quit.'

The Major rolled her sleeves back and stuck her elbows on the table. 'Did you know Hitler planned to have his victory celebration in the Astoria? I heard they had menus printed.'

'Maybe now's a good time to dust them off,' said Natalya.

The comment riled Belikova. 'You call us fascists but do you see any camps?' She took out her Grach and laid it on the table.

Dahl took another breath and puffed out his cheeks as he exhaled: 'Have you ever been in love, Natalya?'

She bristled at the question. He may be drunk but it was still damned insulting. 'It's a psychosis brought on by hormones.'

Belikova lifted a glass of vodka to her. 'Bravo!'

Natalya took one of Lyudmila's cigarettes, holding it in two hands to stop it shaking. Dahl leant across the table to light it. He seemed calm, presumably thanks to all the vodka and whisky.

Belikova cracked her knuckles. 'So when do we get to the part where you tell us this hotel receptionist is Zena's mother?'

Dahl ran an index finger along the rim of his glass.

'Thorsten?'

'The Major is right.'

'You said she was an orphan,' Natalya said, barely suppressing her anger. 'Was Kristina the real reason Zena came here?'

'No, it can't be – I told Zena both her parents were dead.'

Belikova inspected her fingernails. 'Nice story to tell a little girl, considering you pulled it from a chicken's arse.'

Natalya puffed on the cigarette, feeling disgusted with herself for smoking again. 'So you let her come here without any security?'

'I forgot Dahl's a billionaire? How much are you really worth?' Belikova tapped her cigarette again.

Natalya gave the Swede a warning glance not to say too much. Nahodkin saw it and he swiped her face with the back of his hand knocking her to the floor. Her chair clattered against the tiles. She got up, glaring angrily at him as she righted the chair and sat down.

'You want to take on someone your own size?' growled Dahl.

A smile twitched on Nahodkin's lips. 'Anytime.'

She rubbed her cheek. 'Why did you let Zena come here without any security?'

'It wasn't a risk. She hated being in the public eye so no one outside of a few small circles knew who she was.' Dahl topped up his glass with whisky.'

Chapter 34

'You need to stop drinking.'

He laughed to himself and prodded his chest with the glass. 'It doesn't matter. He's going to kill me.'

Major Belikova sucked deeply on her cigarette then tapped off the ash. 'This is going to be interesting.'

Natalya leaned forwards in her seat. 'Who?'

Dahl held his glass in the air as if expecting someone to appear at his elbow and refill it for him. He withdrew it awkwardly. 'The man you saw on television. I've never met him but I saw his picture a long time ago. His name is Yuri Volkov.'

Natalya let out a sarcastic laugh. Dahl didn't need to answer; everything had fallen into place. 'He's Kristina's husband, isn't he? You fell in love with a gangster's wife. Thorsten, you fucking idiot. I'm surprised you're still alive.'

'I concur,' added Major Belikova.

Natalya stared at the television; it had moved on to show the latest Donald Trump revelations, but she was thinking about the man with the bristly hair. 'Zena was two years old in 1999, you can't be her father.'

Dahl sank in his chair as if his two metre-frame could possibly become less conspicuous. 'No, I'm not her father.'

'Did you steal her?'

Belikova ran a tongue over her teeth, 'There's no need to get excited, Captain. He won't face any charges – as long as he's a good boy. I would be more worried for yourself. Unless you do as I ask, it will be you in prison and your stepson, Anton, fighting Ukrainian fascists in the Donbass People's Militia.'

'You can't do that!' Tears were in her eyes, betraying her weakness. She tried to blink them away and they rolled down her cheeks.

Belikova twisted her head. 'Nahodkin, did you hear anything?'

'Not me.'

'So let's get this right,' said the Major, 'Zena is Yuri and Kristina Volkov's child?'

There was an uncomfortable silence, punctuated by the television in the apartment next door as the volume was turned up to near maximum volume. Nahodkin finished off Lyudmila's vodka, sniffed at the whisky bottle then put it down with a look of disdain.

'Her birth name was Ksenia…Zena was the closest equivalent.'

'Thorsten,' Natalya hissed, 'did you steal their child?'

'No.'

'But she wasn't yours.'

'This isn't easy,' Dahl said. 'The last person I told was my father, over seventeen years ago.'

'Just tell me the fucking truth for once.'

He tried to placate her. 'Anatoly told me not to trust you, but I wish I had done it sooner.'

She snapped: 'Don't flatter me, Thorsten. If you hadn't lied, Felix Axelsson and Yulia Federova might still be alive. I thought Zena had been abducted and you didn't feel it was relevant to mention you once screwed a gangster's wife? Are you stupid? You didn't think it was worth telling me you stole his fucking child?'

'Please let me explain.'

'Hey, Nahodkin? Give the Captain her clip back, I think she's going to shoot him.'

'Keep it, I don't trust myself.'

Dahl offered a weak smile as if she had made a joke; Natalya glared at him until the smile died on his face. 'I didn't tell you about Yuri because I didn't think he was a threat. Kristina and I were careful. Yuri never knew I had Zena.'

'Well, I'd say he does now,' said Belikova.

'Yes,' Dahl poured more whisky, 'he does now.'

Natalya heaved a sigh. How had she got herself into this mess? She needed to warn Mikhail about Anton.

Belikova sucked on her cigarette. 'I adore love stories. What happened after Kristina left the Astoria?'

Dahl was morose though he had no right to be. Zena was alive and the FSB weren't threatening to send her to a war zone. 'I thought Kristina had done it to break off our affair. At the beginning of October I left for Yekaterinburg – Anatoly had discovered a gas pipeline manufacturer going out of business with no debts and a full order book.' He shook his head in amazement. 'When I returned to the Astoria, a letter was waiting for me. It was from Kristina, she told me her husband had been arrested. She had left a mobile number and told me to only use it for urgent messages.'

He leaned back in his chair. 'I asked to see her straight away. The next day I got a reply telling me to meet her at a café near the Eliseyev Emporium. It was the middle of December and she was dressed like a Siberian Yupik. She couldn't stay long – her husband had assigned a pair of young bulls to guard her and she had managed to lose them.'

'And?' asked Belikova.

'They were not there to protect her; they were her jailers.'

'For Christ's sake, Thorsten,' shouted Natalya, 'not them, her. What did she want?'

'She was in shock – her husband had been charged with killing a man.'

'What had he done?'

'She thought Yuri was a businessman, maybe a little crooked sometimes, but she had no idea he was trafficking girls from Moldavia. One of them was the thirteen-year-old daughter of a local police chief. He managed to track down Yuri then got murdered for his trouble. The chief's family caused a scene. Yuri got seven years.'

'So while he was away you tried to steal his wife?'

'It wasn't like that,' he snapped. 'Kristina asked for my help. Yuri used to beat her. While he was away she was kept as a prisoner in her own house.' He held up his glass to check the contents, then finished the remains of his whisky and reached for the bottle.

Natalya pulled it away. She measured one finger of whisky into his glass then handed it back to him. 'Now slow down.'

'Natalya, how can you understand when you've never been in love?' He turned in his chair, knocking over the glass and spilling whisky across the table. He picked it up and cradled it in his hands. There were dregs of whisky left and he put the glass to his lips. 'I still haven't told you everything.'

Natalya rolled her eyes in contempt. She figured it was the reaction he'd wanted all along. Dahl needed her to despise him in order to consolidate the way he felt about himself.

'You don't understand,' he repeated, then grabbed the bottle and cradled it in his arms. 'I killed Kristina.'

35

After his big announcement, Dahl fell silent.

'So, to recap.' Belikova said. 'Mister Dahl has confessed to kidnapping a child and killing her mother. There are a number of unanswered questions, chiefly: why is he still alive? But, actually, I have little interest in that. What I want is—'

Dahl shook himself from his reverie. 'Me?'

Belikova clapped. 'A dancing dog, how delightful. No, my preference is to put a bullet in your head and blame it on the homo. Regrettably, I am constrained by orders.'

'I haven't got anything left to give.'

Belikova put her hand on her heart. 'My poor rich man, you don't understand the Russian way. Let me explain.' She gave Dahl the smile of a bear observing salmon swimming upstream. 'The FSB has many divisions. There is counter-terrorism, border control, and internal security to name a few. My own is called the Economic Crimes Directorate. Until recently we have been out of favour with the president. Now we have an opportunity to embrace his warm breast and suck the cream from his teat.'

'It's always about money and yet you call yourselves patriots.' Natalya said.

Nahodkin appeared at her elbow.

'No, leave her. See if the old woman has got any beers.'

Nahodkin returned a moment later and shook his head. 'No beer.' He leaned past Natalya with deliberate slowness to take the lighter from the table.

'That's a shame,' the Major said. 'Now let me finish my story. On Sunday night, my colonel tells me the police have found a dead girl in St. Petersburg and there's a rumour her father is having difficulty selling his Russian companies. We put the two together and decide the girl's death is connected to an extortion attempt. He orders me to intercept the criminals—'

'So you can steal his companies yourself. You're too late – Thorsten ransomed them for Zena yesterday morning.'

'Shit,' the Major hissed. 'Dostoynov didn't tell me this.'

'And I might have stopped the exchange if you hadn't been so busy trying to scare me off the case.'

Belikova was unmoved. 'You were in the way, nothing personal. We'll just have to take them using another method. I assume Volkov is behind it?'

'It makes sense,' Natalya said grudgingly.

'Yuri was the kidnapper?' Dahl asked, shaking himself from his stupor.

'Yes,' said Natalya, irritated with the Swede, 'that's how he answered the proof of life question; he simply asked Zena.'

Belikova addressed Dahl in English. 'If you cooperate, you can go home.'

'That's not enough, I want Zena.' He stabbed himself in the chest with his finger.

'You can't have her, she's with her real father.'

'I would give my life for her,' Dahl slurred.

'Pointless but sweet,' said Nahodkin.

'Actually,' Natalya said, 'Zena is an adult so it's up to her if she wants to see you. There is one way I can help you though.'

'What?' Dahl asked.

'I have contacts in the Punishment Fulfilment Service. I can get you moved to a prison near her.'

'I've already told you, he's not going anywhere,' said Belikova.

'Doesn't anyone care that he stole a child and confessed to killing her mother?'

'Hey, what happened to the mother?' asked Nahodkin. 'I thought you were in love with her. Did you get bored? I get like that sometimes.'

'That's why I need to see Zena. I need to explain myself to her.'

'That's one conversation I'd like to hear,' said Belikova.

Chapter 35

'Come with me.' Belikova led Natalya into Lyudmila's kitchen. 'I've got a job for you, Captain. It's going to be more dangerous than a dip in Lake Karachay without a lead bathing suit, but if you do it right I'll leave you and your stepson alone.'

'What is it?'

'I want you to find everything Dahl gave to Volkov and give them to me.'

'Why not do it yourself?'

Belikova yawned. 'Isn't it obvious? If I screw up the President will hear and I'll freeze my tits chasing bootleggers in Irkutsk.'

'What about me?' she asked, stepping back into the living room. 'What choice do I have?'

Nahodkin slid the clip of her Makarov across the table to her, then lit another cigarette. 'Basically, none.'

36

It was late now. The sun was at its lowest ebb, barely visible over the horizon and the lampposts were still grey and unlit. In her mirror, headlights followed at a discreet distance; she didn't care enough to try to lose them. The analogue clock on the Volvo's dashboard showed one a.m. but it was always slow and she hurried to catch the Palace Bridge before it was raised. She found a parking place on the road, then climbed out of her Volvo and slammed the door. As she crossed the street, the empty night carried the noise of another car door closing. A moment later, the huge bulk of Nahodkin stepped into the open to show himself before disappearing in the shadows.

She climbed the stairs wearily and at the third floor heard dance music that grew louder as she approached her apartment door.

She let herself in. 'Misha?' she called.

'Here, Angel,' he shouted.

Mikhail was sitting in his customary chair next to a fresh collection of Ochakovo bottles on the coffee table.

'Hey, did you see the Sven on the news? Can you believe Zena's alive...and Dahl?' Mikhail shook his head. 'What a bastard.'

She ignored him. 'What's with the shit music?'

'The radio.'

'Then why—'

Mikhail beckoned her over then pointed to his phone on the table. She leant over so he could cup a hand to her ear. 'They can hear us even if it's switched off,' he said. 'I'm making their ears bleed.'

Another time and she might have dismissed his comments as paranoia. Now, she went to the kitchen, returning with some silver foil. After tearing off a sheet, she wrapped Mikhail's phone before doing the same to hers. She put both devices inside her microwave oven and closed the door.

She tapped the power button on his stereo to kill the music. 'Misha, don't make me listen to that shit again.'

'What have you done?'

'A Faraday cage kills the phone signals. It's not perfect but it'll do the job. Just don't switch the microwave on.'

'You were always the smart one.'

'No, I read it on an American website.' She looked around and saw how tidy it had become in her absence. 'Misha, it's late, why haven't you gone to bed?'

She heard a toilet flush then taps running as someone washed their hands.

Her eyebrows came together. 'Is someone else here?'

The toilet door opened and Rogov stepped out. He wafted his hand in the air. 'Shit, I think something died in there, Misha.'

Mikhail coughed.

'Natalya, what are you—'

An Ochakovo bottle arced in the air before bouncing off Rogov's skull. He staggered and held an arm out to ward off more blows.

Another was in her hand before she knew it. Mikhail was tugging on her arm. 'Tasha, No!'

'That bastard set me up.' She tried to jerk her hand clear from Mikhail's grip but he was too strong and took the bottle from her.

'I'm sorry, boss.' Rogov's hair began to glisten. He dabbed his head with the back of his sleeve then frowned at the red smear on his shirt.

'You want me to stitch that for you? I've got some knitting needles here.'

'Stepan was doing as he was told by Dostoynov.'

'Rogov, you tried to put me away.'

Mikhail was speaking in a reassuring manner that made her even angrier. 'Angel, they were going to sack him.'

She looked around for something new to throw. A glass ashtray looked solid enough. She tipped out the ash and cigarette butts onto the table then felt its reassuring weight.

'Angel, don't – you could kill him.'

'That's the idea.'

Mikhail placed his hands on her shoulders and turned her gently before enveloping her with his arms in an embrace or restraint; she wasn't sure which but it still felt good. The heat from her anger was cooling, turning into guilt.

In Lyudmila's apartment, Thorsten Dahl had asked if she had ever been in love and she had responded by calling it a psychosis. As he held her, Mikhail's stomach filled the space between her breasts and lower ribs, fitting perfectly. She remembered how, in bed, he cradled her from behind and his outstretched fingers were the same length as hers; his chin touched the top of her head. Mikhail was an old cardigan that was snug in the right places. She felt nauseous, remembering that she loved the stupid, big-bellied ment.

'I'm OK, Misha.'

His arms relaxed and she pulled free then twisted to pitch the glass ashtray Frisbee-style at Rogov. This time her aim was sure, it caught him in his gut and she had the satisfaction of seeing him double over, clutching the wall for support.

Her arms went up in surrender. 'I've stopped now…promise.'

Mikhail seemed oblivious to his friend's pain. 'As I was saying, Angel. Stepan was trying to help.'

'By making it look as if I was threatening Yulia Federova. Was it you who got her neighbour to lie?'

Rogov straightened. 'Dostoynov spoke to him – it was nothing to do with me.'

'Don't get angry with Stepan, he's keeping me informed. He's on your side.'

'Can I use this?' Rogov had stepped into the toilet and retrieved a hand towel,

'Sure,' said Mikhail, and Rogov pressed the towel against his bleeding scalp.

'Give me your phone.' She held out her hand.

'Shit, boss, this really hurts.' He winced as he reached into a trouser pocket with his free hand and handed her his mobile. She placed it in the microwave oven with the other two.

Rogov sat down heavily in the chair next to Mikhail's. He stretched over the table to pick up a near-empty Ochakovo.

'I thought Muslims didn't drink?'

'This one does.'

Curiously, she sensed that for once he was telling the truth. Rogov seemed to exist between two contradictory positions, unable to be one thing or the other. And it wasn't just him, the whole country was doing it. She doubted Colonel Vasiliev's United Russia badge was any less genuine than his old membership card for The People's Freedom Party; Primakov was gay yet lived a life of denial as a straight man; Mikhail had wanted to be a decent *ment* but was compromised by corruption. As for her, she pretended to be a European liberal while bribing her way through life like everyone else. That's what happened when old KGB men were put in charge of a country. News studios pretended propaganda was the truth. Elections pretended to be fair. Everyone pretended to be someone else, and nobody knew who they were any more.

'What's going on, Tasha?' Mikhail asked, taking his seat.

'Where's Anton?'

'Still at Dinara's.'

'He's in danger.'

Mikhail shook himself out of his lethargy; the Ochakovo bottle in his hand forgotten. 'What?'

'Unless I do what they say, the FSB are going to wrap him in a uniform and present him as a gift to the Donbass People's Militia.'

Mikhail was silent and his pupils seemed to shrink.

'The FSB are evil bastards,' volunteered Rogov.

She went to the kitchen and opened a bottle of Satrapezo before pouring out a generous measure into a wine glass. In the fridge she took an Ochakovo, ripping off its ring-pull and dropping it in the bin.

Her intention had been to give the beer to Mikhail but Rogov looked pathetic holding a bloody towel to his head. She placed it in front of Rogov as a gesture of goodwill and put her wine glass on the table before making an elaborate bow.

'Now we're all friends again,' Mikhail said. 'What's going on?'

'Can I trust you both?'

'You can trust me and most of the time I trust Stepan.'

'Well, if that's the best I'll get.' She saw a pack of Sobranie Classics on the table and took one.

'Still smoking?' Mikhail arched an eyebrow.

She ignored him and leant towards Rogov's extended lighter, keeping her hair away from his bloodstained hand.

She sucked in the smoke and exhaled heavily. 'Zena's real father is called Yuri Volkov; he was a gangster in the 1990s.'

Mikhail sat down and reached for his cigarettes. 'Yeah, I saw him on the news outside some DNA clinic. He said he was a businessman but he has that look about him. They say Dahl stole Zena when she was two years old. I hope that mudak gets what he deserves.'

She frowned. 'You know something? I don't understand why Volkov didn't take Zena back years ago – it makes no sense. Also, why is Thorsten even alive?'

Mikhail snorted and shook his head. 'Volkov and Dahl can fuck themselves for all I care. Why is the FSB threatening Anton to squeeze you?'

She puffed on the Sobranie. 'Remember I told you that Dahl gave up his company seals and documents as a ransom for Zena? Well, Volkov was behind it.'

'That makes sense,' said Mikhail.

'The FSB want me to get them back.'

'*You?*'

Rogov said it with such a pompous tone she was tempted to hit him again with the ashtray.

She had never seen Mikhail look so concerned. 'How are you going to get the documents?'

'I'm not sure yet.'

'Angel, whatever you do it won't be safe.'

Rogov's belly rippled as he let out a sardonic laugh. 'Now you won't be needing it, boss, can I have that fancy wine of yours?'

Mikhail glared at him and Rogov held up his hands in surrender.

'Only joking, she's got balls though.'

'They weren't there the last time I looked. Besides, I won't be alone.'

She smiled at Rogov. He looked even paler than usual and she wasn't convinced it was due to blood loss.

Mikhail patted Rogov's knee. 'Of course we'll help, won't we, Stepan?'

'If I get the documents, Volkov will come after me. I need someone to stop him.'

'That's me,' offered Mikhail.

'Thanks.' She puffed on the Sobranie. 'And I need to get Zena to safety.' She turned to Rogov who didn't react.

'Stepan is going to kidnap Zena Dahl?' Mikhail put a hand on his head. 'Well, at least it won't be a novel experience for the girl.'

'She's an adult. All you need to do is persuade her to go home. Thorsten is at her apartment, entertaining some FSB guests.'

'Any idea where Zena is now?' asked Rogov.

'No, you need to find where Volkov lives.'

She closed her eyes and felt sleep try to overwhelm her. 'Rogov, you remember that nice lady at the office in Sestroretsk?'

'The sixty-year-old virgin? I told you she didn't know anything.'

'That's because we didn't have the right questions. Now we do. Zena's real name is Ksenia Volkova, her parents are Kristina and Yuri Volkov. Whisper sweet things to the lady and check out any address she gives you. Go through births, marriages, and deaths.'

Mikhail lit up the Sobranie. 'Deaths?'

'Thorsten Dahl left with Zena in December 1999. Before then, he killed her mother.'

Mikhail glared at her. 'You're joking. We should be placing his head on a spike and you want us to give him Zena?'

'Boss, I feel the same. From what I saw on TV, that piece of shit needs to take a bullet.'

'And you believe everything you watch on television?' She raised a hand in defence. 'If you ask me she was a lot better off with Dahl. Volkov was not going to be father of the year – he was a sex trafficker for God's sake; he did prison time in Krasnoyarsk for killing a police chief.'

Mikhail asked, 'And who told you that? Dahl?'

'Dahl's weak but he's a good man – I believe him.'

'But, still.' Mikhail shook his head and drew on his Sobranie.

'I know it looks bad for Thorsten, but it's what I'm doing. You have to trust me…like I'm trusting you.'

Rogov rubbed the blood off his hands with the towel. 'I can't do it.'

Mikhail put a hand on his knee again. 'I don't want to hear it, Stepan. You owe Natalya for not defending her in front of Dostoynov – the Colonel told me what happened. What about Primakov?'

She didn't know what to say. Leo had set her up but then Rogov hadn't exactly been on her side either. It was also churlish to take it personally when very few people were strong enough to go against the authorities.

Mikhail sensed her indecision. 'Let's keep Primakov out of it, he is a scientist after all.'

'Agreed,' she added. 'We all need some sleep. Rogov, head to Sestroretsk first thing and go to all the addresses you can find for Volkov. If you come across him, keep out of the way and tell Misha immediately.'

Rogov didn't move. 'You need to go home. Oksana will be worried.'

'I think she prefers it when I'm out.'

She arched an eyebrow. 'That wasn't what I was saying.'

'Oh.' Rogov finally took the hint and she watched him perform an elaborate stretch in the chair.

His shirt was hanging out and spotted with blood, there was a congealed mess in his hair, and his eyes were red from tiredness and drinking. 'Oksana doesn't know what she's missing,' she added.

'Yeah, right.'

Rogov drained his Ochakovo.

37

Mikhail's snores woke her but it was time to get up anyway. Four hours in bed had been barely enough and she had slept for less than two by the time she had calmed her racing mind. She took a quick shower, getting dressed in the bathroom before retrieving her phone from the microwave.

'Hey,' she kissed Mikhail on the lips.

His eyes remained closed. 'You're up,' he mumbled.

'It's already after eight.'

He dragged his fingers over his face as if he was rubbing his skin off. 'Jesus. What day is it?'

'Friday.'

'Come back Tasha.'

'To bed?'

'Yes, and all of it.'

'Give me a reason.'

Mikhail opened his eyes. 'The pawnbroker's widow.' He stretched like a child with his arms extended. 'I found her yesterday. She lives in Poselok Lenina.' He sat upright, showing his almost hairless chest. 'I've been thinking about it. When this is over, I'll give her the money I was paid to keep the two *bratki* out of prison… I'll tell her the truth.'

'She won't forgive you.'

He fixed her with his grey-blue eyes that for once didn't seem wolfish. 'I'm not looking for forgiveness,' he said; she wasn't convinced.

'You'll do that if I come back?'

'I'll do it anyway.'

She kissed him again. His hand worked its way under her shirt and cupped her breast; his left arm slipped around her waist to pull her closer to him. She put a hand on his chest to stop herself falling. 'Misha, I have to go.'

Outside, there was a heavy squally rain and she stole a raincoat from the back of the apartment door; it was Mikhail's and came down to her knees but she took it anyway. In a pocket she found a pack of his cigarettes and a lighter. She caught her breath at the bottom of the stairs then put one of his Sobranies to her lips. If the FSB or Volkov killed her, at least she wouldn't have to go through weeks of torture to break her reignited nicotine addiction. She smiled grimly at the thought as she pulled the coat's hood up before running for cover to her Volvo. For part of the journey she sang along to her Leningrad CD, hoping it would hide the foreboding she felt, or at least drown out the monotonous screeching of her worn wiper blades; it did little to mask either.

The downpour caused the morning traffic to be heavier than usual on Nevsky Prospekt but she was still able to observe a Mercedes SUV sticking close to her, even after she had slowed down and given it an opportunity to overtake. She presumed it belonged to Nahodkin, but the rain and tinted glass made it impossible to know for sure. His role, she figured, was much like that of his NKVD predecessors: to hold the front line and stop deserters by any means necessary.

She parked and got out, feeling the calves of her jeans grow damp and stiff as they absorbed the horizontal rain. At Vosstaniya, she kept her head down and her body tensed to buttress herself against the spray that came with every gust of wind. As she passed Dahl's headquarters, she tilted her head to see under the oversized hood of the raincoat. The exterior glass was water-smeared and she had to squint to see the man in the moon, the red-haired security guard at the crescent-shaped reception desk. He was there, in his brown uniform, and staring at his phone looking bored.

She kept on walking. At the end of the block was a padlocked metal gate that led, in all likelihood, to the back entrances of several buildings like a lot of the older streets in *Piter.* The archway above the gate looked as though it might provide some cover from the deluge and she took shelter under it, feeling for the soggy packet of Mikhail's Sobranies. She examined them one-by-one until she found a dry specimen then blew on the lighter to clear it of water.

The cigarette lit first time and she puffed on it while re-examining the reasons that had brought her to the building. In the 1990s the mafia took over most of the major industries; they stole company documents and seal presses, and had tame politicians and korruptsioner in the Federal Tax Service ready to sign everything over to them. Anatoly Lagunov had spent eighteen years hiding Dahl's businesses in plain sight; that took a lot of skill and he would have a good idea of which corrupt government officials needed sight of the documents to legitimise Volkov's takeover.

She sucked on the Sobranie, feeling the hit from the nicotine. Above street level, the blocks rose five storeys. She felt vulnerable and leant against the archway wall while she studied the rows of balconies with stone balustrades and windows in shade. Apart from those administrative formalities, the company was as good as Volkov's and it was inconceivable that he wouldn't have someone here, keeping an eye on his new acquisition. Perhaps they were already watching her, their curiosity drawn to a woman loitering in the pouring rain. On the opposite street an old woman cradled a small dog in her arms while queueing on the steps of a bakery. A mixed group of four office workers approach her in a diamond formation; they hurried past with their shoulders hunched and heads down, paying her no attention. There was no one who remotely fitted the profile of a gangster. She shook her head quickly – she really was becoming paranoid.

In her experience, criminals tended to favour luxury cars or SUVs. She scanned the street but the rain had made all but the dirtiest and most decrepit vehicles look like possibilities. Still, to see none had a crew or even a driver at the wheel was reassuring.

Satisfied there was no obvious danger, she stubbed the cigarette on the pavement then doubled back. At Dahl's headquarters she pressed the buzzer, disturbing the security guard who looked up from his phone. Natalya pulled out her ID card and pressed it against the glass. The door clicked and she went inside. 'Senior Detective Ivanova,' she called out, wondering briefly how many more times she would get to say it. She approached the desk. 'Oleg isn't it?'

He nodded.

'Is Mister Lagunov in?'

'He's clearing his desk.'

'Why?'

'I don't know anything…he doesn't speak to me.'

As a direct employee of Thorsten Dahl it made sense for Lagunov to get out. She was surprised he hadn't left on Wednesday when Dahl gave away the documents and presses.

'What about other idle chatter, Oleg? What have people been saying?'

He leaned towards her and lowered his voice in the faux-reluctant manner of a practised gossip. 'Daria, Mister Lagunov's secretary, well…she told me the new owners didn't want him. I always thought he was in charge but Daria told me it was that Sven on television.'

'Yes, Daria's right. His name is Thorsten Dahl.' It was hardly a state secret and might buy her a little grace.

'It was in the papers this morning about how he took that girl. He pretended she was his daughter.'

'I can't talk about it.'

'Well, it's sick. He's a paedophile if you ask me.'

She shook her head, there was no point arguing with someone who believed what they read in the newspapers. Besides, with Oleg, any defence of Dahl she offered could be halfway around *Piter* before the day was out.

'I saw her,' he blurted out.

She turned, catching a guilty expression on his face for gossiping. 'Who?'

'That girl on television.'

'You mean Zena?'

'That was her Swedish name. You can't call her that—'

'You saw Ksenia Volkova here?

Chapter 37

He nodded.

'When?'

'Not for a long time.' Oleg glanced at the sun chandelier. 'Maybe September last year. I remember she came when they were replacing the bulbs. She only came once and Daria was waiting for her. She said…'

Oleg trailed off.

'What did she say?' Her voice came out sharper and louder than she had intended but Oleg was distracted. He twisted his head then flicked his eyes to her to indicate she should follow his gaze.

Over her shoulder she saw a man wearing a leather cap and a leather jacket; he was bald and had a long, straight nose, reminding her of the actor from Day Watch, Gosha Kutsenko. There was an ID badge hanging over his neck and he held it up.

'He's supposed to be with maintenance,' he whispered, 'but something isn't right.'

The resemblance to the actor confused her momentarily, and stopped her from seeing him for what he really was – a gangster. He removed his cap in an easy-going manner.

Her hand went to her hip, reaching for her Makarov. She found it instantly but it was inaccessible beneath Mikhail's raincoat. The Gosha Kutsenko lookalike pulled out a pistol from the pocket of his overalls.

'Come with me, Detective.'

38

The gangster led her down the stairwell then pressed his ID badge against a door sensor. As she entered the enclosed courtyard at the rear, the building's high walls blocked the wind while huge steel drainpipes directed torrents of water off the roofs and into gullies. There was no bad without the good, she thought, even if the only positive aspect to this miserable affair was a little protection from the driving rain. The bald man pulled her wrists behind her back and took out a cable tie.

'You won't get away with this.'

He fixed the nylon strip in place then yanked it tight. 'I've heard that before.' He patted her down, lifting the bottom of Mikhail's raincoat to remove her Makarov from its holster and her iPhone from her jeans pocket.

There was a dirty white van in the courtyard, the doors were open and she could see the interior was bare except for a PVC-covered bench running lengthways on the right-hand side. He pulled a black hood over her head then shoved her forwards. Her shins caught the van's metal step bringing tears to her eyes.

'Get in.'

She stayed on the wet floor, 'No.'

A gun was jammed in her face, the barrel grinding against her cheek bone.

'Get in or I'll put a bullet through you.'

She guessed he had killed Felix Axelsson, leaving the circular mark around the entry wound. It meant he wasn't bluffing. She got to her feet and stood on the step that had caught her shins, then ducked inside.

She heard a door open. Someone had been sitting in the van's passenger seat. There was a murmur of conversation then boots scuffed on the floor as he climbed in the back with her. The doors were slammed shut and the engine started. She took a deep breath to calm herself but it had the opposite effect – the hood had lingering traces of perfume and the iron of blood. Her fingers groped for the edge of the bench seat.

'Not there. Get on the floor.' It was a deep, rough voice and she wondered if it was Yuri Volkov.

'Where are you taking me?'

He said nothing.

They travelled for ten metres or so, then stopped. The driver's door opened and she heard the creak of gate hinges.

A shoe heel pressed between her shoulder blades.

She twisted against them. 'Volkov, get off me.'

He laughed and the weight was gone. So it was him.

Riling him wasn't going to help though. 'You know I was trying to find Zena too. We're on the same side.'

'You stupid bitch,' he said, 'you can't even say her name.'

The van drove over a kerb and her forehead smacked the metal floor. 'Her real name is Ksenia Yuryevna Volkova.'

'Who are you?' he spat. 'A *ment* out of her depth. You don't know anything.'

The van turned right, then left. 'Then tell me.'

'Why should I? You were going to take Ksenia back to that prick Dahl.'

She slid back as the van accelerated hard then braked, pitching her forward. She was thrown to the left as the car turned right. The Gosha Kutsenko lookalike at the wheel was a native *Pitertsy* or else he favoured his chances in the Russia Rally Cup. At least his aggressive driving made it easier to work out the direction of travel. She was certain they were on Liteyny Prospekt heading north.

The van hit a straight patch of road and the high-pitched scream from its abused engine dropped to a whine. She pushed herself against the wall, opposite Volkov on the bench seat, splaying her legs to stop herself being thrown around. She took another breath, catching cheap perfume – after all these years he was still trafficking women. The hood was for the ones who fought back.

'Why did you leave Ksenia with Dahl?' she asked.

'None of your fucking business.'

'I know you're going to kill me. You've done it before. Didn't you get seven years in Krasnoyarsk? Seven years, that still left plenty of time to get your daughter. You could have come for Ksenia a decade ago.'

He paused. 'Clever ment.'

'So Ksenia was nine then.'

'You're questioning me, cheeky bitch? You know why I didn't come for her and kill that Sven piz'da when I got out?' Volkov snorted and spat noisily.

The moisture from her breath was bringing out the blood in the mask, it wasn't a good omen.

'It was on Defender of the Fatherland Day. I was stuck at the workshop in Krasnoyarsk taking this fucking GAZ-44 to pieces. One of the guards came up and told me my wife and daughter were dead – then he ordered me to carry on working.'

'That was February the twenty-third, 2000?'

'Yes…they'd been dead a few months by then. I hired a couple of bulls to look after Kristina and Ksenia when I was inside – they were killed for fucking up. The guard said the *menti* found my wife half-eaten and Ksenia's body had been taken by wolves. I was trapped in a human sewer with their deaths for company. I couldn't speak of it to anyone. Inmates love news like that – it's a knife to them.'

The van accelerated, and over the stink of the hood she smelled the sea – they were crossing the Neva on Liteyny Bridge. She tried to remember the sequence of directions. The theory at least was clear – knowing the destination improved the odds of survival. But she doubted it had helped in more than a handful of cases. Instead of spending their final moments with memories of children or lovers, how many victims had wasted their time plotting traffic lights and turnings?

'So you didn't know Zena – Ksenia – was alive?'

'No, but does it matter? She's doing fine now. You know I was watching her?' He laughed; it was a deep, unsettling sound.

Natalya tried to focus on Volkov as well as the road. 'You were there the night Ksenia went missing?'

'Dahl, that stupid cunt, what was he thinking letting her run around the city on her own?' He exhaled heavily; it sounded like a pair of piston bellows. 'It wasn't how I wanted it. Two *gopnik* scum were on her... well, those roosters will be crowing soon.'

'You saved her from them?'

'The ungrateful bitch keeps whining about going home. I told her this is her fucking home now and she needs to get used to it.' He snorted and spat. 'I thought it would be different but she's not a little girl any more. Nah, I've said enough.'

Maybe she would be the lucky one and knowing the route was going to save her. At the end of the bridge the E18 looped in a tight, three-quarter bend to the right if they were heading north. She felt the van turn and pushed her feet flat on the floor as she was squeezed against the bare metal wall. It was north – she didn't know whether to be relieved or not.

'What happened to Yulia Federova?'

'That wasn't me.'

In the darkness, Volkov was silent but he had to be lying. The Hermès Sellier Kelly – that powder blue handbag of Zena's – hadn't got to the murder scene on its own. It could only have come from him.

'Then who did it?'

'The driver.'

She was stunned by the casual admission. 'The one who looks like Gosha Kutsenko? What's his name?'

'Where you're going, ment, you don't need to know.'

'Why kill Yulia, she didn't do anything.'

'It was a favour.' He brought up phlegm and spat noisily. 'My wife, Elizaveta; she runs a business taking pictures for catalogues. I used her email to make that stupid little bitch think she had won a free fashion shoot.'

In the darkness of the hood it was easy to conjure up the image of Yulia leaving the Krestovsky Metro station in her designer clothes. She must have thought her luck had changed. 'Why did your driver burn her and leave Ksenia's handbag behind? Why did you want people to think Ksenia was dead?'

'Enough. It's my turn.'

The road straightened and the engine whined as they accelerated. She struggled to hear what Volkov was saying and twisted her head. 'I hear that Sven prick is still in *Piter.* Tell me where he is and I'll make it quick for you.'

They were on the E18, she was sure of it. The driver had discovered the gear stick and the ride became smoother.

'Start talking.'

There were two distinct double-beeps. Her mobile had received a text message – the driver must have given Volkov her phone.

'Shit,' she muttered under her breath.

Volkov grabbed her feet and dragged her towards him. Her lips scraped against a bolt fixed to the floor and she cried out. He pushed her face down with a palm then yanked her arms up by the wrists until she screamed out. She felt him grip her right thumb; he pressed it against something flat. She squirmed, realising too late that it was her mobile's fingerprint reader – he was in her iPhone. He let go and she fell on her face.

'Thank you for your cooperation,' Volkov said. 'That message was from Stepan Rogov – your fat sergeant.'

How did he know so much about her?

'Do you want to hear it?' The derision in Volkov's voice was unmistakeable.

'Yes.'

'He says the sixty-year-old virgin is putting out.'

The van braked hard and she jerked forwards. Her body folded against the metal wall. Volkov waited until she propped herself up.

'Now what the fuck did he mean by that?'

The van accelerated and she had to shout to be heard over the whine of the engine. 'Stepan is screwing a librarian.'

Volkov dragged her back to the centre of the van and turned her face-down. 'I'm typing a reply. What shall I say? I know, how about: "Stepan, you are disgusting."?'

Chapter 38

He was quiet for a moment, then, 'There, I've sent it. Let's wait.'

She tried to calm her breathing and tasted blood on her lips from the bolt on the floor. The next woman to wear the hood would taste it too. Her phone double-beeped to indicate a new message had been received.

There was a crack of the seat as Volkov's weight shifted. 'Stepan agrees with your description of his character...Now for another one.'

He was leaning over her as he typed; his breath smelled of raw onions.

'Stepan', he recited, 'where is Thorsten Dahl?'

'There. Now let's see who talks first – you or the sergeant.'

She felt a crushing weight on her hips as he sat on them, grinding her into the floor. Something hard cracked the back of her skull.

'You bastard,' she cried out.

In the blackness of the hood she saw white flashes; a split second later the pain followed – it felt as if her head had been ripped open.

'Tell me where Dahl is and I'll make it quick for you. Believe me, that's a good offer.'

If she failed, the FSB would hand Anton to the Donbass People's Militia. She pictured his corpse being tossed into a makeshift grave and fixed the image in her mind. She would die before she let that happen.

Her phone beeped again.

39

Needles of rain fell on the metal roof, sounding like ball bearings. Her cheek was pressed against gritty cloth, and she felt curiously refreshed. At least she did until her head exploded in pain, bringing with it the memories of her failed mission to save Anton. There was no feeling in her hands where the cable tie had cut off her circulation. She turned her face to wipe the blood from her lips onto the hood.

Before the van stopped there had been a long silence that lasted for thirty minutes or more, followed by an excruciating blow. It was good she could remember her head being smashed – less chance of brain damage – not so good that with every heartbeat a volcanic eruption went off inside her skull. She listened intently but could only hear the rain.

'Volkov?'

He said nothing.

'Are you there?'

Her head pounded for five explosive beats.

'Hey, you with the shrivelled dick.'

There was no creak of boots. No kick. No punch. No onion breath. No crack on the head with the barrel of a gun or whatever he had used – she was alone.

She scrambled onto her front then brought her legs forward to manoeuvre herself to standing. At once, she felt dizzy, turning in time to slump on the bench seat. She tipped her head between her knees as ten thousand wasps swarmed in her body's empty shell. A few stale perfume breaths and they started to fade. She gripped the top of the hood between her knees and slowly straightened her body. Her ears rubbed against the material as the hood came loose, then fell to the floor.

Chapter 39

The windowless van was just as dark as before but the air was fresher and she sucked it in greedily. There was a lull in the rain; herring gulls squawked noisily above her.

Even if she could, she fought the desire to get out and run away – her arms were tied and she had little idea what was waiting for her. She rotated her shoulders to draw some circulation into them, then froze. There were footsteps behind the van. They stopped then she heard a twist of gravel behind her. A gun fired a metre from her head, its echo in the van the toll of a bell.

Frantically, she brushed her body against the walls, hoping to find something sharp to cut through the cable tie. She dropped to the floor and pushed herself under the bench, feeling with her cheeks for any metal with an edge. Her foot caught the bolt on the floor which had torn her lips. She scrambled to it and turned on her back to drag the cable tie over the bolt. She braced her feet against the base of the bench seat and strained. Her shoulders drew behind her like a bow, thrusting her pelvis in the air. A volcano at the base of her skull erupted and she knew she couldn't go on. She collapsed to the floor.

The rain had stopped and the herring gulls were quiet too – no doubt alarmed by the gunshot. She'd made enough noise but Volkov or his driver hadn't come for her. She used the bolt to work the cable tie into the narrowest part of her wrists. It bought a centimetre's worth of space and she used the gap to work the tie with the bolt as far as it would go on the fleshy part of one thumb. She placed her feet against the bench seat again, and strained. Her back arched and her shoulder blades came together. The cable tie slipped, then she fell backwards as it came free.

Natalya crawled to the van's rear door, rubbing her wrists urgently to bring the circulation back. There was heat, then a stinging pain, and she massaged and stretched her fingers until they were only half-numb. She patted the door until she found the release catch. Her fingers curled around a steel lever and the door groaned as it opened. She climbed out, squinting in the bright light. A spray of rain mixed with seawater caught her in the face, the salt finding its way onto her lips and scalp sending fresh electricity through her nerves.

The van was on a coastal road. Stretched ahead of her, a row of eight or ten grand houses with gates and private drives faced the agitated Baltic. Behind, kilometres of winding road hugged the shoreline. A spray of brine brought fresh knife jabs of pain. Escape wasn't an option, however tempting, when she still had to find Dahl's documents. Without them, Anton would never be safe.

She edged forwards, thinking of the driver. In the van, Volkov had admitted sending the Gosha Kutsenko lookalike to kill Yulia Federova. It left more questions than answers but there was no time to consider them. On the driver's side she glimpsed a leather cap protruding through the open window. The cab smelled of cigarettes and the acrid odour of a bullet's propellant. She crept lower, praying he was too distracted to notice her.

She had the element of surprise, but it was hardly a comfort when he had his gun as well as hers. One more step then she checked again. He hadn't moved. She pressed herself against the door. The wind caught Mikhail's raincoat making it flap noisily like a canvas sail. The leather cap was still. She shifted position to see his face in the wing mirror – he was slumped forwards. She stood up.

An "O" of frozen surprise was on the driver's mouth. On the side of his head, a bullet had left a neat black hole in his leather cap. The relief made her want to laugh out loud. She opened the door and prised a gun from the dead man's hand. It had a full clip and "CZ 75 P-01" etched along the barrel. It was a well-made Czech pistol that had worked its way from the police force and onto the black market. She ripped off Mikhail's raincoat and threw it to the floor, then fixed the dead man's gun to the holster on her belt.

Her teeth chattered and she shivered although it was warm enough. A fresh spray of rain caught her as she started walking. Tall grasses gave way to a deserted beach, and with the beach came the houses; the first one she passed had an ornamental fountain and a Maybach on the drive, but where had Volkov gone?

An ancient vagrant wearing a blazer with a nautical badge was hiding from the squally showers under a decaying bus shelter that hadn't been used in years.

'Police – have you seen anyone come this way?'

He didn't react and she touched him lightly on the shoulder, making him jump.

'Please, where did he go?'

He turned to show a weathered face and patches of grey hair through burnt skin, then dismissed her with a flick of his finger towards the end of the street where the beach turned back to grass and the houses stopped. Even in the mist she could see little cover for someone of Volkov's size. She nodded a thanks, realising the old man was unreliable.

A phone started ringing. She recognised the tone and started running to the van, guessing it had come from there. Flares exploded in her head with each footfall. A few seconds later the ringtone was drowned out by a howl of wind.

On the passenger side, the window was stained red and when she pulled open the door, drips of coagulated blood shook free of the dashboard. She heard her mobile beep to alert her to a new text message and she reached for the glove compartment. Inside she discovered her iPhone. A text on the screen alerted her to a missed call from Mikhail. At the side of the van she sheltered from the rain and called him.

'Misha? Is it important?'

'Hey Angel. I did what you asked. That crazy woman cost me my wallet and balls... she's going.'

It took her a moment to realise he was speaking of Dinara. She was leaving the country with Anton and a pile of Mikhail's money.

'Thank God,' she said.

He paused. 'Have you found the documents?'

'I'm not even close.' The van door slammed with the wind. 'Volkov found me.'

'Jesus…are you OK?'

'Yeah,' she looked at the dead man through the window, 'I had a guardian angel. Actually, he might be an Angel of Death, it's unclear.'

'Anton's safe, just get away.'

'From the FSB? He'll never be safe if I don't do this.'

'Wait for me.' She heard echoes of footsteps and guessed he was racing down the stairs. 'Tell me where you are.'

'Go north on the E18 – I'll text you the address when I find it. Where's Rogov?'

'I don't know, he's not answering. I'm worried Tasha, everything's fucked.'

'Bring Primakov – just the two of you. Don't involve Dostoynov.'

'Angel, stay where you are.'

'I can't. Something's happening.'

She ended the call.

Before Volkov had hit her, there had been a text on her phone. She opened her messages to find her most recent conversation with Rogov:

The sixty-year-old virgin is putting out.

That was his adolescent way of saying the woman at the ZAGS office was being helpful. In the van, she had deliberately referred to Rogov as "Stepan". Volkov had copied her, not realising she never called her sergeant by his first name. That must have given Rogov a clue that something was wrong. Volkov's second text had then asked "Stepan" for Dahl's whereabouts when she had already told him the Swede was in Zena's apartment. That wasn't a clue so much as a hammer blow to Rogov's forehead that she had been compromised.

She checked Rogov's reply and allowed herself a smile. The address he'd given to Volkov was in Sestroretsk, where Zena had gone to the ZAGS office with Yulia. She guessed he'd got it from his sixty-year-old virgin. It made perfect sense too, because Dahl was just about brave and stupid enough to go there looking for Zena – it was Volkov's own house. She forwarded the address to Mikhail as a gunshot rang out from one of the properties, then two more followed in rapid succession.

40

Heavy gates blocked the entrance and the steel fence surrounding the property had spikes that were meant to look decorative to a casual observer yet lethal to anyone thinking seriously of climbing it. She noticed a broken branch on the ground and looked up to see a security camera knocked out of alignment so that it focused away from the main gates and out to the Baltic. She tried the gates and was relieved to find them unlocked.

Her feet crunched on gravel and she quickly moved onto the grass verge, seeking out cover among the trees that skirted the driveway. She ducked from one to another holding the Czech pistol outstretched in both hands and angled towards the ground. The house, as she approached it, was three storeys with a light blue wooden façade and white shuttered windows. It looked more like a holiday home than a permanent residence and she wondered if that accounted for the silence in the rest of the street. At the entrance was a solid oak door with steps leading up to it and a pair of sculpted, stone tigers on either side – it was ajar.

As she entered the house, a squall brought a spray inside, soaking her shirt. The hallway was wide and tiled, with a staircase to the right. She saw three open doors: two to the left and one ahead. She jerked her head inside the first, seeing a Persian rug over stained floorboards and a black leather corner unit. There was no one there and she moved to the next, finding an empty dining room. Straight ahead, she saw wet footsteps on the floor and followed them to a kitchen: it was handmade and centred around a stove that was old and spotless. A large pan lay on a work surface filled with vinegar next to a row of empty pickling jars.

The kitchen led to an external door which was clattering in the wind. A woman lay face down on the garden path outside. She had tan tights and moccasin-style slippers, and wore yellow, rubber kitchen gloves on her hands. Natalya stopped to feel for the woman's carotid pulse and observed a thick line of red, cauterised skin where a bullet had grazed her neck. Another two had left glistening holes in her sea-green cashmere top; they were three centimetres apart and had hit her from behind, the shooter targeting her heart. Natalya removed her fingers from the neck. The body was warm; there was no pulse.

Volkov cried out from one of the floors above her, his voice raging and anguished. She ran to the hallway, taking the stairs two at a time. At the first landing, she counted six rooms and stopped to listen. There was laboured breathing coming from the left and she drew closer to an open door. Next to the jamb, she saw an upturned wicker chair.

The floorboard under her foot creaked. She threw herself down the steps as a bullet zipped past her ear, embedding in the wall with a puff of plaster. The stairway exploded, sending splinters sharp as needles into her right shoulder. She lay sprawled on the landing and edged towards the bannister for cover.

'Police!' she shouted.

She heard Nahodkin's voice. 'I thought you were one of Volkov's.'

He was half-hidden by the door, holding out a gun on a relaxed arm. His Grach was tucked in his waistband and she noticed the pistol in his hand had a brown Bakelite grip. She knew with certainty that Nahodkin wasn't her guardian angel – he had her Makarov.

She guessed the rest. She would be Nahodkin's final victim and Major Belikova would label her a crooked *ment* who had killed Volkov and his wife because she liked Dahl's money too much; it was a neat way of taking the FSB out of the picture.

'Come on ment, I won't shoot.'

'I'm unarmed.' she called.

He tracked her voice and more plaster exploded over her head. Another bullet cut through the balustrade and embedded in the wall to her right. It was too close. She slid further down the stairs on her belly.

'Stupid bitch.'

Nahodkin stepped out of the doorway and she heard a familiar click – the small, eight-round magazine of her Makarov was empty. He reached for the Grach in his waistband. She aimed at his wide torso and fired. One bullet missed, the other caught him in the gut and he staggered.

'I lied,' she called.

She ducked down as he fired repeatedly, sending splinters into her face and arms. There was a lull though she knew his clip would be far from finished. She raised her head once to check his position, then lowered it and emptied the Czech pistol at the doorway.

There had been the sound of a heavy body falling but Nahodkin was wily, and there was no guarantee he was dead, or even that he was alone. A full minute went by, then she crept slowly up the stairs, keeping low.

She found the FSB agent on his back, his body still twitching. She kicked his Grach beyond reach though there was little need when his face was already a ghostly white and a lake of blood was seeping through the floorboards beneath him. Beyond him lay Yuri Volkov, tipped out of the upturned wicker chair. The back of the gangster's head was concave, and behind him a silk sheet was spattered with blood and grey matter. She hoped Nahodkin had delivered the coup de grâce but she wouldn't lose any sleep if it had been her.

On the wall to the left of a vanity dresser was a print of an Amur tiger with its glass shattered and a gaping wound to the eye. The picture was swinging perpendicular to the wall, attached by a hidden hinge in the frame. Behind it, a safe with a number pad was exposed and empty. She was surprised Volkov had given up the code so easily. Perhaps, facing certain death, he'd decided to spare himself the pain.

A rucksack lay beyond Nahodkin's outstretched arm. Inside, she found a plastic folder with certificates and a number of devices that looked like a cross between a stapler and a pair of pliers – presumably these were the presses used to create Thorsten Dahl's company seals. She pulled it over her aching shoulders and fastened it in place. Her Makarov had been tossed to the floorboards; she bent down to tuck it in her holster, then pushed the empty CZ 75 in her waistband.

Looking around the bedroom, it was hard to reconcile Yuri Volkov's psychopathic qualities with the petit bourgeois décor. Apart from the silk sheets, there were drapes with a bamboo pattern and a chandelier with electric candles. Above the vanity dresser there was a flower-bordered picture with the embroidered words "Visiting is Good but Home *Is* Better".

She checked the other rooms on the landing then took the stairs to the top of the house; it was blocked by a single door. She tried the handle but it was locked.

'Police. Open up!'

The house was silent now and she pulled a toothpick sized splinter from her forearm.

She counted ten seconds then put her shoulder to the door. The seal presses in the backpack rattled and a wrenching pain persuaded her not to do it a second time. She raised her foot and kicked at the lock. The door blew open.

The top floor was an attic room with framed black and white prints of Parisian street scenes from the Fifties and pictures of Hollywood stars of the same era. On the back of the door was a photograph of the members of One Direction wearing multi-coloured clothes.

By a bed interlaced with fairy lights was a wardrobe. She tapped on the door with her knuckles then stepped back. 'You can come out now,' she called in English.

There was a creak then a door opened. Zena Dahl stepped out of the wardrobe, her blonde hair was wild and there were lines on her face where tears had cut through her makeup.

'It's alright, Zena,' Natalya said, continuing in English. 'You're safe. Are you hurt?'

'No.'

Chapter 40

Natalya nodded. 'I'll take you anywhere you want to go.' She held Zena in her arms. The girl was stiff and unresponsive.

'I'm a police officer. My name is Natalya Ivanova. Do you want me to take you back to Sweden?'

Zena Dahl mumbled something and Natalya had to ask for her to repeat it.

'I can't.'

'It won't be safe to stay here.'

Zena nodded slowly.

Natalya looked at the poster, 'You like One Direction?'

Zena was silent for a long time then she said, 'Yuri mistook me for a twelve-year-old.'

'Your father?' Natalya asked tentatively.

'Yuri.' Zena corrected her.

'Was all this done for you?'

Zena nodded.

'And it was like this when you first arrived here?'

Zena nodded again. 'Yes.'

Natalya heard a car pull up then the sound of the garden gates creaking open. Heavy footsteps were on the stairs, along with heavy breathing.

'Oh fuck,' she heard Rogov call out from the floor below.

'I'm up here,' she called. 'Don't shoot.'

She heard him come up the stairs then he appeared in the doorway.

'Shit, boss, I can't believe it. Everyone's—'

'Dead.' Zena finished for him.

Natalya glared at the sergeant then turned to Zena. 'He's right, a man killed Yuri.'

'I heard it.'

Zena didn't seem upset but her movements were slow and she wondered how much the girl could absorb.

'What about Elizaveta?'

'Yuri's wife?' Natalya asked.

Zena nodded.

'She's gone too. I'm sorry.' Natalya put an arm around Zena to steer her out of the room then noticed she was shivering, most likely from shock. She took a blanket off the bed and draped it over the girl's shoulders. By the bedside was a picture on a rosewood cabinet. It was a black and white photograph of a bride in a white lace wedding dress with the faintest of smiles.

'Is this your mother, Kristina?'

'Yes.'

'She's beautiful…you look like her.'

'Do you think so?' Zena said.

'Yes, I do.'

The air seemed to deflate from the girl. 'My father – Thorsten – he lied to me.'

'I know.'

Zena's tears came. Natalya nodded to Rogov who brought over a box of tissues from the windowsill. She pulled one out and handed it to the girl.

'Yuri said Thorsten killed my mother and took me away.'

'What do you think?' She squeezed the girl's shoulder affectionately and winced with the movement.

'I didn't trust him…Yuri I mean. He wouldn't let me go out. He said it was to protect me.'

'Some men like to control. I heard he did that to your mother too.'

'My mother.' Zena's voice was so quiet it almost a breath. 'Did Thorsten kill her?'

Natalya sighed. 'I think he loved her.'

Zena nodded to herself.

She sent Rogov ahead to block off the view to Volkov's bedroom while she helped Zena down the stairs. Outside, the rain had stopped and puddles glistened with the sun's reflection. Apart from the gulls it was still quiet and she wondered if the occupants of the other houses were at the White Nights festivities in the city. It was an ideal time of year for gunshots to go unreported.

'You two wait here,' she said to Rogov, not wanting Zena to see the mess Nahodkin had made of Volkov's driver. At the back of the van she found Mikhail's discarded raincoat and removed the soggy remainder of his Sobranies from the pocket. She found onc that was smokeable and lit it then wandered back.

Rogov took out one of his Winston's. 'What do we do now, boss?'

'Take her to your car. I'll join you in a minute.' She removed the backpack and held it out to him. 'And put this in the boot.'

The sirens came soon after she had extinguished the cigarette. Mikhail's Mercedes came into view and he sprinted from it when it had barely stopped. His gun was in his hands and he ducked behind the van for cover.

She watched him from a low stone wall, resting her back on the gates of Volkov's house. 'I bet I look sexy,' she called over.

He stood up slowly, then ran to her and wrapped her in his arms. 'Like an extra in a zombie movie.'

They had barely moved when Primakov arrived in his van. She watched him fiddle with his silver case before extracting a pair of blue overshoes from it. For some reason it seemed the funniest thing she had seen in a long time.

'Captain, are you hurt?' Primakov asked.

'I'm fine.'

Mikhail sat on the wall by her side, his arm around her. 'What's going on, Natalya?'

'I got Dahl's company things. They are in Rogov's car. I need you both to stay here and clean up.'

'Angel, what are you talking about?'

She wondered why she felt so composed when she had just killed a man.

'Yuri Volkov and his wife were murdered by an FSB agent. I think you've already met him, Leo' – Primakov looked away – 'he killed them with my gun.'

Mikhail rubbed a hand across his eyes. 'Shit, that's great.'

'My guess is the FSB couldn't rely on Volkov to keep his mouth quiet. When it was over, I was meant to take the blame.'

'So where is this bastard? I'll put a bullet in him myself.'

'He's dead. I got to him first.'

Mikhail lit a cigarette and looked at her with something approaching awe. 'Jesus Christ. You said he was FSB.'

'It won't make him any less dead.'

'Do you have any idea what they'll do to you?'

'This is why I need you.' She took out the CZ 75 from the waistband of her jeans. 'This one killed the FSB agent.' She slapped it in Primakov's ungloved hand; he looked horrified. She removed her Makarov from its holster and handed it to Mikhail. 'This one killed Volkov and his wife…and the driver of the van was probably killed by the agent's Grach. I need you to fix things before Dostoynov finds out and reaches the conclusion I've gone on a killing spree. All the better if you can make the FSB agent look innocent.'

'That's easy,' said Mikhail, 'We'll pile all the bodies inside and burn the fucking house to the ground.'

'No, Major, with respect. That won't work.'

'Of course it will – as long as Vasiliev assigns the case to me.'

'Please Major, we have to do this right.'

She stood, 'I'm going now boys.' She kissed Mikhail on the lips.

'You taste of blood.'

'I'm a zombie. That's what we taste like.'

'Are we good, Angel?'

'We're better than that. I'll see you home tonight.'

'You're the expert, Leo.' she said to Primakov as she walked away. 'Don't let him bully you.'

Rogov was at the wheel, smoking through the open window of the driver's seat. He tossed the cigarette onto the pavement. 'Where are we going, boss?'

'Back to *Piter*.' She glanced at his Makarov. 'And we're going to need that.'

41

On Vasilyevsky Island, Rogov parked his unmarked Primera outside Veselnaya Ulitsa.

Natalya groaned as she took Nahodkin's rucksack from the boot and slung it onto her aching shoulders.

She bent down to address Zena through the window of the back seat then realised she had no words of comfort for the girl. The curtains in the neighbouring apartment twitched as she approached; this time she knew it wouldn't be Lyudmila Kuznetsova watching but one of the FSB agents.

'Hello,' she called out.

Major Belikova opened the door, aiming a Grach at her belly. 'So, here is the late Detective Ivanova,' she said in her sharp voice.

'I've got one of those too, but let's keep it civilised.'

On cue, Rogov leaned over the bonnet of the Primera, his long-sleeved shirt partially obscuring the barrel of his Makarov. He waved at the major with his free hand.

Belikova stepped back to let her inside the hallway. 'Where's Nahodkin?'

'I killed him. To be fair, he was trying to kill me at the time. I've got some people cleaning up the mess he left behind in Volkov's house. With any luck they'll clean his conscience too.'

Belikova pursed her lips. 'You did well, he was one of my best.'

Natalya unhooked the rucksack from her shoulders and dropped it on the floor. 'Where's her father?'

Belikova arched a single eyebrow. 'Her *father*?'

'Let's not play games.'

'Now you're being boring.' Belikova hammered on the door of Zena's apartment with her fist. 'Hey, Demutsky, wake up – you're getting evicted.'

She nudged the rucksack towards Belikova with her foot.

'Is that it?' The Major tucked the Grach in her holster and opened the bag. She removed the plastic wallet and flicked through the papers, then examined the seal presses.

'Hey, Demutsky?' Belikova called through Zena's apartment door. 'Today would be nice. I want to be out of this provincial shithole.'

The door opened, shaking silver fingerprint powder to the floor. The thin agent yawned.

'Get your coat. Hurry up.'

He disappeared, then re-emerged clutching a brown leather jacket. Behind him she could see an anxious Dahl, who appeared to be unharmed.

'Our Swedish friend has agreed to keep his mouth shut,' said Belikova, 'and you kept your end of the deal.' She lifted the rucksack onto her shoulders. 'Tell me, Ivanova, weren't you tempted to sell them yourself? You must know a few criminals.'

'No,' said Natalya, 'I never even thought of it.'

Belikova pulled on the door. 'An honourable ment,' she sniffed and walked away, muttering something unintelligible.

She was on the E18 heading north, escorting Zena and Thorsten to the Finnish border; from there, Anatoly Lagunov had agreed to take them the rest of the way to Stockholm. Rogov was at the wheel with Dahl next to him, his huge frame folded to allow her to fit in the seat behind without crushing her knees. By her side, Zena was taciturn as they drove past the turning for Sestroretsk.

Natalya looked out of the rear window and saw a *gelik*, the nickname for a Mercedes Geländewagon. Those fancy jeeps were expensive; a basic model cost over a hundred thousand euros – though money wasn't a problem for the FSB graduates who liked to flout traffic regulations in their *geliki*. This one had a tinted windscreen and she caught a Moscow region code of "99" on the number plate. There was a possibility it was the same one she'd seen in the morning on the way to Dahl's old headquarters. Had Major Belikova assigned a new agent to make sure Thorsten and Zena left the country, or had she planned something more sinister?

She tapped Rogov on the shoulder. 'Does this thing go any faster?'

He took the hint, and she glanced behind to see the Mercedes pick up speed; it overtook a bus to catch up, then ducked behind a white, VW estate.

Dahl twisted in his seat to speak to her. 'Those boys in prison for Zena's murder.'

'It's a SIZO,' she corrected him, 'a pre-detention facility.'

'Well, I'd like to set up an appeal fund for them.'

She vaguely promised to make some preliminary enquiries but the process always took months; by then, it was more than likely that both boys would be dead from drug abuse or from the hands of other prisoners.

The car was silent again and her thoughts returned to Mikhail. She hoped Colonel Vasiliev was tearing up her letter of resignation. That left Mikhail in an awkward position. It was unfair to make him give up his chance of running the Directorate; not only that, she imagined life would be intolerable for everyone if Dostoynov took over. She could submit a request to transfer to a local station, perhaps the one in Admiralty, where there were fewer social problems than the outlying districts. It sounded promising but she couldn't give up everything she had worked so hard for. They were no closer to a resolution.

She looked for the Mercedes again. She hadn't seen the *gelik* in nearly an hour but it didn't take a genius to know which direction their Primera was heading – if it was following them, maintaining visual contact wasn't necessary.

Rogov stopped at a garage to get fuel where Dahl made admiring comments about the Primera ("it goes very well, is it very fuel efficient?") though it must have been a heap of junk compared to the vehicles he was chauffeured around in. To her, the entire journey seemed an exercise in talking about everything except what was on their minds.

They set off again. After approximately twenty minutes Dahl turned to her. 'Captain, can we pull over, please?'

'I'd prefer to keep going. We'll be at the border soon.'

'Now please. It won't take long.'

She gave the order to Rogov who braked harshly, skidding into a layby with a spray of gravel and dust to express his displeasure. Dahl was first out, followed by Zena.

'Boss, what's going on? I don't like it.'

'Nor do I.' She glanced at his waist but couldn't see Rogov's Makarov for his belly. 'Are you armed?'

'Yeah, boss.'

'Good.'

Dahl walked ahead with Zena sauntering behind – unwilling to join her father or fall back to them. The road climbed as they approached a bridge. Pine trees that had been at ground level fell away until they drew near the tips of their crowns. She watched Dahl jog across the tarmac then stop where the bank met the road again.

They caught up to him. 'What is it, Thorsten?' she asked.

He clasped a hand to his forehead and looked to the river's edge. 'There,' he said, as much to himself, pointing to an area of thick undergrowth.

Dahl started lowering himself down the embankment. Zena stood at the top watching him. A few metres behind, Rogov offered Natalya one of his Winstons; she took it.

'Boss, we should leave him. He might be going for a shit.'

They smoked as Dahl clambered down, clinging onto shrubs and saplings for support. He reached the bottom then looked up at them expectantly, beckoning them with his arm.

'Oh crap, he wants us,' she said.

'I'll wait up here, boss – if you don't mind.'

Having seen Rogov's poor attempt to master a few flights of stairs, she didn't mind at all. 'Keep your gun ready. If anyone comes near, be prepared for trouble.'

She stubbed out her cigarette and offered a hand to Zena. Together, they gripped the foliage as Dahl had done, and lowered themselves down.

'Thorsten,' she called out. 'Wait for us.'

The day's rain had turned the slope to mud and they struggled to stay upright. Zena slipped and Natalya cried out after straining her shoulders to grab the girl's arm.

'Thorsten, what are you doing? This is crazy.'

They reached the bottom and she scraped the edges of her shoes against a rock to remove the cloying earth. Dahl was ten metres away, he had found a branch and was using it like a machete to clear a path through the foliage. They trailed after him reluctantly.

'It's still here,' Dahl called. His eyes were wild and there was something close to madness in them.

His hand rested on the roof of a car that had rusted a vivid orange with age. Now she was near, she could see he was crying openly. It made her feel more Russian than she had in a long time, and she fought against the desire to slap him for being so weak.

'Kristina just needed help,' he said.

Zena looked angry and she was fighting to contain herself. She threw Swedish words at Thorsten like stones and it wasn't difficult to guess their meaning; Natalya imagined they went something like: "I don't want to hear that shit".

'That's your decision, but I'll tell you the truth anyway,' he replied in English. 'You see that?' He pointed through the car's open door to a square of rusted springs poking through bright green moss. 'I drove that car once. It's a *Zhiguli*. You were in there, fast asleep on your mother's lap.'

Natalya could see the girl was struggling. 'You took me away!' she yelled.

'Yes,' Dahl dabbed at his eyes, 'I did. Your father was no good.' He went to brush Zena's hair with a palm and she jerked her head back. 'He smuggled girls younger than you. Your mother discovered that when he was arrested.'

Zena shook her head. 'Yuri said you killed her and took me away.'

'I was helping you both to escape in this thing.' He patted the Zhiguli. 'We were going for the border crossing at *Torfyanovka*.'

'Why didn't you fly?' Natalya asked.

'Yuri did other smuggling too. Kristina thought he had men at the airport.'

'You killed her,' Zena said.

Dahl's jaw clenched. 'We were five minutes away from the border.' He pointed to the top of the bank. 'It's my fault, I was going too fast. The car skidded on ice; we came off the bridge and ended up here.' His voice caught. 'Your mother was gone. I found you in the footwell, wrapped in a blanket and pressed against a bag of clothes.'

'So you stole me,' Zena spat.

'Don't you understand?' he pleaded. 'If I had only saved myself, you would have frozen to death.'

Zena glowered at him.

'Yuri was in prison. What else was I to do?' Fresh tears ran down his face. 'I wrapped you in a blanket and carried you to *Torfyanovka*. My father sent a man to help us over the border.'

'Why didn't you take Zena to one of her relatives?' Natalya asked.

'Because that monster might have claimed her when he got out of prison. Anatoly told me the newspapers were saying Ksenia Volkova had been dragged away by wolves. I began to think of Zena as another girl; one I had found in an orphanage. Yuri's daughter was dead.'

'And that's what everyone believed?'

'People thought I had been naïve to take on a child alone but no one questioned the story. My father knew the truth of course – he expressed his displeasure at my recklessness but then he grew to love Zena and eventually let the matter drop.'

'Boss?' Rogov shouted from the top of the bridge. 'Are you done?'

She raised her hand and waved. 'Coming,' she called.

42

The traffic approaching the border crossing was busy despite the ban on foot passengers to stem the flow of refugees and migrants entering the EU. Rogov stopped in front of a barrier and a woman in a green camouflage uniform with a thick, black ponytail came out of an orange hut. On the other side, in a parking area, Anatoly Lagunov was already waiting; he was leaning on the bonnet of his black BMW reading a newspaper.

'Is this the crossing?' Zena asked.

'No.' Rogov laughed. 'It's a checkpoint. In the army, I was stationed in one of these for six weeks.' He pointed at the guard approaching them. 'She'll pass on our details to *Torfyanovka* so if we take too long or haven't got the same number of passengers they'll have a welcoming committee ready.'

'Thanks for the warning,' Natalya said. She held out her police ID card, then pointed to Dahl and Zena. 'These two are getting separate transport across the border in that BMW – she nodded in the direction of Lagunov's car – 'Can you make sure they are not delayed at *Torfyanovka*?'

'Yes, Captain.' The guard took their registration number and raised the barrier for them to continue.

They pulled up next to the BMW and got out of the Primera. Dahl gave his lawyer a bear hug. 'Anatoly it's good to see you. Thank you for coming.'

Lagunov looked discomfited by the embrace.

'Is everybody ready?' Natalya asked.

'Yes, I think so,' Dahl said; Zena nodded.

Rogov lit another cigarette and Natalya took one from him, then regretted it – she was already feeling like a human ashtray. 'Zena, if you don't mind, I have some questions before you disappear.'

She caught Zena raising her eyebrows and tilting her head in a sarcastic gesture that reminded her of Anton. She hoped Dinara wasn't taking him away on holiday for too long.

Thorsten put a protective arm around Zena, and she leaned into him. 'Don't you think she's been through enough, Captain?'

'It won't take long.' She turned to Zena. 'Why did you come to Russia?'

'To study.'

'Yes, but why St. Petersburg?'

'I liked the course.'

'Is that the whole truth, Zena,' she said.

Lagunov checked his watch. 'I'm sorry to interrupt but the security at *Torfyanovka* will be a nightmare if we take any longer and we need to catch the *Naantali* ferry tonight.'

'Then you'll have to wait,' Natalya said bluntly. She sucked on the Winston then coughed. 'So why did you come to Russia, Zena?'

'Why does this matter? We've got her back,' said Dahl.

'Just answer the Captain,' said Rogov, 'then we can all go home.'

Zena fiddled with her hair, taking out a band and straightening it into a ponytail. She seemed unhappy with the result and repeated it. 'I got this random email. I thought it was junk but it had my name and told me to find the orphanage I came from. I searched on the internet for hours but there wasn't anything in Krasnoye Selo; not even closed ones.'

Dahl spoke quietly and calmly as if defusing a bomb. 'But I've told you the truth now, Zena. We know there was no orphanage.'

Natalya stubbed out the cigarette on the tarmac. 'Then what happened?'

'I replied telling them there wasn't one. A few days later I got an email; it said my natural father was alive. It had a scanned wedding photo attached. I could see myself in the bride's face. Even the man had this thick, blond hair like mine, and the same nose. I just knew they were my parents.'

'You never said anything to me,' said Dahl.

'They told me not to trust you.'

Chapter 42

'So you came to Russia to find your father?'

'They said I should find an excuse to come. There was a course at the university I liked so it wasn't difficult.'

Natalya turned to Dahl. 'When did you decide to sell your companies?'

Lagunov paced. 'We've got a twelve-hour journey ahead of us. Can we do this another time?'

'Early last year,' Dahl said, 'around February. The exchange rates were making them unprofitable.'

'And, Zena, when did you start receiving these emails?'

'March last year.'

Dahl held out his hand to Zena. 'Captain…Natalya, I won't forget what you've done for us but we do have to go.'

'It was my job,' she nodded curtly then turned to the Primera.

She watched Zena and Thorsten climb into the back of the BMW then the car accelerated away as Lagunov tried to make up for lost time.

'So that's that.' Rogov stubbed out his cigarette.

He turned the Primera in the parking area and she got in. Seconds later they stopped at the barrier to wait for the guard to let them leave. The Mercedes *gelik* with the tinted windows pulled up at the crossing. The region code was "99" on the number plate and she was sure it was the same one that had been following them earlier. Behind it, traffic was steadily building.

The guard waved them on.

'Wait, Rogov.'

The electronic windows on the Mercedes SUV lowered for the guard. Natalya looked inside – there was an old Indian woman at the wheel and a girl of eleven or twelve sat next to her. Clearly, they were not FSB agents.

'It doesn't matter. Let's go home.'

Rogov pressed a preset station on the radio and the car filled with static. He turned it off again.

'Why did you ask me to wait?'

'That Mercedes.' She shook her head. 'I thought it was following us. Being a *ment* makes you paranoid.'

Rogov thought for a moment. 'Criminals too, paranoia makes them do stupid things. That's how we catch them half the time.'

After ten minutes they passed the bridge where Thorsten had crashed the Zhiguli all those years ago, killing Zena's mother and setting in motion a train of events that led to the loss of his companies and the deaths of six people.

She thought about the Mercedes again; it was hard to let go of the fact that she had been positive the *gelik* was following them. Criminals too, Rogov had said. Paranoia was the outward projection of internal stresses. It created delusions. The *menti* were overly suspicious and consequently, criminals panicked as if they were about to be discovered. One paranoia feeding another.

'Stop the car!' Natalya yelled. 'We have to go back.'

'Boss, can't we go home?'

'Rogov, turn the fucking car around now.'

43

She fixed the magnetic flasher to the roof, the blue light illuminating the cars queueing at the checkpoint. The guard with the ponytail raised the barrier and waved them through. The traffic heading north was busy and Rogov drove on the opposite side of the road, forcing his way back in when oncoming vehicles hurtled towards them.

'Get out the way, moron!' Rogov made a swiping motion with his hand at a caravan that had seen the emergency lights and braked to a halt in front of them, blocking the lane. The elderly driver raised his arms to show there was nowhere for him to go.

Rogov swore then took the Primera off the road and onto a muddy verge. The traffic built up behind the caravan and the Primera's wheels span as it fishtailed in the dirt. After fifty metres he found a gap and rejoined the highway as it widened, then the road split to separate private from commercial traffic.

At the *Torfyanovka* crossing they faced a row of booths, each one with a barrier and several cars waiting. A border guard, who could have passed for Rogov with his belly and pasty face, hurried out and waved his arms at the waiting vehicles to let them cut through. His random gestures sent the cars in all directions, making the situation worse.

She got out and stood on the Primera's sill for a better view. There were hundreds of cars at the crossing working through similar booths; none of them resembled Lagunov's BMW.

'They've gone through,' she shouted above the siren. 'We need to move.'

She climbed in as he reversed the Primera to take them around a car of blond-haired Nordics blocking their path. Rogov's lost twin raised the barrier and they were through into the no man's land a few kilometres before the actual border. Cars heading for Finland were queuing all the way and he sped past them on the opposite carriageway. A black car broke out of the line and accelerated away.

'That's it!' she yelled.

The BMW squeezed past an oncoming van, ripping off Lagunov's wing mirror. Rogov hit the horn. 'Why doesn't the stupid bastard stop?'

Ahead was a sign – the border was five hundred metres away. The road in front of the BMW was clear all the way and the distance between them was widening.

'Fuck,' she hissed, 'we're too late.'

She flicked off the siren.

Rogov didn't slow. She turned and saw a malicious glint in his eyes. 'Boss,' he shouted, 'Look!'

An eighteen-wheeler with "Vladivostok Auto Spares" stencilled on the side was parked at the border; it pulled out of the queue and started turning to block off the highway.

'Come on!' she screamed.

The lorry moved with torturously slow speed. The cab twisted, then it reversed and straightened. The BMW headed for a gap. The eighteen-wheeler edged forward to seal the road. Lagunov's car braked harder than she thought possible. It shuddered to a halt two metres from the lorry's cab.

Rogov stamped on the brakes. Lagunov was already running out, and they were out of the Nissan after him. If he crossed the border they would never get him back. Lagunov would insist he had been the victim of an FSB conspiracy, with just enough evidence to make Interpol reluctant to enforce a Red Notice. He was too far ahead, already rounding the lorry's cab.

Lagunov stopped. The driver of the eighteen wheeler blocked his path with a tyre lever in one hand.

Dahl was on him too. 'I told you to stop. You could have killed us all.'

Natalya fought to control her breathing. 'Lagunov was working with Volkov.'

Chapter 43

The Swede twisted his fist in Lagunov's shirt to tighten his grip and the lawyer squirmed as he fought to free himself. The lorry driver saw he was no longer needed and climbed back in his cab, waving briefly to her and Rogov.

'Thorsten! Let me go, damn you. I was trying to save you. The Russian police are corrupt.'

She ignored him and turned to Dahl. 'Why did the sale of your companies fall through?'

Dahl rubbed his free hand over his face; he looked as tired as she felt. 'The buyer was already nervous then his auditors found fraud.'

'My guess is, Lagunov was helping himself,' she said.

Lagunov twisted his neck. 'Get your hand off me, Thorsten!'

'It's alright, let him go. If you move, Lagunov…' She pointed at Rogov who had taken out his Makarov.

'You wouldn't dare.' Lagunov straightened his shirt. 'When I'm finished with you, you'll be lucky to have a job as a security guard.'

'Don't run, he really will shoot you. That's what we do to murder suspects.'

'Murder?' The word made him recoil. 'I haven't killed anyone.'

'Then how did Volkov know Zena was alive?'

Lagunov looked to Dahl. 'How should I know? I don't care either. The real story is Kristina jerked him off. All she wanted was to get away from Volkov, and Thorsten ended up with her child like a pussy.'

Dahl cocked his hand into a fist and smashed it into the side of his lawyer's head. Lagunov's feet lifted off the ground and he landed heavily on the tarmac, his body twisted.

'Still think I'm a pussy?' Dahl yelled over his lawyer's prone body. 'The man who got us over the border, I thought it must have been him but he had no idea Volkov was Zena's father. It was you. Why did you tell Volkov, Anatoly?'

Lagunov was dazed. He got slowly to his feet then dabbed his brow with the back of a hand.

Natalya asked, 'Rogov, have you got your bracelets?'

'Yeah.' The sergeant unclipped a set of handcuffs from his belt and fixed them to Lagunov's wrists.

As the lorry moved, there was a chorus of horns from the Finnish side; behind them, the motorists were oddly respectful and Natalya turned to see half a dozen border guards edging between the cars as they made their way towards them. She waved a thank you at the lorry driver and didn't think he'd noticed until a tattooed arm extended from the open window of his cab and gave her a thumbs-up sign.

'So, why did you tell Volkov about Zena?' Dahl asked.

Lagunov's mouth had taken on the crooked shape of a sneer. 'You paid nothing for those companies then ran away. I gave up my life for them. They turned a profit because I made them turn a profit. They are worth a hundred times your original investment because of me. And what did I get? You rewarded me like a regular salaryman.'

Rogov rested a heavy hand on Lagunov's shoulder and squeezed it. 'And I pay my taxes, but that doesn't make me President of the Republic.'

Natalya said, 'You panicked when Thorsten told you he was selling the companies. Were you angry that you couldn't keep stealing from them or were you worried the buyer would find out?'

The lawyer stared back at her, hatred radiating from him like a heat shimmer. 'You are nobody. A corrupt little mouse who tried to grab some cheese from a trap.'

She ignored the accusation. 'You needed the company documents and Thorsten out of the way so you found Volkov and told him his daughter, Ksenia, was alive. You had him arrange the fake kidnapping then insisted that Thorsten went in person to the ransom exchange.'

'Where's your evidence?' Lagunov demanded. 'You have nothing.'

'I have a witness. Originally I thought Zena had been kidnapped and Thorsten had sent you to her apartment to see if she really was missing. The truth is, you panicked. You thought there was something there to connect her to you. How did you get inside? Zena had one set of keys and her neighbour had the other.'

'Yuri took my keys,' Zena said. 'He said he was going to get some things from my apartment but he forgot.'

Natalya held out the flat of her hand to Lagunov. 'There's your evidence.'

'You don't scare me. I'll tell you something else if you like – it was me who sent those emails to Zena. Thorsten's job was done. He'd been the parent of a cuckoo child. It was time for her to go back to her real father. Where's the crime in that?'

'I think Volkov screwed you after the ransom exchange. Why did he have the company documents, and not you? I bet you offered him money but it wasn't enough. Once he smelled how much the companies were worth he wanted them too.'

Lagunov's sneer had gone, it was replaced by self-pity. Most criminals, when it came to it, were selfish and blamed everything and everyone except themselves. 'The FSB have Thorsten's companies now.' He let out a shrill laugh. 'Why don't you arrest them?'

Rogov gave him an unsettling grin. 'The same reason you won't say anything – because the FSB do some evil shit.'

Natalya turned to Zena. 'You had a handbag – a Hermès Sellier Kelly. What happened to it?'

Zena frowned, 'I don't know. Yuri said I'd lost it before he found me. I was so drunk.'

'Did you know a body was found on Krestovsky Island?'

'I heard it on the radio. Yuri told me it was a trap. The police were saying it was me so I would come out into the open.' She glanced at Dahl, then looked away, embarrassed. 'You don't know what it was like. It was so hard to do anything he didn't want me to do.'

'The girl in the park was Yulia Federova,' said Natalya.

Zena's hand went to her mouth, 'No!'

'A man working for Yuri killed her.'

The girl looked stunned; she was staring into the middle distance. 'Yulia is dead?'

'Yes.'

'Why?'

'She was helping you to look for your parents. Lagunov was

worried Yulia might lead me to Volkov and expose everything.'

'I didn't want to cause my father any embarrassment. I told her not to say anything.'

'She didn't,' Natalya put an arm over Zena's shoulders, 'but Lagunov thought she would. I was asking him awkward questions about the adoption and her death stopped the investigation into your disappearance. We thought she was you because her body was burned and they left your Hermès handbag near it.'

Zena frowned, 'Are you saying Anatoly had Yulia killed?'

'Yes.'

Zena faced Lagunov, 'You killed my friend?'

Lagunov shook his head, 'I didn't'

Natalya got in between them before it turned ugly.

'Get off me!' Zena tried to brush Natalya way.

Lagunov stepped back then taunted her, 'Your real father was a thug, it looks like you've got his genes all right.'

Natalya strained to hold Zena. 'For God's sake put him inside.' Rogov shoved him roughly into the back of the Primera.

She tried to placate the girl. 'He's going to prison for a long time.'

'Yeah, and it's not like one of your Sven holiday camps,' added Rogov.

She said goodbye to Thorsten and Zena then climbed into the Primera. Rogov drove onto a verge to let the backlog of cars clear. Soon the air stank of exhaust fumes and was filled with a cacophony of horns as motorists competed for the opening spaces. She watched Thorsten Dahl hold open the door of the BMW for Zena. Before climbing in, she hugged him. A few minutes later she saw the black car edge slowly into the traffic.

'How long are we going to be here, boss?'

'Just wait.'

It took another twenty minutes for the BMW to cross the border and just once, Natalya thought, she saw Zena turn to wave but the car was too far away by then.

The sky had grown dark again and was threatening rain. Rogov opened his window a crack then lit a cigarette. He grinned, expecting her to order him to put it out. His smile looked unnatural, she thought, like an air steward's – only without the orthodonture to back it up.

'Can we go now, boss?'

'You really are an insolent bastard, Rogov.'

He grinned even more.

Coming soon...

BLACK WOLF

G D Abson

Natalya Ivanova is investigating the death of a young woman found near a wealthy dacha community, when the victim is identified as a member of the Decembrists – a secretive group of anti-corruption activists.

Natalya's investigation is handed over to the Russian FBI, but she knows they won't look for the killer of a "traitor". Another Decembrist goes missing and she is forced to work secretly on the case. Soon, there's an unbearable cost to her unofficial investigation – finding the killer means losing her family.

Also by Mirror Books

Losing Leah

Sue Welfare

A DEBUT CRIME THRILLER FROM AN AWARD-WINNING SUNDAY TIMES BESTSELLING AUTHOR AND TV DRAMATIST.

On a cold, dark February morning, Chris and Leah Hills stop for coffee at an isolated service station a stone's throw from the Welsh Borders. While Leah heads inside, Chris locks the car and goes in to order their drinks. Minutes pass. Chris waits and waits, but Leah doesn't come back.

When Sergeant Mel Daley and her boss, Detective Inspector Harry Baker, arrive to begin a search for the missing woman, their investigation calls everything into question. Is she alive? Did she leave the service station with someone else? Did Leah ever even leave Norfolk? While her husband becomes more frantic, the pair begin to unravel a tangle of dark secrets from the past.

Perfect for fans of Robert Galbraith and The Girl On The Train.

Also by Mirror Books

A Mayfair 100 murder-mystery

Murder in Belgravia

Lynn Brittney

London, 1915. Ten months into the First World War and the City is flooded with women taking over the work vacated by men.

Chief Inspector Peter Beech, a young man invalided out of the war in one of the first battles, is investigating the murder of an aristocrat and the man's wife will only speak to a woman about the unpleasant details of the case. Beech persuades the Chief Commissioner to allow him to set up a clandestine team to deal with this case and pulls together a small crew of hand-picked women and professional policemen. Their telephone number: Mayfair 100.

Delving into the seedier parts of WWI London, the team investigate brothels and criminal gangs and underground drug rings that supply heroin to the upper classes. Will the Mayfair 100 gang solve the murder? If they do, will they be allowed to continue working as a team?

The first in an exciting series of fascinatingly-detailed stories involving the Mayfair 100 crimebusting team working London's streets during the First World War.

Mirror Books

Also by Mirror Books

A Song for Bridget

Phyllis Whitsell

THE UNFORGETTABLE TRUE STORY BEHIND SUNDAY TIMES BESTSELLING MEMOIR, FINDING TIPPERARY MARY.

A brutal and touching account of the life of Bridget 'Tipperary Mary' Larkin.

She faced poverty, bereavement, cruelty and abandonment many times over yet never lost the heart to pursue true love.

Returning to rural Ireland in 1938 and a young girl full of hope and expectation, A Song for Bridget recounts a series of tragic events that eventually bring her to Manchester and Birmingham and a desperate daily struggle to survive.

Bridget's haunting story, told for her by her daughter, is a perfect example of both the fragility and resilience of the human spirit.

Mirror Books

Also by Mirror Books

Playland

Anthony Daly

The voice of one man from within a dark scandal that nestled in the heart of London's Soho in the 1970s

Travelling to a new city to escape The Troubles in his native Northern Ireland, Tony Daly accepted a job in Foyles Bookshop. However, his naivety saw him fall foul of predators, looking for young men to sexually exploit.

Tony spent years hiding the secret of his abuse at the hands of some of the most influential men in the country. But finally, his lost voice ripped through the safe family life he had built over 40 years.

Stylishly written and politically explosive, this is the haunting true story of a young man's descent into a hell designed to satisfy the powerful. A world which destroyed the lives of everyone involved.

"Tony Daly's horrific story demands to be heard - his journey into the very heart of a corrupt and perverted establishment is simply off the scale ..."
– PAUL FRIFT, FILM MAKER/PRODUCER ITV'S 'VICTORIA'

Mirror Books